BURN THE SKY

PART 2: REDEMPTION

Printed in Australia

First Printing: July 2022

Shawline Publishing Group Pty Ltd
www.shawlinepublishing.com.au

Paperback ISBN- 9781922751454

Ebook ISBN- 9781922751522

NATIONAL LIBRARY OF AUSTRALIA

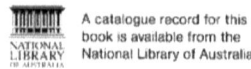

A catalogue record for this book is available from the National Library of Australia

To our sister, Kylie. This is a story of survival and determination, something about which you know all too well.

CONTENTS:

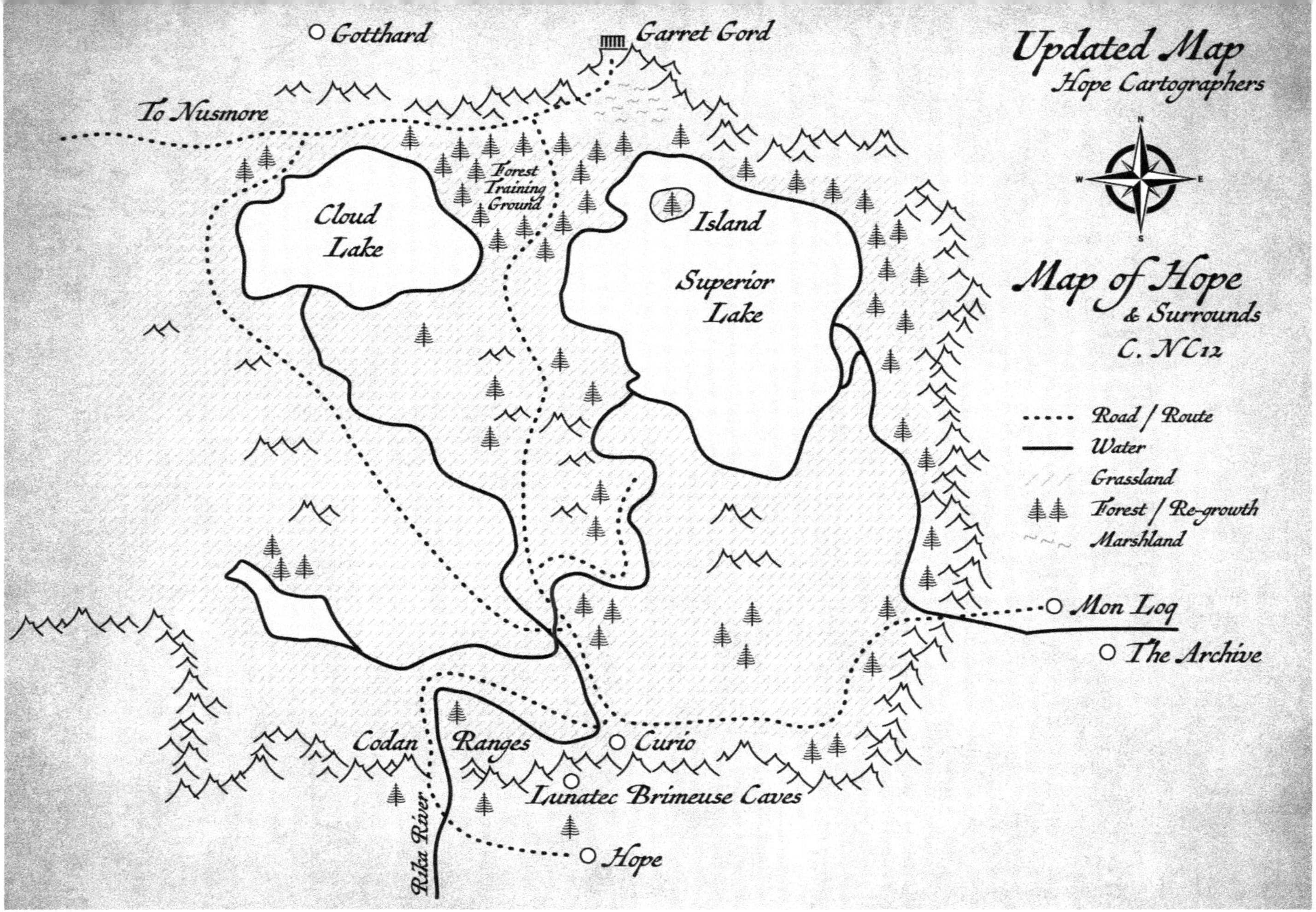

Updated Map
Hope Cartographers
N
E
S
W
Map of Hope
& Surrounds
C. NC12
Road / Route
Water
Grassland
Forest / Re-growth
Marshland
Gotthard
Garret Gord
To Nusmore
Forest Training Ground
Cloud Lake
Island
Superior Lake
Mon Loq
The Archive
Codan
Ranges
Curio
Lunatec Brimeuse Caves
Rika River
Hope

BURN THE SKY

PART 2: REDEMPTION

My name is Jayne. At seven, my family, home, and everything I ever knew and loved was destroyed by nuclear fire. I was rescued by a stranger and taken to a shelter where I was told I'd be going to someplace better. But as I experienced what remained of the world I once knew, I began to question, what does better actually mean? Now, as I sit writing this, reflecting on the last seven cycles, I'm left wondering what will happen next? With Sera no longer able to take me on adventures as she once had, and a strangely armoured man hunting us, I can only hope better comes soon.

01 HIDE AND SEEK

NEW CALENDAR - NC06

It's cool, dark and quiet inside the air ducts, just the way I like it. The silence, punctuated by the rhythmic whoop-whoop of the surface fans, is both soothing and exciting. While crouching in the stillness inside this labyrinth of metal tunnels, I imagine being inside the living, breathing bronchioles of the complex, feeding fresh air into every room—rooms I can explore. Occasionally, sounds drift from the adjacent rooms through the vents, and I wonder what may be going on within.

For the last three cycles, I've been exploring the complex using these ducts, except for the apartments, which have their own isolated ventilation systems. But everything else, it's like my own secret passage into the deep, dark recesses of Garret Gord.

This night, I've stopped outside a room where every time I've come here, it's always dark. This is as far as the light goes, so I've not dared to enter this room or venture further—until now. Curiosity has finally gotten the better of me, and I really want to know what lies beyond.

Light reflected into the duct from the room back a ways makes it difficult to sense what occupies the dark, and I've been crouching here for so long, trying to peer through the vent louvres, my legs have gone numb.

One thing I've learned since almost stepping on a sleeping guard is, don't exit into a room without light. Unlike other vents, the catch holding this one closed isn't budging; its movement, restricted either by time or something else. The grill and latch feel no different, it just seems to need more encouragement.

Careful not to make a sound, I rummage through my shoulder bag and pull out my trusty vent cover opener—a tool I made myself. It's a long thin piece of metal, rolled at one end and fashioned to quickly open vent covers from the outside. This grill is taking a bit more prying, and, in my attempt to get the catch to release, I create more noise than intended.

Light from a room I'd just passed turns on, illuminating the metal tunnel further.

'Hey, Creatch, did you hear that?' a voice says.

'I can't hear nothin' over your snorin',' another voice, possibly Creatch, responds.

'What you complaining about? You were asleep. Anyways, if you're awake now, you'd've heard that noise coming from the vent.'

'It's probably just rodentia. Go back to sleep.'

'Nah, this don't sound like no rodentia. How'd you open it?' The first voice says as the vent jiggles.

'I don't think you can.'

This time, they seem more intent on opening the grill as a person-shaped object moves between the light and the vent, grabs hold of the cover and shakes it hard.

With the stubborn grill to the neighbouring room beckoning to be opened, I return my attention to it. One firm knock, and it swings open, emitting a low, vibrating squeal before disappearing beyond my reach into absolute darkness. In my attempt to grab the grill to stop the noise, I overbalance and fall the one meta drop to the floor, landing face and hands first onto the hard, concrete floor. 'Ouch,' I groan through gritted teeth.

The room has a powdery smell of forgetfulness and neglect, and it tickles my nostrils, bringing on the urge to sneeze. Try as I might stifle it, I hold my nose, but in my next breath, the itching returns, increasing to an unbearable crescendo.

'*Ah-choo!*' Then again. '*Ah*-CHOO!'

'A sneeze,' the first voice says out of the open air vent. 'Surely you heard that?'

Creatch muffles something in reply.

'It was a sneeze, alright, and it sounds like it come from next door.'

'Shak,' I swear under my breath. *In a few moments, I'm going to have company.*

The neighbouring door opens, and a slit of light spills under the gap in the door, illuminating the room enough to reveal six large wooden crates sitting in a thick layer of fibrous dust. Footsteps stop outside, and the handle jiggles while I take cover behind one of the wooden boxes.

'Frakin' Kacir, it's locked,' the first voice curses.

'Why do you have to always profane?' the other protests, 'you know I'm a believer.'

'Get over it, Creatch. Have you got the keys?'

'Be easier to just kick it in.'

'Frak you. It's a solid metal door.'

There is no way I'm sticking around for them to find those keys.

By now, my eyes have adjusted to the minimal light. The vent cover almost touches the adjacent wall, and it drones with a horrible jarring noise when it's moved.

'Hear that?' the voice outside says, 'you got the right key yet?'

I spit into my fingers and rub saliva into the small hinges as lubrication. With a little work, it moves more quietly.

While Creatch and friend jingle with their keys, attempting to find the correct one, I get the flock out of there, climbing back into the vent and pulling the cover closed behind.

Leaving the two men with the locked door, I venture deeper into the blackness. The long tunnel has eluded me so far; it's about time I discover where it leads. A few metas in, and without a light source of any kind, I can't even see the end of my nose. It feels like the walls are closing in, and I question my decision to come this way. Using my hands to feel my way along the duct, I get the sense no other rooms exist in this part of the complex—at least, no vents exit here. I keep crawling through the blackness, upwards and onwards, until an enticing golden glow dancing in the distance draws me toward it.

At first, I think my eyes are playing tricks, but as I shuffle closer, the light becomes brighter and faint voices echo through the duct, gradually becoming louder.

'What is done is done, Patriarch. What more can I do?' a familiar voice says.

I drop to my belly and slide silently towards the vent, pulling myself up to the cover to peer through. Beyond the louvres, Sera is sitting in the small wooden chair in a very well-furnished office, talking with the white-haired, bearded man I recognise as the Patriarch. From behind his fancy desk, the old man gesticulates wildly. 'You could give me a reason not to retire you,' he scolds her. 'Look at you. You're a useless cripple. Fraking useless. You can't even walk straight, let alone do whatever it is you people do. What am I supposed to do with that? Tell me?'

Despite the rants directed at her, Sera remains seemingly unperturbed, with a serene expression on her face and her hands resting in her lap. 'What do you want me to say, Elihus?' she says in a calm voice. 'I have already apologised.'

'That isn't good enough. You should have known better. Your excuses mean nothing to me. And they're certainly not going to repair the damage you have done to my position in Hope. I don't appreciate having to explain myself to that… imbecile of a Surprime. Have six cycles of inactivity melted your brain and made you soft? These are not the actions of a seasoned professional. It's amateurish. And to think I once considered you my best.'

'No need to be harsh,' Sera retorts, still with that calm demeanour. 'I completed the mission. Do you want me to go back and retrieve my knife? Is that it?'

He steps around his desk and sits on the edge just in front of her. 'Insolent woman!' he spits, lifting a hand to strike her across the face. Sera closes her eyes, bracing for the slap, but he reaches out and strokes her face instead. 'Good thing for you, I've had some time to think over this predicament. I am of two minds about what to do with you. Part of me wants to see you punished for your insolence—the other part knows you may still have more to offer.' His fingers wander toward the neckline of her top, pulling it away so he can peer down. 'You could serve me in other ways…'

She slaps his hand away.

It seems the act provokes him, and he grips her chin firmly between his fingers, holding her head. They stare into each other's eyes before he forcefully plants his lips on hers.

Sera resists, but the chair restricts her movement.

I can't watch and turn away, but when I hear Sera laugh, I almost press my face against the cover to see why. By then, Elihus has returned to his chair, and Sera is rubbing her jaw with a sardonic grin on her face. 'Oh, come now, Elihus. You and I both know that will not work out well for you.'

'Gah!' he retorts, dismissively flicking his arm. 'You and that retched protection order. *He* may protect you, but that doesn't include that little tramp of yours.'

That comment seems to have penetrated Sera's cool exterior as her disposition changes to something much more threatening. 'You leave Jayne out of this!' she snaps.

'That got your attention,' he says, white beard bristling with his smug grin.

Sera scowls at him. 'If you lay one fat finger on her—'

'*Or*, you will do what?'

'Jayne is under *my* protection. I may walk with a cane, but I can still tear off your testicles and make you eat them. Nothing has changed.'

'I beg to differ. You are not in control here. I am! This is MY House. I WILL DO WHATEVER I PLEASE. Or do you not get that, MonLantry?'

The look on Sera's face is one of utter repugnance. 'Speak plain, Elihus.'

'Things happen,' he says, with another one of those sly grins. 'I know you've taken affection to your little tramp. It's a good thing for you she's come this far. It would be unfortunate should anything happen to her. I guess we'll soon see just how much further she will get.'

'Is that a threat?'

'No. It's a statement of fact. *Your* idle threats, on the other hand, don't scare me. If I want her, she will be mine, you understand? Now, you will submit her for testing like all the others. *If* she survives, we'll see how useful you both are then. Now get out.'

'Patriarch,' she says with disdain, collecting her cane propped up beside her and hobbling towards the door.

'Oh, and MonLantry, you're not off the hook yet, not by a long shot. Prove to me you can be useful, and I'll agree to leave *her* alone. But disappoint me again, and that order will not be enough to protect either of you.'

As the door closes, a pang of guilt rises from the pit of my stomach. Concerned for Sera, I scramble for home, trying not to think about what I just saw.

The hall outside the apartment is quiet as usual. Slipping from the vent, I take the four steps to my door, gripping the handle with my heartbeat thumping in my ears like a drum.

'If you didn't still have her… if she survives, we'll see how useful you both are then.'

What does it all mean?

The silence is too much. While I stand there, gathering the confidence to open the door, a familiar sound interrupts the stillness. Over my shoulder is the large wooden door to the neighbouring apartment where I had seen the blue-eyed girl. It stands ajar, and a single unblinking eye watches me from within. I turn the handle to my door, flash the owner of the eye a smile, and then slip inside.

Upon entering, Sera's at the dining table, cupping a mug of tei and looking forlorn, as though lost. Despite her normally impenetrable exterior, it would seem that her altercation with the Patriarch had hit her hard. She snatches a used tissue from the table and hides it up her sleeve. *Like I didn't notice.* Her glistening brown eyes are puffy red, and she attempts a smile as I approach. 'Hi, Jayne. Come sit with me.'

Discretely shoving my bag under the table, I take my seat beside her. 'Are you okay?'

Beneath her hands is a piece of crumpled paper that she's clearly pretending to conceal. 'Better now,' she replies, picking strands of dust from my clothing. 'Where have you been?'

'Just exploring. What's this?' I ask, tilting forward for a better look at the paper visible between her fingers. It's a torn page from *The Hope Chronicle*, dated, Lunaday 2, Reincarner 06, with the headline:

Gaius Sempro Murdered

Sera peels her hands away, exposing a black and white picture of a respectable-looking, middle-aged man with dark hair and a warm smile.

'Consequences,' she replies.

The article reads;

Gaius Sempro, much-loved founder and long-serving Administrator of Hope, was found murdered yesterday evening. His body was discovered in one of the offices of the recently opened Town Hall. It's alleged the murder weapon, a knife, was still present at the scene. His death comes as a shock after he was favoured to win the first election for the position of Virtuous Surprime by a landslide vote. His successor and close friend, Sage Solon, said, 'This is a great and terrible loss to our community. Gaius was more than an

Administrator to us; he was also a friend, a father figure and a mentor. His presence will be sorely missed.'

Authorities are still yet to reveal any information on their investigations but say they have some leads towards finding the killer…

'I don't understand. What am I looking at?' It can't be a coincidence Sera just so happens to have a newspaper from Hope dated the day after we were near there. 'Has this got anything to do with us?'

'Afraid so.' Sera scratches her head in the way she does when she's anxious. 'The person they are looking for is me, Jayne. I killed Gaius Sempro.'

Her admission hits me like a punch to the guts. 'What? You're serious?'

'Yes.'

'So, ahh…'

'Jayne, I am only telling you this because you would have found out about it, eventually. I would rather you heard it from me than someone wanting to stir trouble.'

I turn to look her in the eye. 'But you *killed* someone? Why?'

'It is… complicated.'

'What's that supposed to mean?'

She sighs and, fumbling with the page, avoids my gaze. I don't think I've ever seen Sera lost for words before. 'I have never had to explain it to a person such as yourself, but I will try,' she says.

'Sera, you're scaring me.'

'I am sorry.' She takes a deep breath, and her expression becomes more serious. 'The reason I did it is that I was contracted to.'

'But why? Why would you do that?'

'Because Jayne, I am… an assassin.'

'What?!' I gasp.

'An assassin.'

'I heard what you said, but what?'

'I am just as all the other women are here. We are ordered to fulfil contracts, and so that is what we do.'

I'd never considered her to be a killer, let alone something like this. Sera has always been kind-hearted, friendly and nurturing, at least to me.

But an assassin?

'So, you kill people… for money?'

'Those are not the words I would use, but essentially yes. However, instead of being paid money, we are paid by way of this lifestyle. That is how it is for us all.'

My mouth hangs agape in disbelief. 'Huh. So, is that why we were chased down the mountain?'

'Yes. Well, I can only assume so.'

'And is that how you lost your knife?'

'Yes, I had no choice but to leave it behind.' Her response seems so casual—like we are discussing the weather.

While I know from her serious expression she's telling the truth, I still can't bring myself to believe it. 'I still don't understand, though. Why would you do this, and why are you telling me now?'

Her hand reaches for mine, and I pull away, uncertain if I can handle being comforted by someone who has just told me they're a killer.

'I am still the same person you met five cycles ago. This changes nothing. I am telling you this now because it is time you learned the truth, well, *some* of the truth at least.'

'What truth?'

'Garret Gord is not what you think.'

'No shak!'

'Jayne, please listen. This is important. Garret Gord is a training complex for female assassins. You, among others, are here to be trained.'

'Trained? To be like you?'

'Yes.' Sera's face remains unyielding against her statements, but I sense confliction in her voice.

'Wow. So, all the camping and Shitak'na that was…'

'Survival and combat training. And there will be more.'

'What if I don't want to be an assassin? Don't I get a choice?'

Her shoulders uncharacteristically slump, and her gaze falls to her hands resting on the table. 'Sorry, no.'

'But, why?'

'That, I'm afraid, I cannot answer. When I was your age, I wanted to be a chef, but we cannot always get what we want.'

'No kidding. You seem to be pretty good with knives though…'

Her chuckle breaks the seriousness, but only momentarily.

When she returns her gaze to me, her eyes glisten with fresh tears. 'The fact of the matter is, I am not even supposed to be telling you this. I fear I have already said too much, and that could get us both into a lot of strife. All I know is, I have been contracted to raise you and care for you as your guardian so that one day when you graduate, you will join our elite ranks.'

'Elite? So, I can be ordered to go kill people just like you? Is that it?'

'If you want to put it that way.'

I don't know what to think about that. Having Sera tell me she's only caring for me because she's been ordered to makes me sick. Clenching and unclenching my fists beneath the table, I try to keep my anger from bubbling up and resist the urge to storm out of the apartment. 'SO, I'm *just* another contract to you? Is that it?'

'No,' she replies, using that calm exterior trick on me, and I can see why it got the Patriarch so riled up. 'That is not true, and you know that. It may be true for some, but not for me.'

'But you just said you've been raising me because you have to. Was all this talk about loving me a lie?'

'You are just twisting my words. That's not what I said at all.'

'What about all those cycles ago when you first came to see me in Gotthard and told me I was going to someplace better? Is this what you really meant, or was that just a lie too?'

'I have never lied to you, Jayne. I may not have told you the whole truth, but I never lied. And I was not lying when I said you can help make this a better world.'

'How is killing people making this a better world?'

'We do not ask questions; we follow orders. We must trust our leaders know what they are doing.'

'And how did that work out for this man, Gaius Sempro?' I yell, poking at the picture on the page. 'What did that article say, "A friend, a father figure and a mentor"? Sounds to me our leaders got it wrong. And so did you!'

'I don't know,' Sera says, bowing her head. 'We cannot be expected to understand the complex decisions our leaders have to make.'

'So why did you do it? Why did you kill this man? Because they ordered you to?'

'Yes. But you must understand, it's not that simple.'

'Then, explain it to me!'

She sighs, leaning across the table so she can get closer. 'I have lived in Garret Gord for almost my whole life. Like you, I was an orphan—only I was five when my parents died in a car accident, not a nuclear war. The State sent me to a horribly strict orphanage where I was punished for even the most minor etiquette misdemeanours. Then, when I was ten, Elihus Kinton came to the orphanage. He adopted me and three other girls and brought us back here, where we began our training. He told us we would change the world for the better by eliminating bad people from it. Over the cycles, the facility grew, and he became known as the Patriarch. When we graduated, he sent us out on top-secret missions to do things nobody else dared. For that is why we were trained. That was our purpose. We brought down empires and helped establish new ones, all the while the world carried on, never knowing we even existed. We never knew the reasons for our missions, who we were impacting or whether what we were actually doing was right.'

'How does that make it right?'

'That is irrelevant. Here in Garret Gord, we live by a strict code and are told to obey without question. I have always accepted that as truth, and that is why I carried out those orders. For whatever reason, this Gaius Sempro had to be eliminated. That is all I know. That is all I am ever allowed to know. I can only gather he was targeted because strategically, he needed to be neutralised—put out of the way. Wrong or right, someone believes that, and as an asset, I am expected to believe that as well.'

'But *why*?'

At that moment, Sera hesitates, and I can tell the question has given her pause.

'When you came into my life, it changed me. I thought raising a child would make me soft. That somehow, I would lose my edge and myself in the process. Even when a stranger told me all those cycles ago I would have a child, and it would change my life, I despised them for bringing it up. But I have come to realise having you in my life has been the best thing that has ever happened to me. And it is since that mission I now know why. I wish I could explain it better, and I know I am doing a pretty poor job. All you need to understand is everything I do, Jayne, I do for you.'

'How is killing an innocent man got anything to do with me?'

'That is the only explanation I can offer you. I know it is difficult to understand why I did what I did—why Gaius had to die—and I know it does not make it right, but that is not for me to decide. You just have to trust me.'

'That's rich coming from someone who keeps telling me to not trust anyone.'

'Jayne,' she sighs, 'I cannot make you understand, but it is what it is. You may not like or agree with what goes on around here, but this is your life now, and we have to make the most of it.'

'Like how? Why do I just have to accept orders?'

'Because you do. You are very intelligent, Jayne, and I can see you have the need to understand everything that goes on around you. That is very admirable, and you should never lose that. Some things, however, are just not meant for us to understand. It pains me to watch you go through this, so the best advice I can offer you now is to accept it. It may be hard, but you must trust me. It is better that way.'

After her conversation with the Patriarch, I'm surprised to hear her say that, but it's starting to make more sense now. Still, there's no way I can tell her what I overheard, and I'm done arguing with her. Maybe it's better if I just accept it—I'm going to be an assassin. Maybe it's not all that bad. 'Okay, so, it is what it is. What now? What will happen to you?'

'Well, I keep training you like I always have. As for me, you do not need to worry about that.'

The expression on her face says there's more to this story. But if I know one thing about Sera, there's no point in probing further; she's already changed subjects in her mind. I offer her a slight grin and nod in acknowledgement, and it helps ease the tension.

Sera's shoulders relax, and with apprehension, she asks, 'so, are you ready to do this?'

'If I'm to do this, I want to do it my way.'

'If you insist. There are strict rules, but I am sure we can work within them.'

'We?'

'Of course, you are not doing this entirely on your own. Gosh, no, we are a team and are in this together. That is what I am here for.'

'Okay,' I reply. 'Then yes. I… we can do this.'

02 SAGE ADVICE

Sage adjusted the large lapels on his stately, long-flowing, deep-red robes. As he did, he glanced with affection at the beaming woman in the front row clutching their three-day-old daughter.

Four long days had passed since the election, and a lot had happened since then.

The birth of his daughter had been the shining light amongst an otherwise bleak time in Hope's short history. The town was still coming to terms with the tumultuous events, particularly the horrific murder of their beloved administrator, Gaius Sempro. Despite their sombreness, the townspeople flocked to the town hall to witness the swearing-in of their new Surprime.

'And I give you Sage Solon, first Virtuous Surprime of Hope,' Orian announced, concluding her introductory speech and gesturing to Sage, who waited nervously at her side. He turned and bowed before her, allowing her to drape a large golden chain of pressed metal discs over his shoulders.

Engraved in cursive script on the first disc was Sage's name, marking him as the position's official holder. The central amulet featured an image of cupped hands, forming wings supporting the likeness of the new town hall, behind which emblazoned rays of a sunshine crest, depicting the emergence of Hope into a new dawn. Beneath that, a waving five-part ribbon read:

Hagalaz Othila ᚺᛟᛈᛖ Peorth Ehwaz

In the old tongue, it meant Rebirth, Heritage, Life, Traveller; four words that personified Hope.

Complete with political jewellery, Sage stepped up to the podium, looking the very picture of nobility, and he hated it.

He cleared his throat and prepared to recite his practised speech, pausing momentarily for the audience's subdued applause.

'Family, friends, good people of Hope,' he said with a painted smile, taking care to avoid a recurrence of his last disastrous speech but also conscious of the conditions under which he stood there. 'I am both honoured and saddened to accept the position of Virtuous Surprime. This, as you know, is a bittersweet day. Gaius should be the first name on this chain, not mine. He should be the one standing here, and it breaks my heart every time I think of why he isn't.' Sage allowed a wave of grief to wash over him, looking out at the gathered crowd to see he wasn't the only one stifling back tears. He gritted his teeth and continued. 'If you will allow me before I begin with the formalities, I'd like to first say a few words in honour of Gaius.'

The crowd stilled while Sage extracted a piece of paper from inside his robes and placed it on the podium, smoothing it down with the palms of his hands. 'I think you all know my track record with speeches,' he said light-heartedly, hoping it would relieve some of the awkwardness. 'So, this time, I've asked Orian to help me. I think it's pretty well right.' He cleared his throat again and took a deep breath. 'Gaius was a great man,' he said, the words formed even without the aid of his notes. 'Hope would not be here without him. I look around at all of you gathered here today, and I can't see a single person whose life Gaius hasn't touched and made the better for it.

'When I came to Hope in 02, I, like most of you, was a lost and desperate refugee, hungry, sick and in need of warm shelter. Gaius and Rika took me in, cared for me and gave me food and a home. They didn't care or even ask where I came from—they just accepted me as a person who needed their help. Because that's what they did. Gaius was more than a friend or mentor to me—he was like a father. He saw something in me I couldn't see in myself, and ever since, he had only ever striven to make me a better version of myself.

He had a vision for Hope, too,' Sage continued. 'Both Rika and Gaius dreamed of making this place a town. A place where people can come and forget the world they've left behind and focus on something better. He always said, "What's passed is past. Everything happens for a reason," and while we may want to shut away from the horrific events of the past, they don't define us. Instead, like

Gaius, they shape us and encourage us to learn, grow, move forward and become better versions of ourselves. I only wish to carry on this legacy so that I may not only provide a better place for my beautiful wife and new baby daughter but for us all. It saddens me Gaius could not have been here to meet her. So, with that, I pledge to you, as the first Virtuous Surprime of Hope, I will make Hope a better version of itself. I vow to carry on Gaius and Rika's vision and see their dream for Hope realised.' Sage wiped away the tears under each eye, and while he hesitated, it appeared there wasn't a dry eye in the crowd. The gathering gave him a delayed cheer, and it lightened his heart to know that even in their grief, he had given them something to cheer about.

As the cheers faded, Sage spoke again. 'Gentle people of Hope. In my first act as Surprime, I will dissolve the Council—'

Applause melted into gasps and exchanges of confused glances.

'But,' he continued, raising his palms to the gathering to reassure them, 'in its place, I will establish ministries of representatives who will help me govern the new Hope. Each one dedicated to seeing a part of that vision made real. Allow me to introduce your new Hope Peoples' Ministry.' Sage directed his arm toward the line-up of people standing in the wings, each stepping forward when he announced them.

'Treasurer, Abril Tope.

Minister for Defence, Artimus Wyrm.

Minister for Education, Elihus Kinton.

Minister for Property and Development, Indira Tryce.

Minister for Science and Research, Garan Tope.

Minister for Health, Alessandra MonBrelstaff.

Minister for Food and Resources, Niklas Martell.

And of course, our Speaker and Vice-Surprime, the wonderful Ms Orian Gracyn.'

They all wore new, tailored robes similar to Sage but in black, while Orian, whose position was only lesser to Sage's, wore blue.

When the applause died down, Sage concluded his speech. 'I know that in the coming cycles, my ministry, your ministry, will do you all proud. It is all Gaius and Rika would have hoped for. That's why we call our home Hope.'

The crowd erupted in glorious ovation, which continued as Sage said his thank-yous and shook the hands of his ministry. While they dispersed, Sage descended the steps to join his young family at the foot, where those who remained flocked around him to shake his hand in congratulations.

When the last person had pressed their hand to Sage's, Jaylyn leaned in closer to whisper in his ear. 'When do I get to congratulate the Surprime?'

'Better make it later. My wife might see us,' he joked.

'Your speech was beautiful, my love,' she said, kissing him with affection on the cheek. She adjusted the cloth-wrapped bundle nestled in a sling against her chest. 'And I must say, those robes are really sexy on you.'

'What, these old rags,' he chuckled, plucking at them, 'you really think so?'

'Seriously, I think Gaius would be proud,' she said, her eyes glistening with pride. 'Are you okay, though?'

'What do you mean?'

'Well, you know, after everything that's happened over the last few days, you look five cycles older…'

Sage choked out a chuckle. 'Thanks, and you're supposed to be on my side.'

'I'm proud of you, Sage Solon, first Virtuous Surprime of Hope.'

'Don't speak too soon. I've not done anything yet,' Sage smiled, trying not to let her comment trigger him. 'Thank you, my babe.' He kissed her on the lips and then gave his tiny daughter a kiss on the forehead. 'It's just a shame she missed him by a day. I was really looking forward to Gaius becoming a "grandfather".'

'Ohh!' Abril's familiar shrill voice came from behind. She was making her way towards Sage and his family, her eyes fixed on the tiny bundle cradled around Jaylyn's body. 'I'd heard she'd come but hadn't had a chance to meet our newest Hope resident yet.'

Jaylyn pulled the side of the sling over, exposing the fine, fuzzy blonde hair of her daughter and, with the affection that only a proud mother could give, beamed at Abril.

'The first child of the Surprime. She's adorable,' Abril said.

'With all the excitement, she's asleep at the moment. I think she just wanted to see her daddy get sworn in,' Jaylyn said.

Abril touched the bundle supported in the wrap. 'What's her name?'

'Averyx,' Sage replied. 'After my mother.'

'Averyx Solon, that's a beautiful name,' Abril said, smiling at the baby's adoring parents. She then looked down and crooned at the sleepy bundle. 'Hi there, Averyx. Aren't you a little cutie?'

'If you will excuse me,' Sage said, finding a moment to take his leave, 'there's something I have to do.' He kissed his wife again. 'It begins. Love you. I'll see you tonight.'

'You've got a good one there,' Sage overheard Abril say as he strode away. 'I always believed he would make a great father…'

Following the ceremony, Sage retreated to the quiet of the cemetery to visit Gaius's final resting place. Jaxson, dressed in a smart, new black and red-piped formal uniform of the Surprime Guard, accompanied him, and together, they stood side by side at the large headstone. Engraved into the polished stone, emblazoned in gold, were the words:

Here lies Gaius Sempro, husband to Rika, father of Hope.
May he forever find peace.
AP1894 – NC05

'I can only hope to do as well as you would have,' Sage said, wiping a tear from his eye. Beside him, Jaxson stifled back tears of his own.

'I failed him,' Jaxson despaired with a sullen expression.

'No, you didn't,' Sage said. 'You couldn't have known this was going to happen. None of us did.'

'Yes, but I was his personal guard. It was my job to protect him. I've never lost a charge under my watch, even the ones I didn't respect. But Gaius, he was more than just a charge to me. And I let him get killed.'

Sage patted his closest friend on the back. 'This is not your fault, Jaxson. Don't make it so.' The words were as much for his benefit as they were for Jaxson. After all, the feeling was mutual.

'Thanks, man,' Jaxson said as Sage pulled him into a firm embrace.

Footsteps crunched over the ground behind them, startling the two men. Jaxson unclipped his pistol and drew it as they separated and spun around.

'Gentlemen,' Orian said, holding her palms out by her sides and approaching with caution. 'It's just me.'

Sage relaxed, and Jaxson re-holstered his weapon, both trying to conceal they'd been crying.

'Apologies for the intrusion,' she said, moving closer to stand before Gaius's grave. 'I didn't mean to startle you.'

'It's fine, Orian,' Sage replied. 'We were just paying our respects.'

She smiled an affectionate, melancholy smile. 'That was a beautiful speech, by the way. Gaius would be proud.'

Sage bowed his head. 'Are you sure about that? You wrote it.'

'But it came from you. I just crafted it into something… intelligible.'

'Ha!' he laughed, 'I can just imagine my tombstone: "Here lies Sage Solon. He had a way with words"!'

'Do you know how many speeches I've written for others over the cycles?'

He considered that for a moment.

Orian continued. 'It was just part of the job. But out of them all, yours would have to have been the most sincere.'

Sage sighed, his sadness and doubt returning. 'What am I doing, Orian? I'm not made for this.'

'Don't be silly,' she said, rubbing him on the arm. 'You seem to be doing just fine.'

'I've got my hands pretty full right now. Besides, I never asked for this. When I put my name forward, I only did it because *he* wanted me to.' Sage flicked a hand at Gaius's grave. 'Probably so he didn't have to,' *the coward*, he added the last two words mentally. It wasn't that he was angry at Gaius, but the man always had ways of forcing him into things he didn't feel ready for.

'I remember an impetuous young man who only a few cycles ago risked his own life to save a burgeoning village. While we sheltered in safety, this man braved a military attack. He single-handedly negotiated a deal that saved all our lives. If there are two things I've learned over the cycles, first, you never get to choose the manner in which life decides to challenge you. Second, great people often do not seek out power. Circumstances push them into it.'

'*Great*? No, I don't think so. That was him.'

'I beg to differ,' she said. 'I've seen how you've risen to these recent challenges. How you've handled the investigation, the devotion you have shown to your family, and how you've balanced that with your new responsibilities as Surprime. Sage, you may not think you can ever measure up to Gaius, but you don't have to. We can't all be like him, and if you think that's what he wanted, you've completely missed the point. He wanted you to be a better version of yourself, not him. And from where I'm standing, you've done just that.'

To Sage, her words carried much wisdom and foresight, resonating something within him he knew to be true.

'She's right, brother,' Jaxson said. 'If it weren't for you, my brains would have been splattered all over the pavement. I can't think of a better person to lead us than you.'

'Thanks, man,' Sage said, slapping him on the back. All this emotional talk made him feel uncomfortable. He gazed at his feet with embarrassment, scuffing the ground with a shoe, contemplating what they had said. After a moment, he lifted his head to the cool afternoon breeze. 'You're right,' he said. 'You both are. And I'm grateful. Thank you.'

Orian smiled and gave a slight nod while Jaxson brimmed with newfound energy. Sage felt a weight had been lifted, although, in his heart, he knew there was still a long way to go. But with these two at his side, he would undoubtedly be able to face whatever challenges came his way.

'You know, Sage. You remind me a lot of him. That day I arrived in Hope, and you insisted on checking the trucks before helping the wounded—that's something he would have done. He was never one to shirk responsibility. It wasn't because you didn't care about my people. You could have easily taken my word for it and allowed me to harry you into abandoning your security protocols, but you didn't. You considered the safety of your own people first. Like him, you're prepared to make the tough decisions and pursue what you believe is right. I admire that. And that's what's going to make you a great Surprime.'

Sage scratched his head in embarrassment. He wasn't used to people complimenting him like this. People looked up to him, sure, but he had always figured that was because he just did things that needed doing. That's what he had been trained to do. He never had to question himself like this in his previous job. In many ways, he felt more comfortable working alone, but hearing Orian say these things gave him hope he was walking the right path. Nobody, however, could train him to be comfortable with it.

'He was also impulsive,' she added with an affectionate smile. 'You know he proposed to me within twenty decs of our meeting?'

'Gaius? Really? That sly pup!'

'We were seventeen, and it was our school graduation party. He said, "you want to get married someday?" which at the time I remember thinking was a bit presumptuous and odd, but I liked that. I also think the amount he'd had to drink and the environment may have had something to do with it. Anyway, he seemed nice, was kind and *really* handsome, so we became friends. After a few treys, he offered me his spare room, and I moved in. Not long after, he enlisted in the military, and after six cycles of only seeing him for short bursts here and there, I realised I was in love with him. So, I eventually accepted his proposal, and we married soon after.'

While Orian's story had lightened the mood, from the wavering of her voice, they were getting into sensitive territory again.

'You really loved him, didn't you?' he asked.

She nodded, then turned to face him, eyeing him in his formal robes. 'He was very proud of you, you know, and would be thrilled to see you as Surprime.'

Sage smiled an awkward smile. 'Thank you, Orian. And thanks, old man,' he said, glancing at the headstone.

'Anyway, I came to find you. Artimus says the Hunter has returned.'

Sage, Orian and Jaxson stood at the door to Artimus's office, where the burly minister, looking out of place in his robes, sat deep in thought behind a worn timber desk.

Standing bold about a meta from the desk was a rugged man even larger than the Admiral.

That must be the Hunter, Sage thought, observing the man's peculiar, well-worn armour. He couldn't help but notice the numerous scratches and indents peppering the layers of camouflage paint, appearing as though it had seen its share of battles.

Sage's attention then drifted to the rifle slung over the man's shoulder where its short, thick black barrel protruded a little over his head, while the ejection port seemed large enough for a round the size of Sage's thumb. With carefully concealed admiration, Sage could only imagine what it would be like to fire just one shot from that beast.

The weathered man spoke with blunted affect. 'I followed their tracks to a bridge crossing the Rangy River. There was a discarded sled, bloody bandages and tyre tracks where a vehicle picked them up.'

'Who's they?' Artimus asked.

'A woman and a girl about twelve.'

'And they had help?'

'You have my report.'

Artimus scratched his head. 'So, the child was injured?'

'No.'

By now, Artimus's face had turned red. 'How could you not catch them?' he yelled, slamming his hands on the desk as he stood. 'You allowed an injured woman and a child to beat you?' His eyes darted to Sage standing in the doorway. 'Surprime, so glad you could join us.'

Sage entered, conscious of the bloodstain which still marked the floor where Gaius took his last breath. He shied away from it and approached Artimus, even more wary of the heavily armoured man, taking care not to block the space between him and the door. He knew people like that prefered their exits clear and tended to charge through anyone who may be standing in their way, even if that person happened to be the Surprime.

Sage stood a comfortable distance from Hunter at the side of the desk, which was mostly bare except for the murder weapon and an odd, coverless book.

'Hunter here was just telling me he chased Gaius's killers down the mountain towards the deserted town of Curio. He lost them in an avalanche after he decided to drop the mountain on them. They got away.' He picked up the coverless book and threw it to Sage. 'They left this, though. Well, that and a pile of tinned canis food.'

'*Be Yond the Horizon*,' Sage recited the title. 'I haven't read that one. Where's the cover?'

'Don't know, don't care, probably somewhere in the cave where he found it,' Artimus flicked a finger towards Hunter.

'I'll find them,' Hunter growled. 'They're out there.'

'Which direction were they heading?' Sage asked.

Artimus replied, 'According to Hunter, the tyre tracks headed north-east up the Rangy towards Superior Lake.'

'Anyone got a map?'

Artimus turned to the wall behind him, lifted aside a few pieces of paper pinned to it with string and revealed a map.

Sage approached and considered it. 'That's toward the Garret mountains,' he said, running his finger up the blue line depicting the river. 'There's nothing out there!'

Artimus slapped a thick envelope on the edge of the desk and pushed it towards Hunter. 'Your payment,' he said. 'That's more than your services on this occasion deserve. You WILL find them. That is our arrangement.'

Hunter grunted, took his parcel and strode past Jaxson and Orian on his way out of the office, his armour and equipment barely making a sound as he left.

'Where did you find him?' Sage asked. 'He's got the personality of a block of wood.'

'He's been in my service for some time. It's not a story I'm interested in telling,' Artimus replied rather bluntly.

'Alright, I just hope he's worth what we're paying.' Sage's eyes drifted to the stain on the floor again. 'Why did you set yourself up in here?'

Artimus glanced at Orian. 'I have my reasons.'

At that moment, Jaxson stepped forward. 'As head of the Surprime Guard, I need to know, was the attack on Gaius or the position?'

'You heard the report, so now you know as much as I do,' Artimus said.

'Well, it looks like you have everything under control,' Sage said. 'I have a meeting with LunaTec in five decs, so I have to go.'

'Just wait a dec!' Artimus roared, his sudden aggression catching Sage by surprise. 'You may be Surprime, but HomeGuard report to me!'

Sage paused. 'Is there a problem, Artimus?'

'Only that I learned this morning I lost a truck and eight good soldiers, and yet I have no recollection of sending them.'

'Perhaps you should cut back on the ale.'

Artimus slammed the desk. 'HomeGuard is my operation. We have an agreement!'

'Yes,' Sage said calmly, 'but you are Defence Minister and the ministry report to me. Whatever *this* is, just sort it out.'

Without a second thought, Sage left Artimus to fume.

Orian followed Sage down the hallway, through the antechamber and into the Surprime's office, which sat adjacent to the main hall. She closed the door, leaving Jaxson to stand guard outside.

'That went well,' he said with sarcasm, slipping out of his ministerial regalia. He hung the robes on a stand by the door, passed the chain to Orian, and grabbed his trusty red coat. Breathing a sigh of relief, he threw it over his shoulders and adjusted his shirt collar in the mirror on the wall before slumping in his leather chair behind his dark polished timber desk.

'That's Artimus, I'm afraid,' Orian said with sympathy.

'You say that like it's normal. You've worked with him?'

'Unfortunately, I have, yes, but that was a long time ago,' she replied with a grim look.

'And was he like this?'

'No, not at first. When I met him, after Gaius, well, you know, Artimus was a well-respected Admiral. He was also handsome and charming, with a wife and a baby girl—I even met them once. Then something happened, and he disappeared for a trey. When he came back, he had that burn covering half his face, his wife and daughter had died, and he… changed.'

'Oh, I didn't know. That's terrible,' Sage said. Thinking about his own family, he couldn't even imagine the grief that would have caused. 'I know I shouldn't ask this, but that night when… you know… happened, you were interrogating him and alluded to something he did. What was that about?'

'You're right. You shouldn't. Please forgive me, Sage, but do you mind if we talk about something else? I feel like you're interrogating me.'

'I'm sorry, Orian, I didn't mean that. I just need to know it's not going to be a problem.'

'I can't speak for Artimus, but we can only hope it won't. Anyway, I just wanted to prepare you for your meeting with LunaTec. Cristal will be here soon. Here are the financial reports.' She slid a manila folder across the desk to him. 'Congratulations on the new baby girl, by the way. If you need anything else, I'll be in my office.'

03 ILONA

Dirty yellowed fingers drift across a map of the forested area surrounding Garret Gord as the truck bounces over the rough, corrugated track. 'Your drop point will be here,' the cantankerous guard says, half-heartedly relaying instructions. Wedged between his fingers is a smouldering brown stick wafting tendrils of acrid smoke. It reeks almost as bad as he does. 'That's one cendec drive from the Gord. 'ere's your map and compass.' He crumples up the map, thrusts it along with a small globe suspended in liquid into my hand. Still, I'm more intrigued by the nasty-looking scar down the side of his face, giving him the appearance he's wearing Sera's ornametics. I'm sure he catches me gawking because he gives me a dirty look. 'Now shove off,' he says before reclining against the wall and pulling his grey woollen hat down over his eyes.

Uncrumpling the map to examine it, it doesn't seem right. The driveway to the Gord runs almost south-east, but the map reads south-south-west. 'Excuse me?'

"His grumpiness" lifts a corner of his hat to impart a nasty glare.

'You gave me a mag-compass, but I think the map is true north.'

'Well, if the map's true, follow that,' he grumbles, crossing his burly arms before resuming his repose.

Right. I groan inwardly.

An awkward silence descends upon the truck, and I'm urged to make pleasant conversation. 'Have you worked at Garret Gord long?'

'Long 'nuff.' He doesn't bother moving this time.

'You're not much of a talker, are you? What's your name?'

The man lifts his hat again and shoots me an even colder glare. 'My orders are to see you to the drop. That's all. You're not my friend, and I don't care 'bout you. Now, shut up and let me get some sleep.'

'Yer, but what do your friends call you? I'm Jayne.'

'V'nom.'

I stifle a laugh.

'Wot? You got a problem with my name?'

'Is that with or without the "e"?' I giggle. 'Only raiders have names like that. I would have thought your name would be something more like Bob or Barry, but okay, V'nom.'

The man bares his yellow-stained teeth and points one of those grubby fingers at me. 'Well, I'm gonna call you dinner, the next girl I pick up, I'll call breakfast, and I'm gonna have myself a feast.' He licks his lips and then rests a hand on the pistol in the holster draped over his shoulder. 'But if you don't shut up and let me sleep, I may just eat you now.'

The uniform may be Garret Gord, but he certainly isn't. If I didn't know better, he's a raider. Or at least he was. *Why would Garret Gord hire raiders?*

We come to a stop, and V'nom drags himself off the bench to kick open the rear door. Fresh afternoon air floods the truck, and I breathe it in, glad to be relieved from V'nom's horrible stench. The chill tickles my exposed skin, and I pull my fur-lined coat tighter, throw my small pack over a shoulder and stand to leave.

'I'll have the pack,' he demands, blocking my exit, 'and that nice coat.'

'But they're mine.'

'They're the Gord's. I'm seein' they're returned.' He smiles a grisly smile that tilts his scar towards his thinning hairline just visible under his hat.

With a huff, I swing the bag off my shoulder, twist and slam it into his face. It catches him by surprise, and while he flounders, I dart past, leap off the step and land into a shoulder roll. 'Nah, I think I'll keep them. Thanks.'

'You rotten boart,' he cries.

'See ya, V'nom,' I wave, sliding down an embankment and out of sight.

'You're dead!' he yells, and that's the last I hear from him.

The embankment leads to a running stream where a jumping fish snatches something from the air and splashes into the middle of an eddy. As much as I'd like to stay and watch, I'm more concerned with putting distance between myself and the truck.

I keep moving away from the fish and running water until the throb of the truck engine fades in the distance.

First up, food. Good thing Sera lent me her belt knife. She would have died of horror if she saw me cutting down a sapling with one of my throwing knives.

In the fading light, I construct a multi-pronged spear from a fibrous green sapling, catch a fish and set up a neat fire next to the creek in a secluded location to cook.

The sweet aroma of fish baking over the glowing coals fills the rocky nook, and my mouth waters in anticipation. Reaching into my bag, I pull out a small container of salt and spices to season it, and it makes me think about what Sera said.

'When I was your age, I wanted to be a chef. We don't always get what we want.'

Well, Sera, you may not be a chef, but you certainly taught me a thing or two about cooking.

The thought makes me contemplate what I would have wanted to be if I weren't being trained as an assassin.

Dad was an astrogeological engineer, although I was too young to understand what that meant at the time. He used to bring home scale models of asteroids and told me they contained so many rich minerals that mining them would supply all of Jorth's metal needs for hundreds, even thousands of cycles. 'One day, we would live in space,' he used to say, and then he would go on about how the great Gaia'Ta left to live amongst the stars.

Mum worked for the government in some high-level position. She was always so secretive about her work I never knew what she actually did. I believed I would do something like that too someday, but the war changed all that.

Distracted by my introspection and the delicious-smelling fish, I almost eat it. Then, I remember what I'd learned about the dangers of cooking and eating in the same place. So instead, I wrap it in a preserve sheet for later. After tucking the parcel in my pack, I prepare to extinguish the fire just as a rock tumbles down the embankment and splashes with a plonk into the water.

Instinctively, I melt into the nearest foliage and hide behind the large root ball of a fallen tree.

From the shadows, a dark-haired girl about my age, dressed in rugged Gord-issue camo gear like me, shuffles around the slope and drops by the sputtering fire.

She picks up nearby sticks and feeds the fading embers before disappearing and returning a short time later with an armful more. In no time, the flames pick up, illuminating the face of the entire rock formation. The girl perches herself in its warm glow with a look of satisfaction, pulls out what appears to be a collection of local berries, removes her gloves, and contemplates the forage she has laid out on her pack before her.

'I know what I did wrong,' she says, in a soft and whimsical voice loud enough for me to hear. She sounds sad, almost as though she's in pain. As the fire licks at its food, she stares into the dancing flames.

The night is bitterly cold, but with the fire now blazing like the sun, I'm not surprised the strange girl removes her jacket, exposing a slender, petite figure. 'I know you're watching,' she says without turning. 'When I arrived, the ground was still warm where you sat.'

It was as if she were inviting me to give up my hiding place and join her by the fire, but resisting the urge, I remain hidden in the dark.

'Don't trust anyone,' I can almost hear Sera's voice say. *'People are wicked and can't be trusted.'*

'I won't hurt you, I promise,' the girl says. 'It was an amateur move, I know. I just want someone to talk to.'

Tempting, but… *'They will try to take advantage of you.'*

'I'm Ilona.' She sifts through her collection of berries, picks up a yellow one and lifts it to her mouth.

'Stop!' I yell before realising I'd said it.

'You *are* out there,' she says, returning the berry to her collection. 'I'm glad you are.'

The fire looks so warm and inviting. All I want to do is join her, but my training and conditioning reject the thought. As I shift from my hiding place and move in closer, she looks in my direction, and I fear she's seen me. She turns her head away, shielding her eyes as if to say, "I can't see you." Despite everything, I don't feel threatened by this girl. If anything, she could use my help.

Something about her seems familiar, and then it dawns. She's the owner of the blue eyes that watch me in the hall. I could recognise that sorrowful gaze anywhere.

'Can you tell me what I can eat then? I'm hungry,' she says.

With my attention split between the enormous fire, staying alert to my surroundings, and now realising who this girl is, I'm too distracted and respond without thinking. 'Jayne.'

'What did you say?' she says, lowering her hand and turning to face me with a puzzled expression. Those eyes glisten in the firelight like sapphires, revealing a smooth, oval face more beautiful than I imagined. It startles me to find someone like her out here in the wilds like this.

'I'm Jayne.'

'Nice to talk to you, Jayne.' As though realising she was now looking at me, she turns back to the fire and continues chattering away—her voice droning on as I slip out of earshot to scout the surrounding area. Light from the fire casts frolicking shadows all over the rock face. It's entertaining to watch, and I can understand why she has become mesmerised by it.

Harsh voices shout something indiscernible in the distance, and I turn to flaming torches leaping towards the beacon of lit rock. Raiders!

Ilona! I have to warn her.

Without hesitation, I dart for the narrowest part of the creek downstream from the camp, leap over the water, and sprint along the bank. 'RUN! RUN NOW!'

Charging through the campsite, I seize Ilona's pack, spilling her collection of berries, and keep on running, hoping she'll follow.

'Hey, that's my food,' she cries as I disappear into the darkness and drop behind the tree root again.

'Jayne,' she calls from the circle of light, casually fitting her jacket and gloves. 'Where are you?'

The torchlights grow nearer, and I pray they might not yet have seen us.

'Get over here,' I snap. 'Get out of the light.'

She takes a few steps forward. 'But the fire? It's warm.'

'Raiders are coming!'

Ilona turns around in a stupor. Before she settles her feet, I dash back out, grab her by the arm and heave her into the cover of darkness.

The instant we duck behind the root ball, four raiders barge into the ring of firelight.

'No one's here,' a woman's muffled voice grumbles.

Ilona stoops behind me, and the two of us peer through the gnarled root watching the foul people scour the camp.

'Looks like we just missed 'em,' a man says, pointing at the berries strewn across the ground.

'Ha! Easy meal then,' another male voice sniggers.

'Spread out and go find them,' the woman says.

'We have to go before they find us,' I whisper.

Ilona stares silently at the raiders like she's never seen them before. I shove her pack into her arms, and she follows me to a suitable tree about half a decametre away.

The moment I motion for her to climb the tree, she looks at me as though I'd asked her to eat it.

'You want me to climb *that*?'

'Yes.'

'But, why?'

'Just do it, please, before they find us standing here.'

Ilona grabs hold of the trunk and, with my help, hoists herself up onto the closest branch. Together we climb, and it appears Ilona isn't a confident climber either. Still, she keeps going until we reach a branch a suitable height above ground. There, from our safe perch, we straddle the branch watching the raiders scurrying around below until they give up and settle beside the fire.

'What just happened?' Ilona asks after they'd gone.

'You almost became their meal.'

'Oh,' she slumps, 'how was I supposed to know they were there?'

'You *don't*. That's why you don't attract them. And that big fire, that attracted them, alright!'

'But I wanted to be warm.'

'So did I, but open fires are for cooking, and that's all. At least that's what I've learned.'

'Cooking? You may have eaten, but I'm still hungry. You spilled all my food back there. What am I supposed to eat now?'

'I didn't—' I begin to say, but as she grips her bag tighter, a yellow berry rolls out of a fold.

'Oh, look! You're not going to knock this one into a fire.'

'Will you stop trying to kill yourself,' I scold her, grabbing her wrist. Her ignorance is shocking.

'Wha? Let go of me,' she complains, struggling against my grip.

'Take your glove off.'

'No.'

'Just do it, please.'

'But it's cold without—' she protests. 'Okay, fine,' she concedes, then removes a glove. 'Now what?'

'Give the berry a squish between your fingers.'

'But I want to eat it. I'm so hungry.'

'If you squash it in your fingers and then feel you still want to eat it, I won't stop you.'

She stares longingly at the berry and then gives it a press.

'Harder. Break the skin and let the juices touch you.'

Ilona sighs and the yellow berry bursts open between her fingers, its extract dripping all over her hand and onto the branch. 'See, it's okay.'

'Give it a moment.'

'Oh,' she says with surprise, dropping it. 'I can't feel my fingers or palm.'

'See, that's a torporberry. If you'd eaten that, it would have paralysed you for a day or more, and if you survived, you wouldn't have remembered even consuming it. Wash your fingers off with water from your canteen. The feeling should return in a cendec or two.'

'How'd you know that?' she says, rinsing her hand.

'How don't you know that? Didn't your guardian teach you anything? Didn't she take you camping?'

Ilona puts away her canteen and rubs her shoulder bashfully. 'My guardian… um, no. She gave me books to read, but I've never done anything like this. This is the first time I've even been outside.'

'What? Why?'

'Um… I don't want to talk about it.'

She stares back toward the camp where a bonfire now blazes. 'Maybe it would have been best if you just left me there.'

'Don't be silly. You wouldn't be saying that if you've seen the raiders like I've seen them.'

'They don't look too bad.'

'You think?' I snort. 'You really have no idea, do you?'

'Why are you helping me? You could have just walked away. I thought you did before you rushed me.'

'I didn't rush you. I saved you. Believe me, you don't want to end up in their hands. I've seen what they do to their captives. It gave me night terrors for a trey.'

Ilona mumbles something under her breath, gazing absently at the dancing light on the rock. She fumbles to hold my hand around her waist. She seems to have relaxed, even making herself comfortable in my arms. 'Why are you holding me like this?' she asks. 'It's… nice.'

'Why so many questions?'

She doesn't answer but instead grips my hand firmer.

'Hey, look!' she says suddenly, gazing up at the night sky. 'It's a billingar moon tonight. I've read that's something you don't see very often.'

Sure enough, just visible through the trees is a second glowing yellow sphere—Jorth's smaller and rarely seen second moon. It's just starting to add light to its brother's already illuminating the forest.

'I can hardly remember the two moons being up at the same time,' I agree, marvelling at it. 'It *is* rare. And beautiful.'

'Have you seen it before?'

'A billingar moon? Once, when I was little. Dad told me the story of how Embla, our planet's smaller moon, got bullied by her bigger brother, Askr. That's why we don't see them together very often.'

'That's a silly story.'

'I guess. But when you're five, it sounds perfectly reasonable.'

We quietly laugh, and I'm grateful for the distraction. Even though I'd prevented her from eating the poisoned berries, I couldn't help feeling sorry for her, especially given I'd denied her of her dinner, however disastrous it would have been. 'Hey, would you like to share my fish?'

On the second morning, I awaken to the sun breaking over the horizon, illuminating that part of the sky in a soft orange glow and shrouding the landscape in a slight purplish tinge. This time of the day is always the most peaceful and calming. Different species of aves awaken to serenade the sun from its hiding place beneath the horizon and bring light to the day. When the dawn performance is over, Ilona and I untie ourselves from the tree and prepare to push on toward the Gord.

'I'm hungry,' she complains not long after heading out. 'Do you have any more of that fish?'

'No. We ate it all.' Glancing around, I spot a large piece of purple fungi growing on a tree trunk, pluck it off and offer it to her. She gives me a look eerily reminiscent of the expression I gave Sera the first time she did that with me.

'What's this?' she asks.

'Food. You eat it.'

'Eww,' she says, crinkling her nose in disgust. 'I'm not eating that!'

'Suit yourself,' I shrug, taking a bite out of the frilly purple mushroom. 'It's really not that bad.'

When she sees I'm fine after eating it, she unscrunches her face and snatches the rest from my grasp. Then, with eyes squeezed tight, she shoves the mushroom into her mouth.

I'm half expecting her to throw it back up, but when she chews on it, she gives me that all too familiar look of pleasant surprise.

'That's not bad,' she says with a cheeky smile, tearing off more from the tree. 'It's… nutty.'

'I thought you might say that. But don't eat too much. It can… ahem, give you a good cleansing.'

Over the next few cendecs, I teach her more of the skills Sera taught me. When the sun starts to make its way back towards the horizon, we find a suitable tree for sleeping, then set up a snare trap along a tomadai run before filling our canteens in a nearby freshwater stream. The steady flowing stream leads out to a large lake where we stop to rest and catch some fish for dinner.

It's there that Ilona pulls out her map and compass. 'Ah, we're going the wrong way,' she says, noticeably stressed.

'What do you mean?'

'We're at the wrong lake,' she says, pointing at the map. 'See, we should be here.'

I pull out my map and compass for comparison and immediately see what has her so distraught. 'Oh, you didn't pick up on the compass being magnetic north and the map being true?'

'Well, let's follow the map then,' she says straight-faced.

'Come on, I'll show you how to make a proper fire, and I'll explain about the map along the way.'

Later, when we tie ourselves to our branches for the night, Ilona's mood seems to have lightened. 'Who are you, Jayne?'

'What do you mean by that?'

'Where did you come from?' she asks, somewhat whimsically.

'You mean Garret Gord?'

'No, before that.'

The question seems to have come from out of nowhere, and I scratch my head, wondering how best to answer. 'Well, I spent about a cycle in an underground bunker, but before that, I lived in Plulvale in Nusmore Provence with my parents before the bombs…'

'Do you remember them?'

'It's hard sometimes to picture their faces, but when I'm sad, I think of the warmth of their hugs and how that made me feel. I still miss them.' Even after all this time, talking about it brings about a pang of emotion, and I choke back tears. 'What about you?'

'I'm tired now. I want to sleep.'

'You don't want to tell me about—'

'I don't want to talk about it,' she snaps. 'No one can tell me I'm alright. I'm just an unwanted child with a stupid head, used and then thrown away. Nobody wants someone like that.'

'Hey, you shouldn't talk about yourself that way. Besides, you started this conversation.'

'Why? It's true. Today has been the best day I can ever remember, and tomorrow I have to return to that place and go back to being alone again. I wish they would just marry me off like one of those people in the storybooks. Nobody will want someone who almost poisoned themself or got eaten by cannibals. I'm even more stupid than *she* says I am. So, if you don't mind, I want to get some sleep.'

'I don't think that's true,' I try to reassure her. 'When I first went camping with Sera, I didn't know these things either. You wouldn't believe all the stupid things I did. She had to teach me all this stuff. You can't be stupid if you just didn't know.'

'Who's Sera?'

'My guardian.'

'She sounds nice. I wish I had a guardian like her.'

I thought about that for a moment. Sera *was* nice until I found out she's a cold-blooded killer. But then, I guess we all are, or soon will be. Ilona clearly has had a far different experience.

'Jayne, did your Sera ever tell you not to trust anyone?'

'Yes, that's one of the first things she told me.'

'Then why haven't you left me behind?'

'Because you look like you need help. I don't think helping someone is against the rules, and you haven't tried to hurt me, so I guess...'

'Thank you,' she whispers and rolls onto her side, away from me.

I hope it helps, but you're welcome.

When I awaken, Ilona lies still tied to her branch, serene and as comfortable as one can be under the circumstances. Her slow breath condenses in the chilly morning air. Compared to yesterday, her face is soft and relaxed, lacking all the cares that had clearly been stressing her. Mindful not to wake her, I climb down to check the traps and find a strangled tomadai.

While I prepare the carcass for breakfast, seasoning and splaying out the meat on a trellis of damp green sticks to cook, Ilona awakens, and I send her off to collect firewood. She takes to the task with enthusiasm reminiscent of my early trips with Sera, even relishing in the opportunity to re-ignite the fire using my bracelet. We quickly cook, bundle up our meal, and cover up the pit with dirt before the smoke and the aroma of cooked meat travels too far.

Ilona glares at me forlornly when I place the warm bundles in our packs, but I stress we need to place enough distance between us and the fire before we can safely sit down to eat. After about a cendecs' walking, my stomach rumbles.

'Are you hungry?' I ask, channelling Sera's mannerisms. At least it strikes me as something Sera would say.

Ilona's eyes widen with delight. 'I thought you'd never ask,' she says. 'I'm starving.'

She's even smiling. I hand her a leg of meat laid out on a big green leaf, and she gnaws at it like a wild animal. 'I'm sorry about last night,' she says after swallowing her first mouthful. 'I didn't mean to bite at you like that. It's just…'

'It's okay, I understand.'

'You do?'

No, but I want her to think so. I want her to feel comfortable, even happy. Tearing off some meat for myself, I shrug and sit back beside her. 'Things will work out, I'm sure of it.'

'This is really good,' she says. 'Thank you for this and for everything. You really saved me—in more ways than one.' She leans in close and kisses me on the cheek, dirt and all.

'What was that for?' I ask in surprise.

She smiles. 'I felt like it. In a different life…' she trails off before turning away and nibbling at her meal in silence.

Strange girl.

The last leg of our journey back to the Gord takes only two more cendecs. Ilona's spirits seem to have lifted again until we approach the steep roadway leading up towards the gates, and she sees the wood pole fence. It's at that moment she stops, and the recluse returns. 'What if we don't go back?' she asks furtively. 'What if we just turn around now and go somewhere else?'

'Somewhere else?' I reply, scanning the surrounding forest. 'Where would we go?'

'Who cares? Anywhere?'

'Why?'

'What do you think they'll do when we get back? Do you think they'll allow us to stay friends?'

'Um, I guess not.'

'Then let's run.'

'I see your point, but there really isn't anywhere we can go. I'd prefer to stick it out here than spend any more time dodging raiders, boarts, and Progenitors knows what else.'

'I guess you're right,' she concedes and boots a stone along the track.

'But that doesn't mean we can't stay friends. Nobody has to find out.'

She nods. 'Well, it was nice meeting you, Jayne. And thank you again for saving me. I won't forget that. This has been the best few days I've had in cycles.' She gives me a quick hug and then runs ahead.

Ilona enters through the front gates, and with trepidation, I follow—at a distance. It's apparent they expected our arrival as both Sera and Ilona's guardian stand outside the guardhouse with plain, indecipherable expressions. I would have expected relief, even happiness from them. After all, they sent us out there into the deadly wilds, and we returned alive. But it's not. Whatever they're thinking, they're keeping it to themselves.

Ilona's guardian, a stern-faced woman of about Sera's age but Ilona's height, steps forward and slaps her across the face. From Ilona's silent, submissive response, this interaction is not unusual, and I get a sense of what she was talking about. Without so much as a word or nod, the stout, vicious woman grabs Ilona's arm and drags her across the compound.

'Well, that's nice,' I say to Sera with sarcasm, but she just frowns at me as though storm clouds are gathering. 'Is something wrong?'

'We shall soon see,' she replies sternly. 'Get inside.'

04 HOUSE RULES

Our apartment door closes, and Sera pulls me into a firm hug. 'I am so glad you are safe,' she says, her voice wavering on the verge of tears. 'Of course, I knew you would make it. I am so proud of you.'

Conscious of all the sweat and mud, Sera's still hugging me, although she doesn't seem perturbed by the dirt messing up her beautiful clothing. In her arms, everything feels alright again. Despite that, something nags at me. 'What was that out there?'

'Appearances,' is all she says. 'Now, go wash up. I have made pie, and it is almost ready. We will discuss it after.'

Three days without a shower, clean clothes and Sera's wholesome, home-cooked meals, I take the time to relish in these luxuries, grateful I have them to come back to. But as my thoughts wander to Ilona and what she said, it makes me wonder what she's doing now and whether she's enjoying the same comforts.

After dinner, Sera collects my empty plate, from which I seem to be trying to remove all traces of food. 'Anything the matter?' she asks.

'Just thinking,' I reply, not interested in discussing it with her. Instead, there's something else. 'What did you mean by appearances before?'

She sets the plates into the sink and returns to the table. 'We must remain impartial, unemotional. Our connection to our daughters is strictly professional. It is only behind closed doors where we are permitted to connect with you in any way we wish.'

As if on cue, there's a knock at the door, and Sera opens it to find one of the Patriarch's burly personal guards standing there.

'The Patriarch will see you in his office. Bring the girl,' he says, then leaves.

Sera turns to me, and now her expression is one of concern. 'You heard the man. We shall not keep the Patriarch waiting.'

Sera guides me to the far end of the second level and up a sloping corridor that seems to go on forever. Suspended from the ceiling and spanning the corridor's length is the boxy metal air duct, presumably through which I had travelled this passageway before. Now I can see why there aren't any vents here. There are no rooms along this section except for one at the very end where faint voices carry on an unintelligible conversation. A sense of foreboding descends upon me as memories of being called into Nanneral's office come to mind.

The door opens inward, providing a different perspective of a room I had only seen from above. It's filled with a strange assortment of expensive-looking pieces of artwork, stone heads and, on the wall by a large window, a sinister-looking black cane with a golden fist at one end. Ilona and her guardian are already waiting inside. They stand in front of the big timber desk behind which the man with the ridiculous long flowing sleeves is leaning, his knuckles pressing into its surface. From the bitter expression on his white-bearded face, it's clear this is not a casual visit. But that's nothing compared to the scowl Ilona's guardian is expressing.

Ilona stands between her guardian and the desk with her head bowed in submission. Sera signals for me to go stand beside her.

The Patriarch glares at the two of us with furious eyes. 'It has been brought to my attention that two of my students collaborated during this initial trial. As you are all aware, that is forbidden. You two,' the Patriarch points at us, 'explain your actions.'

I glance sidelong at Ilona and assume she's probably doing the same as I, choosing her next words carefully.

'Answer me!' he spits.

'Raiders crashed my camp,' I reply, speaking out before Ilona can respond. There is no way I will let her take the blame, nor do I intend on taking it either. But someone must make them see we've done nothing wrong.

'I fled, and that's when I ran into her.' I glance at Ilona, and she returns my gaze with a questioning look. 'If by "collaborated" you mean helped, yes I did, but only to prevent them from looking further, finding us both and tracking us back here.'

'What is your name, girl?' the Patriarch asks.

'Jayne,' I reply.

'Ah, yes, the infamous Jayne Doe, prodigal daughter of Seraphin MonLantry.' He says my name with an acerbic quality, then turns his attention to my companion. 'You girl, and what is your name?'

'Ilona,' she gives a meek reply, once again gazing at the desk.

'Care to reply to me and not my furniture.'

'Ilona,' she repeats, this time looking at him.

'There you go, daughter of Weaons Shaddix.'

At that moment, he steps out from behind the desk to approach us, standing so close, his potent aftershave is eye-watering. I can clearly distinguish the intricate gold patterns in the stitching of his very-expensive-looking waistcoat. This is clearly a man of affluent quality but exceptionally poor taste.

'This is my House,' he says, stepping between us and the desk. 'Consider yourselves honoured to be here. Only twenty-eight have been chosen, as you have, and are destined to do great things. There will be a number that won't make it through, so their failure should motivate you. You just have to think to yourselves, "*which will you be*?" My expectations are simple; commit, obey, train well and make me proud. Compliance will be rewarded, and insubordination will be punished. Do I make myself clear?'

'Yes,' we reply in unison.

'The appropriate response is, yes, sir.'

'Yes, sir.'

'Better. There are five simple rules in *my* House. You are expected to know them verbatim. Tell me, Miss Jayne, Miss Ilona, what is rule four?'

'Never trust anyone,' we rattle off together.

'Rendering help and collaboration of any kind is a form of trust and, therefore, a breach of rule four.'

'But we were just escaping the raiders,' I interject.

'Do NOT interrupt me!' he snaps. 'The purpose of this test was to determine your ability to operate alone. By collaborating, you have voided that purpose and, therefore, effectively failed. Under normal circumstances, you would have been sent straight to the box. However, given the ingenuity you demonstrated in escaping the threat without exposing yourselves or this establishment, it warrants clemency. Therefore, as this is your first offence, I will pardon you. But let this be a lesson to you. You will not be afforded such leniency again. I will leave it in your guardians' hands to determine the punishment most suitable for you. Mark my words, though, should this happen again, it will be into the box with you.'

'Yes, sir,' we chorus.

'Good.'

'Dismissed.'

With a sigh of relief, I return to Sera, and we turn to leave.

'MonLantry,' he says before we reach the door. Sera doesn't turn back. Instead, she watches me like a mother ursus with her cub. He walks up to me with a smirk and strokes my face with the back of his hand. I catch Sera scowl. 'This one has spunk—I'll give you that. She shows promise, the kind of promise my House needs.'

His touch makes me feel dirtier than the full three days out there in the wilds, and I get a sense of what Sera has gone through.

'Consider our agreement valid, *for now*,' he continues. 'I will be keeping a close eye on you. *Both* of you. Impress me, and Jayne will remain in my good graces. But remember, disappoint me, and you will experience fury only Gotthard himself can equal.'

05 CLOAK AND DAGGER

NC07

Artimus adjusted his breather, pulled his jacket tighter, flicked on his flashlight, and entered the darkness. It had been many cycles since he walked the familiar concrete tunnels of this underground Skoyca military facility. Back in those days, this place was a hive of activity, with people scampering this way and that, carrying important documents and saluting him everywhere he went. Today, only the occasional rodentia scurried these dank passages. At least it was quiet. Only the rhythmic drumming of dripping water, his footsteps and the low squeal of his radiation meter echoed here.

As he strode through the turbid blackness, guided by the circle of his flashlight, it reflected off pools of fetid water collected in eroded pits along the ground. It amazed him how six cycles of abandonment and exposure to mild nuclear radiation can lay even concrete to waste. He headed towards a room marked 'electrical plant' and hoped enough power remained in the generator to get him through this expedition. Like the rest of the facility, its door, locked ajar from rust, looked as though it had seen better days. He squeezed inside, examined the switchboard, pulled the lever marked 'Aux Mains', and engaged the backup generator with a loud metallic bang. To his relief, the electrical buzzing sound of power flowing through the circuits joined the dripping water. Interspersed fluorescent lights sequentially illuminated the area and corridor outside in a flickering, sickly yellow glow. He switched off his torch, clipped it to his belt and then headed for an unmarked door, buried deep in the bowels of the complex: *The Archive.*

This was a room for which he possessed one of only a few keys.

As he stood at that unmarked rusted metal door with the key in hand, he contemplated what he would find inside. He half expected to find the room flooded or worse. Instead, as the big door swung inward with a jarring screech, all it revealed was a musty room filled with wall-to-wall card cabinets and hundreds of stacked locked metal boxes caked in cycles of grime. He checked the radiation counter once more. The needle hadn't moved from the left end of its semi-circle gauge. 'Low to nominal. Good,' he said, setting the boxy device down on a rotting desk nearby.

This area had been one of the first locations hit by the enemy during the war, and nuclear radiation hotspots were still prevalent. Fortunately for Artimus, this particular facility survived the bombing. Others nearby, including his old offices, weren't so lucky.

He approached the first row of badly corroded metal cabinets and pried open a rusty drawer. The contents inside had weathered worse. Half of the cards resembled yellow muck, and the rest were damp and barely legible. Artimus lifted an intact card to the light and squinted to read the faded letters typed across its surface. *Illegible, more like it,* he thought, returning the card to its grave.

'This will take a while,' he muttered, turning to survey the six hundred meta square room.

Picking the handheld comms unit off his belt, he spoke into it. 'Cargo is ready for pickup. Get in here. Out.'

Moments later, six masked soldiers wearing neat green and black HomeGuard uniforms appeared at the doorway bearing trolleys. 'Take all the boxes. Leave the cabinets,' Artimus ordered. 'I want this place emptied.'

'Yes, sir.' They touched their right fists to their foreheads, palm out in salute, and set to work.

As the day drew to a close, Artimus observed his team fill up the last of his trucks, and they drove the two cendec journey back to Hope. There, Artimus retired to his office, where his crew cleaned and neatly stacked the locked archive boxes, ordered by pre-war date, along all the walls. When they were finished, virtually all the floor space was occupied. With mixed apprehension and anticipation, he collected the first box, placed it on his desk and opened the lid, smiling at the faint click of the key cracking the lock.

A trey passed, and Artimus had barely made a dent in the towering city of archive boxes occupying his office. Like most days recently, he sat hunched over his basic wooden desk by the back wall, under the light of his lamp with an open box and its contents splayed out neatly before him.

He picked up an aged green folder, reminiscing on the words *'Operation Atropos'* written in bold lettering across its cover. He opened it to reveal a stack of mission reports. The top one read;

****Transmission begins****
Timestamp: AP 1925-02-50 2:60
Sender: Lt Commander [redacted]
Message: After investigating the crashed vessel, it has been determined it is not of Jorth origin. Upon arrival at the site, an area cordon was established, blocking access to the vessel. Hostile forces intercepted, and Commander [redacted] was K.I.A. during the ensuing skirmish. Six large, polished metal objects were among the salvage taken by the enemy. These could not be recovered at this time. No occupants were discovered in or around the vessel. Assumed escaped or captured. Remaining salvage relocated to [redacted]. On behalf of the Skoyca Government Alliance, the vessel and all objects it contained have been declared Skoyca Government property. Following Commander [redacted]'s death, until orders otherwise received, Operation Atropos continues under LC [redacted]'s command, ensuring investigations into missing property continue.
****Transmission ends****

Artimus closed the file and placed it on the pile of read documents. *Oh, how I wish to return to those days,* he thought, but then he picked up the next folder, and that made him shudder. He unconsciously rubbed a hand over his tortured skin while he stared at the words '*Operation Parasol*', typed in large lettering, and with *'Terminated'* overstamped in red across the cover. He knew his name would also be redacted in here.

Parasol was a covert operation that involved testing noxious chemical compounds from the air over the enemy—not his preferred method of warfare, but the decision was not his to make.

And as a freshly promoted Admiral, he took command of the operation to show what he was capable of.

The folder triggered memories of that fateful day in Centraal AP1945 when Artimus had driven out to his top-secret chemical factory to undertake what was supposed to be a routine inspection. But, as his vehicle rounded the bend, the entire facility went up in a bright flash, followed by a massive fireball that obliterated everything within close vicinity. Artimus awoke days later in hospital, lucky to have survived the explosion. The entire right side of his face was not all he lost. Upon seeing his disfigured face, his wife, who had come to visit, took their daughter and ran as far away as she could. A tendawn later, Artimus received the chilling report that both had perished in an air-raid attack. That left Artimus just a little unhinged, and he shuddered to think about what happened next.

He slammed the file shut and tossed the wretched thing into the newly installed fireplace.

The next folder was the first he had come across without a title, as though it had been misfiled. The initial pages contained basic office administration in a military facility, followed by other random meeting itineraries and a to-do list prepared for a General Luck. This General appeared to have had the worst day;

General Luck task admin, subject: Overheads.

1. *Waste management.*
2. *Deal with contractors.*
3. *Pest control.*
4. *Fire control testing.*
5. ...

The list was barely legible, typed on a stained and half-deteriorated scrap of paper. Most tasks made little sense, yet having carried out many of these types of orders, Artimus could hazard a guess what some of it meant.

A crisp piece of paper at the back of the file had the simple title; '*Dispersion pattern*'. Its contents contained a list of what appeared to be serial numbers and names. This had been the first piece of paper where his name had not been redacted.

He picked up his mug of tei. It had gone cold, but he still drank it and, over the lip of the mug, examined the page.

The list displayed thirty-nine names, his second from the top, just below his commanding officer of the time.

NL38722Q - Captain - Leaton, S.
NL38723Q - Commander (Spec. Op.) - Wyrm, A.

His eyes also drifted to the entry near the bottom, causing him to choke on his drink.

NL38759Q - Sergeant (Spec. Op.) - Wyrm, J.

Focus, he berated himself, struggling to force the memory back into the compartment he had built for it long ago.

He set down his mug and examined the serial number beside his name. Without having to check, he knew it wasn't a pistol or personnel number—he knew his without needing to look them up.

As he turned to the final page, it hit him with a spark of adrenaline. There, on the yellowed sheet of paper, was a scale schematic of a knife. Not just any knife, a large, reverse-barb bladed hunting knife so intricate, its appearance seemed to contradict its purpose.

Artimus's gaze lifted to the head of his desk where the unsheathed knife that had been used to end Gaius's life rested. The knife had a similar appearance to the one he had lost many cycles ago, one that had caused Orian to mistakenly identify him as Gaius's killer. There was no mistake; it matched the design on the page perfectly.

He picked it up by its flecked opaline handle, pondering on it for a moment. Something about its design caught his interest. Reaching into his drawer, he pulled out a magnifying glass to examine the drawing more closely.

According to the schematic, the handle appeared to have something hidden underneath.

It was ornate, for sure, but Artimus didn't care for its beauty. To him, it was the symbolism of possessing such a knife that mattered. Being awarded one earned him status, more so than just a medal in a box. 'Operation Canorus,' he recalled under his breath. 'Dangerous but exciting days.'

Whoever was the previous owner of this weapon would normally have earned his respect, but not this person. Now, it was a piece of evidence occupying his waking moments.

Artimus rotated the knife between his thumb and forefinger, inspecting the intricate acid etching on the blade. It still glistened red. 'It's a shame,' he said in a low voice as he wrapped the blade in his jacket and smacked the handle against the edge of his desk, denting the timber, then again and again until the handle cracked between the two rivets. One more hit and the opaline material broke away to reveal what he had been expecting to find. He looked closely at the half-naked metal tang. The handle hid the number, as per the design. He lifted the magnifying glass so he could read it.

NL38761Q.

He ran his finger down the list to find the serial number.

NL38761Q - (BLANK) - MonLantry, S.

'Who is S. MonLantry?' he muttered, 'and what happened to your rank?'

A knock at his open door startled him from his concentration. Minister Kinton leaned around the corner with only his arm and head protruding into view.

'How long have you been there, Kinton?' Artimus asked bluntly.

'Well, good morn to you too, Artimus,' Elihus replied with a haughty, condescending tone.

Artimus set the broken knife and magnifying glass down. 'What do you want?'

'Ah, the Gaius knife,' Elihus said, strolling over for a closer look and picking up the blade, much to Artimus's dissatisfaction. 'Oh, it's broken.'

Artimus glowered at the man with his massive sleeves draping over his desk, disturbing his neat and orderly paperwork.

'Put it down, Kinton, before you cut yourself. I don't want your blood all over my desk.'

'Oh, I'm terribly sorry,' he said with a feigned apology, placing the blade back and withdrawing his arms. As he did, his sleeve pulled the page of names onto the floor. Elihus bent to pick it up. 'Is this a list of suspects?' he probed, reading it much to Artimus's displeasure. 'It seems your name is here as well.'

Artimus slapped both hands on his desk as he stood and snatched the paper from the incorrigible minister's hands.

'That is none of your business,' he snapped.

Elihus ignored Artimus's outburst and turned his attention to the room. 'Hmm, so, I see you *have* gone crazy,' he said, flicking a hand at the wall behind Artimus's desk where seemingly random bits of paper were pinned up in a haphazard fashion among a web of interconnected pieces of string. 'Why are you persisting with this futile endeavour?' he scoffed, 'and for whom? Him?' He glanced at the discoloured floorboards between the fireplace and the door. 'Or for you?'

'Is there something you want, Kinton?' Artimus growled.

'No, not particularly,' Elihus replied as he resumed strolling about the room, wiping a finger across the top of one of the archive boxes, which now bore a fresh coating of dust. 'I just happened to be passing by when I heard a noise and came to see what it was. Good thing I did, too, by the looks of it. My goodness, man, this place could make a dump look tidy.'

'Thank you, Elihus, for that unhelpful observation. Now, if you're about finished, take your ridiculous sleeves and get out. I have work to do.'

'What in the Progenitor's name is going on down here?' Sage demanded as he entered the confined space. 'Are you two arguing again?'

'Oh, great,' Artimus said, exasperated, 'did you *need* something, Surprime, or did you come to check on me too? You know I have my hands full right now. Not only am I running the people who let you two sleep safely at night, but I'm also conducting a murder investigation, you know, in case you've forgotten.'

Sage gave Artimus a cold look. 'I can see that, Artimus, but do you really want to talk to me about busy?'

Artimus glared at him.

'If you need help, I can always send Conrad in here.'

'Conrad,' Artimus snorted. 'That little rodentia-faced errand boy of yours, Sage? Ahh, no, thank you. I'll be fine.'

'You know, Artimus,' Elihus piped up, 'if you're feeling stressed, I may have something that could help with that. If you know what I mean?'

Artimus turned his glare back to Elihus. 'Kinton, you insufferable idiot,' he spat. 'No. Just, no. I've had about enough of your help. Or anyone else's "help", for that matter. What I need is to be left alone to do my job!'

'Suit yourself. You just seem tense,' Elihus shrugged, brushing off Artimus's stare.

That just made Artimus fume more. 'Tense!' he growled. 'You think this is tense? No, Kinton, tense is finding out my HomeGuard officers keep disappearing after receiving secret orders to go on personal security missions.'

Elihus shrugged again. 'Dangerous things reside beyond these parts. What can I say?' he said whimsically.

Sage flashed the Education Minister a quizzical look. 'What are you talking about?'

Artimus replied, 'News has come to me that Elihus Kinton here is the one responsible for ordering my HomeGuard personnel out without my prior authorisation. He's been sending them on "personal errands".'

'So that's what that was about?' Sage said.

'To find Gaius's killer, I might add,' Elihus countered.

'I don't care if you ordered them to help a little old lady cross the road. You are *not* authorised to make such an order. Let me be clear, little man,' Artimus roared, rising from his chair again to leer over his desk at Elihus. 'HomeGuard is not yours or anyone else's personal security. You will leave their command to me. Got that?'

'Well, that's just a tad unnecessary, but yes, Minister, I have "got it" clear as day,' Elihus replied in a snobbish tone. 'And here I was thinking I was doing you a favour.'

Artimus facepalmed. 'Eight missing personnel and a vehicle is not doing me a favour. I had already dispatched four units to scour the area for Gaius's killer. They all came back with nothing. But thanks to your "favour", because I didn't know where that unit you sent went, I couldn't even send a unit to go look for them. Eight families had to be notified their loved ones weren't coming home. I hope you're satisfied, Kinton. You are Education Minister. Stick to doing whatever it is you do and keep out of my business.'

'Righto, message received, Captain,' Elihus mocked, feigning a salute with the wrong hand.

'Don't do that,' Artimus snarled, his face turning red.

'Look,' Sage interjected before Artimus could tear the little bearded man a new one, 'I know you're stressed. Let's just calm down. Artimus is Defence Minister, and he has control of HomeGuard resources. Kinton, should you wish to utilise those resources, arrange it with Artimus. And Artimus, please try to *relax*.'

'Relax? Only a cycle ago, you taped me to a chair and threw me in a storage closet. And now, when I do the very thing you demanded I do, you want me to relax?'

'I'm not telling you to stop, Artimus. Just calm down a bit,' Sage implored. 'I know you've been working hard looking into Gaius's death—'

'*Murder*,' Artimus snapped.

'And I appreciate it. The whole town does. But don't you think you're working at this a bit too hard?'

'You, yourself, set me this task. You insisted I find the murderer so I can clear my name. So that's what I'm doing. No, Sage, I *will* not back down. I will see this through, whatever it takes.'

'Artimus, it's almost been a full cycle since… it happened,' Sage said, looking forlornly at the gruesome stain on the bare patch of floor between the fireplace and the door. 'How much closer are you to solving this? And, you do know, we could have at least replaced the floorboards.'

'You obviously don't understand then,' Artimus said with more emotion than he'd intended. Artimus wasn't sentimental. Despite what he knew Sage thought, he'd left the place where Gaius once lay clear as a visual reminder of his commitment, more so than his respect for the man.

'I understand you moved into this room the first opportunity you could,' Sage said, squeezing past Elihus to move closer to Artimus's desk. 'You disappear for days at a time, returning with truckloads of files, and you obsess over them for most of your waking cendecs. We want to find the killer just as much as anyone else, but the case has gone cold. Even Hunter couldn't find them.'

Artimus slammed his hand down on the paperwork, the timber desk echoing his aggravation. 'Hunter isn't an investigator. Once he lost track of them, the trail went cold. It's as if they just disappeared.' Artimus shuffled a few files on his desk and picked up a neater, more recent-looking folder. 'It's all in there,' he said, holding it out.

Sage went to take the file, but Elihus snatched it before he had the chance. Unperturbed by the Surprime and Defence Minister glaring at him, Elihus skimmed the report. 'Let me get this straight,' he chortled. 'Your Hunter, supposedly the meanest tracker in all of Hope, got bested by an injured woman and a girl? Oh, that's gold.' He closed the folder and handed it to Sage as though passing it off to an underling. Sage brushed off the disrespectful comment, took the file and began flicking through it himself.

'I didn't ask for your opinion, Kinton,' Artimus growled.

'And what about the mountains? Sage inquired. 'Did you find anything there?'

'No,' Artimus replied. 'Those mountains are hostile territory, and trying to find them there would be like looking for a shadow in the black. The case may be cold, but I'm not done yet, not by a long shot.'

'Well, I hope you know what you're looking for,' Elihus said with a smirk, eyeing the vast number of boxes stacked up against the walls.

Sage casually picked up a second folder from Artimus's unread pile. It was titled 'Operation Canorus'. The moment Artimus saw it, his eyebrow lifted.

'Just look at these files,' Sage said, flicking through it. 'Redacted beyond readable. Take this one, a profile of someone named Seraphin MonLantry, who's quite possibly dead after all these cycles. Look, most of—'

Artimus's good eye twitched at the name. He reached out and snapped the folder closed in Sage's hands, catching it as it dropped.

'I think the chances of finding whatever fiendish individual did this are long gone. This is just a waste of time and space,' Elihus said.

'It's not a waste of time, Elihus,' Sage corrected him. 'I just want Artimus to take a step away for a while. Focus on other things, then come back with a clearer mind.'

'As do I, Surprime,' Elihus backpedalled. 'I just think he's got his work cut out for him, is all. And who's to say any of this will yield anything of use? But what would I know? I'm just a humble Education Minister. Anyway, it looks like you have everything in order. Good morn, Surprime. Minister.' And with a flourish of his flag-like sleeves, Elihus drifted out the door.

'That's an odd man,' Sage commented when Elihus was out of earshot. 'I have no idea what Gaius saw in him.'

'Now that's something we can both agree on,' Artimus chuckled, then went serious again. 'Sage, I know this looks like a mess, but trust me, I have everything under control. Keep that man out of my business, and I promise you, I will find Gaius's killer.'

'Okay then, if you insist. But keep me informed. I want regular updates.'

'Yes, of course.'

'Good morn to you, Artimus,' Sage said, turning to leave. 'And, for goodness sake, man, take a shower.'

As Sage's footsteps faded down the hallway, Artimus's attention drifted to the open *Operation Canorus* file on his desk. The monochromatic profile image of an attractive, dark-haired woman stared back at him.

'*Seraphin MonLantry*, so that's your name?' he said, pinning the page to his wall. 'Wherever you are hiding, I *will* find you.'

06 TRAINING

Excerpt from Book of the Progenitors:

Some fight demons; others need not, for they can convince the demons to fight themselves. Such was the way of Martok Wyllt, the spectre with many faces, master of deceit and conjurer of mystical fancy. When the generals of the army of the damned sought to render the world asunder and scatter the blood and bones of every mortal gaian across the lands, it was Martok, summoned by Xisnys and Gotthard themselves to destroy the army and their heathen plan. Under the guise of one of their own, Martok descended the camp, drank tankards of ale and had merriment with the generals earning him favour. Five days and five nights, Martok entertained, beguiling them with compelling tales of heroism, vanquishes and retched conquests. Convinced were they by Martok's conviction of their enemy's plot, they dismissed their own plans as folly. And so it was that on the sixth day, Martok, with the generals on his leash, called forth their army and marched toward certain annihilation.

'Jayne! Breakfast is ready,' Sera's voice calls from the other room.

I adjust my slim-fitting grey top in the mirror and follow my nose out to the kitchen, where Sera is cooking up one of her masterpieces.

Glancing down at the delectable contents of the bowl she sets on the table before me, it's her Mon Loq porrij; Gord-grown grains cooked in cultured milk and served with fruits, nuts and seeds. What makes this dish special is Sera's floral homemade blossom syrup, which she uses to sweeten it, made from flowers grown right here in the apartment.

'So, how do I look?' I ask, showing off my new training outfit.

'You look… fierce,' she replies with a grin, and I can tell she's enjoying this. I, on the other hand, think it's silly.

'Why is it all grey? And does it have to be *this* tight?' I ask, plucking at the form-fitting leggings.

'Grey is nondescript, and as for the firmness, it has to be tight. It minimises bruising and helps your injuries heal quicker.'

'Injuries?'

'Oh, before I forget,' she says, conveniently changing subjects and hobbling over to the sideboard to retrieve a neatly wrapped parcel. 'I got you a little first-day-of-training gift.'

Within the handmade wrappings is a brightly coloured hard-cover notebook. Flicking through it, I look up at Sera with an expression as equally blank as the pages.

'It is not much, I know,' she says. 'But I thought it would be a good idea to keep a journal to document your training progress, so you have something to look back on later. You never know; it might prove useful.'

With a gigantic smile, I wrap my arms around her. 'Thank you, Sera.'

She places a scribe on the table beside my bowl, and I immediately scrawl my name on the inside cover. Then taking a mouthful of breakfast, not wanting to waste this opportunity, I start writing…

DAY 1

I was both excited and terrified at the prospect of beginning training. Sera advised me to keep this diary as a record of my progress. She already warned it'll be both gruelling and rewarding, depending on the effort I put in. Not sure if that should comfort or horrify me, but she said she'll support me the best she can, which quells some anxiety at least. Four cycles I've lived at Garret Gord, and for much of that time, I'd thought Sera and I were the only people here. That's aside from Ilona, whom I haven't seen since the forest, the Patriarch and the guards. Oh, the guards, those useless imbeciles. Where have they come from? They both look and smell like reformed raiders, and it churns my stomach every time I have to deal with them.

The morn was clear, and despite the brisk chill and slight dampness, it was a fine day for outdoor training. Twenty-eight of us assembled on the large, flat, bare patch of the compound called the Field. All the others seemed to be about my age, and we were all dressed in our new training garb; thick grey tights, grey and white fur-lined hooded coats, and shin-length black combat boots. The only form of identification we wore was a patch above our left breast numbered one to twenty-eight. I am number ten.

Those creeps who call themselves guards couldn't keep their eyes off us, hooting and bellowing like a pack of wild animals. Wouldn't I just love to have smacked one of them in their grotesque, toothless faces and show them what the female of the species can do!

Despite our proximity, none of us spoke to one another. Instead, we waited in silence, sizing each other up like rivals. At the other end of the row, and with a patch numbered twenty-eight, is Ilona. I'd recognise that meek, dark-haired girl anywhere. The cheeky grin says she saw me too, but then it faded, and her eyes fixed on her boots again.

Our instructor for today was Blackthorn, a frighteningly loud woman with very short blonde hair, high cheekbones and a permanent scowl. From the moment she marched out to greet us, I got the impression she's the kind of person who would wear combat boots to bed. Needless to say, I wouldn't want to be a boart against her in a fight.

'ATTEN-TION!' she bellowed, startling us from our various states of attentiveness- somewhere between brimming with excitement and excruciating boredom.

'Feet together, back straight, shoulders back…' she ranted on. By the time her string of instructions were done, we all stood as though we had rigid sticks up our butts.

There are five rules at Garret Gord, something Instructor Blackthorn, like the Patriarch before her, made it clear we are expected to obey without question. Sera's already made me go through them ad nauseam. To ensure they are permanently imprinted on our memories, Blackthorn had us yell them out forward and backward at least ten times. I don't think we'll forget them anytime soon. In case anyone reads this later, this is the code I am now living by;

1. *Protect and obey the Patriarch and the chain of command*
2. *Do no harm unless ordered otherwise*

3. Protect one's self
4. Never trust anyone
5. No unchecked weapons, explosives or fire

One other thing- the mission is key; no compromises, whatever that means. I'm sure that'll make sense someday, but right now, it's a kind of mission statement. If only we knew what said mission was.

It was at this point the Patriarch emerged, and in all his outrageous ostentatiousness. Even so much as being driven out onto the Field in his newly polished green car—the very same car Sera and I liberated from the raider camp. We weren't allowed to keep it, so he commandeered it as'it was his right'. Still, I'm sure he could have walked that hundred or so metas himself, supposing his feet weren't painted on. Perhaps he couldn't hold his butt cheeks together that far?

Blackthorn had the audacity to introduce him as 'his graciousness, the Patriarch, father to Garret Gord and our respected leader'. After my introduction to him, I'd say creepy old fossil.

For ten excruciating decs, we endured the staged pomp to stroke the old man's ego, allowing him to make his proclamation, then examine us like a child admiring his playthings.

His speech went something along the lines of the arrogant rhetoric he spat at Ilona and me the day before.

As he marched the line, a foul taste rose in the back of my throat. For some reason, his eyes didn't much leave Ilona once he'd seen her. He even paused to stroke her face like he did with me in his office that time. My encounters with the Patriarch have so far only been short, but they've been more than enough for me to determine his character. Those wandering hands, the beady eyes and exuding self-effacing arrogance. Put simply, I despise him.

'Do not disappoint me,' he said, waving those ridiculous sleeves. He then got back into his car and was driven away.

The rumble of the car's engine barely diminished when Blackthorn ordered us to break up into pairs. The dumbstruck looks on the other girls' faces revealed the order had caught them by surprise. Over five cycles, I imagine few had seen *another person, much less trained with them. So, while the others milled about in confusion, treating each other as though they had some kind of virus, Ilona and I gravitated to each other.*

We sparred for most of the morning, judging each other's level of skill, learning their tells and trying not to cause harm. It appeared Ilona's guardian had taught her some variation of Shitak'na, but her technique was sloppy. From the telegraphed punches and poor form, it's clear Ilona's guardian hasn't been as studious with her training as Sera has been with mine. It begs the question, what has her guardian been teaching her? I tried to help improve her technique by practising jabs and blocks, focusing on precision over force and, to my satisfaction, her abilities improved. As did her confidence.

Then Blackthorn came to visit. After spending time with the other groups, she stood, hands clasped behind her back, watching us. It's unnerving having your every move scrutinised like that.

'You two,' she yelled. 'Show me that again.'

Ilona seemed worried, shuffled her feet into 'level' stance—the starting position of the Shitak'na water style, then delivered a slow-paced strike to my face. Just as we had practised, I deflected it without effort.

'Pathetic,' the instructor roared. 'I could do better in my sleep. This time hit her. I want you to want to hurt her!'

Ilona reset, clenched her fist and struck again. The swiftness of her manoeuvre surprised me as I lay sprawled in the dirt, dazed and clutching my jaw.

The other girls burst into raucous laughter. Poor Ilona, the remorseful expression on her face told me she hadn't expected that either.

Blackthorn seemed to approve, but that permanent scowl deepened as she warned, 'If I ever catch either of you pulling punches again, I will have the class use you as training dummies, and you can learn what real punches feel like.'

Recess couldn't come soon enough. We dragged ourselves over to the mess—a mobile kitchen where we lined up in order of number to collect our food on formed metal trays. The dining area is nothing but a bare patch of dirt surrounded by a newly erected, high cross-hatch wire fence. With no tables or chairs on which to sit, we took our slop and went to find a solitary place in the warm sun. As I entered the pen-like courtyard, I found a small spot in a corner and sat cross-legged on the bare ground to eat in silence. By the time Ilona arrived, she had found herself without a sunny place to sit.

She approached the other girls, and they growled, hissed and shooed her away as if she were some kind of pest. When she came my way, everyone was staring, presumably to see what I would do. Standing, I leaned toward her and shouted, 'You weak, pathetic wimp!' Startled, she looked at me with eyes on the verge of tears. 'Play along. Just follow my lead,' I whispered. While it upset me to have to force Ilona to give up her food, it was a necessary performance for the prying eyes.

We had eaten about half our food when Number Two, a slender girl with short-cropped blonde hair like Blackthorn's and a remarkably similar sour face, came over and kicked dirt all through our lunch. To be fair, it probably improved the flavour.

She attempted to goad us, calling us pathetic little tomadai who can't throw decent punches.

'Pair with me,' she said, directing the challenge at me, 'and I'll show you how to fight.'

I declined, taking a bite from my gritty bread roll instead.

But Number Two wasn't going to take 'no' for an answer.

Ilona later told me she's Instructor Blackthorn's daughter, and her appearance all made sense. Seems she's taken the title 'daughter' a bit more seriously than most.

During afternoon training, we paired up again. This time, Number Two made good on her promise to partner with me and pushed Ilona aside.

'Look, it's the girl with more fire in her hair than she has in her gut,' she said, as though her taunts of my hair colour somehow should be an insult.

I take my stance. Of course, instructor Blackthorn noticed my change in sparring partner and congratulated us both as though it was something of an upgrade.

At that point, Blackthorn asked for my name. I thought it odd, given we had to have been wearing numbers for a reason. When I replied, that curious scowl deepened again.

Apparently, according to Blackthorn, I need a strong opponent to teach me what 'true combat is.' That's when I learned Number Two's name; Alyx.

As we go a few rounds with Blackthorn glaring at us, it's obvious she was showing my partner favouritism. Each time she threw a punch or a kick, Blackthorn was quick to congratulate her while I nursed yet another bruise. Seems Ilona was right about them being guardian and daughter.

I'm floored by Alyx's skill and learned quickly she's stronger, faster and more aggressive.

After Alyx attempted one more leg sweep, and I dive rolled out of the way, Blackthorn stepped forward and considered me once more with that scowl.

She demanded to know who trained me.

Reluctant as I was to say, Blackthorn was insistent, so I answered the question.

At hearing Sera's name, Blackthorn chuckled. Alyx called her a weak bikkja and other things I won't repeat in this journal.

Her callous disregard toward a guardian had me stunned. Not even Blackthorn intervened. And while I tried to understand why, all Blackthorn responded with was 'Forget it, tomadai. Focus on your form. Beseech the Progenitors, we can make a better fighter out of you.'

I shall remember those words.

As I hauled my tired and battered body home, Sera tended to my wounds in that gentle manner she does. I was surprised to find her earlier comment about the tightness of the outfits happened to be true—seems they really do help minimise the bruising. She set down a nice bowl of hot stew and fresh-baked bread. Unlike the rest of the food in this place, Sera's always tastes delicious, and I consider myself possibly the luckiest daughter here. Whilst I sit at the dining table writing this journal entry, I can't help but think about what Alyx and Instructor Blackthorn had said…

'Sera?' I ask, pushing the notebook aside.

'Can it wait? I am a little busy right now.'

'Okay, never mind.'

'It is okay, Jayne. I shall be there in a dec.' She limps around the kitchen, humming softly to herself while she finishes up what she's doing. The timer on the oven goes 'ding', and she reaches in to pull out a tray of piping hot goodies.

'Are those cocao biscuits?' I ask as their tantalising aroma floods from the oven and fills the apartment. 'Damn, your baking smells good.'

'Watch your language,' she chides, albeit flippantly. 'But they do smell damn good, though, do they not?'

She places two on a plate and brings them over. They're hot and floppy, just how I like them.

'Now, what were you saying?' she asks, pulling out the chair beside me to sit.

'Ah, um, it's something the others said today. They said some unflattering things about you.'

'Hmm, did they just? What did they say?'

'They said you were weak and a failure. That you did something wrong, and now you're a disgrace.'

'I see. And do you believe them?'

'Well, no. Of course not. But I wanted to beat their heads in so bad. If they weren't stronger or faster than me, I probably would have.'

'Stronger? Faster? Jayne, have I taught you nothing? What purpose would "beating their heads in serve", anyway? You should know by now it is not about a person's strength, or speed or skill. It is about how they use it that matters.' She taps me on the forehead. 'Your strength comes from up here. That is the muscle you must use, and if you do so wisely, you can rise to any challenge.'

'That's all good and well, but just how am I supposed to do that?'

Sera strolls to the bookshelf, selects a tome I instantly recognise as *The Book of the Progenitors* and flicks it open to a page. 'Consider Progenitor Martok Wyllt,' she says, placing the hefty, leather-bound book on the table and pushing it over for me to see. On the page is an image of a well-built man wearing a flowing black cloak and an intricate mask depicting many faces.

'What, the Progenitor of deception?'

'Martok was the master of disguise. So skilled was he, many believed he was more than one person. No one ever knew what he truly looked like. He was able to use his skills of deceit, illusion and misdirection to confound and defeat any foe. It is one of the reasons Xisnys and Gotthard relied upon him to help them defeat the Army of the Damned. Never underestimate the power of the mind.'

'But Instructor Blackthorn…'

'Ah-ha, that explains it then.'

'What?'

'Blackthorn, she was your instructor today, was she?'

'Yes. Why am I getting a sense there's some history between you two?'

'Nothing you need concern yourself with.'

'Sera, she called you a bikkja.'

She smiles and takes a biscuit. 'She did, did she? And, you think that should insult me, do you?'

'Yeah, shouldn't it?'

'Let us see. A bikkja in the old tongue means *female canis*: A formidable hunter, fiercely loyal, incredibly intelligent, and a powerful fighter capable of taking down a full-grown male ursus. What do you think?'

'But she used it as a derogatory word. I so wanted to defend your honour, but I was ashamed I couldn't. I felt like I couldn't protect one of these biscuits from a child.'

Sera chuckles. 'She may have, but I think the meaning is lost on her. While I thank you for jumping to my defence, it is unnecessary. Put it this way, it is not much of an insult if I am not insulted, is it?' She smiles and takes a bite of the biscuit. 'Mmm, these are good. My best batch in some time, I think.'

'But…'

'I would not worry about Blackthorn. I will let you in on a little secret. When we were your age—Progenitors, I hate saying that—Vina and I were, well, rivals. She has always been a competitive individual who believed brawn trumps brains, yet on most occasions, I would prove her wrong.'

I move in closer to listen to Sera's story.

'It was our final test,' she continues. 'The two of us were in the forest and came face to face with a lone boart. It hunted us for a day and a half, determined to make us its dinner. Vina tried to take it down with spears and knives, but she learned that would not work when she almost ended up gored. It was at that point I offered a different tactic and convinced her, albeit reluctantly, to follow my plan.

'By using a row of sharpened stakes to line the bottom of a natural pit and a cover of woven branches and leaves, we set our trap. We lured the unsuspecting creature over, offering ourselves up as bait. Right until the moment it was struggling at the bottom of our pit, she never believed the plan would work. We feasted on roast boart that night, yet I still do not think it sunk in for her how we had defeated it.'

'Wow, I had no idea you and Blackthorn...'

'There is a lot you do not know. Just whatever you do, never tell her I told you this. The lesson here is not *how* to use your skills—it is *when*. Though they may train us for violence, it is not always the right solution. Mental strength can be just as powerful, so never dismiss it outright. It might just save your life.'

Training day two—the morning is brisk, and a thick fog covers the Field. Our instructor is late, and Ilona is missing. Twenty-seven of us line up at arms reach apart with our coats pulled tight, waiting.

Where's Ilona?

A shadowy figure lumbers from the apartment block and traverses the Field towards us.

Can't be.

They come nearer, and the obscured figure materialises into Sera, who hobbles with the aid of her cane toward the mound where Blackthorn stood yesterday. 'Good morn. I am Instructor MonLantry,' she bellows in that tone I only hear when I'm in trouble and gets right down to business. 'Who here can tell me an effective way to disable an opponent?'

'With a pistol, sir,' Alyx sniggers.

A few of the surrounding girls giggle in response.

'Perhaps,' Sera replies, 'but what if you do not have one?'

'Why wouldn't I? I always carry one,' Alyx replies in a curt tone.

'Do you have one now?'

'Well, no, of course not. I'm not stupid to bring a pistol to class.'

The other girls try to conceal their laughter behind cupped hands.

'Okay, so you do not always carry one. I will ignore the fact you just lied to an instructor, and let us say in our scenario, you do not have one either. There will be times when you cannot rely on weapons. What do you do then?'

'Take one from someone else,' she says, seeming to revel in the humour.

Sera remains calm, her cool demeanour never wavering. 'Do you see anyone else here with a pistol?'

Alyx points to a guard standing at the edge of the Field. 'He's got one.'

The guard shifts nervously away from the training grounds.

'And how do you propose to do that?' Sera counters.

'Kick 'em in the head,' Alyx laughs.

'Okay, care to demonstrate?' Sera stands back, thrusts her cane into the hand of the nearest girl and waves Alyx forward.

Alyx glances around at the rest of us with a smarmy look on her face, pushes up the sleeves of her jacket and assumes her combat stance.

Sera grounds her feet and assumes the steady crouch stance of the rock form, Shihung'na, allowing her thighs to take the strain of her weight instead of her damaged knee.

Without a word, Alyx begins leaping around, throwing kicks in the air and dancing about in a display of combat bravado, showing off to the crowd before launching her attack.

A high kick swings toward Sera's head, and her forearm blocks it, returning with a fast jab to the inside of Alyx's thigh.

Alyx staggers backwards. With renewed determination, she steps in for a second kick.

Sera lifts her thigh to block Alyx's strike to her guarded knee.

With a jolt, Sera stops Alyx's next punch mid-air, gripping her wrist and whipping her hand to strike three times in rapid succession at Alyx's upper arm. That wipes the smirk from her face. With a look of abhorrent shock, Alyx pulls away, unable to lift her limb.

'What have you done?' she howls. 'I can't move my arm.'

'Say again, Number Two? I did not hear you?'

'What are you, deaf? I said I can't move.'

'Number Two,' Sera barks, 'I will give you a dead left arm to match your right if you continue your attitude.'

Alyx grits her teeth. 'Yes, sir.'

'Good, and that is how you disable an opponent without weapons.' Sera retrieves her cane and orders Alyx back in line. 'And, Number Two, do not fear. It will wear off as you move.'

The other girls share astonished glances as Alyx, doing her best imitation of a Blackthorn scowl, moves back into position, rubbing her arm.

'What you witnessed,' Sera says, addressing the group again, 'is Shihung'na, the solid rock form and one of four close to medium range fighting modalities specifically designed to draw in and disable one's opponent. The others are; Shitak'na, the flowing water form; Shibag'na, the light air form and Shatak'na, the fierce fire form. Each invokes the natural environmental energies of Jorth. This is the basic technique. To demonstrate further, I call on student Number Ten. Please step forward, Jayne.'

Is it hot all of a sudden?

Alyx's glare seems intent on burning holes in my back as I take her place out front.

'Okay, Jayne, show me a block grab,' Sera says, dropping into stance. She throws a controlled punch, which I block and hold before releasing for the next example. 'Good. Now let us show them some more advanced techniques.'

Sera's face becomes stern with concentration, and I ready myself for her attack.

Together, we demonstrate different variations of offence and defence manoeuvres, each time increasing in difficulty, making me test the limits of the training Sera has already given me.

Puffing from the exertion, we reset for a fifth time, and before I can catch my breath, Sera strikes again. I move to block, catching Sera's arm and hold it out to the side. But then, in a wash of landscape, she disappears from view. Stars speckle my vision, and the edges fade to black. All colour washes from the world, and then…

Sprawled on the ground, something gently caresses my hand. Upon opening my eyes, Ilona's beautiful but blurry face is the first thing I see.

'Jayne, are you with us?' Sera calls, supporting my head.

Then the realisation dawns—Sera choke-locked me out!

I can't believe it. How could she, of all people, do that to me?

Still dazed, I roll away and struggle to stand.

'Jayne…' Sera says, reaching forward to help.

After what she did, I bat her hand away and put as much distance between us as I can. 'Just stay away from me.'

Ilona and I sit together in the same sunny spot at recess as the previous day. She seems more timid than usual. 'Where've you been? I didn't see you at line-up this morn.'

'Just stuff.' Her finger traces out concentric circles in the dirt, and she seems more engaged with that than answering the question.

'When did you arrive? I didn't see you show up.'

'I came while you were in the choke. Why did she do that?'

'Dunno,' I sigh, rubbing my neck. The thought of it still has me fuming.

'She's your guardian, right?'

'Yeah. Some guardian, huh?'

'So, I said,' a voice comes from behind. 'What's the frak a cripple running a combat training session, anyway? It's absurd.' Alyx stands with a group of other girls. 'Maybe the teacher's pet can tell us. What of it, teacher's pet?' She throws a rock, and it skims off my knee, hitting the fence.

'Go away, Alyx. I'm not interested.'

'How does it feel to be the laughingstock of the group? The only one of us who's had a nap during training, *and* it's only our second day.' Alyx and her posse giggle like a flock of water-aves. 'And oh, look, the tardy one has returned. The prodigal daughter and little miss tardy.'

'Shut up, Alyx.'

'Or what, you'll try your fainting move on me?'

'What's your problem?'

'My problem? You want to know what my problem is? Weak little thviets like you, that's what. Both you and your pathetic guardian who couldn't teach a class if the students were imbeciles. My arm is still numb, thanks to her. I should have just kicked her in the head when I had the chance.'

'Why didn't you?'

'I don't attack cripples. They're too easy.'

'And that's what it looked like, too.'

'I heard she botched a job. If she can't work, what makes her qualified to teach?'

'Shut up!' I yell, balling my fists.

'Whattya gonna do, call your mummy?'

Unbearable rage wells up inside, and before I know it, Alyx lies pinned to the ground, straining against my weight.

Hands wrench at my shoulders, attempting to pull me away, but it only gives Alyx room to retaliate and unleash a furious burst of fists and knees. Each time she strikes, I deflect, and the fight descends into an all-out brawl, with the two of us rolling about in the dirt.

Large hands wrestle us apart—I barely notice the two guards swoop in and pry us from our hated grip on each other.

'I'll get you for that, psycho,' Alyx spits, trying to break free.

'Both of you, stop it this instant!' Sera booms. Even with her cane, she can stride at a pace when she has the need.

'She started it!' I glower at Alyx, who is still trying, and failing, to wrestle out of the guard's strong grip.

'Number Ten,' Sera yells, 'what's the matter with you?'

'I don't know, Sera,' I say with sarcasm, 'maybe my brain got miswired from you choking me out earlier. Alyx was just reminding me how amusing it was.'

Sera levels her voice and her gaze. 'I *can't* have you speaking to me that way. You know better than that.'

'Do I? Well, maybe knowing better isn't good enough, *sir*.'

'Number Ten, if you continue like this, I will have no choice but to send you to the box.'

'Then do it. It might be the only decent thing you've done all day.'

She scowls with an intensity I don't think I've ever seen on her before. It's a mix of disappointment and something else I can't put my finger on, and it startles me more than the threat of being sent to the box. 'Guards!' she yells, turning away. 'Take Number Ten to the box. Leave her there until I say she has had enough. Perhaps some time alone with her thoughts will mellow her anger.'

Sera doesn't even give me the courtesy of a glance as the guards drag me away.

The box is a basic squat metal cube buried most of the way into an unshaded part of the Field. It's hot and smelly, and there's barely enough room for one person. Comfortable is not an option, and with only a thin slot in its side, there's nothing to do but sit cramped in this wretched pit and watch as the other girls and Alyx train with Sera. *My* Sera.

HOW DARE SHE DO THIS TO ME! After everything I've done to stand up for her!

If I were any angrier, my head would explode. Before I realise it, my knuckles bleed from punching the walls of this miserable metal coffin. The metallic smell of blood and the unbearable pain forces me to stop. At that moment, my attention is drawn to the untouchable world beyond the slot. Out there, in the Field, twenty-seven girls flow through motions so familiar I can close my eyes and follow along. Tears stream down my cheeks, and I realise I am missing out. Sera had spent much of my initial days teaching me this, and yet here I am.

As I observe them, a different side of Sera emerges, one that is not constrained by personal attachment or empathy. I realise she isn't training them like she trained me. With them, she is stern, almost aggressive. There's none of that gentle kindness or nurturing she afforded me when I misstepped or failed to complete a form properly. It's as if not having me there has somehow set her free and allowed her to be the person she is, not the person she wants me to see. So, I sit here in silence, watching, waiting and learning.

Night falls, and the temperature plummets, causing the metal to leach away any warmth I fight to retain. With only the clothes I was thrown in here with, I begin to shiver.

In the darkness, footsteps approach, carrying through the silent night. A figure with dark hair and a familiar face peeks through the slot. Ilona!

'Hi Jayne,' she says, squatting in front of my narrow little window. 'I heard you were still here, so I thought I'd sneak out. How you doing?'

'Oh yeah, not bad, really. Need to pee, but other than that, I'm doing fine.'

'Well, my guardian thinks I'm taking out the scrap bin, so…' she lifts a small bucket for me to see.

'Isn't the compost heap on the other side of camp?'

'Yeah, well, I kinda didn't go that way, did I? And I didn't want anyone to find it, so I'll just dispose of it on my way back.'

'Why did you come?'

'I wanted to see you, silly.'

'Thank you, I guess. How was training?'

'Yeah, alright. Better than yesterday. Your guardian is one hard arse, I'll tell you that. But she's nice. Nicer than mine, and Blackthorn, that's for sure. You're so lucky.'

'Lucky, yeah,' I say with sarcasm. 'Say, about yesterday. What happened? Last thing, you got called off to the Patriarch's office, and then you were… different today. Is anything wrong?'

'I don't want to talk about it.'

'Well, okay. But you know, I *am* in a box. I'm kinda a captive audience right now. If you want to talk, I'm right here. Not going anywhere.'

'Thanks, but I'm fine. Really. Oh, sheeze,' she says, jumping up, 'there's someone coming. Gotta go. Catch you later, Jayne.'

'You too. Thanks for visiting.'

Her footsteps fade in the distance as another heavier pair comes my way, jingling what sounds like keys.

'You in the box,' a gruff voice says as the lid opens. 'Go home before I chase you back.'

Once out of that confined space, my legs wobble, and I can barely stand, let alone walk. If it wasn't for my full bladder, I'd be in no hurry to return home.

The heavy front door opens, and Sera, as usual, is sitting at the dining table with one of her papers. In front of her are two steaming cups of tei. She sees me and pushes one across the table.

'I'm not thirsty, thanks,' I grumble, heading for the bathroom. That's a lie, of course, but I'm not prepared to accept anything from *her*.

'Jayne, wait.'

Despite my current sentiment, it's how she spoke that stills my stride.

'I know what you are thinking,' she says, standing and retrieving the first-aid kit from atop the icebox. 'But it is not true.'

'What, that you really are a liar or a lousy person or both? I'm not interested. Going for a shower.'

'Please, Jayne.'

'*What?*'

'Surely you would have figured it out by now?'

'Enough with the riddles. I'm tired. You not only humiliated me in front of Alyx and all those other girls, but when I fought to defend your honour, you threw me in a box?'

'That last bit was all you. Please sit down.'

The tei's sweet, herbal aroma draws me in, and with reluctance, I take the seat across from her.

'Jayne, please listen. Everything I do, I do to protect you.'

She reaches out to take my hands, but I pull them away with a huff. 'Could've fooled me. You know my head's still spinning.'

'I am sorry about that. But I chose you because you were the only one I could trust.'

'Well, that isn't something we've practised before. You should have warned me!'

'Yes, I should have. And I will make sure I do that next time.'

'Next time? Oh-no, Sera. There's not going to be a next time.'

'Listen to me, please—this is serious. But first, let me look after those hands.'

With a sigh, I give in and let her treat my split knuckles. While she works, she continues speaking. 'This place, I told you, is not what it seems.'

'I know. It's a training camp for assassins. You already told me that.'

'Yes, but it is more than that. All those girls you see out there, not all of them will survive here. Two already have not.'

'What?' I exclaim, pulling away in astonishment, but Sera gently retakes my hands and finishes cleaning the wounds.

'You thought there were twenty-eight girls,' she continues somberly. 'That is not true. There were thirty. That last solo trip to the forest, two girls perished. And that was just a trial.'

'What happened?'

'I do not know. But if you think I am being hard on you now, you do not know what is coming.'

'Well then, how many more of us will disappear before this is all over?'

'That I know neither. All I can tell you is with me, you have a fighting chance of avoiding being one of them.'

'So, you think I should be grateful?'

'It would not go astray. I told you we are a team, and I meant it. My job is to get you through this, and I promise to do my best to keep you alive. I do not have to be kind to you or care to protect you from all the sharp edges of this place. But I do, and I do it because I choose to.'

'I still don't know how I'm supposed to feel about that. After you brought me here and did all these things, it's hard to know what to think or feel.'

'Believe me, I understand, and it does not help that I cannot tell you half the things I want to. I only want to protect you. It may not look that way, but it is the truth.'

'Is that why you sent me to the box?'

'I have my reasons. Would it help if I said yes?'

I shrug a response.

'This is more than just about survival. I want to give you every chance to succeed, too. You have the potential to be one of the best assets this facility has ever seen. Even the Patriarch sees that.'

'So, you sent me to the box?'

She sighs. 'I sent you to the box because I wanted you to learn a more valuable lesson than what I was teaching the other girls. Remember what I told you about strength? You are a powerfully astute person. You are playful, energetic, caring, enthusiastic, and passionate, all wonderful attributes that are so rare here. These are your strengths, but they can also be used against you. As I keep saying, you must use your strengths wisely. By spending time in solitary like you did today, I hoped to teach you mindfulness—the ability to channel your emotional energy. Watching the world go on around you can be a very cathartic experience. You will have felt a full range of emotions today, and this is the first step to understanding and controlling them, so they do not control you. When you can learn to channel your emotional energy, you have the power to overcome anything. That is why I put you in the box.'

'You could have just told me.'

'And what good would that have done? Sometimes you need to experience the lesson to truly learn it. Anyway,' she says, stroking a hand through my hair. 'It is late, and you said you are tired. Just think about what I said. Finish your tei, then wash up. There is some food for you on the stove.'

As I sit sipping my tei, contemplating today's events, thoughts swirl through my mind. Despite how tired and sore I am, I enter it all down in my diary. While I do that, I can't help but wonder. If that's what day two is like here, what on Jorth awaits me tomorrow?

07 REVELATIONS

DAY 197

We had another accident at training today. After four cendecs on the obstacle course, traversing barbed wire lined mud pits, crawling through dark waterlogged tunnels, and climbing ropes and high vertical walls, we transferred to the urban simulation.

Exhausted and caked head to toe in mud, I stood on the sideline and watched as the others came through. While I rested, breaking open a ration pack and hydrating, Number Seventeen, possibly the most athletic of the group and eager to get the jump on the rest, decided to continue.

She darted up the wall of the replica building to the second storey, where she hung precariously from an open window. While she managed to swing herself in, her rifle, which was slung over her shoulder, caught on the frame, and I guess with all the mud on her hands, she slipped and fell.

Time seemed to slow as she plummeted, arms and legs flailing, with a sickening thud to the ground below—it still gives me chills.

Blackthorn was furious, yelling at her to 'get up' before realising she wasn't going to and called the medics. From where I stood, I had no idea if she was okay. I hope she is.

Six was right behind Seventeen when it happened. She saw everything. When Six reached the shooting range later, she didn't even hit the target. It's clear the incident had rattled her. She's normally one of the best, so I can't imagine how she's feeling tonight.

Tomorrow's lesson should be held by DelTasker again. She teaches knife handling and 'resilience under duress', aka torture training. Can't say I ever look forward to her classes.

'Do you have time to talk?' Sera says, emerging from the VT room where she'd been watching her shows, to join me at the dining table. 'Oh, you are writing…'

'No, it's okay. Just finished,' I reply, setting down my scribe.

'I am interested to see how your studies are going.'

I glance at the half-written history essay on the table. 'Fine.'

'Why do I get the impression you are procrastinating again?'

'Because I'm putting it off until the morrow.'

'Jayne, I asked for that essay a trey ago.'

Setting aside my journal, with great reluctance, I reach for the history notebook. 'I know, but history is so *boring*.'

'History is only boring to those who do not wish to understand its value,' Sera says, dropping into that tone she does when she goes into one of her sayings. She disappears into her bedroom and returns a moment later, carrying a thick, leather-bound folio. 'It serves as a stout reminder of past mistakes, so it does not doom us to repeat them.'

She sets the collection of documents on the table, and I marvel at its thick size.

'But isn't history written by the victors? I mean, if in war one party is wiped out, they're not going to be the ones to write the story of how it happened, are they?'

'You would be surprised. You make an interesting point, though. Half the problem is not obtaining information but obtaining *quality and reliable* information. And especially now, without libraries or publicly available records, there's nobody to preserve its authenticity. After a time, a lot of it often conveniently gets lost or altered. Hence, if we are to preserve the *true* account of events, we must document it ourselves. I have done my best to do this—collect as much information from reliable sources as I can. That way, I have something back to which I can refer.'

'Why?' I ask, puzzled.

'Why not. Call it a hobby if you will, but I think it is important to preserve history.'

'What's that, then?'

'This…' she says, untying the leather cord from around a metal clasp and spreading the cover out on the table, 'is an archive of sorts—my collection of records from some of history's more notable events. When I started this project a little over twenty cycles ago, it was for my own personal record to understand our motivations and that of our enemies. However, it never really served that purpose. I see this being of more use to you now.'

'I still don't understand how this will help me? What's the point in digging around in the past when the past can't be changed?'

'While the past may be immutable, we can use our knowledge of it to shape the future. As a culture, we tend to move in cycles. As generations go by, the same things motivate us as they once did our ancestors; greed, power, control, vengeance. Yet because experiences are not heritable, like our hair or eye colour, we do not remember what our ancestors endured fighting over them. For this reason, we end up making the same mistakes. That is why war is cyclical. The Progenitor wars, the Faction war and all the skirmishes in between, they are all the same. We remember the valour and glory but conveniently forget the pain and suffering. And when that goes away, we become complacent, and the cycle starts all over again.'

She flicks over a few pages until she uncovers a yellowed newspaper clipping and pushes the folder across the table so I can see.

The Aster Herald

Lunaday 91 Centraal 1945

Tensions escalate: Cedreau destroys Hillfar. Skoyca declares war.

At 04:53, Cedreau forces launched a major nuclear strike against the Skoyca government-protected town of Hillfar in Mon Loq province. Hillfar has a resident population of 200 thousand. Many remain unaccounted for. Authorities fear the worst.

Admiral Capener of the Aurora Liberation Army, on behalf of the Skoyca Government Alliance, has declared the Cedreau Coalition militia's actions against the Skoyca people as an act of war. 'We are doing everything we can to evacuate the residents of Hillfar and the surrounding area, but we also cannot allow this vile act to go unpunished. The Lafir government is officially on notice,' Admiral Capenar said.

'So, this marked the start of the Faction war?'

She nods. 'Yes, but it was a very short war. Not long after that, the Skoyca Government Alliance retaliated, bombing other Cedreau Coalition-held provinces of Oclave, Aswela and Nusmore. After that, very little remained.'

'Nusmore? That's where I lived. It was the Skoyca who did all this? Bombed my home?'

'The Cedreau were the ones to throw the first punch, so to speak, but both sides were as responsible as each other. What happened is the result of both their actions.'

'But why? Why did they attack?'

'There were a number of reasons, mostly to control power and contested resources. Sound familiar?'

'The Cedreau sound like horrible people. I'm not surprised the Skoyca retaliated.'

'Do not be too quick to judge. My childhood home was in Hillfar, up the valley by a river in the province of Mon Loq. I may not have lived there when it happened, but I still have fond memories of the place. Where you were a citizen of Skoyca, I was Lafir. Do you think me horrible?'

'No, of course I don't.'

'Just because someone happens to be associated with your enemy does not make them the enemy. We cannot fully understand our enemies or find them where we expect. That is why we follow orders. We are meant to leave that responsibility to our superiors.'

As she says that, I flick through the pages of collected clippings, notes, photos and articles,

all stained and ragged with age. 'Well,' she adds, 'that is how it is supposed to work.'

'Then, who won?'

'Won what?' she asks, seemingly distracted.

'The war, who won?'

'Do you see any winners?' she replies. '*Nobody* won this war. Both sides bombed themselves into oblivion, and so here we are.'

'So, what caused the war in the first place?'

She pulls over the folder and starts flicking through it to a page displaying a picture of a rock and featuring the heading, *'Megloinium: The Progenitors' Power.'*

'The Cedreau and Aurora factions had been fighting over it for quite some time. Both had attempted to further research in energy technologies, but neither controlled enough resources to achieve it. That is why they partnered with rival governments. The Aurora Mining Corporation's Liberation Army allied themselves with the Skoycan government. It became the Skoyca Government Alliance or SGA, while the Cedreau Corporation, also a mining company, partnered with the Lafir government and became the Cedrean Coalition or CC. Both governments believed having corporations controlling their militaries would strengthen their authority. It gave them the appearance the government had power, but in actuality, it was the corporations that effectively controlled them.'

'But what is Meglon—?'

'Megloinium. It is a highly volatile compound mined for its superior energy potential. Just a tiny amount can power a city for a cycle. It is also extremely rare. Both sides constantly accused each other of mining it to make weapons. Their concerns were warranted because, as it would happen, that was the case.'

'Is that what they used to bomb my home?'

'The SGA had recently acquired a quantity of refined megloinium thermonuclear warheads. Judging by the fallout, it is highly likely that was what they used in the attack, yes.'

'What about you? Where were you before the war?'

'Here. I've always been here.'

'Then how do you know so much? There's nothing about that in here.'

'Ahh,' she says, 'that is not part of the lesson.'

'Why not?'

'Because I do not wish to talk about it. Please move on.'

'Has it got anything to do with *Project Vesuvius*?'

At the mention of the words, Sera's eyes widen, and she glares at me as though I'd just insulted her. 'How do you know about that?'

I point at a stack of books in the bookcase. 'I found references to it in one of those periodicals.'

She sighs. 'I am sorry, Jayne. I think that is enough for tonight.'

'Didn't you just say, "history serves as a reminder of past mistakes, so we don't repeat them"?'

'Yes, but this is not what I meant.'

'But you did say, if I'm going to understand what I'm getting myself into, I should learn from your history.'

Sera glances with nervous apprehension at the papers spread out over the table. 'Do you want some tei? I'm going to make some tei.'

'Sera…' I say, resting my hand on hers like she does sometimes to calm me. The action stays her, but her body language betrays her, and she looks at me very troubled, like a tomadai caught in a trap. 'What is it?'

'You are right, Jayne. You should also know that some things are just best left buried in the past.'

'Why? What's it about *Project Vesuvius* that's got you so rattled?'

'You really want to know?' she says, and I'm guessing she's hoping I'll just let it go. But this is one box she left out in the open—it was inevitable I would eventually crack the lid. Until now, Sera's been reserved about certain aspects of her past, guarded at even the mention of it, so it would seem strange she would take this much interest in history. What could have possibly happened that would make someone who's usually so calm and collected clam up like this?

I nod my response.

She sighs and straightens in her chair. 'It has got me rattled, as you so eloquently put it, because it involved my first real love. *And* my first kill.'

'So, you were involved with *Project Vesuvius*?'

'Not exactly. Look, if you insist on me telling you this, I must warn you, this is no dreamtale.'

'Okay, but I think I can handle it,' I reply, getting comfortable to listen as she tells her story.

'That is not what concerns me, but here goes. The cycle was AP1936. *Vesuvius* was a top-secret CC research and development project aimed at refining and weaponising high-grade megloinium. Stocks were rare, even back then, so they were exploring ways of maximising its destructive potential.'

'What has that got to do with you?'

'I am getting to that,' she replies simply. 'The Skoyca government alliance contracted me as part of a team to infiltrate the project and steal their research. They called it *Operation Canorus*. I was assigned to the Vesuvius's director as a nanny to her newborn daughter. My role was to distract her and glean as much information about her and the project as I could. Then, when the time came, I had to kill her. An easy assignment, or so I thought.'

'Then what happened?'

'I succeeded.'

'You did your job. What's wrong with that?'

'We fell in love.'

'Oh.'

'Oh, is an understatement,' she says, her voice quavering. 'You have to understand, I expected things to be simple. But invariably, they never turn out that way. Back then, I was a strong, independent young woman—impetuous and fiercely ambitious. I never expected I would end up falling desperately in love with someone I was contracted to kill.' She pauses to take a breath and compose herself. From the furrow in her brow and the sorrow in her soft brown eyes, retelling this story isn't coming easy, but she glances at me and continues. 'Her name was Loriana Marquess. She was the most gentle-hearted and passionate woman I had ever known. From her file, she was recently widowed and vulnerable—an easy target. But after two cycles of living with her, spending time together and helping her raise her gorgeous daughter, the lie became truth, and I could not help but become attached. The hardest part was knowing someday, they would call upon me to end it. Somehow, I had convinced myself the ruse was real, and for a while, I believed everything would work out. That somehow, they would just forget about us and leave us be. Then my orders came through, and there was no denying it. Oh, I resisted. I did not want to go through with it and did everything I could to avoid it. But in the end, the mission took priority, and I did what I was there to do.'

'Oh, Progenitors!' I say with aghast. 'So, you were the one who had to kill her?'

Sera nodded.

'And nobody else could do it?'

'No. That was my task and mine alone.'

'And you're okay with that?'

'Does it look like I am okay with it? No, Jayne, I was not okay with it, and I am still not okay with it. It haunts me every single day.'

'Then why did you?'

'Because it is, as I said. It is what I have always said. I followed orders.'

'Screw the orders! If you knew what it meant, why would you? Why didn't you question them?'

'It is not our place to question orders. That is who we are, Jayne. We do as they instruct us. That is all.'

'What do you think would have happened had you not succeeded? What if you *didn't* follow the orders and let her live?'

'Jayne, I cannot speculate about could-have-beens.'

'But surely you think about that?'

'I do, but after all these cycles, there is only so much contemplating "what ifs" a person can do before they drive themselves mad.'

'You just said it, though. This war ended in the destruction of *both* sides. I've read about this. It's called *Mutually Assured Destruction.* Had you succeeded and the Skoyca *That* obtained their meg-whatever, maybe the Cedreau would have bombed them into oblivion, and we would have one side exterminate the other instead of both.'

'You have a very strange way of thinking, Jayne. But who is to say the Cedreau were any better than the Skoyca? Both wanted control of the megloinium for nefarious purposes. Perhaps they did the world a favour? All I know is, I had a role to play in the events that led to the destruction of the world, and all I got to show for it was a knife. I am not happy about it, but you wanted to know, so there it is.'

'*That* knife?' I ask, referring to the beautifully intricate knife Sera had lost while in Hope.

She nods solemnly. 'Yes.'

'They gave you a knife? *For that*?'

'That was part of our payment. Now you see why I did not care much for it.'

'Hmm. What about the little girl—the director's daughter—whatever happened to her?'

The enduring sadness in Sera's eyes deepens at the question. The only time I've seen anything like it was when Lou Doe couldn't save Amity. Sera lifts her head in defiance, choking back tears I know are just aching to burst out. 'The facility and the Marquess family home were destroyed,' she says after a moment. 'The child was not my target, and I could not leave her there to die, so I took her and brought her back here. The moment I entered the compound, she was taken from me. I have not seen her since.'

'Does this mean she could be one of us?'

'Perhaps, but I don't know what became of her. We guardians seldom speak, and she would have been far too young to remember.'

'If they had ordered you to kill her, would you have done it?'

'Jayne, please do not ask questions for which you will not want to know the answer,' she snaps.

I think I already know the answer, and it chills me to the core thinking about it.

We sit in silence while I process this shocking revelation. Part of me feels Sera is somehow relieved by telling her story, as though she has waited this long to confess and is somehow seeking forgiveness. Her eyes bear the shame of her actions, and it's heavy. But I think she would be waiting a lifetime to find absolution for this. There's one thing she's right about, though, and knowing this terrifies me; that I, too, am destined to follow this path. If I ever have to face these situations as Sera has, I have to make better choices.

I just have to.

Gathering all my fortitude, I ask her one last question. 'So, if they ordered you to kill me right now, would you do it?'

Her head whips up with her eyes wide with shock. I can almost hear her say, 'how dare you?'

The expression is short-lived, though, for as soon as it appears, she turns away. 'Jayne, I don't want to talk about this anymore,' she says tersely. '*I am* tired. This is enough for tonight.'

She rises from her seat and collects up her folio to leave, but I catch her by the sleeve. 'Please, tell me.'

'*I'm* not answering that question. Goodnight Jayne.'

'Why, *Seraphin MonLantry*? Does that mean you would?'

There's a long silence as she takes two steps toward her room. A hundred cycles would have been shorter than the enduring wait tightening my chest and knotting up my guts.

When she finally turns, her hair is glued to her glistening cheeks, and she stares directly at me. 'I am no longer that person.'

08 IDENTITIES

NC09

One would think the home of Hope's Virtuous Surprime would be opulent and lush, especially given it housed the town's leader. But for Sage and his young family, it wasn't. Sage never had an interest in the grandiose and insisted he shouldn't enjoy special treatment, ensuring the needs of his people came first.

For their contributions to the community, all of Hope's citizens were supplied with a comfortable home, good local-made clothes and wholesome, locally sourced food. Nobody went without—just the way an honest town should be. If anyone wanted more, there was money—in the form of Hopemarks—which could be earned through trade. But, as everybody was already well cared for, money was more of a luxury than a necessity.

Sage pondered on this while he pottered about his moderate kitchen, dressed in his pyjamas and dressing gown. In the darkened glass window above the sink, he casually observed his dull reflection carrying out the motions of preparing a fresh pot of kahwah. As he poured boiling water over the grinds, he savoured the aroma of the dark brew before adding milk to his own and some sweetener to another.

The moment the bedroom door opened, Jaylyn stirred, his wife's groggy hazel eyes following him while he crossed the room.

'Morn,' he said, setting the piping cups down on the side table and giving her a gentle kiss.

'Is it that time already?' she said, yawning.

'Not quite. I have to get in early. No doubt Artimus slept at his desk again. Ever since I left him with the investigation, he's been camping out in that office, living off ration packs. I've never seen such a detrimentally determined, single-minded person in all my life.'

Jaylyn gave him an ironic look. 'Really?'

'You know what I mean,' he added. 'He's not the easiest person to manage.'

'Speak for yourself, my love,' she gently mocked.

Sprawled out over his side of the bed was Averyx. His two-cycle-old daughter rolled over, rubbed her eyes and, upon seeing Sage, yelled out, 'Daddy!' clambering over her mother to wrap her arms around him. With light blonde hair, brown eyes and features like his, there was no mistaking he was her father.

Sage picked her up in a hug and sat on the edge of the bed, giving her a tickle. 'You're getting so big and heavy. Soon I won't be able to pick you up.'

Her giggles filled the room as she squirmed before he turned his attention back to his wife.

'So long as he doesn't expect you to join him,' Jaylyn said, watching on with delight. 'Send him by the co-op. I'll make sure he has something decent to eat.'

'Of course. I'll pass on the message.'

'And don't forget, our reservation's at 7:90. Anja is looking after Averyx at her place, so it'll just be the two of us.'

He smiled a cheeky smile and kissed her again. 'Already looking forward to it. Love you.'

While the sun lazily peeked through the clouds, Sage, now dressed in his smart business attire, slipped out his front door, where his chauffeur, and Jaxson, in his red-piped Surprime guard uniform, waited.

Already in the car was his young, auburn-haired assistant Conrad, who passed him a leather-bound folder containing papers about as exciting as the bottom of his shoe. 'Sir, you have a full agenda today. First up, you have a meeting with the Transport Collective. They're still complaining about raiders. Then you have a meeting with LunaTec. Also, some of the townsfolk are petitioning for a change to the barter system.'

'What?' Sage said, raising an eyebrow. 'They're not happy with it?'

'No. They're saying it's unbalanced.'

'Unbalanced?' Sage shook his head. 'Who's the contact? I want to talk to them. Please set up a meeting.'

'Yes, sir—'

'Do I have *any* spare time today?'

Conrad ran his finger down the sheet. 'Not until this afternoon, sir.'

'Good. I want to check on Artimus. Schedule a meeting with him in his office. And when you speak with him, tell him I want him to go by the co-op and get something decent to eat. I know he's been holed up in that office living off ration packs.'

'Not that he'll listen to me, but I'll do my best, sir.'

'And Conrad,' Sage added, producing a crisp folder. 'I need you to get him to sign these papers. Today if you can.'

The sunlight was fading over Hope when Sage finally traversed the dark corridor towards Artimus's office. Stuffy stale air lined with the acrid stench of sweat and musty old papers escaped the moment Sage pushed open the door. He flicked on the desk lamp, illuminating the neat but cluttered desk where his defence minister lay, face down, with his head resting on his folded arms.

Sage coughed, politely trying to avoid drawing attention to the fact he'd once again caught Artimus sleeping at his desk.

Artimus's head dropped onto the desk with a thump, then he sat up like nothing had happened.

'What do you want?' he grumbled.

Sage awkwardly averted his eyes so he didn't laugh. 'I like what you've done with the place,' he said sardonically, shifting his attention to Artimus's 'crazy' wall, which had grown since he'd last seen it. The sprawling mural of paper and string now covered a large section of the wall behind the desk. It featured documents, photographs and handwritten notes connecting the knife, something called '*Operation Canorus*', the coverless book, and a black-and-white photograph of a woman labelled with the name '*Seraphin MonLantry*'.

When he turned his attention back to his minister, Sage couldn't help but notice Artimus's distinctly unkempt appearance. Judging by the man's wild hair, crinkled green and black army fatigues and the fact he clearly hadn't shaved in some time, Sage figured Artimus had barely even left this office. *Detrimentally determined* didn't even come close to describing him.

'When was the last time you had a shower?' Sage asked.

Artimus rubbed a hand over the stubble covering his face. 'Sage, did you come here to judge me, or was there something you wanted?'

'Well, hello to you too, Artimus. Is it too much to ask after the welfare of one of my ministers?'

'I don't need your or anyone else's charity.'

Sage ignored Artimus's comment. 'I see you at least got out of this room?' he said, referring to the half-eaten bowl of stew sitting at the end of the desk.

'I was getting tired of MREs,' Artimus shrugged. 'They're okay, but this has more taste.'

'Wait, did you just compare my wife's cooking to a ration pack?'

Artimus gave him a wry look. 'Well, if she starts making ration packs, let me know. Anything else?'

'I'll forget you said that, but there goes your invitation to dinner. How goes the investigation?' Sage replied, changing subjects and brushing off his impulse to order the man home.

Artimus sighed, leaning an elbow on the armrest of his chair and looking up at Sage with indifference. 'What do you think?'

'I recall saying a cycle ago you can have help if you need it.'

'And I recall saying, no thank you. Sage, I *said* I'll do this. I just need more time.'

'You've had two cycles, Artimus. I'm willing to give you more. Take all the time you need, in fact, but I shouldn't need to remind you of your other responsibilities.'

'I'm aware of that. And it's under control. You'll be happy to know these are the last,' Artimus said, pointing at the twenty-odd boxes stacked against the walls. The room did seem less cramped than the last time Sage visited.

'Does this mean you're almost done, then?'

'If by done, you mean going through all these boxes, yes.'

'That reminds me. I've been meaning to ask. Where are the others? Dare I ask what you've been doing with them once you've finished with them?'

'The bunker,' Artimus said with a straight face.

'The bunker!' Sage protested. 'But Artimus, that's for emergencies.'

'Are you serious? When was the last time we used it? Six cycles ago? And, thanks to me, we haven't needed it since. Besides, how many people did Hope have then? A little over seven hundred? Hope is now more than double that size. Everyone would have to breathe in at the same time to close the door.'

'We might still need it.'

'No, Sage, we won't. HomeGuard is more than capable of protecting Hope.'

'That sounds familiar. I remember having this conversation once.'

'Lucky for you, I'm not an impetuous young vice-administrator.'

Sage gave a wry smile. The reference to his disastrous defeat at the hands of a peculiar band of raiders still gnawed at him. That 'impetuousness' had cost him his role as defensive administrator of Hope and almost all their lives as well. If it wasn't for Artimus, swooping in and saving the day as he had, Hope would've ended up a very different place. He buried the thought and took the gibe. 'Ah well. As it happens, Hope was in the market for a stubborn old Admiral.'

'Age brings wisdom,' Artimus said with a sly grin.

'And crazy by the looks of it,' Sage joked, referring to the wall of interconnected documents.

'All while saving your…' Artimus shuffled papers around on his desk. 'What was I going to say?'

Sage brushed it off. Seems the Admiral could take a joke as well as he could. As much as Sage could continue this banter, time was getting on, so he resumed his original line of conversation. 'Hmm, so what about your investigation? What happens now?'

'Well,' Artimus said, glancing musingly up at the wall. 'There are a few things that don't make sense.'

'Like what?'

'It doesn't matter.'

'Maybe I can help? I am Surprime, after all.'

Artimus scoffed. 'With respect, you may be Surprime, but I don't expect you to know everything.'

'Try me.'

'Okay, let me know if these ring any bells: *"Hildr"*, *"GG"*, and *"Patriarch"*.'

Sage stared at him with a blank expression before opening his mouth.

'I didn't think so.'

Sage huffed. 'I *do* have people who can look into it.'

'No, Sage. You focus on… other things.'

But Sage was still looking at Artimus's crazy wall, and it was then he pointed out the black-and-white photograph of the dark-haired woman at its centre. 'Who's Seraphin MonLantry?'

'Ah yes,' Artimus replied with a frown. 'That's one elusive woman. I've linked her to the murder weapon—she's our prime suspect—but I can't for the life of me figure out where she's hiding. Or what her connection with Gaius could be.'

'I see,' Sage said. 'So, why would Orian mistakenly think the knife was yours? Why would this woman also have a knife like that?'

'It's a long story. The short of it is, we were both involved in the same operation.'

'And yet you didn't recognise her?'

'Just because we were part of the same operation doesn't mean we knew each other.'

'And this was *Operation Canorus*?' Sage probed, pointing out the words connected to the photo of the MonLantry woman by red string.

'You're quite perceptive, Sage. Maybe you should take over the investigation?' Artimus replied in a dry tone. 'There's nothing more to glean from that than this was her knife. That's all.'

'Right. So, you don't know where she could be now?'

'No,' Artimus said.

'And you're sure there's nothing I can do to help?'

'Sage, if anyone has the resources to hunt her down, it's me. She's out there. *I'll* find her. After all, it's my job and I'll take care of it.'

'Well, speaking of *your job,*' Sage said, switching subjects, as it was clear Artimus wasn't going to discuss the investigation any further. Other, more pressing matters needed the minister's attention. 'The hospital is almost complete, and you need to run security for its unveiling. I had Conrad leave some documents with you to review and sign this morn. Are you done with them yet?'

'Huh?' Artimus asked, and now he was the one with the blank expression. He began searching under the heap of papers piled up on his desk that used to be neatly arranged. He picked up a stack and moved them from one side to the other. 'What were they again?'

'Security plans for the hospital opening next tendawn.'

'Argh,' Artimus complained. 'Are you kidding me? That's next tendawn?'

'Yes, and we discussed this. I need those plans reviewed and signed today. So, if you would please?'

'Right, I know they're here somewhere…'

Just as Artimus was moving documents around, a stray file caught Sage's attention. He slid the aged folder towards himself and pulled out a photograph that was poking out of its side.

'What's this?' he asked, opening the cover to peek at its contents.

Artimus briefly glanced up from his search to look at the file under Sage's hand. 'Oh, yeah, I left that one aside for you,' he said. 'Figured you might find it interesting.'

It was a personnel file. Written across the top in bold black text was the name '*Sempro, Gaius.*' Sage examined the photo. It bore the faded black-and-white image of a younger Gaius Sempro wearing the bars and military dress uniform of a captain.

Progenitors, that's Gaius? He's so young! Sage thought.

The moment he saw the crossed rifle insignia of the Aurora Liberation Army printed on the page, he snapped the file shut. 'There's a reason we don't talk about the past, Artimus,' he said, sliding the file back to its original place.

'That's easy for you to say. You're not the one hunting ghosts,' Artimus replied dryly. 'You knew, though, didn't you?'

'Knew what?'

Artimus reached into his drawer and slid another file across the desk.

Unlike Gaius's personnel file, this one was a weighty but plain, aged manila folder with the words 'Classified' stamped in red across the cover. Sage opened it. Looking back at him was an image of a much younger version of himself, only this wasn't a personnel file—it was a dossier, a complete and unsympathetic record of all the events the SGA had secretly chronicled on him. The image had been taken from a distance, showing him dressed in a special ops uniform carrying his rifle and surrounded by a crowd of people. Beside the photo, the page read:

ENEMY CASEFILE: N7-3178
Faction: Cedreau Corporation Military
Name: Sage Solon
Rank: Commander (Special Ops)
Specialisation: Long-range target shooter, covert marksman
Classification: Extremely Dangerous

```
Mission directive: Kill or Detain
```

The following pages contained information on missions he had been involved in, people with whom he had worked and even been close. Every page was stamped with; *'Cedreau Operative: Extremely Dangerous'* in red across the header.

'Seems you were a popular person back then. Looking at the date, I wonder how much longer your career would have lasted,' Artimus said with a grim smirk, leaning back in his chair. 'That one's on the house.'

Sage looked at Artimus with incredulity. 'What is this?'

'My bargaining chip. Well, it *was*.'

'What are you playing at? Have you any idea what this would do to Hope if it ever got out?'

'Yes, which is why it's yours to do with whatever you please.'

That had Sage dumbfounded. 'Why?'

'Consider it a professional courtesy. It was war. We all did things we weren't proud of. Some worse than others,' he said simply. To Sage, it almost looked as though Artimus was ashamed as if the man was ever capable of such an emotion. 'The fact of the matter is, we are not at war anymore. That means there is no longer a need for that, and you got Orian off my back. I think that makes us even.' Artimus stood and took the two steps over to the fireplace, where he retrieved a rifle that was propped up against it. Sage instantly recognised it as his own—the one Artimus confiscated the day he arrived. He laid the weapon on the desk and sat back down. 'I knew you were good,' he continued, 'and I'd suspected what you may have been the moment I met you, but I've seen that's not the person you are now. Whatever you think of me, I'm here to maintain peace, not destroy it.'

Sage blinked, stunned by Artimus's admission. 'No,' he said, clasping his hands behind his back. 'I can't. Besides, you earned it. "The honourable know when they have been beat by a worthier foe".' That was another one of Gaius's favourite quotes. 'You keep it. This man,' he tapped the file, 'died in the war. That weapon belonged to him. It has no use to me, so do with it as you see fit.'

'Alright,' Artimus replied, reaching forward to pick it up. He swept aside a few pieces of paper to reveal a more recent stapled document. 'Ha, found them. Now, if you don't mind, you wanted me to review these. Please close the door on your way out.'

Sage took his dossier and turned to leave. 'Thank you, Artimus,' he said, grabbing the door handle.

'For what?' Artimus replied, not even bothering to look up.

Sage went to respond, but Artimus had already buried himself back in his paperwork.

Standing in the dimly lit hall outside Artimus's office, Sage glanced down at the folder in his hand. He had never expected this. Back in those days, he was elite—one of the Cedreau's finest—but despite his skill, to him, it was just a job. Flicking through it, this folder listed the names of all the people he had assassinated; the high-profile targets, politicians and military strategists. He remembered every single one, yet it also represented his own death. He was a marked man, and it chilled him to realise that had the bombs not dropped and the war not ended the way it had, his name could have been marked on the deceased rolls, too. That realisation, thinking about his current life with his wife and daughter, was sobering.

He hurried down the corridor to his offices, where Conrad, who was busy finishing up for the day, greeted him on his way through. Sage closed the door and tossed the folder on his desk before throwing himself in his comfortable padded leather chair. Taking a quiet moment, he gazed out the window to clear his mind. Already, the sun had dipped below the horizon, so he flicked on his desk lamp. As he did, it illuminated the bookcase housing his prized collection of pre-war artefacts and miniature model cars. Sitting pride of place among them was a broken mug that read "world's best da". It was one of the first things his daughter had handpicked and gifted to him herself. The memory of it made him smile, giving him a brief respite from the horrid thing that sat on the desk before him.

It taunted him like a box of nightmares he'd thought had been securely buried and forgotten. Gaius couldn't escape his past, so it was naive to think he could too.

Sitting back, he pondered on that folder for a while, biting his thumbnail in quiet introspection.

How did Artimus find this? Where did it come from?

Sage lifted the cover once more, cautious as though it may

explode.

Extremely dangerous? Me? Did they really come this close to…?

A gentle knock made him jump. 'Surprime, sir,' Conrad said, popping his head around the door. 'Your wife's here.'

As he said that, Jaylyn appeared in the doorway, making Sage's breath catch in his throat. She was stunning in a gorgeous, knee-length black dress and tailored, red fur-trimmed coat to match his own. Seeing her instantly lifted his spirits. Seeing her dressed like that could have almost made him forget what was troubling him. He was so used to seeing her in her comfortable co-op uniform and apron. But with her soft brown hair cascading over slender shoulders, the sweet fragrance of sugar blossom and the subtle touch of ornametics, she looked like she'd just stepped out of a pre-war feature.

Without waiting for an answer, she strode into the room and seated herself in the guest chair opposite him.

'Thanks, Conrad,' Sage said. 'And go home. It's late. Thank you for your work today.' He turned his attention to Jaylyn and smiled.

'Yes, sir,' the young assistant replied, closing the door behind him.

'Hello, my darling,' Jaylyn said in a soft, seductive voice. 'You look tired.'

'Something like that,' he replied, his attention caught between the dossier and the exceedingly exquisite woman seated across the desk from him.

'Hopefully, not too tired for our date night,' she said. 'I thought I'd come here and surprise you. Are you almost done?'

'Almost. You look beautiful tonight, by the way.'

'Thank you. What's this?' she asked, reaching for the ragged folder.

He quickly pulled it away. 'Nothing,' he said, picking it up then, opening the door to the fireplace and tossing it in. He gazed intently as the pages curled and burned behind the glass, only waking from his distant reverie when something soft touched his face.

'I'm sorry, babe,' he said, realising with a start that Jaylyn was now on his side of the desk, leaning against it in a flirtatious pose.

'Just dealing with some work stuff. I'm almost done.'

'Do you want to talk about it?'

He sighed. 'No. Not really.'

'Then maybe there's something else I can do?' she said, bending down to deliver a passionate kiss on his lips while slipping a hand up Sage's inner thigh.

'Surprime, I must speak with you this instant…' Elihus Kinton raged as he barged through the door, startling Sage and Jaylyn from their intimate moment. He saw them and stopped, a devious grin appearing on his crinkled old face. 'Oh, I am sorry, Surprime. Excuse my intrusion, Miss…?'

Jaylyn stood, straightened her dress, and glared at the minister in much the same fashion as Sage. 'Solon,' she replied curtly, resting a hand lightly on her husband's shoulder. '*Mrs* Solon.'

'Elihus, you know my wife, Jaylyn,' Sage said.

'Ah, yes, of course,' Elihus stammered. 'My dear, would you—'

'Can't this wait until tomorrow?' Sage cut him off, rising from his seat to leave.

Elihus shot Sage an irritated look, following him to the stand where Sage retrieved his trusty red coat. 'But Surprime, this is really a matter of urgency.'

Sage shrugged on his coat and then turned to the old man. 'With you, Elihus, *everything's* urgent. What could possibly be so important that it can't wait until tomorrow?'

Elihus moved in closer and spoke in a low voice as though trying to prevent anyone from overhearing. 'It's the budget. It's simply insufficient. An outrage really…'

Sage merely patted the shorter man on the shoulder in mock sympathy. 'That does sound outrage-ish,' he said, herding Elihus towards the door. 'Tell you what. Come back tomorrow, make an appointment with Conrad, and *then* we can discuss your budget concerns. Until then…' he opened the door and gestured for Elihus to leave. 'Grace even.'

The education minister was clearly not impressed by the audible huff and nose raised skyward as he marched out of the office. But Sage didn't care. It'd been a long time since he and Jaylyn had had a night together. He afforded himself this simple but rare luxury and wasn't going to allow this pompous old fool to interfere. Without giving Elihus or the burning file in the hearth a further thought, Sage flicked off the light, took his wife by the arm and walked out. Hope's troubles could wait until morning.

09 RESEARCH

Quinn Staff reviewed his schematics again, ran his graphite blackened fingers through his unkempt blonde hair and turned to inspect the circuit board on the workbench beside him. 'Something's not right,' he muttered to himself. 'What's not right?' Blinking hard, he tried to clear the fog from his exhaustion-addled vision while he struggled to trace a finger along a track from one transistor to another.

'Need some help?' his teenage niece, Ester, asked from the workbench on the opposite side of the room. She wasn't really his niece, but after Commander had adopted Ester and brought her here, Quinn and Cristal had looked after her. After a few days, she just started calling him *uncle*. At first, he found it strange, but it did make it easier to explain, so it stuck.

Clad in blue overalls, large, brass-rimmed goggles and steel-capped boots, she swivelled on her stool, soldering iron in hand, to face him. Laid out on the bench beside her was a dish-sized green circuit board she'd been working on.

Ever since Quinn agreed to allow her to assist him, she'd spent much of her free time in his lab. When she wasn't with him, Quinn knew she was likely with Commander, performing brain-numbing complex mental calculations that gave even him a headache. She seemed to revel in the simple manual tasks Quinn assigned her, assembling circuit boards, screwing together pieces of equipment and keeping him supplied with fresh cups of kahwah. She even occasionally helped him with his calculations. That, he knew she enjoyed the most—relishing in the smug satisfaction of again reminding him how much smarter she was than him.

'Last one,' she said, tapping the smoking hot iron on a damp sponge and returning it to its cradle. Stepping over to examine her handiwork, he placed his screwdriver on the bench and, putting on a set of thick-rimmed eyeglasses, leaned in to get a better look. Upon seeing the little globules of solidified metal lined up in two near-perfect rows, connecting an EPROM to the board, he couldn't help but smile. It was her neatest yet.

'Nice work!' he complimented. 'Aren't you just becoming the neat little lab tech?'

A knock at the open door startled them.

'Oh, flamin' fire,' he swore, sweeping the screwdriver off the bench onto the concrete floor, narrowly missing his boot.

Ester giggled, earning her a scowl from him.

'Phew, you look nice,' he said, whipping the glasses from his face and glancing up at Cristal's slender figure standing in the doorway. With her long layered brown hair cascading down a lacy cobalt blue knee-length dress and bodice, she looked like a courtier at a ball. Even after seven cycles, he still hadn't gotten used to seeing her out of her Cedrean uniform, especially as she now wore outfits he found quite provocative.

'You look… the same as yesterday,' she replied with a wink in Ester's direction. 'Is he behaving?'

'Nope,' Ester replied with a grin. 'He's been staring at those schematics for four cendecs already.'

'Alright, smarty-pants,' he said, glaring at her. 'You see if you can get this thing working.'

'It's still not working?' Cristal said. 'You *do* know Commander is doing his rounds today?'

'Puddlegoo! It's next tendawn. I've got a full ten days till then.'

'Nope, it's today.'

Quinn picked up the screwdriver and set it into the leather holster belted to his thigh. He then dodged Cristal and several benches covered in circuit boards, blueprints and miscellaneous bits and pieces to pat down a wall plastered in handwritten notes. Hidden beneath a page of complex calculations, he found what he was looking for. 'Now, I hope you're just pulling a boart tail,' he said, examining the calendar. 'What date is it?'

'Reincarner, 21,' she replied, crossing her arms.

He rolled up his oil-stained shirtsleeves and ran his index finger over the calendar. 'Ah, pile of pebbles!'

Ester giggled at Quinn's mild swearing.

'Better get to it then,' Cristal said with a smirk.

'Ah, I'll figure something out,' he said, letting the paper drop back over the calendar again. He turned to face Ester, scratching his head in contemplation. 'Now, where did I put that screwdriver?'

Quinn's lab was the messiest it had ever been. Since Commander set up the LunaTec complex in the Brimeuse caves around Hope, he tasked Quinn with getting the object they retrieved from the downed ship working.

He glanced towards the windows at the opposite end of his lab. Partially obscured with sticky notes, they looked out at a deep, rough-cut cavern that used to be part of the old mining tunnels where the massive alien cylinder now lay chained down, horizontal on the custom-made rig of Quinn's own design.

'Are you any closer to figuring out how it works or not?' Cristal asked, having followed his gaze.

Quinn shook his head. 'I still haven't the foggiest what it is, let alone how it works. If the big man could just give me a clue, any clue at all, that would be marvellous.'

'Does that mean you haven't progressed since last inspection?'

'See all this?' he gestured at the piles of paperwork and schematics covering every flat surface of the lab. 'I've designed these boards to interface with whatever that thing is. If only I knew what it was and what it did, then maybe…' he threw up his hands in frustration.

'There's got to be something you can report?'

'I've figured out it turns on.'

She scoffed. 'That's all?'

'My, aren't we pushy today? If you must know, I managed to get the end cover off at last—what are you doing here, anyway? Shouldn't you be in Hope?'

'The ministry closed session for the day to prepare for the hospital unveiling.'

'That's today?'

'What do you care?'

He shrugged. 'Meh, I do like to know what's going on every once in a while. Speaking of, how've you been lately?'

'Nice try, changing the subject,' she scorned, waving her finger at him. 'You said…'

'I know what I said. I'm just asking how you are, that's all. You've been pretty sick since we left the tower.'

She reached for and idly fidgeted with one of the tools on his bench. 'Since you asked, it's fine, thanks,' she sighed. 'It comes and goes. There's that constant lethargy, but today seems to be a little better than most.'

'Have you seen a doctor? I mean, you've been sick more than not.'

'Yes, but Doctor Tsao hasn't found any reason for the sickness. She just says it's stress. Can we drop this, please?'

'I'm only concerned for your health.'

'That's nice, Quinn, but can we please get back on topic?'

'What's more to say?'

'So, you really are no closer to figuring out what that thing is we recovered from that weird ship?'

Quinn removed his thick, brass-rimmed goggles from atop his head and pushed back his wild hair from his eyes. 'Hang on, what, so it's not Diosday today?'

Cristal chuckled. 'Have you slept at all recently? Today's Freoday, you missed two days.'

He returned to the bench where he had been working, pushed aside some paper, retrieved his mug, took a sip, and, with a screwed-up face, spat it back into the mug. 'Ugh, that's cold. Didn't you just top this up?' he asked Ester, tilting his mug at her.

'Yeah, two cendecs ago,' she scoffed, then returned to her work.

Cristal took the mug out of his hands. 'You need to spend time in your bed tonight and not wherever it is you've been sleeping. And cut back on the kahwah.'

'Now, who's looking out for who?'

She plucked at his vest. 'Someone has to keep you on track.'

'Oh, really? You know what I think? You have feelings for me,' he said, grinning at her like a mischievous child.

'Ah, no,' she laughed, her response echoed by a snort of laughter that came from Ester's direction. Cristal turned to place the mug on a less cluttered part of the bench.

'Face it, you do. You have feelings for me,' he said, following in such proximity that when she turned, he could relish in her startled expression.

'Not on your life, grease boy,' she scoffed, turning to look him straight in the eye.

He sniggered. Despite her disappointing reaction, Quinn still enjoyed these moments of playful banter. He was about to fire back with a witty retort when he noticed something odd.

She averted her gaze.

'Hey, Cristal. What was that?' he asked, pointing at her eyes.

'What was what?'

'Can you look at me again?'

'No.'

'I mean it. Look at me for a midec.'

'Why?'

'I thought I saw something.'

'Enough with these games, alright?'

'Seriously, I thought I saw flecks or something move about in your eyes. I swear I've seen something like that before, but…'

'You swear, do you?' she mocked. 'Now you're definitely seeing things. Get some sleep, Quinn. You're hallucinating.'

'No, I'm not kidding. Cristal, can you please look at me again?'

'Fine,' she said, turning so he could look at her eyes. 'You try any funny business, and you'll be slapped into next tendawn.'

'What the…?' he said.

Light streaming through the open entrance to the lab dimmed as Commander's giant form appeared in the doorway. He ducked his head to enter and harrumphed, standing to examine Quinn's messy workspace.

Quinn and Cristal snapped to attention, striking a fist to their left pecs to deliver their boss a firm salute. Although they no longer served in the corporate military or wore uniforms, the ex-Watchtower crew still observed military formalities. The only difference was Commander now wore a tailored black suit and gold-embellished waistcoat, but it may as well have been his military uniform, for even after all these cycles, Quinn still found the man intimidating.

Ester was standing, too, although less formally.

'At ease,' Commander boomed at them, approaching the bench nearest the door where Ester was working. He picked up the circuit board she'd been soldering, turned it over and examined her work. 'Clean,' he said, eliciting a proud grin from the teenager, then turned his attention to Quinn. 'Report.'

'Well, ahh… Sir,' Quinn stammered, scratching his head. 'The device draws power and stores it in what I can only describe as an ultra-capacitor array and outputs a field—a radiative flux. I've managed to connect the primary bus with the console interface to access the systems. Still, the technology's vastly different to what I'm used to. I can't for the life of me figure out what any of it does.'

Commander strode over to Quinn's schematics, picked one up and mused over it for a while. 'You're handling it fine.'

'Thanks?' Quinn leaned over the big man's forearm to get closer to the schematic. 'Ah, yeah. That. I've been experimenting with these different boards to get the system readout to work on the terminal. The coding is in a strange syntax, and I keep getting compilation errors. So far, nothing's remotely compatible. I found the power input, though.' He looked at Cristal and shrugged. 'You know, sir, it would really help if I knew what it was. I mean, that's assuming you know what it is. You did seem to know what you were doing when you—'

'Power it up,' Commander interrupted.

'Sir, I can't recommend that,' Quinn countered nervously. 'I just finished telling you I have no idea—'

'Power it up,' Commander insisted in a low voice, glaring as though boring a hole through him. 'Unless you fraxed it, let's call it a relocation test.'

'A what? Ahh…' Quinn moaned, turning back to his bench, seeing the mug of cold black kahwah. He picked it up and swallowed a mouthful of the bitter drink. 'Oh, that's a wake-up,' he spluttered, catching the dribble down his chin with his free hand, and returned the mug to its place on the pile of papers. 'S'pose now's a good time to test your interface board, Es.'

She picked up the board and carefully handed it to him.

'Righteo, sir, ladies,' he said, finding the door handle under pinned-up papers and gesturing for the others to follow.

The door led out to a rigid metal platform, fixed to the lab's brick exterior and overlooking a cavernous space with rough-cut stone walls disappearing into darkness in either direction. At its centre, illuminated by industrial lights hanging from the cave ceiling, was the smooth cylindrical object sitting parallel to the platform on its heavy-duty metal frame bolted to the ground.

Thick cables snaked from one end, across the rough ground and up the platform's supporting structure to a large power junction box on the wall. From there, smaller wires ran into the back of a bulky computerised console that jutted out from the wall at one end of the platform. Quinn had pulled it away from the wall to access the circuit boards inside, but by the list of numbers and the words "Failure to communicate" printed across the bottom of its monochromatic green screen, he'd had little success.

'I call this device the "Quantum Vacuum of Life",' Quinn said in a droll tone, glancing over at his messy lab. 'It seems to take my time away from other, more productive things I could be doing. It could also be called the "Quantum Vacuum of Kahwah".'

'What's a quantum?' Cristal asked.

'When I turn the power on, at a distance, things get spooky.'

'Yes, but what does that mean?'

Quinn shrugged. 'I don't really know. The air in the cavern changes. It's hard to explain.'

'Don't explain,' Commander ordered. 'Demonstrate.'

'You sure, sir?' Quinn asked, waiting for an answer. Commander's cold stare was the only answer he was going to get. 'Right! Okay then.' He brushed his sweaty, blackened hands on his brown vest. 'Es, you want to check those cables while I tuck this card in?' he asked, gesturing down the ladder at the cables snaking from the exposed end of the enormous cylinder. He then stepped up to the console, where he inserted the freshly-soldered circuit board into its assigned slot. As he did, Ester slipped down the metal ladders to the cave floor.

'Careful with that,' he called to her.

She gave him a thumbs-up, then returned to the platform by the open door where the others were standing.

Commander's stony face didn't change as his eyes followed their actions.

'Oh, wait,' Quinn said, rushing back into his office once more, returning with two sets of round brass-rimmed goggles and handing a pair each to Commander and Cristal. 'Put these on. Okay, then. Buckle yourselves in and get ready. You're in for a wild ride.'

Quinn's wit echoed off Commander's emotionless face. He gave a nervous smirk, put his own goggles back on, and took his place by the console. 'Sir, I'm going to start with five per cent power. With this latest board—'

'Just turn it on,' Commander interrupted. 'On my order, increase the power in five per cent increments.'

'Sir, I can't tell if our generators can handle the output required to fully power… this,' he complained. 'I've never gone past point five, but here goes.'

Quinn pulled the lever on the Y-shaped knife switch with a clack, then turned the disc-shaped power dial to 0.5. As he did, the console and power box emitted a hum of activity. Small multicoloured lights seemed to glow from beneath the strange cylinder's smooth metallic skin.

Glancing up at Ester at the railing, she clapped with excitement. Her board worked! And, from Cristal's expression, she seemed equally impressed. It was a stark contrast to Commander, however, who stood rigid as usual beside them.

'Bring the power up to ten per cent,' Commander ordered.

With trepidation, the engineer turned the dial to 1.

'Higher.'

The hum increased an octave, getting louder as more power flowed into the device. Commander ordered for more.

With the dial resting at 3, Quinn said, 'Sir, umm, we're at thirty per cent capacity.'

'Engineer Staff, this is where you make history.'

'Yes, sir.' Quinn turned the dial to the next increment, and the hum became a buzz.

When the pointer on the dial hid the number 4, the cavern lights started jostling. An invisible force exerted upon the three standing on the platform, pressing against their bodies as though gravity had turned sideways. Papers and other loose items slipped off the console to the floor. 'Sir?' Quinn asked, his voice wavering with increased nervousness.

'The generators and fuses are still holding,' Commander said, his face showing no emotional tell. 'You'll know when to stop.'

Quinn moved the dial to 4.5, and the dangling lights lifted toward the rock ceiling. At 5, the globes held motionless against the rock. As the pressure of the invisible force increased, Cristal and Ester grabbed the safety rail with a firm grip while Quinn held onto the console. Commander merely leaned into the force like it was a stiff breeze.

At 5.5, the hanging globes exploded under the pressure, plunging the cavern into darkness.

'Sir?' Quinn shouted in desperation over the cacophonous buzz of electronics.

Emergency lighting activated, bathing the cavern in a sinister red glow and shadowing parts of Commander's sharp facial features, making his face appear sunken like he was a creature from a children's horror story. He didn't look away, only readjusted his feet to lean further forward.

'Okay, sir,' Quinn continued, 'I'm increasing to sixty per cent.'

The door to the lab slammed open, and the heavy console scratched at the metal flooring as it slid towards the wall.

Ester hooked her arms and feet around the balustrade to keep herself steady, but Cristal appeared to not be having as good a time.

'Um, Quinn,' she cried before her feet slipped out from underneath her, and she looked as though she was hanging from the railing. She held on for dear life while Commander, unperturbed, placed one foot forward and leaned in more.

Ignoring Cristal's pleas, Commander demanded Quinn continue. 'More!'

Beyond the open door, the lab lights flickered. Quinn turned the dial to 6.5.

'Quinn…!' Cristal cried out as her grip slipped, and she plummeted through the doorway.

'Again, more!' Commander bellowed.

'Sir, I can't do that,' Quinn yelled over the roaring of the device. The pressure had him pinned against the wall, unable to move.

Just then, there came an ear-splitting scream. Quinn tilted his head just in time to see the balustrade Ester was gripping onto break away. Commander reached out to grab her, but his arm missed her by a mere finger's width as she plummeted like Cristal, her body striking the frame as she fell.

Then, seemingly ignoring what had happened, Commander adjusted his footing and stepped onto a section of brick wall beneath the lab windows. He trod like he was walking on flat ground toward the console, reached out past his immobilised engineer as though he wasn't there, and rotated the dial to 8…

10 TREMORS

Orian stepped up to the makeshift podium, her long grey hair flicking over her shoulder in the brisk wind. 'Please give a warm sunny welcome to the Virtuous Surprime, Sage Solon!' she announced.

The crowd applauded while Sage, dressed in his official regalia, took his place behind the podium on the temporary stage. Behind him stood a newly constructed three-storey brick building, the first of its kind in Hope. 'What a beautiful day this is,' he said, briefly raising his arms aloft to embrace the sun's warmth. 'Thank you, Orian,' he said, turning to address her, then returned his attention to the waiting crowd. 'And welcome, Admirable Ministers, friends, family, good people of Hope. Thank you, everyone, for coming out to join me on this beautiful day to celebrate this momentous occasion.'

As he stood tall at the podium, he glanced at his ministry seated on the stage beside him and grinned. 'It feels like it was not so long ago we were opening a building, and I was standing before you all, making an infamously disastrous speech. I assure you, I'll probably not live that down. Anyway, I've put a little more preparation into this one.'

He lifted his chin to project his voice, took a deep breath, and continued.

'This building,' he said, raising his arm to present the building in much the same manner as Gaius once did, 'is eight cycles in the making. It's also the crown jewel of the plan our founders, Rika and Gaius Sempro, had for this town—a plan I have vowed to complete.' The crowd cheered, and he waited for them to finish before continuing.

'As you all know, we have a saying in Hope; "what's passed is past". We don't normally dwell on history, but there's a story that

I know Gaius—if he were still here with us today—would have wanted to be told. It is the story of how this building came into being, and as part of its glorious unveiling, I will tell it to you now.

'Before the war, Gaius Sempro suffered a tragedy. He was hospitalised and declared dead.' He glanced at Orian as he said that, knowing how it may make her feel, but she just smiled and nodded, and he carried on. 'The one person who saw him through it was a physical therapist, Rika Vennlocke. She worked with him for cycles while he recovered from his injuries. They married, and she took his name. When the war eventually broke out, Rika and Gaius fled together. They came here and made a home, taking in refugees no matter where they came from. Rika patched up their injuries, treated their sicknesses and ensured they were fed, while Gaius gave them a bed, a roof over their heads and, for some, a purpose.

'When I came to Hope in 01, hypothermia was the least of my troubles. I was in bad shape. Like everyone else, Rika saw to me, treated me without judgement and nursed me back to health. She always said she wished she could have had a proper hospital and not a tent in which to work her miracles. Today, that wish has come true. Because of them, we stand here now. Friends, family, great people of Hope, I proudly present to you the Sempro Memorial Hospital of Hope; A tribute to Rika and Gaius Sempro, the mother and father of Hope who saved us all.'

He clapped, and enthusiastic applause erupted from the crowd.

'There's more to this story,' he continued after the applause died down. 'I wasn't the only one Rika helped that day. Doctor Lexi Colyar was with me. After Rika helped her and saw she could use help, Doctor Colyar graciously obliged, later helping Rika establish a clinic. When our beloved mother of Hope tragically passed, it was Colyar who confidently stepped up to continue Rika's work. With her two nurses, she treated everything from hangovers, broken bones, cuts, and bruises to radiation sickness and birthing babies, including my own. Her clinic has since grown into a field hospital with six nurses, a birthing doula, and two junior doctors on its staff.

'So, before we cut the ceremonial ribbon, I have an announcement to make. A great hospital deserves a great Chief Surgeon. I can think of no one more accomplished and dedicated to run our new hospital than Doctor Colyar. Therefore, it is with great pleasure I invite Health Minister Alessandra MonBrelstaff to the stage to officially appoint our new Hospital Chief Surgeon.'

To Sage's left, a middle-aged woman wearing ministerial black robes with long flowing blonde hair stepped forward. Sage took a step back to allow the minister to take her place at the podium.

'Thank you, Virtuous Surprime, Admirable Ministers. It is with great pleasure,' she announced in a strong voice, 'I appoint Doctor Lexi Colyar to the position of Chief Surgeon of the Sempro Memorial Hospital of Hope.' At the mention of her name, the tall Doctor Colyar in a smart grey pantsuit and white doctor's coat rose from her chair in the front row and ascended the stage. The minister continued her oration. 'Since her arrival in Hope, the good doctor has been an inspiration to all the medical staff and me at the Hope field hospital. It is with great honour I make this appointment today. Everyone, please join me in congratulating Doctor Colyar.'

Once again, the crowd cheered as Orian held out a box containing a pressed metal pendant on a blue ribbon. Minister MonBrelstaff removed the pendant and placed it around the Doctor's neck. Doctor Colyar bowed to the crowd as they continued to applaud her.

'And now,' the minister concluded, 'I will ask his Virtuous Surprime and our new Chief Surgeon to assist me in formally opening the new hospital.'

Sage stepped toward the podium once more and turned to Orian, who now held out a gold tasselled green velvet pillow bearing an ornate knife. The knife held an amber jewel in the pommel, with embossed lines like sunbeams streaming down the polished timber handle, warming the trees embellished on the thick guard. Its acid-etched blade featured wavy lines signifying the tree's roots—a symbol of life.

'Our bladesmith has been hard at work making this,' he proclaimed with pride, lifting the ceremonial knife from its bed and presenting it with its blade pointing upwards to the crowd. 'The jewel "Aster" shines down over the landscape, providing life over the cold blade below.'

Orian leaned in and whispered something in his ear.

'Oh,' he chuckled, inverting the knife so that its jewel was on top. 'I should be holding it like this.'

As though made manifest by some divine intervention, the ground began to shake. Nervous tension rippled throughout the gathered crowd and those on stage as they turned to one another in confusion. At first, it was nothing more than a deep rumbling that shook the air and vibrated the stage beneath Sage's feet. Still, the rumbling grew louder, the windows of the new hospital began to rattle, and the gathered crowd, unsure whether to flee or stay, grew increasingly anxious. The mysterious rumbling intensified, and the doors to the hospital banged until they unlatched, held together only by their ceremonial ribbon.

An uneasy nausea overcame Sage, who gripped his head, which felt like it would explode. Several people in the crowd, it seemed, had also been overwhelmed as they collapsed, and Sage fought against the intense pressure to keep himself from collapsing too. Beneath his feet, the makeshift stage's timber vibrated like a speaker, only adding to his anxiety. Behind him, bricks and mortar from the building crumbled, raining down on the stage at first like snow, but then in larger chunks.

'Jorth tremors!' someone shouted, causing people to flee in all directions.

Suddenly, a massive gap split the bricks from the hospital's upper floor, drawing a horrified gasp from the startled onlookers. Bricks and debris rained down on the stage below, narrowly missing Sage and Orian.

Minister MonBrelstaff disappeared into the seething mass of bodies while Sage pushed Orian into Jaxson to rush her to safety. It left Sage exposed to the crushing danger from above. It was Artimus who sprung forward to tackle the Surprime, lifting him from his feet and collecting Colyar on the way. Artimus's knee collapsed under their combined weight. They tumbled onto the grass, clearing the stage just in time before a pile of bricks smashed onto the podium, crushing it where they had only just been standing.

The last thing Sage remembered was a thunderous roar belting from the building's upper floor, followed by a deafening bang that tore the universe asunder.

11 DEVELOPMENT

Quinn awoke to a noise he hoped he'd never hear again. With a grunt, he rolled over to find the source. Commander had his back to him and was emitting a thunderous roar that echoed throughout the chamber. *Was he…laughing?* Quinn thought, clutching his pounding head.

Waiting for feeling to return to his limbs, he rolled onto his side and nearly threw up. 'Ugh,' he groaned loudly. 'It feels like I've been sat on until I passed out.' Using the railing for support, he clambered to his feet, finding the cavern still bathed in the emergency lighting's sinister red hue.

'That couldn't have gone any better,' Commander boomed, slapping the startled engineer on the back and almost knocking him over the balustrade. *At least* he's *happy.*

'When Spriggs wakes,' Commander said, pointing to a bench along the back wall, 'send her to my office.' Then, with no further comment, he stepped through the door and left.

Dazed, Quinn stumbled into the lab as though he'd spent the night drinking, trying to focus his vision on the bench and the dark pile beneath it he was sure hadn't been there before. He was used to the room being messy, but this was a whole new kind of messy. All his benches and their contents were clustered against the wall opposite the cavern door as though the room had been upended. A mound of papers beneath the bench where Commander had pointed groaned. It was then it all came flooding back.

Quinn gasped, dropping to his knees and throwing debris aside to search for Cristal and his young protégé. Shifting the mess, he found them both lying in a crumpled heap of mixed fabrics and hair. Ester lay unconscious on top of Cristal, who it seemed had cushioned her fall. Quinn quickly checked her over—to the best of his knowledge, she seemed fine—but Cristal lay wedged behind the unconscious teen clutching her arm with an agonised expression on her normally serene face.

'Ow,' she whimpered as Quinn reached in to pull Ester off her. 'It feels broken.'

'Yeah, I'm no doctor,' he said, spotting the lump on Cristal's wrist where a lump shouldn't be. 'I think I agree with you.'

'It hurts like mad, and the fingers don't move,' she cried.

'Come on, we need to get you both to medical.' He carefully reached in and grabbed Cristal's good arm and pulled her to her feet.

Ester was heavier than Quinn expected, and with Cristal hobbling alongside, it was lucky medical wasn't too far away.

'What does breaking your arm feel like?' he enquired, trying to fill the uncomfortable silence. 'I broke my nose in a bar fight once, but not anything major.'

Cristal gave a pained chuckle. 'Well, you know what,' she said, 'it frak'n hurts.'

'Oh, so like the way I felt the next morning?'

'Quinn,' she said, 'you were in a bar fight?'

'Ah, yer, quite embarrassing. I tried to start a fight with a table that spilled my drink.'

'A what?'

'I don't remember much, but yep, a table.'

'Huh. Well, if you're trying to help make this situation feel better, it's working. So, the nose then? Come on, tell it all.'

'Well, the table pushed back, I think', Quinn said, voice strained from the weight in his arms. 'It knocked me into this wall of a person.'

'And he punched you out for spilling his drink?'

Quinn chuckled. 'It wouldn't be embarrassing if that happened. No, he pushed me away, and I fell face-first on another table, then the floor when it collapsed. I broke my nose somewhere in between and spent the rest of the night in lockup, throwing up. I didn't realise it was broken for an entire day.'

Cristal laughed despite her obvious pain. 'Has anyone told you, you're a strange one, Quinn Staff?'

'All the time.'

∞

Ester stirred. Opening her eyes, she caught the blurry vision of the LunaTec medical clinic as someone carried her in and gently set her down on a chair beside Cristal. She was holding her wrist and looked like Ester felt. 'Ugh,' she moaned, then winced, clutching her ribs. 'Ow. It hurts to breathe. Why does it hurt to breathe?'

'You've probably broken a rib,' Quinn said gently. 'You hit the door frame pretty hard.'

'What?! How?' she said, glancing up at him in shock. 'What happened?'

'That's the part I don't know,' he replied. 'But you and Cristal got hurt.'

Trying to take her mind off the pain, Ester glanced around, hoping to find something more uplifting than sterile grey-yellow walls. It reminded her of Gotthard, right down to the sparse furniture and an odour that smelled distinctly like floor cleaner, which Ester found particularly discomforting. The only exception was the "work safely at work" posters stuck to the horrid walls. *Why does everywhere have to be so tepid*? she thought to herself, recalling the time she ended up in the med clinic at Gotthard. She'd just turned eight, and while out playing with her best friend Jayne, trying not to annoy the grown-ups, they'd found a maintenance scaffold. Jayne dared Ester to climb it. It seemed like a good idea right until the part where her foot slipped, and she fell the two meta drop to the concrete floor, landing with an agonising crack on her left arm. The pain was excruciating, but that was nothing compared to the fury she faced when her mother found out. That was the first time she'd ever broken a bone.

Now, as she sat there, taking short, sharp breaths between bouts of breathtaking pain, she wished it had been the only time. At least, in some strange way, the memory reminded her of Jayne, and that helped. She hadn't thought about her old friend in quite some time. If only she were here now, trying to cheer Ester up as she'd done all those cycles ago.

Where are you now? She thought sadly. *You'd find this funny, for sure.*

Ester sighed, earning a concerned look from Cristal.

'Everything alright?' she asked.

'Yeah, I mean, no. I don't know.'

At that moment, a woman wearing dark blue scrubs and a white LunaTec branded doctor's coat emerged from one of the small rooms along a nearby corridor. 'Hello,' she said, pinning back her long golden layered hair revealing her nametag; Doctor Macie Whitelock. 'What's happened here?'

'We had an… accident,' Cristal replied. 'Tess's chest hurts—she may have cracked a rib. And this arm may be broken.'

For reasons Ester didn't fully understand, Cristal referred to her as Tess. She liked her name but thought it prudent not to protest.

'I see,' the doctor mused. 'Well, come with me, and I'll take a look at you.'

'Okay,' Cristal said dubiously, 'but what happened to Doctor Tsao? She normally sees us.'

'Doctor Tsao is in Hope today assisting with the new hospital. But I promise I'll take good care of you. Please, come on through, both of you,' she said, motioning them into her room.

'I'll just wait out here,' Quinn said, yawning and taking a seat in the reception area.

Nursing their wounds, Cristal and Ester followed the doctor like two forlorn little pups.

The sterility extended to this small room and was furnished like all the other doctors' offices Ester had been in before.

'Young Tess, please take a seat on the bed,' the woman said in a soft voice. 'Ms Spriggs, if you can take a seat, I'll see to you in a moment.'

Ester winced as the doctor examined her, prodding gently at the nasty-looking bruise developing on her side. After handing Ester an ice pack for the bruise and some pain medication, the doctor concluded that Ester had indeed cracked a rib. Knowing what was wrong didn't make Ester feel any better, especially considering she'd have to "take it easy" for the next few tendaws and allow it to heal on its own. That probably meant spending more time doing boring things. When the doctor had finished with Ester, she turned to Cristal.

'Let's have a look at that arm of yours.'

Cristal lifted her arm, but as she did, she seemed perplexed.

'That's weird,' she said, poking at it. 'There was a big lump here before. But it's gone now.'

'Does it hurt?' the doctor asked, gently manipulating Cristal's arm and monitoring her for a reaction.

'No,' she replied. 'Not anymore. But, it did before.'

'What if I press here?'

Cristal shook her head.

The doctor continued to examine the spot where Cristal had pointed out, moving it some more, but surprisingly, Cristal didn't even wince.

'That's very strange,' Cristal protested. 'When it happened, it hurt badly, and there definitely was a lump there. The fingers wouldn't even move.'

'Hmm,' the doctor mused. 'There's no lump now, and it seems you're no longer in pain, so it's fair to say it's maybe sprained, but it's definitely not broken. All I can suggest is bandage it, and if the pain returns, come back and see me. Okay?'

Cristal gazed at her arm and then the doctor in disbelief.

'Is there anything more I can do for you?'

'No, thank you, Doctor,' Cristal said, seeming lost.

She wasn't the only one struck by the supposed miracle. But whatever had happened to Cristal, somehow her arm had miraculously healed itself, all in the time it had taken for the doctor to examine it. Ester knew her Aunt wasn't the kind of person to make up things like this. There had to be some reasonable explanation. Whatever that was, it kicked the butt of medical science.

As the doctor led them back into the waiting area, Quinn remained there, slumped in a chair, quietly snoring. From the long hours he'd been working, and the copious quantities of kahwah Ester had been feeding him, it almost seemed a shame to wake him. He jolted when Ester lightly touched his shoulder.

'You're back?' he asked, brushing off the fact he'd dozed off.

Cristal strode past him and straight out the door, forcing him to leap from the chair to catch up. Ester stifled a groan and followed them out.

'Are you going to tell me or not?' he demanded as they were halfway down the corridor. 'What's the prognosis? Will the arm have to come off or not?'

Cristal stopped, turning on him so fast Ester could almost see him concertina. 'It's humiliating; that's what it is!'

'Huh?'

'There's nothing wrong with it. See…' She demonstrated by holding her arm out, rotating her wrist and wiggling her fingers a few times for good measure. She even allowed Quinn to gently grip her arm.

'That's impossible!' he said. 'It definitely looked broken to me.'

'Yeah, well, it's not now. And that doctor…argh.'

'Didn't she believe you?'

'Well, she didn't say it in so many words, but you can be sure she was thinking it.'

'But…'

'Quinn,' she insisted, 'there's no way this could've been imagined.'

'Maybe humour *is* the best medicine?' he replied with a cheeky grin.

Cristal didn't seem impressed. 'What humour?'

'Never mind. Does it still hurt?'

'Not at all, and you know what's weird? That lethargy's gone now, too. In fact, gotta say, never felt better. At least, not since leaving the 'tower. It's difficult to describe.'

'Wanna try breaking your arm again?' he joked.

'Not on your life!' she said.

'You two, please don't make me laugh,' Ester groaned.

'Tess, maybe you should go get some rest?' Cristal suggested, focusing the attention on her.

'Ah, not on *your* life,' Ester said, copying Cristal. 'I need to know what happened as much as you do.' At this point, Ester had to convince even herself of her words. After all, having spent so many cendecs assisting Quinn on the project, a good proportion of the work was hers. Despite needing to rest her aching body, anticipation was painful enough. Figuring the pain meds should tide her over, she would be fine if she didn't move too quickly or breathe too deeply. She had to learn the results of their first major test personally.

As they approached the red-bathed lab, Quinn stopped still. 'There's something I wanna check out first.'

Cristal and Ester followed him in with caution, taking care not to trip over the junk cluttering the doorway.

'Shame this room didn't fix itself,' Ester said, observing how everything was strangely piled up like the contents of a box of pebbles that had been tipped on its end, then set flat again.

Quinn dug out a couple of battery-operated torches from a nearby bench and handed one to Cristal before heading towards the darkened cavern.

'Commander was… I think laughing when I woke up,' he continued.

'Get out of Hope,' Ester said. 'He did what?'

'Yeah, I know. It's not a sound I wanna ever hear again either. But he found something down there funny.'

'Funny? Commander? He doesn't *do* funny,' Cristal said. 'Anyway, you're not going in there alone.'

'Wow, some fair force put into that,' Quinn said, touching the splintered timber doorframe. 'Come outside. He stood just here at the rail, looking that way into the dark.'

Cristal squinted in the direction Quinn pointed. 'What's that?' she asked.

'What's what?' he said.

She flicked on the torch and pointed it toward the rear of the cavern. Its light barely penetrated the darkness. 'Can't you see the flat surface there?'

'What are you looking at? I can't see squat.'

'Right there,' she insisted, jiggling the torch about.

'I think breaking your arm did something to your eyesight.'

'Go down there and have a look yourself.'

'You're pulling me a boart tail,' he complained, flicking on his torch and descending the ladders to the cavern floor. Cristal followed while Ester waited on the platform.

She watched as the two trod over the uneven ground toward the rear of the natural opening. As the torchlight spilled across the rock wall, Ester could just make out the formation of elongated shapes and unnaturally flat surfaces jutting out like they'd grown there. She was certain she'd never seen them there before.

'There! See that?' Cristal said, her voice echoing around the chamber. She shone the torchlight over a flat white surface. 'There are words here, too. What's an "emorial hos"?'

Ester walked toward the edge of the platform, eyes fixed forward. But something fluttering caught in her peripheral vision. It was then that Ester noticed it. It was a stray, torn piece of paper stuck to the end of the balustrade.

That's weird, she thought, shuffling over to inspect it. *What's this doing here?* Clutching her aching ribs, she gingerly knelt to pick it up, and tilting it in the limited light, she read the lettering on its surface.

'Hey guys,' she said, as loud as her ribs would allow. 'I think you should come see this.'

Within moments, Cristal and Quinn were standing beside her, shining their torches on the little slip of paper. 'It's a letterhead from the "Sempro Memorial Hospital of Hope",' Ester said.

'How'd that get here… Oh, that's not right.'

'What?' Quinn asked, looking up at them. His expression changed at the realisation it was a stupid question. 'Which direction is Hope from here?'

'About one-three-four and a half degrees, give or take a point,' Ester replied without needing to think.

'Roughly the same direction this cavern faces,' Quinn said, pointing his torchlight to the other end of the formation.

'Sage might have some questions that need deflecting,' Cristal said, thrusting the torch into Ester's hand. 'Gotta go.'

'Oh,' Quinn yelled back, 'Commander was looking for you earlier. You might want to stop by his office first.'

'Right,' she replied.

'And Cristal,' he said, catching her before she disappeared through the door. 'Good luck.'

12 INTERLUDE

Cristal jogged down the corridor, delighting in her restored energy. It was as if eight cycles had been turned back, and she was young again—not that she was that old. Trying to retain her decorum, she stilled her excitement and quickly made her way through LunaTec's warren-esque corridors past staff wearing LT emblazoned uniforms toward a prominent office at the heart of the complex.

She knocked on the large solid doors to the Commander's office, and his deep resounding voice reverberated in reply. Despite its size, the door swung effortlessly inward as she stepped inside.

Within those doors was a spacious office sparsely furnished with a studded leather couch, a couple of timber bookcases filled with various books, and a small collection of strange objects for which Cristal couldn't fathom a use. The man himself sat behind an enormous, antique wood desk in an equally large, studded leather chair. This room was fitting of a man such as him; simple yet practical—a stark contrast to Quinn's lab or her own office.

'Sir, you called?'

'Close the door,' he said, strangely eyeing her up and down.

She approached the desk with apprehension, wondering why he had summoned her knowing she had work to do in Hope.

'At ease, Spriggs,' he said in a less formal tone. 'Tell me, how long have we known each other?'

That was unexpected, especially considering she thought he'd called her there to discuss what had happened in the cave. Despite that, she knew the answer and responded automatically. 'Eleven cycles, one trey, five tendaws, give or take a day.'

'Do you want some time to think about that?'

Perhaps that was a little overeager, she thought, clearing her throat. 'No, sir.'

'Then, you have known me long enough to know that whatever happens in this room stays in this room. Understood?'

'Yes, sir.'

'Relax, Spriggs,' he said, leaning over behind his desk to remove an item from a safe he usually kept locked. He stood, joined her on the other side of the desk, and leaned against it. Compared to him, she felt tiny. At almost 1.8 metas in height, Cristal wasn't short, but her head only came up to Commander's chest and standing this close, he was all muscle and sinew.

'Do you know what this is?' he asked, setting a small transparent tube of swirling metallic-black liquid on the desk beside him.

'Ahh,' she stammered, 'do you mind?'

He gestured, allowing her to reach over and carefully pick it up to get a better look.

As she drew closer, his irresistible scent tickled at her senses, and she wanted to linger.

'It's one of the vials we retrieved from the crashed ship back in 01,' she replied after taking a comfortable step back.

'Correct. But do you know *what* it is?'

She looked at the vial again and shrugged. The strange substance inside moved almost like it was alive. 'No idea. Sorry, sir.'

'That,' he said, gently plucking the vial from her hand, 'is a highly sophisticated bio-nanotechnology. One cubic micrometa of this substance can heal flesh, cure disease, and even knit bone.'

Her eyes widened, but she dared not interrupt.

'It can also inhibit the ageing process. Tell me, Spriggs, how old do you think I am?'

'Um,' she stammered again, examining his chiselled, ruggedly handsome features. She'd never thought about his age before. 'About forty-five?'

'I am precisely one hundred and ninety-three.'

'Gracious Progenitors!' she gasped, and he smiled a curious smile. 'How is that even possible?'

'All in good time.'

'And, you said it can *knit* bone? Is that…'

'Yes,' he replied simply. 'I injected you with a small dose shortly after we left the crash site. I needed to see how your physiology would respond.'

'Huh? Forgive the forwardness, sir, but you did what?' she asked, involuntarily rubbing the spot on her neck where she recalled thinking something had stung her.

'Your reaction… wasn't what I'd anticipated. People who lack the required genetics… respond differently.'

'Is that the reason for this sickness all this time?'

'Yes.'

'And you knew?'

'Yes.'

'Huh. But why?'

'I have my reasons. Suffice to say, you benefitted from them, anyway. Your arm is healed.'

'You knew about that?'

'I know a lot of things. Now that the nanites have fulfilled their purpose, they have been rendered inert. Your system will process them as though a foreign body. You will suffer no further ill effects.'

'Why are you saying this now?'

'That vial is among only three I recovered from the vessel. It was necessary to test you, but in so doing, I have limited my supply. I have come to realise that for my mission to succeed, I must have an alternative plan.'

'That doesn't make any sense. You can't get any more?'

'No. I waited twenty-two cycles for that ship. There won't be another.'

'How do you know for sure?'

He turned away, and she knew she wasn't going to get an answer. But it did give her a moment to ponder. All these cycles, she'd been suffering a mysterious illness only to discover it had been inflicted upon her and by this man—*her* commanding officer, no less. He'd injected her with an alien substance without her consent as some kind of experiment. Everything about that should have made her angry, but something inside quelled her. 'But why?' she asked, hoping he would be forthcoming with more answers.

'Cristal,' he said. 'Why do you think I spared your life?'

He'd used her first name, and it instantly shattered her thoughts, forcing the question that had kept her up at night to slip from her mind. She opened her mouth to answer, but no words came out.

'Let me ask another way. Do you desire me sexually?'

Her face flushed at the provocativeness of the unexpected question. From the moment they met, she considered him attractive. She always fell for the alpha male types. It was possibly the reason she felt nervous in his presence. Now, as she looked at him, casually leaning against the desk, muscles bulging through his tight-fitting tailored shirt and black suit pants with what appeared to be a slightly curious smile on his face, he was different. It was the most expressive she'd ever seen him.

'You can answer honestly,' he added, prompting her for a response.

'What if the answer is no?' she replied nervously.

'Then you will walk out of here, and this conversation never happened.' Then he tilted his head with a knowing expression. 'But that's not your answer.'

Her blush didn't fade, and she dropped her chin, staring at the desk to cool off, only to realise her gaze had fallen between his thick, treetrunk-sized thighs. Her face flushed hot, and she couldn't look at him. 'Yes, sir.'

He put the vial in his pocket and moved closer, bending over to whisper in her ear. 'Then you can drop the Sir. While you are here, alone with me, you may call me Fafnir.'

'Fafnir?' she asked. 'Is that your real name?'

He nodded. 'Fafnir Mylaekar.'

Cristal looked up, staring into his eyes. 'Fafnir Mylaekar,' she repeated the name under her breath.

He sat on the edge of his desk again to bring his face in line with hers. 'Cristal, kiss me.'

Did he really just tell me to kiss him? She thought, the warmth in her face intensifying, flowing down through her body and becoming a subtle pulsating between her thighs. *Where? How? Just do it.* Before she could overthink it, she leaned in and pressed her lips to his. It was only brief, and when she pulled back, his expression was unchanged.

'You can do better than that,' he said. 'Try again.'

This time she opened herself to the secret desires she had locked up for him and let the feeling flow free. It's not like she'd get another chance. She rested her hands on his thick, sturdy shoulders, their lips locked, and she kissed him. This time, his spicy aroma awoke something within her, her pulse raced, and she found herself kissing him with a passion she'd reserved for her dreams. To her surprise, he reciprocated, embracing the kiss and holding her firmly by the waist while her knees weakened. She held the kiss for as long as she dared, and when he pulled away, he wore a grin.

'That's better,' he whispered. 'Now, what else can you do?'

Chest against chest, his firm but gentle voice reverberated through her.

Only in her wildest dreams had she ever imagined getting this close to him and doing what she knew he was asking.

The buttons on his shirt opened with ease, and she slipped a hand inside, caressing his smooth, tanned muscles. His deep dark eyes swarmed with speckles in a way Quinn had described with hers. Then she felt something peculiar. Examining where her fingers ran, beneath his semi-translucent skin, a network of thin blue wires crisscrossed through the fibres of his muscle, like an intricate electrical circuit connecting tiny nodes. She traced a wire with a fingertip.

'What's this?' she asked.

He grabbed her hand gently and placed it on his belt buckle. 'Focus.'

His words left her breathless, and with the pounding rhythm of her heart, she pulled at the buckle.

Most would be on top of her already, clawing at her undergarments, but Fafnir was patient and calculating, responding only when required. He waited for her to make the moves, observing her and allowing her to respond according to her impulses.

She squeezed her eyes shut, then unbuckling his belt, reached inside. 'Oh my!' she gasped.

Fafnir pressed against her, ran his hands down her dress to its hem and then up her legs, lifting the silky material to her waist. Allowing her undergarments to drop, he picked her up like a delicate flower and lowered her onto the desk.

For what seemed like a lifetime, Cristal waited. She ached for him to make his move, losing herself to the intense pulsating between her thighs.

His hands pulled her in by the small of her back. Then she felt him, her breath caught, and all conscious thought wiped from her mind. Right now, she didn't care about the incident or Hope, for at this moment, she had completely surrendered to the fantasy come true.

13 FORBIDDEN FRUIT

Sera must have slept in this morn, as she's usually in the kitchen busily making breakfast. But not today. The clock on the wall says it's 3:12—class starts at 3:33. With only twenty-one decs to prepare some breakfast, I set aside my diary, throw some pulses and dried fruits into a bowl with milk and sit at the table to eat.

That's when Sera's bedroom door opens. 'It's about time—' I shout, but the rest of the words escape me when a man sporting dishevelled blonde hair and wearing only a startled look streaks from her room to the front door. The only thing shielding his dignity is the ball of clothes he's clutching.

Sera drifts into the living room moments later, casually tying up her bright floral robe.

'Who was that?' I ask, watching the stranger's bare buttocks disappear through our closing front door.

'I think he said his name was Buck,' she says, sauntering barefoot into the kitchen as though nothing untoward had happened.

'Ah, like that tells me anything.'

'What?' she says defensively. 'I am a woman. I have needs too, you know.'

'Okay.' I shrug and return to my breakfast.

Sera prepares us both some tei and sits next to me in her usual spot at the head of the table.

'So, how long have you been seeing Mr Buck naked?' I ask, trying to say it with a straight face.

She giggles. 'Oh, since about last night.'

'Sera!' I say, feigning shock.

'Dear Jayne,' she replies with a sly smile. 'One of these days, you will understand.'

'One of these days, huh?'

'How old are you now? Fifteen?'

'I'm Sixteen, Sera. You baked me a cake, remember?'

'Of course, I know that.' She giggles again like a child. Seems her romp with Buck has addled her mind. 'So, you are old enough to understand that sometimes people desire the company of others for more than just friendship.'

'Yes, but we're not supposed to trust others. Rule number four, right?'

'Oh, you do not have to trust someone to sleep with them,' she replies with a nonchalant expression.

'Wow, okay, I didn't see that coming. Where exactly are you going with this?'

That nonchalant expression changes into something awkward, and she glares at me over the rim of her cup like she's about to recount her night in lewd detail. 'Well, when two people—'

'I know about sex, Sera.'

She sighs, visibly relieved.

'Those textbooks you left for me are pretty graphic. It's not like you've really helped me with that kind of stuff. I had to learn about menstruation on my own. Thanks for that, by the way.'

'I am sorry, Jayne. There are some things at which I am not particularly proficient. Sex education and female physiology are two of them.'

'You seem to have given Buck a decent lesson.'

'Jayne!'

'What?'

'I am not the only one around here having secret rendezvous.'

'And what's that supposed to mean?'

'I shall let you figure that out.'

The first class of the day is weapons crafting with Shaddix. I thought Instructor Blackthorn was a hard arse, but Instructor Shaddix; she's a maniac. Like fire and accelerant, hers is a fitting personality for someone who teaches weapons crafting and explosive technics. This is a woman whose stature is comically paradoxical to how loud she can yell. Shorter than most of her students, I'm certain she compensates for it with her temper.

Despite the instructor, this class is one of my favourites. There's something soothingly meditative about making your own ammunition. Maybe it's the quietness and the time for concentration, or perhaps it's because I can stand at my bench and watch Ilona work. With her long black hair tied back and beads of sweat glistening off her flawless olive-toned forehead, I can't help it. Prying my eyes away, I glance down at my work.

The scale reads 5.7671; one more grain and this slug is ready for packing.

'Excellent work, Number Ten,' Instructor Shaddix says, seemingly materialising from out of nowhere to lean over my arm.

Her unexpected appearance startles me, causing half the pouch of grains to scatter over the workbench. 'Ah, boartcrud,' I swear. It's almost like she timed it.

'Made a mess there. Better clean that up before we lose any more of those precious grains,' Shaddix sneers. Once she's had enough leering over my shoulder, she resumes pacing along the line of workbenches of the weapons workshop, eyeing us like a predatory ave over stray tomadai.

Crimping the last slug, I tap the finished set of five out into a tray. While I wait for the others to finish, I remove my protective goggles and scratch my initials into each casing.

Shaddix reaches Ilona's workbench across from my position and leans in, just like she had with me.

'Shoddy, Number Twenty-eight,' Shaddix growls. 'You'll be lucky if any of those fire straight. Guess we'll see soon enough, won't we?'

'Yes, Instructor,' Ilona mutters. Shaddix continues her rounds, leaving Ilona to crimp off the slugs and lay them out for inspection.

Behind the instructor's back, Ilona glances up and flicks me a quick and discrete sign with her fingers; *See you at break.*

Some things are best left unanswered, like what this beige square is on my lunch tray. Nestled between a bread roll pretending to be a rock and some sad-looking piece of fruit, it resembles a reconstituted omelette filled with dried, canned meat. It probably tastes just as bad as it looks. After all these cycles, the oafs in the kitchen still can't cook—what they make is reminiscent of the uninspiring meals served at Gotthard. Oh, what I would do for some of Sera's bean cake right now. At least they've finally provided tables and fixed seating in the outdoor eating area, so we no longer have to sit in the dirt.

'Hey there,' Ilona says as she takes the only other chair at my table.

'How d'you go?' I ask, taking a bite of my stale bread roll.

'Yeah,' she shrugs. 'I'm never going to impress her, so I don't bother trying.'

'That's shak.'

'Meh, I just hope they don't blow up in my face.'

'I'm sure they're fine. I'll even trade you some—that's how sure I am.'

'Thanks, but I think I'll be right.' *Don't want trouble*, she adds with a discreet flick of her fingers using our unique but limited form of non-verbal communication.

'Is she always like that?'

'Yes, well, most of the time.'

'Why? I walked by your bench after you made them. They look as good as mine.'

'Because,' she sighs and, completing the sentence with her fingers, says, *She don't like me.*

'That's tough. How is it I got Sera, and you got…' I glance around, then mouth, 'that psychopath?'

'Beats me. Sera's awesome,' Ilona says, biting the edge off one of those disgusting beige squares and promptly throwing the offensive thing back onto her tray. 'Ugh. Even Shaddix gives me better food than this.'

'I know. What is that thing anyway?'

'Dunno, but it tastes like something I picked up with my boot.'

'Thanks for the warning.'

I push the inedible lumps of food about my tray and decide I'm better off waiting for dinner. It's then that a thought occurs to me. 'Hey,' I ask, sliding the tray aside to lean on the table, 'has Shaddix ever had visitors over?'

'Visitors?' Ilona replies, 'I don't know what you mean.'

'Ah, never mind. It was just something Sera said this morning. It was strange.'

'Oh, you mean *those* kinds of visitors?' Ilona chuckles. 'Heck no. I heard about *that*, but I've never seen her with anyone. Could you imagine Shaddix doing *that*? Ew, gross.'

We giggle together, trying not to draw unwanted attention.

A guard patrols by our table, and we return to pretending to eat in silence, reduced to mainly communicating through our simple hand signals.

At the sound of the buzzer, our break ends, and I tap three fingers on the table. *Same time, same place?*

Ilona responds by rubbing the side of her nose with her right thumb. *Yes.*

The firing range is set—a bare section of the Field at the rear of the compound with paper targets intermittently spaced at fifty meta intervals. One by one, we each select a single-shot rifle from the lockbox brought up from the armoury and line up for instructions.

'Students,' Instructor Shaddix bellows, 'you have all made your ammunition. Now you will see how well they fire.' She paces along the line, considering each one of us carefully.

'You will start at five hundred metas, increasing by increments of fifty metas until you have spent all your rounds. You will be scored on distance and accuracy. If you can successfully hit the target at seven hundred metas, you will pass this course with distinction. Hit the target at six hundred, and you'll receive a pass grade. Fail to hit at six hundred, and you will fail this course. Today's test is the first of many which will contribute to your overall grade. Should you fail today's test, it will result in a negative mark against your overall record and potential overall disqualification. Disqualification will result in banishment from the program. I should not need to remind you what that means. Is that understood?'

'Sir, yes, sir,' we chorus.

'You have two decs to check over your weapon and collect your slugs. Take your positions at the range and fire when ready.'

Cradling the long-barrelled target rifle in my arm, I take position beside Ilona. Then, putting on my earmuffs, kneel down, setting the metal box labelled 'Ten' containing my slugs behind the line marked in the compacted dirt. With mixed trepidation and pride, I open the box. Inside rest five newly-crafted slugs. The moment I take them from the box, something is wrong. They're smooth. Too smooth. Rolling a round between my fingers, I feel for my engraved initials, but they are missing. A quick inspection of the others reveals my initials are missing from them as well. There had to be some kind of mistake—these slugs aren't mine. Looking around at the other girls taking their positions, I catch Alyx standing five places from me, grinning broadly. There's no mistake.

She switched my slugs!

Alyx loads a slug into her rifle, takes aim and fires a near-perfect shot. She lifts two fingers at me before firing again. Oh, what I wouldn't do to smack that acetic grin off her smug, scrawny face.

She takes another shot and raises three fingers.

My blood begins to boil, and I avert my gaze to prevent doing something I'll end up regretting. Instead, I take a breath and focus on the target ahead.

Just get it done.

What's up? Ilona signs, apparently noticing the invisible steam rising from my ears.

'I think Alyx switched my slugs,' I mouth over the intermittent rifle shots.

'Shak,' she replies just as Alyx prepares to take her fourth shot. 'What you going to do?'

'Nothing, I'm just going to have to use these.' I show her the slugs. At least they *look* fine.

'You can do this. You're a great shot. Even with her slugs, you can do—'

'Number Ten, is there something wrong?' Instructor Shaddix barks from the other end of the line.

'No, sir,' I yell back.

'Good. Then what are you waiting for? Load your weapon and fire.'

Okay, you can do this.

The weight doesn't feel right, but I load the first slug into the chamber, close the breech and take aim, adjusting the sights. The paper target featuring black and red concentric rings, five hundred metas down range, flutters in the light breeze, beckoning me to hit it.

With the deftest touch, I squeeze the trigger. The weapon kicks back into my shoulder, and the slug rips a hole in the target. It's a satisfactory hit, but I have shot enough rounds at five hundred metas to know the slug should have hit dead centre. Instead, it hit lower, only just inside the second innermost ring.

Like before, I load, aim for the five-fifty, correct for the wind, take a slow, steady breath and ease back the trigger.

The slug nicks the edge of the target, right where it's secured to its frame.

I compensated for the wind. At least, I think I did.

There's something about these rounds; a flaw that almost cost me the shot, and I'm concerned the next won't be so lucky.

Alyx watches on with keen interest. Having already exhausted her rounds, completing six hundred metas, she's safely passed. But with three slugs left to go and the last one only just hitting the target, I'm far from saying the same.

I won't let her beat me.

After this, I will have only two chances left.

It must *not miss.*

This time I take added precaution and focus on every step, mindfully working through the process, hoping it will assure a successful outcome. Wrapping the rifle strap around my upper arm and wrist and using a knee for support, I grip the forestock and squeeze the trigger.

The slug misses.

'Frak,' I swear under my breath, forcefully ejecting the spent shell.

Two slugs left.

With any hope of passing with distinction gone, all I can hope for now is that six hundred.

Loading my second-last slug into the chamber, my hands tremble. Sera taught me breathing techniques to deal with nervous tension, and I take a moment to close my eyes and breathe.

I am one with the target. Focus. You can do this.

The unmarked six hundred meta target taunts me, and I raise the rifle once more.

Like before, the slug disappears, leaving the target undamaged.

My stomach churns, and I despondently let the rifle barrel drop. I can almost feel the stale bread roll trying to make a reappearance. At least I didn't eat the beige square.

Alyx sniggers from her position in line while I eject the spent shell. One last round rests in the box like it's possessed. Its shoddy construction is almost sentient, as though it's deliberately mocking me while it bores a hole into the bottom of its container. There's no way I'm firing that thing, and the indecision digs at me like a knife in the guts.

There is no way I'm going to hit that target with this damned slug. But I can't miss. This is my last chance.

Beside me, Ilona's hand flicks a gesture. If it weren't for my moment of indecision, I probably would've missed it. *Take*, she taps on her rifle. Then a second time, and from the corner of my eye, I catch her drop a slug by my foot.

I don't want her charity, but I have little choice. Hoping no one's looking, I snatch the last slug from its metal box, pretend to fumble and drop it beside hers. Then, swiping up Ilona's slug, I unsympathetically press the demon slug into the dirt with the heel of my boot.

Hands trembling and with my heart pounding like drums in my ears, I close my eyes and focus.

Calm. Stay calm. You've got this. You're one with the target.

Fighting every nervous muscle twitch, I open my eyes, raise the rifle and fire. The rifle recoils and my fate now rests with the trajectory of that one last slug.

'How was training today?' Sera asks as I slip through the door of our apartment, plonking myself down next to her on the couch. She presses a button on the box-shaped remote to mute the VT.

'What on Jorth are you watching?' I ask.

Silent images of scantily dressed women in skimpy but elaborate outfits court a pretty-looking man. Their plunging necklines leave nothing to the imagination. From my brief glimpse, the women appear to be fighting over him in an amusing display of pointed fingers, flailing arms and shouted words. I can only imagine what they're yelling.

'It's "*The Unattached*",' she replies shamelessly. 'It was one of my guilty pleasures from before the war. I still like to watch my recordings of it from time to time for a laugh.'

'It looks hideous.'

'It is,' she chuckles.

'Do you want anything to drink?' I ask, becoming disinterested.

'I have a drink here, thanks. So?'

'So?' I ask, and Sera glares at me with expectation.

'Your weapons crafting and target-shooting final. How did it go?'

'Oh, that,' I reply and hand her a crumpled piece of paper from my pocket.

She examines it for a moment, then throws her arms around me, squeezing me in a tight hug. 'Congratulations Jayne! You passed. That is fantastic!'

But I'm not as excited. The piece of paper contains my score, revealing I'd only just passed the test. 'It should have been a perfect distinction. I could've easily done it blindfolded.'

'Then what happened?'

'I wish I knew,' I reply sullenly. 'If it's okay, I think I might just eat and study in my room tonight,' I say, getting up from the couch and heading to the kitchen.

'Is something wrong?' Sera asks with concern.

'No. Just not feeling great.'

'Fair enough. If you want to talk, you know I will listen.'

The cendecs drag by, and I keep checking my bedside clock. Finally, when it reads 8:30, I leave my room, go out into the kitchen and grab the compost bucket from under the sink.

Sera still sits on the couch, watching her pointless shows. This one has two teams out in the wilderness running a made-up course, scoring points.

'Just taking out the scraps,' I say, darting past to the front door.

'Alright, but Jayne,' she adds, her voice containing that tone she uses when she's alluding to something, 'if you are going out, be careful.'

With a nod, I quickly open the door and slip out.

The corridor is dark and empty, and as I head toward the vents, I scan the area up and down to be sure I'm alone. Then, levering the vent cover open, set the bucket inside and climb in.

Since I began exploring the ducting system, I reckon I've traversed just about every square meta of it by now. I feel I know it so well, I'm sure I could navigate the interconnecting network of tunnels by feel alone.

After stumbling into the neglected room, my curiosity got the better of me, and so with the aid of a bioluminescent lamp I'd filched from Sera's camping gear, I returned. It turns out the room is a storeroom of sorts. I spent several days investigating the contents of each of the crates, picking their locks to discover the hidden treasures within; bottles of pre-war liquor, risqué magazines and other useless items.

I even cleaned up some of the thick dust, sweeping it aside, collecting it up in my pockets and discarding it when I go outside.

It wasn't long before I let Ilona in on my secret, and since then, we'd been using it as a meeting place where we could sit and talk freely.

As I slip out of the vent into the neglected storeroom, I give the bioluminescent lamp a wind and set it in a shielded spot away from the door.

While I pluck a bottle from a crate, a shuffling noise comes from the vent and Ilona's beautifully serene face emerges from the darkness. Perhaps it's a peculiar trick of the blueish light, but her normally blue eyes now appear greenish-gold.

'Sorry, I'm late,' she says, scrambling out of the shaft. 'Shaddix found out I gave you that slug. She wasn't happy.'

'Oh? Does that mean we're in trouble?'

'I don't think so. Me, perhaps, but I think you're in the clear.'

'I'm sorry, Ilona. The last thing I wanted was to get you in trouble, but thanks for doing that. You really saved me today.'

'It's okay. I'm used to it. Besides, you've saved my butt more than a few times.'

'Anyway, I don't know about you, but I think it's about time we celebrated. This stuff's been sitting here for Progenitors' knows how long. I figured we should try some.'

Ilona stares at the brown bottle in my hand with suspicion. 'Are you sure it's still okay?'

'We'll soon find out.'

Sitting cross-legged facing one another, I pry open the dusty bottle. As soon as the cork lifts away, a rich, intoxicating aroma wafts from its top. Taking a quick swig, the smooth liquid slides down my throat and warms my stomach, releasing a tingling sensation throughout my entire body. 'Oh, it makes me feel like I'm drinking a hug.'

Ilona gazes at me longingly. 'A hug?'

'Here, try a sip. You'll see.'

As I hand her the bottle, she sniffs at it and then cautiously takes a sip. 'You're right. It feels nice. Tastes alright too. What is this stuff?'

'It's called Malt, or so the label says. Whoever locked it in here must really like the stuff.'

'Better hope they don't miss this one then.'

'My guess is it belongs to the Patriarch. Either he has forgotten it's here, or he doesn't come here often. I don't think he'll miss a bottle or two. Besides, it would be worse if it were Shaddix's, right?'

Ilona laughs, then takes another swig.

'Was she very angry?' I ask.

'About the slugs? Not really. She was more pissed finding these.' She retrieves three slug casings from her pocket. Even in the lamplight, I can make out the initials "JD" etched on their sides.

'My slugs! Where'd she find these?' I ask with exasperation.

'She found them at Alyx's position.'

'So that thieving shak-eater *did* switch my slugs?'

'Seems so. But don't expect anything to come from it,' she says, taking a few larger gulps from the bottle.

'Why? She deserves a fail for that.' Relieving the bottle from Ilona, I take a gulp as well.

'I seriously doubt that,' Ilona says.

'Did you see her face when I got that last shot? It looked like a distorted imitation of the dried piece of fruit I had at lunch.' We both chuckle at that. 'If they found her with my slugs, why don't you think they'll punish her?'

Ilona shrugs. 'Haven't you noticed? She's untouchable. For a start, Shaddix and Blackthorn are "friends",' she says, making air quotes with her fingers. 'If you or I had done it, we'd be sent to the box for sure. But Alyx, "little miss can do no wrong", all she'll likely have to do is answer to the Patriarch.'

'Ah-huh.'

'Still, that's bad enough. Personally, I don't know what would be worse, the box or having to face that monster.' This time, Ilona snatches the bottle from my hand and tilts her head back like she's planning on guzzling the rest.

I pry the bottle from her grip, trying to stop her from swallowing it as well. 'Careful. We don't know how potent this stuff is.'

'I don't care. You have no idea. Having to see the Patriarch is so much worse. Even discussing it is making me feel sick.'

'You sure that's not the drink?' The dark bottle feels as though about half its contents remain. Ilona is swaying, and my head feels as though someone has stuffed it with clouds. I decide to re-cork the bottle.

'Hey, I'm drinking that,' Ilona protests.

'I think we've had enough. I'd hate for you to have to explain to Shaddix why you're drunk.'

'Yeah, well, you obviously haven't had to face the Patriarch then,' she slurs.

'So?' I shrug, and it earns me a sour grimace from Ilona.

'It's true then? You've really never been to *his* office?'

'No, well, not since that time we were both there. I caught him telling Sera off once, but I was in the vent. I heard them talking about some kind of agreement. Why?'

'What sort of agreement?'

'I'm not entirely sure, but I think it had to do with the reason I've not been called into his office like you have.'

'Wow. Okay. That makes a lot of sense then.' Ilona gazes despondently at the bottle, but I keep it out of reach.

'What does that mean?'

Ilona shifts nervously like she knows something I don't. 'Sera's protected,' she says eventually. 'At least that's what I've heard. I don't know why or who gave that order, but he can't touch her or you, so it would seem.'

'Touch me? You mean lashings?'

'Lashings are the least of your worries when you go to visit him. The man is a total and utter tyrant. A real sick frak.'

'I'm not sure I follow. He can throw me in the box, but he can't touch me? That doesn't make any sense. I don't like the guy, but I didn't think—'

'Jayne, you have no idea.'

'Then tell me. What are you saying? Has he done something to you?'

The instant I ask the question, her demeanour changes, and she becomes the shy little girl I found in the forest. I thought we'd move past that, but it would seem some habits are harder to kill than a boart. 'I don't want to talk about it,' she snaps, and from the way she's now hugging her knees so tight, whatever it is, it's deeply troubling her. I'm not entirely sure how to respond in such situations. After all, I've never really had a friend like Ilona before, so I shift myself closer to sit beside her and hope it's the right thing to do. 'It's okay, Ilona.' I try to reassure her in as sympathetic a manner as I can. 'It's me, and we're alone. You can tell me.'

'I don't know,' she mumbles.

At least she hasn't rejected me. I don't know what I'd do if she did that. Whatever is disturbing her, I can almost feel it exuding from her, and all I want to do is provide comfort so it doesn't hurt her anymore. 'Ilona. I'm here for you. You're safe with me, I promise.'

Her head drops, her shoulders slump, and her hair falls, shielding her eyes. But I can tell she's crying. I allow her time to gather her thoughts, and then she gazes through the black veil of hair into my eyes. The golden tinge is gone, replaced by a dark grey, almost silver.

'Each time I'm called into his office,' she stammers, with a meek, soft voice, 'he… he does things to me—unpleasant things. I can't describe it. It makes me sick just thinking about it.'

'What? What sort of things?'

Tears stream down her cheeks. 'I don't know. Horrible things. He makes me do…things to him.' She shudders and turns away, taking her time to wipe her eyes, and compose herself.

'What?'

'You're so lucky,' she says, quickly cutting in and diverting the conversation so I can't ask further questions. 'You've got Sera. I bet you can tell her anything.'

'I haven't told her about us. And I won't tell her either.'

She hesitates, and I can tell she's thinking about what I said. Then she looks up at me, and her eye colour changes from liquid silver to blue, like the deep blue I'd seen before. Seeing her eyes do that leaves me with chills.

'How…?'

'Jayne, I think there's something wrong with that drink,' she says, with those mesmerising eyes shifting like water. 'My head feels… funny.'

'It's ethylwater—liquor. Adults drink it. And I'm getting to see why.'

'Whatever it is, it's making me feel… I don't know…good.'

'Well, that's good? Right?'

Ilona cracks a smile, swaying a little more. Without warning, she starts to fall sideways, and I catch her around the waist to keep her upright. With her face buried into my neck, the rich malt on her breath is intoxicating. Whether it's the drink or something else, her closeness awakens something within me, and turning my head to absorb the sensation, Ilona presses her soft lips to mine.

An eternity passes before Ilona pulls away, and she gazes at her lap.

'What was that for?' I ask with an awkward smile.

'I'm sorry. I don't know what came over me. I just wanted to see if it's supposed to feel nice.'

'And?'

'I thought it was nice. You?'

'Same.'

'I like you, Jayne,' she says, tilting her head. 'You're not like the others. You're kind, compassionate and really pretty.'

'You think so?' Her compliment sends warm flushes through my cheeks and down my neck. *Maybe it is the drink*?

'Would you like to do it again?' she asks with a cheeky smile.

The excitement of her lips caressing mine lingers, and it floods my body with strange sensations I've never felt before. *This drink is certainly doing something to me.*

Together, we sit in this dark, dusty room, daring to go against the rules for a moment of happiness. Before I realise it, Ilona leans forward, pulls me into a gentle embrace, and we kiss again. Those mesmerising eyes of hers, now iridescent blue and green, sparkle in the lamplight, and I find myself falling into them like deep, glistening lakes. And that's when it dawns on me; I would do anything for her.

14 LESSONS

Ester stood anxiously in the centre of Commander's roomy office while the slow and steady tick of a metronome bored unrelentingly into her throbbing head. At least the pain detracted from the shallow ache in her chest, where her cracked rib was still healing. It had been three tendaws since the incident in Quinn's lab, yet Commander had taken it as an excuse to double down on her mental arithmetic training.

Tick... tick... tick... tick.

He sat at the corner of his desk, as usual, glaring at her with considered expectation.

'Eighteen and thirteen,' Commander called in his deep, authoritarian voice.

Ester absently tugged at the silver locket around her neck and began. 'Two, three, four.'

Tick.

'Three, zero, four, two.'

Tick.

'Three, nine, five, four, six.'

Tick.

'Five, one, two—'

'Wrong!' Commander shouted, making Ester jump.

Wringing her hands behind her back, she tried not to let her anxiety show.

'Again!' he ordered.

Ester took a deep breath and moistened her lips, bracing herself for another round.

'Seven and twenty-two,' Commander announced.

'One, five, four.'

Tick.

'Three, three, eight, eight.'

Tick.

'Seven, four, five, three, eight—'

'No! Wrong again!' Commander barked, this time slamming his hand on the metronome with such force Ester thought he would crush it. 'You haven't been practising.'

'But I have!'

He raised a hand, cutting off her protest.

Ester's shoulders drooped with exhaustion. She'd spent most of the morning doing these iterative calculations and had reached the point where it almost didn't matter what punishment lay ahead; she just wanted the lesson to end.

'We are done for today,' Commander said, much to Ester's relief. 'You will study Vodhan's theorem and infinitesimal calculatus tonight. We will resume tomorrow. Dismissed!'

'Yes, sir.' Ester grabbed her books from the desk and darted from the room.

Excited she now had the rest of the day to spend as she pleased, she hurried through the corridors of LunaTec's Brimeuse Caves complex, rounded a corner and collided with Cristal, who was coming the other way.

Ester grunted upon impact—it was easy to forget that, unlike Cristal, her injury was still very much a literal pain in the side.

'Whoa, Tess!' Cristal exclaimed, almost dropping the handful of documents she carried.

'Sorry, Aunt Spriggs, I didn't see you there.'

'That's no surprise. And where might you be going in such a hurry?'

'Anywhere, I just want to get out of this place and get some fresh air.'

'Does this mean you've finished your lessons for today?'

'Yes.'

'And how are they going?' Cristal asked, resuming on her way.

Ester followed. 'Ah, yeah, okay, I guess.' Talking about her lessons with Commander wasn't the easiest of subjects. 'I just can't concentrate, and that metronome gives me a headache.'

'He has you doing that for a reason, you know. He always has a reason. Being able to focus despite distraction is a valuable skill. Not everyone can do complex calculations in their head like that,' Cristal said.

'Yeah, but I hate it. Why does *he* insist I do it today of all days?'

'Because it's a school day. Happy Namedawn, by the way. You *do* have the rest of the day free. What are you going to do?'

'Hmm, I was just coming to see you. I was hoping I could spend the day with you.'

'Um, don't know about that, Tess. Just about to head off to a ministry meeting. Not sure if teenage girls would be welcome in the ministerial chambers.'

'Pleeeease! I promise I'll behave myself.'

'You? Behave?' Cristal chuckled. 'Do you really want to come to a boring meeting? It's all politics and dull conversation. What about your rib? Are you up for the trip to Hope?'

'Yes, I'm fine. Besides, do you think staying here listening to Uncle Staff go on about power converters and sauv couplings is any less torturous?'

'Okay, point taken. Suppose it would be an excellent learning experience. And we could spend some time in town after. You may come, but you have to be quiet, okay?'

'Yay!' she burst out with excitement. 'I'll get changed out of this boring uniform.'

The distance between LunaTec and the Hope Ministerial Chambers was a leisurely half-cendec drive down the mountain and across the Rika Bridge bordering the town. The days were becoming warmer, and the river gushed with freshwater from the mountains, brimming with fish. Local fishers who were dotting the bridge with their lines cast for their daily catch gave Cristal and Ester a friendly smile and a wave as they passed.

Ester, now wearing the new turquoise dress Cristal had given her, poked her head out the window, pulled the tie from her hair and allowed her long red curls to flow in the breeze. Delighted by the fresh air, she briefly closed her eyes to face the sun, relishing its warm rays on her skin. A pair of brightly coloured aves flew overhead, chirping and singing; it seemed she wasn't the only one enjoying the fine weather.

As their LunaTec branded utility vehicle rounded the bend into Hope, Ester couldn't help but notice the building covered in a giant green tarpaulin. It seemed to conceal a gaping hole where part of the roof and a large section of wall used to be. 'Wow,' she said, gawking up at it. 'So, that's the hospital. I guess I needn't ask what happened there?'

'Speak not a word of that to anyone,' Cristal replied curtly, barely glancing at it. 'If anyone asks, we don't know what happened. Okay?'

'Yes, Aunt Cristal,' Ester said. Even though she'd witnessed first-hand what had caused that damage, it didn't explain *how* it happened. Still, her aunt had told her to remain quiet, and that's what she was going to do. She was simply happy to be out of the caves for a change. Most of her waking cendecs were spent attending her lessons with Commander, studying or helping Cristal or Quinn with their work around the complex. Occasionally, she'd find the opportunity to venture beyond the doors and spend some time in nature, watching the aves and soaking up the fresh air. Rarely did she get to see Hope. So today, she could think of no better way to spend her namedawn.

When their vehicle pulled up outside the ministerial chambers, two men wearing officious long layered robes were engaged in serious conversation. The man in the red robes had scruffy blonde hair, almost like Quinn's, and bore a gleaming gold pendant of squashed discs around his shoulders.

They didn't appear to be happy to see Cristal, as they turned away the moment she ascended the stairs.

'Good morn Surprime, Minister,' she greeted the men formally.

'Good morn, Attaché Spriggs,' they responded in kind. Then they both noticed Ester, who followed a couple of steps behind.

'I see you've brought a guest,' the man with the fancy necklace said, acknowledging Ester. 'And who might you be?'

'This is my niece, Tess,' Cristal said as the man reached out his hand to shake Ester's.

'Hi,' Ester said. For the moment she held the Surprime's hand, his grip was gentle and warm, and it helped to quell some of her nerves.

'Nice to meet you, Tess. I'm Sage, and this is Elihus.'

'Pleased to meet you, Tess,' the grizzled, white-haired man said in a tone not as welcoming as the Surprime's. Ester could sense from his posture he was not entirely comfortable in her presence.

'Did you come to see what your Aunt does?' Sage asked, smiling a gentle smile.

'Yeah, something like that,' Ester replied, tugging at her locket for comfort, feeling its familiar worn, smooth surface. Despite her tension, she felt more comforted by the Surprime than the older man.

'Good on you, Tess. Welcome. I hope you find it enlightening.' Then he turned. 'We better get in there.'

The two robed men, Cristal and Ester, entered the cavernous ministerial chamber hall. Passing through the thick, carved wooden double doors, Ester stared in wonder at the high ceilings, walls adorned with paintings and all the dignified-looking people milling about. And in the centre spanned a very wide and long polished wooden table that ran almost the length of the room. Two more tables, not as decorative but just as long, skirted the walls.

An official showed Ester to a seat on the outer tables, behind the chair, where a polished metal name block engraved with Cristal's name marked her place. Cristal placed her folio on the table and took her seat.

A tall woman with long, plaited hair, wearing deep blue robes, seemed to almost drift across the room and position herself behind the podium at the head of the table. She briefly spoke to the Surprime with a smile as he took his seat to her right, and she tapped her sphere-shaped gavel twice to bring the room to order. Conversation in the room dropped to a murmur.

'Who's that?' Ester whispered to Cristal, pointing with discretion at the woman leading the room.

Cristal leaned back and replied, 'that's the Vice-Surprime and Speaker, Orian Gracyn. She presides over these meetings to keep this mob in check. Now, you have to be quiet, okay.'

Ester nodded.

Orian tapped the gavel once more. 'Order! Order!' Her voice projected around every corner of the room. 'Virtuous Surprime, Admirable Ministers, officials, and esteemed guests,' Ester imagined she caught a smile from the Vice-Surprime as she said that. 'Please take your places. This Peoples' Ministry meeting is in session.'

The remaining few still standing took their seats, and the chambers' heavy doors closed with a resounding thud.

'I call forth the Virtuous Surprime, Sage Solon, to lead the recitation of the Oath and to commence this, the fifteenth session of the Hope Peoples' Ministry on this, the forty-first day of Centraal in the cycle New Calendar nine.'

Orian stood back from the podium as Surprime Solon rose from his seat, taking her place.

'Please stand for the Oath.' As he asked, everyone rose.

'*We, children of Hope,*
Honour bound and just,
United by strife, together in peace,
Swear to uphold the sanctity of our land,
Foster strength and progress,
To continue that which we have inherited from our forebears;
The Progenitors,
Now and forever,
So it shall be.'

'*So it shall be,*' the room chorused.

'You may be seated.'

The congregation returned to their seats with a brief discussion.

'Welcome everyone,' Sage said, with a little less formality. 'It's so nice to see some fresh faces today. The chambers have never been this full. I will begin with what I assume is on everyone's minds; getting to the bottom of what happened with the Sempro Memorial Hospital.'

An audible babble erupted in the room as people chatted amongst themselves.

'Now, I know—' he spoke over the conversation until it tapered off. 'Now, I know what you're going to say, but before we open the floor to discussion, we have LunaTec's Attaché Cristal Spriggs with us to report on the progress of her people's investigation.' He gestured a hand in Cristal's direction. 'I will now call her to the podium to deliver her report. Ms Spriggs.'

Dozens of scornful eyes glared at her as she took her folio and walked the short distance to the head of the room. Sage returned to his chair.

Cristal pulled out a small printed booklet and notes from her neat stack, straightened her shoulders and raised her chin.

'Thank you, Surprime Solon and good morn, Hope,' she said, her voice as calm as a clear day. 'LunaTec would first like to acknowledge what a tragedy the incident involving the Sempro Memorial Hospital was and that we stand united with you. As fellow citizens of Hope, we are devoted to understanding the cause so we may move forward together.'

A few sniggers bounced about the crowd, but Cristal ignored them and continued.

'Immediately following the incident, LunaTec launched a thorough investigation. We assure you that LunaTec is intent on finding the cause to ensure such a thing does not happen again. A crew of expert engineers, technicians and scientists have spent the last three tendaws scouring the site for answers. That investigation has now concluded.'

She paused and held the booklet out for those gathered in the room to see. 'According to their findings, radiation emitted from new equipment installed in the hospital's west wing reacted with residual pockets of thermonuclear radiation blown here by the recent storms. The reaction resulted in an implosion event that vaporised the wall. It is just fortunate no one was in that part of the building when the incident occurred.'

Puzzled murmurs replaced contemptuous growls.

Unperturbed, she continued. 'The investigation did not find any cause for further concern as this phenomenon is extremely rare and theoretically is unlikely to occur again.'

The room erupted in undirected conversation and shouting as the occupants voiced their disapproval and disbelief.

Why the lie? Ester thought to herself, certain that from what she'd witnessed, it couldn't have been the true reason for the incident. *Perhaps it was a cover story Cristal was ordered to tell them*?

'My thunderous backside!' the grizzled man seated opposite Ester raged, gesturing wildly at Cristal. Ester noticed half his face was disfigured with what looked like a hideous scar. She wondered what could have happened to him to cause a mark like that. It certainly made him seem more menacing, especially with his short-cropped greying-brown hair that was distinctly military in style. But, despite the barrage, Crystal maintained her composure. 'How can you possibly expect us to swallow that ridiculous drivel?'

'Minister Wyrm, that is what the report says,' she rebuffed calmly. 'Your concern is understandable, but this is what the experts have determined.'

'Then explain to me how a wall simply disappears? And not just a small wall, the *entire* façade of the west wing of a three-storey brick building! We are not yesterday's children, Ms Spriggs. That report of yours is a complete and utter load of shak!'

'With all due respect, minister, you may be the Minister of Defence, but you are not a scientist nor an expert in thermonuclear dynamics. Even our scientists had a hard time comprehending it. The sheer forces required to cause such an event would be…' she fumbled through the document for the figures.

'Twelve hundred megapulses,' Ester said it before even she realised it.

'What did someone say?' Orian asked of the room.

'Twelve hundred megapulses,' Ester repeated a little louder. 'It's enough to vaporise concrete, brick and steel. Well, twelve hundred and ninety-two point five megapulses, to be precise.'

Cristal gave Ester a curious look.

'Who is this girl?' Minister Wyrm spat, waving his hand palm up at Ester.

'It doesn't matter, Artimus,' another minister said. Seated beside the defence minister, the scruffy-looking man had a slide rule out and was doing his own calculations. 'It's twelve hundred and ninety-two point five three by my reckonin', he said, brushing his almost white hair out of his eyes. 'The girl's correct.'

'I don't care about the calculations. There's half a building out there, and I demand to know why. I demand to know the truth!'

'Artimus,' the Surprime interjected. 'I think LunaTec has made it clear it was a freak accident.'

'A freak accident that nearly smudged you all over the pavement. If it wasn't for me, we wouldn't be having this argument.'

'I am grateful for that Artimus, truly I am, but we must move past this,' Sage said respectfully, standing in his place. 'This "freak accident" has created angst amongst us, but it has also created more pressing issues that we now need to put our grievances aside to address, like how we will fund the repairs to the hospital. With that wall missing, it's exposed to the elements and is structurally unsound. Patients remain in the old facility that's falling apart and becoming dangerous. With that now at capacity and more people succumbing to the sickness, we don't know how much longer it can stay like this. We need solutions, not more problems. If Cristal is done, I will open the floor to discussion.'

Cristal nodded, gathered her papers and returned to her seat, giving Ester a mixed sigh of relief and acknowledgement as she did.

Orian raised from her chair at the head of the table the moment the chamber exploded into a flurry of intense vocal outrage, accusation and castigation.

'ORDER! ORDER! I will have order in my Chambers,' Orian bellowed, slamming her gavel repeatedly in attempts to calm the room. Still, its echo failed to carry over the rabble.

It was then the defence minister rose from his seat again and slammed his fists to the table. 'Will you screeching pack of cockamandrels shut the frak up!'

The room instantly fell silent, with not a soul daring to utter a word or so much as cough.

'Thank you, Minister,' Orian said, issuing the scar-faced politician a steely glare. She still held the gavel aloft in preparation to strike it again, but as people returned to their seats, so too did the defence minister, leaving Orian speechless.

'Ahem,' the Surprime coughed, taking the podium while Orian, seemingly perturbed, set the gavel down and returned to her seat.

'If I may?' said a woman after an awkward silence.

'The chamber recognises the property and development minister,' the Surprime said, gesturing at the woman with long dark hair seated further down the table. 'Please proceed, Indira.'

'We must focus on rebuilding. Only then can we put this fiasco behind us. We already know how in dire need this town is of a working hospital. But without the construction materials, I'm afraid it will take much longer than we all would hope.'

'That's all good and well, Minister Tryce,' a younger man said, leaping to his feet. 'But how do you propose to do that?'

'You're Resources Minister, Niklas, you tell me?'

'Only last tendawn my office was advised the *MARSAP plant* broke down, again,' Niklas replied.

'Ahem, excuse me,' the older minister, Elihus, interjected. 'But for the laypersons in the room, care to tell us what a MARSAP plant is?'

'Material And Resources Sorting and Processing,' several voices called out in reply.

'And what in the Progenitor's names makes that an issue of importance here?' Elihus protested.

'Because, Minister Kinton,' the resources minister replied with an unsympathetically stern expression. 'Seventy to eighty-five per cent of the materials needed for infrastructure projects, like the hospital, come from recycled materials—materials that plant enables us to produce. Without it, we would be having this conversation in a cramped little room in the dark. Last time, it cost us five thousand hopemarks to get it up and running again. That delayed a number of critical projects and put a lot of Hope citizens out of work. If we can't get that plant working, we won't be building anything, let alone fixing that hospital.'

'Minister Martell,' a petite older woman sitting to the left of the Surprime said. Her name plaque read Abril Tope, Treasurer. She adjusted her thick oblong spectacles on her nose and stood to speak. 'I am aware of the situation with the recycling plant, Minister. Chief Engineer Anaska has already stopped by my office and apprised me of the situation. But I am afraid to say, the ministry coffers have no additional funding. Our budget was exhausted building the hospital. We could go cap in hand back to LunaTec, but I'm afraid I have already tried that.'

The Surprime turned to Cristal. 'Ms Spriggs, is this true? Has LunaTec rejected a request by the Treasury for additional funding?'

'Not exactly, sir,' Cristal replied. 'Treasurer Tope did contact our offices, but the request was denied on the basis LunaTec had already provided funding of fifteen thousand hopemarks for the hospital construction.'

'That's preposterous!' Minister Tryce exclaimed from the other side of the table. 'As Property and Development Minister, I would know if fifteen thousand marks hit my accounts. I can assure you, it has not.'

'Then where did it go?' Surprime Solon exclaimed, looking at the Treasurer. She frantically shuffled through ledger pages, searching for a sign of the missing marks while a few sheets of paper slipped away from her across the table's smooth polish. 'Fifteen thousand marks don't just disappear.'

'What's this?' Minister Wyrm leaned over the table, slid a loose sheet of paper toward himself and examined the page. 'Surprime, this curious purchase order is dated last tendawn, to the value of five thousand hopemarks and is for something called GG.' He flipped over the page to see if there was more, then handed it over to the Surprime. 'At the bottom, I think you'll recognise the scrawly signature.'

'Elihus,' the Surprime said, reading the page. 'Care to explain? What's GG, and why is it worth five thousand hopemarks?'

Elihus considered his fellow minister with an unerringly calm expression. 'If you should know, Minister Wyrm, GG stands for Grade Gratuity, and it's for the teachers to supplement their wages this cycle to ensure the children are adequately protected while they are in the care of my institutions. Furthermore,' he added with a pompous nose held in the air, 'it was allocated to my portfolio well before this whole situation happened. And I don't appreciate the insinuation that I reapportioned the funding by any sort of deception.'

The defence minister slammed his fist on the table again. 'So, what you're saying is your teachers deserve a wage over and above the universal income? We're all scraping for pebbles, and here's Elihus Kinton paying his teachers' bonuses! I'll have you know, Elihus, last week, my office received fourteen, yes, fourteen complaints of raiders breaching the boundary. Raiders, who like to sneak into people's houses and cut their throats while they sleep. I requested funding for additional patrols to keep this town safe, but I was denied. Yet, you, you get play money to give your teachers tips to do what exactly? Make sure the children learn their times tables? This is ridiculous!'

'Your objection is noted, Minister,' Elihus retorted, 'however, you must agree funding is necessary for the safety and security of the children. *Hope's future.*'

'That's my job!' Artimus roared. 'I'm Defence Minister, or had you forgotten?'

'Yes, yes, Minister, but it isn't enough to rely on HomeGuard to protect Hope's future. That responsibility rests with me and *my* ministry. Surely you and everyone here can see that? To refuse my requests for funding would be to refuse protection for your children. Do you wish for your children to be left vulnerable and Hope's future exposed to harm? Of course, you do not!'

'Gentlemen,' the Surprime promptly cut in. 'I think we can all agree this town is doing it tough. Resources are tight, but we will sort this out. I'm going to call a brief intermission to allow people to get some fresh air and perhaps let off some steam.' He glared at Minister Wyrm as he said that. 'We will resume in ten decs.'

With the tap of the Speaker's gavel, the congregation adjourned, and the room filled with loud, animated chatter.

Cristal turned to Ester, her face looking flushed from the pressure.

The shaggy-looking minister with the slide rule stood next to Cristal and addressed Ester. 'That was impressive. How did you do that?'

Ester blinked at him. 'Do what, sir?'

'Come up with those calculations? Did you really work that out in your head?'

She shrugged. 'I dunno, I guess.'

'Well, good on you, girl,' he said, tapping her on the shoulder. 'I'm Garan, by the way, Minister for Science and Research.' He extended his hand for Ester to shake it.

'Tess.'

'You're a bright kid, Tess,' he said with a smile. 'You should be proud of her, Ms Spriggs.'

'Thank you, Minister Tope,' Cristal replied.

'And don't worry about Artimus. We can handle him. He can be a bit of a *you-know-what*.'

'I can be a what?' interrupted Artimus, who, with a noticeable limp, had come from behind Garan to join the conversation.

'Ahem,' Garan coughed. 'I think I'll go get some fresh air. Nice to meet you, Tess. Hope to see you again sometime soon.' And with that, Garan took his walking cane and hobbled towards the door.

'What do you want, Artimus?' Cristal grumbled, gathering up her belongings.

'Only the truth. You may expect these hair-brained simpletons to swallow your cover story, but not me. Thermonuclear implosion? Is that really what the report says?'

'It's what the report says, Artimus,' she said, thrusting the booklet at him. 'Here, read it for yourself.'

Despite her slender stature, she stood defiant against the burly minister. 'Excuse us, Minister, but we need some fresh air—' she pushed past him with a hand covering her mouth and rushed toward the bathrooms, leaving him still holding the report.

Something about how he said the word 'report' gave Ester a moment of phantasm. Glaring up at him while she squeezed past, she was more interested in seeing what was up with Cristal than making small talk with the man who'd just torn strips off her aunt.

As Ester pushed open the bathroom door, the Chief Surgeon, Lexi Colyar, was there, knocking on a closed cubicle door. Ester recognised her from the ministry session. 'Cristal, is everything alright in there?' she said.

'Fine, thank you,' Cristal replied, promptly followed by the sound of retching.

'Sounds like it,' the doctor said. 'Please open the door, Cristal.'

The toilet flushed, and Cristal exited the stall, wiping her mouth. She approached the sink, splashed water over her face and cringed at her pale reflection in the mirror. 'This is supposed to have been cured. We should have gotten over this,' she mumbled to herself.

'Gotten over what?' the doctor asked.

'Nothing. Lexi, please don't pretend you care.'

'Pretend? This isn't pretending. I saw you run in here, and I came after you, genuinely concerned.'

'Please, you've already made it perfectly clear where you stand. You got what you wanted.'

'You mean not talking to me? Cristal, that was cycles ago. I was angry, but I'm no monster. Unlike *him…* '

'Don't speak about him that way,' Cristal snapped, and Ester could recognise from the scowl on her face the '*him*' to whom the doctor referred was someone they both knew. Cristal had spoken very little about her past. She had only mentioned in passing she knew Chief Surgeon Colyar. Still, it would seem from the way this argument was going there was a lot more to it than Ester understood. 'You don't know him. He's not like that.'

The doctor gave a sardonic laugh. 'Are we talking about the same person? Of course, I don't know him like you do. Anyone who did is now dead.'

'And you're still on about that?'

'Aunt Cristal?' Ester interrupted, and Cristal immediately turned to her, softening her expression as though only just realising she was standing there. 'It's okay, Tess. This is a discussion that needs to be had.'

Ester nodded, and Lexi continued, giving Ester a wary, almost apologetic look.

'I will always be on about that. You don't survive the massacre of eleven of your closest friends and almost die yourself and just get over it. Please tell me you're not with him, Cristal?'

'That's none of your business.'

'Cristal?' Lexi enquired, stepping forward, but Cristal brushed her off.

'Leave it, Lexi,' she growled in a stern voice.

'He's dangerous, or haven't you figured that out already? What is it about him, anyway? Why would you stick with a person like that?'

'That has nothing to do with you!' Cristal shouted defensively, turning to face the mirror.

'Oh, I see what this is,' the doctor said. 'I recognise that look. It's the infatuation, isn't it? He's gotten to you?'

'This is ridiculous.'

'Come on, for cycles, you flirted after the Commander. We know you tried to hide it, but we all knew. I didn't give you a hard time about it. I even thought you'd be strangely good for each other.'

The instant the doctor mentioned Commander, Ester knew who the *'him'* was they had been referring to, although it seemed strange Cristal and the doctor were talking about him in this context. Commander had only ever been a parental figure and teacher to Ester. The man rarely showed any sign of emotion.

'Is that so?' Cristal scoffed.

'And remember that crazy guy back at the Academy. What was his name?'

'Marvyn,' Cristal said with a nasal snigger, and Lexi briefly joined her.

'Yes, him! The cultist.'

Cristal spun from the mirror. 'He wasn't a cultist!'

'He was *definitely* a cultist,' the doctor said. 'He belonged to that Sovereign order that believed the Progenitors would one day return and *liberate us all* and that we would all live in kingdoms in the sky. That's what he said. He was dead set determined on indoctrinating you, and he had you like a fish on a line. Until he tried to sacrifice you.'

'Okay, so he was a little unhinged.'

'A little? The guy was flat bed crazy. But who came when you called for help to rescue you from his place?'

'You did.'

'And whose shoulder did you cry on for three days after while you got over the heartbreak?'

'You, but—'

'You bet, Cristal. That was me. Friends do that. *I* did that. We were close friends once, remember? What happened?'

'Things change.'

Lexi gasped, and Ester could tell from the doctor's shocked expression it was an emotional blow. 'Cristal, I *had* to save you then, and I'm *trying* to save you now,' she persisted, her attempts to appeal to Cristal now seeming more desperate. 'Can't you see that? I'm telling you, the Commander is dangerous.'

'Your help is misplaced,' Cristal said, dismissing Lexi's pleas. 'Don't try to save what doesn't need saving.'

'What is it about him that's got you so besotted?'

'Besotted? Is that what you think this is? You know nothing. Leave him alone. He's nothing like you think he is.'

'Nothing?' she hesitated, 'oh my goodness, Cristal, you *are* with him.'

Cristal visibly blushed.

Lexi noticed. 'And you slept with him, didn't you?'

'Not slept.'

'But you *are* pregnant?'

'What?' Cristal replied with aghast.

Lexi gave her a candid look. 'I'm a doctor, Cristal. I can recognise natal sickness when I see it. Is it his?'

Cristal crossed her arms beneath her breasts in the stern manner Ester had seen before when she was done listening. 'That's definitely none of your business.'

'I can help you if you want. Please let me help you.'

'No, Lexi, not this time. Leave us alone. Come on, Tess.' With that, she stormed out of the bathroom, beckoning Ester to follow.

On the steps outside, Ester couldn't keep composed any longer. 'Is what she said in there true? Are you pregnant?'

'Not you too?'

'Please, Aunt Cristal. Surely you can tell me?'

She hesitated. 'Yes. But please keep it down. We only found out a couple of days ago. You must not tell anyone.'

'And is it really *his*?'

'Go, enjoy the day, Ester,' she said, dropping a small handful of hopemarks into Ester's hand. 'That's for lunch. Come back in two cendecs, and please keep this to yourself.' And then she turned and strode back inside the ministerial hall.

Ester's mind reeled. The mere concept of Cristal and Commander having a baby together seemed unfathomable—like a butterfly and a rock. There wasn't even a hint of a relationship between them, so it came as something of a surprise. Thinking about that made her wonder about her own parents and it re-sparked emotions she'd believed were long since buried, reminding her she still missed them terribly. Ester learned long ago the truth about how she came to be in Commander's custody. There was no denying it—he'd kidnapped her. The reason still eluded her, and while the reality of that was cause for much angst, Ester had to concede she had been treated well. Cristal, in particular, cared for Ester as though she were her own daughter, which was why Ester called Cristal 'Aunt.' But she would never be 'Mother' to Ester. That title was already taken.

Ester involuntarily tugged on the silver locket about her neck and flipped open the tiny catch. Nestled within the frame was a minuscule, monochrome photograph of her real parents happily smiling back at her like nothing could ever spoil that moment. So much time had passed, she could barely remember them, especially her father, whom she hadn't seen since she was a young girl. All she could remember of him was tucking her in at night on the rare occasions he was home. This tiny photo was the only lasting memory she had of them, and she treasured it more than anything else in the world. If only she knew where they were, what had become of them, and whether they were even still alive. So many questions. Before the tears could start, she snapped the locket shut and descended the steps into the streets of Hope, eager to embrace the freedom. In no time, all thought of her last conversation with Cristal had slipped from her mind, and she absorbed herself in her new, wondrous surroundings.

Single-storey, part-brick, part-timber buildings with awnings and signs in an assortment of bright colours stood all around her. Electric lampposts lined the green-tinged asphalt main street, upon which a handful of repurposed military vehicles and cars travelled to their unknown destinations. People dressed in well-made but straightforward clothing glided with purpose along the concrete footpaths, scurrying this way and that.

A door opened, and the aroma of fresh baked goods wafted from a shop into the street, making Ester salivate. She took in a deep breath. With its delectable delights on display in the window, her belly rumbled, and she realised she hadn't eaten in some time. She pulled out a few of the coins Cristal had given her and bought something called a butter-crunch—a curly golden pastry that, compared to the bland food prepared in the mass kitchens at LunaTec, was like chewing on a luxuriously sweet, crunchy pillow.

As she savoured the last of the butter-crunch, laughter echoed from a nearby side street and sparking Ester's curiosity, she went to investigate. Wandering to the street's end, she stopped when a red ball about the size of an adult's head bounced off her ankle.

'Hey! You mind throwing that back here?' called a scrawny boy about Ester's age. He had sandy-blonde hair, was wearing baggy but neat-looking clothing and was standing on a bare grassy square along with four other children of varying ages.

Surrounded by buildings, the square had shrubs planted around the edges, concealing it from view, making it a little hidden oasis in the middle of town.

Ester crammed the rest of the pastry into her mouth, delicately picked up the light and squishy ball so as not to aggravate her ribs, and threw it back along the narrow road. It bounced off the neighbouring walls a few times before stopping halfway between her and the boy, drawing pitiful laughter from the small crowd.

'Where did you learn to throw?' he mocked, retrieving the ball.

Ester swallowed hard and moved down the short alley toward the boy so she could answer. 'I didn't.'

'Well, that's obvious. Hey, I don't recognise you from around here. Where you from?'

'From there,' Ester said, pointing at the distant mountain, looming like a gigantic sentinel standing guard over the buildings.

'The mountain?'

Ester nodded.

'Seriously, you live on the mountain?'

'Nope, *in* the mountain.'

'Wow, no wonder we haven't seen you around. The name's Rodi, that's Esmay—my girlfriend, the boy with the red hair is Tobias, that's Helina over there with the dark hair and the little one's Averyx. What's your name?'

'Ester, but people call me Tess.'

'Well, Tess. Welcome to Hope. What brings you to our little slice of paradise?'

'My Aunt's a diplomat.'

'Ahh, I see,' he said with a knowing grin. 'Commiserations. We all have family in the ministry. Averyx's dad is the Surprime, and both my parents are ministers. Mum's the Treasurer, and Dad's the Science and Research Minister. Perhaps you've met them?'

'I've met your dad. He couldn't believe I calculated something faster than him,' Ester said with a grin.

Rodi gave a sarcastic laugh. 'That would've gone down well.'

'He seemed impressed,' Ester said, catching on to the cynicism.

'I'm sure he was. Anyway, can't blame you for not wanting to stay there. That's why we're all here, in this courtyard and not in that hall.'

'Yer,' she replied, happy to be out of there but not so grateful to have left Cristal to be savaged by those flesh-eating scavengers. 'So, what are you playing?' she asked, diverting the conversation.

Rodi chuckled. 'What? Have you been living under a rock?'

Shrugging, Ester glanced toward the mountain again.

'Ah, I guess you *actually have* been living under a rock,' Rodi recanted. 'This is Ace Ball. Well, it will be if I can get more players. You take this ball here,' he said, bouncing the ball with one hand, 'and the Ace throws it at the others, trying to hit them. Whoever gets hit is the new Ace. The less you get hit, the more points you get.'

'Does it hurt?' She absently touched her side, where her ribs were still tender, trying not to wince at the thought of the ball hitting her.

'Only if you don't watch where you're going and run into something. Do you want to play?'

'Ahh,' Ester said, 'I think I'll pass, thanks. I'm not really into ball sports. Besides, I'm not dressed for that.'

At that moment, the pretty, brown-haired girl named Esmay latched herself to Rodi's arm. 'Who's this?' she said snobbishly. The particularly provocative black dress she wore had a plunging neckline that revealed way too much of her golden-tanned chest for Ester's tastes.

'This is Tess,' Rodi said, apparently oblivious to the girl hanging off him like she was a piece of his clothing. 'She's our neighbour from the mountains.'

'The mountains?' Esmay replied with a haughty attitude. 'Like those mountains?'

'Yer, why?' Ester said.

'I guess that makes sense,' Esmay giggled.

Ester frowned. 'What?'

'They don't let you out much, do they?' Esmay sneered, eyeing Ester up and down as though a rival. 'You look pretty pale.'

'I get out,' Ester insisted.

'In *that*?'

'What's wrong with what I'm wearing?' Ester said, glancing down at her new dress. She normally didn't concern herself too much with appearances, preferring comfort over style. Still, she was so thrilled to receive the dress for her namedawn, she just had to wear it out. At least she wasn't dolled-up like this girl Esmay who appeared to be wearing so much ornametics she resembled an actual doll.

Esmay looked about to reply with some terse remark, but Rodi jumped in, seeming to have noticed Ester's discomfort. 'Um, Tess, you said your aunt was a diplomat?'

Ester nodded shyly, still a little put out by Esmay's criticism of her appearance.

Rodi's snooty girlfriend leered at Ester again. 'Ooh, I know who you are now,' she said, 'you're the LunaTec attaché's little girl. What's her name?'

'I'm hardly little. I'm probably the same age as you,' Ester retorted, but Esmay persisted.

'I heard they're holding LunaTec responsible for what happened to the hospital. Looks like your Aunty is in twuble,' Esmay said condescendingly, emphasising the last word by sticking out her bottom lip.

To Ester, it was unnecessarily rude and delinquent, but she wasn't prepared to pick a fight with people she'd only just met.

'Come on, Esmay,' Rodi said, glancing scornfully at his girlfriend. 'Leave the poor girl alone. I'm sorry about that, Tess. You're welcome to join us if you'd like. I'm sure Esmay won't mind.'

Esmay shot him a disapproving look.

'Thanks,' Ester replied, 'but I better be getting back. Say, before I go, you don't happen to know a girl named Jayne by any chance? Red hair—a bit darker than mine, green eyes, about our age?'

'My Rodi doesn't know anybody like that, do you, babes?' Esmay said, wrapping her arms around the boy's neck.

Rodi glanced at his girlfriend before turning his attention back to Ester with a thoughtful look. 'I don't know anyone by that name, sorry.'

'Thanks anyway,' Ester said, unable to hide her disappointment. Though it was clear Rodi was trying to make her feel welcome, Esmay merely batted her eyelids and turned her back like she was dismissing an underling.

'Okay, bye now,' she said, waving Ester away.

This was not the reception Ester had expected. Perhaps it was a bad idea coming here. She had been looking forward to coming to Hope, but to be mocked by a stranger, that stung.

Before Ester could conjure a retort, the moment had passed, Rodi had returned to his game, and Ester stood in the narrow roadway alone once more. It was then she heard an oddly familiar voice call her name from behind.

'Huh?' Ester responded, spinning around. Standing at the entrance to the alleyway was a tall, lean woman dressed in a khaki delivery driver's uniform. She considered Ester with a peculiar familiarity. With a red ponytail poking from beneath a cap, she bore an uncanny resemblance to the description she just gave. Only it couldn't be Jayne. This woman was much older.

'Ester?' the woman with the familiar voice said, advancing toward her. 'It *is* you!'

15 ARTIMUS

NC10

Artimus squinted at his bedside clock, its dim back-lit display showing 0:97. Still one and a half cendecs until dawn. With a discernable groan, he tossed over onto his back again. This had been the second night in a row he hadn't slept. The more he eyed those black digits, brazenly reminding him he was an unwitting conscious passenger in time's slow but definitive sojourn toward morning, the worse his temper became.

Someone once told him if he focused on his breathing, he could clear his mind.

Abril Tope, you are a bizarre woman, he thought, remembering who that someone was.

You're supposed to be clearing your mind, not thinking of her.

Although he had tried this several times—to little avail—he shifted into a more comfortable position to try it once more.

The bedroom door squeaked, and squinting through slitted eyelids, he abandoned any further thought of relaxation and lay still in silence, listening for the sound again. The door opened wider, reflecting a moving beam of light across the room from the streetlamp outside.

That's definitely not the wind.

Artimus focused on the sounds in the room; the wind toying with his curtains through the open window, the floorboards beside his bed creaking under the weight of a careful footstep, and then a faint 'tisk' of a knife leaving its leathery scabbard. It was a sound all too familiar to the veteran.

With clenched fists, he gripped his blanket and cast it like a fisher's net, catching the unknown assailant by surprise. Before they could react, he slid off the bed, pinned them down and punched them until the struggling mass stopped moving.

'It's about time you came,' he hissed, relaxing his grip. 'No one sneaks up on Artimus Wyrm and gets away with it.'

Artimus hefted the dead weight wrapped in his blanket and draped them over his shoulder. 'I was getting tired of wearing my boots to bed.'

Under the early morning's dappled light, Artimus carried his slow breathing bundle to the edge of town. In a less developed quarter, situated close to Artimus's apartment, was a building of simple brick construction with offices out the front and lockup at the rear. It may not look like much, but it was HomeGuard headquarters—a place Artimus could avoid the soul-destroying political matters of Hope's ministerial offices.

He stepped inside one of the small vacant concrete cells and lowered the bundle into a steel-framed canvas cot in the corner. When Artimus pulled back the blood-stained blankets, it revealed the unconscious and battered face of a brunette woman with high cheekbones. Dressed in black and grey camouflage, worn military boots, and with wide adhesive tape covering anything loose or metallic, it was clear she was no opportunistic intruder.

A professional, he thought while he collected a wooden chair and placed it in the cell's doorway, allowing his would-be assassin to sleep off her induced unconsciousness. There he sat and waited.

Almost half a cendec had passed when Artimus stood and poured a mug of kahwah from the cold pot on the bench behind him. He couldn't tell if it was the bitter taste of the drink or the thought of this intruder violating his sleep that made him cringe. As he returned to his sentry, the blanketed mass in the cell stirred.

'Here,' he said, tossing his mug's vile brown contents into the woman's face. 'This should wake you up. Personally, I don't know how people can stomach the stuff.'

With a groan, she lifted a hand to wipe her face and glared at him with the animosity of a caged wild animal.

He leaned forward to make his presence seem more imposing. 'We'll start with a nice, simple question. What's your name?'

'Potential fractured zygomatic and parietal,' the strange woman said. The way she talked without moving her jaw clearly showed she was in pain. 'Deviated septum, cracked temporal and maxillae, and one, no, two broken molars.'

'I'll ask again. What's your name?'

'Broken left clavicle…'

'I don't care about your damage,' Artimus said, unrolling a bundle on his lap and producing her knife, holding it up in admiration. It was a thing of menacing beauty with braided red binding around the handle contrasted against the matte black split metal blade. He'd seen nothing like it before. 'I only care about this and why you were aiming to use it on me.'

The woman ignored him and continued exploring her injuries. 'Contusions, but no broken ribs. No sign of internal hemorrhaging. Internals feel undamaged.'

Artimus bundled up the weapon into its length of cloth and tucked it inside his coat. 'Maybe you'll recognise her,' he said as he held up a picture of the woman he knew as Seraphin MonLantry.

Most would have missed it and so might have Artimus if he hadn't been an expert interrogator in a former life, but the fleeting micro-expression on her face said it all.

'I see. So you *do* know her?' He returned the photo to his breast pocket. 'One way or another, you will tell me where I can find her. But more to the point, why you found it necessary to come visit me in my bed. Most women try bleeding me for drinks first. If you wanted in my bed, you're somewhat attractive, I think. You need only have asked.'

She gave a muffled chuckle through her swollen lips. 'You're not my type, old man.'

'So you aren't just a pretty anatomy and physiology textbook. Care to answer my first question? WHAT'S YOUR NAME?'

She spat blood-filled saliva at him.

'Have it your way,' he said, standing to leave. 'It's just as well you attacked me this night. One more sleepless night like this, and I would've had to summon you from the dead to have this little conversation. Tell me, have you ever seen a grizzly ursus?'

'Beastly and odorous?' she replied with a snigger.

'You forgot, cantankerous. Consider me that ursus.' Artimus withdrew his chair and slammed the cell door shut, locking it behind him with a loud click. 'My blankets are as close as you're going to get. Savour the odour.'

She sat up and threw the blanket at the bars with vehemence.

From the adjoining offices, Lieutenant Wistham entered, wearing a pressed green and black HomeGuard town uniform and shiny black boots. Upon seeing his commanding officer, the young, tall and lanky officer greeted him, right fist to forehead, palm out in customary HomeGuard salute, and a raised eyebrow.

'I wasn't expecting you this early, sir,' he said, lowering his arm as Artimus returned acknowledgement.

Artimus grunted.

'And I see we have a guest,' Wistham added, glancing at the scowling woman occupying the cell. 'What happened to her?'

'Don't ask.'

'She looks like I did that time I got into a bar fight a few cycles back.'

Now Artimus was the one raising the eyebrow.

'Don't worry,' Wistham backpedalled. 'That was before I enlisted. Dad thought I needed discipline…'

'I don't want your life story, Wistham,' Artimus grumbled, pushing past his lieutenant to exit the room and turning up the thermostat to the cells as he left.

Wistham followed. 'It's strange. I remember getting hit in the face with a chair, but that's about it. I know I took some stuff Ferne gave me, but I'm damned if I can remember. I lost a whole day.'

'You don't say?' Artimus mused. 'And what was this stuff Ferne gave you?'

'Dunno. It was just something for the pain. She didn't say what it was.'

'Ferne, the crazy chemist?'

'Yes, sir. She has a shop on Main street, although I think she prefers to be called an apothecarist–'

'Watch the prisoner,' Artimus cut him off. 'I'll be back.'

By the time Artimus stepped out into Hope's Main Street, the sun had risen, and the town bustled with people going about their morning routines. He didn't care about any of them. With a strange woman who wanted to see him dead now occupying his lockup, he was more concerned with finding out why. He strode across the road, barely noticing a large truck rumble by, heading toward the ministerial chambers and Sempro park. He caught the words 'moon' and 'LunaTec' emblazoned on its side but, lost in his own thoughts, ignored the truck and marched on.

Newly constructed brick homes gave way to brightly decorated façades and shopfronts that lined the busy streets of the retail quarter.

Artimus headed for one place in particular—a small green shop with branches and leaves painted to spell out the business's name on the front glass—'Ferne's Apothecary'.

He hoped to find it open.

Ferne reminded him of a more rotund, whimsical version of Abril Tope with her long wavy reddish-brown hair and perky nature. He was more of a man of science and cared little for her form of whimsical medicine. However, she had served Hope with her potions and herbal concoctions for many cycles.

A bell above the door chimed as Artimus entered the quaint shop. The moment he stepped over the threshold, his nostrils were assaulted by a potent odour that appeared to be emanating from a smouldering stick on the counter. Small bottles, candles, coloured rocks and various other items lined the walls and counters. Standing beside a thick slice of a tree trunk that made up the front countertop was the shop's proprietor, Ferne, busy finishing up with another customer. With her brightly multicoloured clothing and bits of random things braided into her hair, her appearance forced Artimus to swallow his conservative sensibilities and just do what he came there to do.

'Well, Artimus, isn't this a blessing?' Ferne said, having noticed Artimus blocking the door. The other customer had to squeeze past him to leave. 'I've never seen you in here before. How can I help you, sweetheart?'

Artimus cringed a little inside. He watched over his shoulder and waited for the other customer to leave before stepping forward to speak. 'I'm after something that can help loosen someone's tongue.'

It was an odd but brazen request. However, Artimus didn't have time for pleasantries.

Ferne took half a step back. 'There is no such thing, Artimus,' she said disapprovingly. 'Don't be silly.'

'Alright then,' he said, having to rethink his tact after seeing her reaction. 'What about pain? Do you have something for that?'

'Are you in pain, my dear? What sort of pain?'

He moved in closer, and her perfume, adding to the pungent incense, irritated his nose even more, nearly making him sneeze. 'It's the knees,' he said in a low voice. 'Must be the change in weather.'

'Oh, dear. Yes, I've had a few enquiries like that lately. With all these cold and then warm days, it's not great on the joints. It causes inflammation, you see. Especially in us "more mature" folks,' she said with a wink, accompanied by a cheeky grin that gave Artimus the impression the woman was flirting with him. 'I've always said the gaian body wasn't designed for sudden changes—'

'Ferne…' Artimus interrupted.

'The tincture, yes, of course. Sorry, dear.' She reached under the counter and pulled out a small opaque green bottle. He reached for it, but she pulled it back, forcing Artimus to listen to her instructions first. 'Now just remember, and this is important,' she said in a light, flowery voice, 'there's five days' worth in that bottle. Too much will suppress your short-term memory, so go easy with it. It can also make you drowsy, so don't drive one of those motor vehicles. Only one spoonful every five or six cendecs should do it. If the pain persists, come back, and I'll adjust the mixture. Okay, lovely?'

'Yes, fine,' he replied, reaching for the bottle again.

'That'll be three hopemarks, sweetheart. Would you like anything else?'

Artimus huffed and fumbled in his pockets for a few coins. Without counting them, he slapped them on the counter. 'Keep the change.'

'Oh, Artimus, aren't you a dear,' she said, passing him the bottle as though presenting him with a precious gift. 'You should notice its effects almost instantly. Any trouble, any trouble at all, come back and see me, 'kay, sweetheart?'

'Excellent. Yes. Thank you. And Ferne,' he added, turning to leave, 'keep this between us.'

'Of course, sweetheart. As with all my treasured customers, your secret is safe with me,' she said with a titillating giggle. 'Remember what I said, though. Go easy with that.'

Artimus grunted a reply.

'It was a pleasure seeing you…' Ferne called out as he left the shop.

A corporal standing guard at the front door of HomeGuard headquarters saluted Artimus as he pushed his way inside.

Wistham was adjusting the electric thermostat for the cells when Artimus entered.

'Leave that alone,' Artimus snapped, almost making the young lieutenant leap off his feet in surprise.

'But sir, the prisoner…?'

'I don't care.'

'Yes, sir. Sir, the prisoner has requested water. Shall I still take this in for her?' Wistham asked, holding up a tin mug.

Artimus grabbed the mug. 'No. Leave it with me. You go find Hunter and tell him I need him back here. Go!'

'Sir!' Wistham saluted before marching out the door.

Artimus set the tin mug on the desk beside a collection of others and a steel jug filled with water, poured in approximately two spoonfuls of Ferne's tincture, sniffed it, gave it a sip, and then tipped in the rest.

Before entering the lockup, Artimus adjusted the thermostat to a more comfortable setting.

'You're still here?' Artimus joked sardonically. 'Is it hot in here, or is it just me?'

The woman lifted her chin, eyeing the mug in Artimus's hand. 'Are you going to give me that, or are you going to let me die of thirst?'

'What, this?' he said, tipping some of it on the floor.

She scowled.

'I'll make you a deal. You tell me your name and what you're doing here, and I'll let you have a drink.'

She growled through her teeth. 'How about you give me that water, and I stop thinking of worse ways to end you, *Artimus Wyrm*?'

'Well, that's brilliant. You know my name. I only know you as the crazy bikkja who tried to get into my bed. *What am I supposed to call you*?'

'Steel.'

'Steel what? First or last name?'

'Steel Bar.'

'Oh, like that, hey? Okay, *crazy bikkja* it is. Have your water.' He shoved the mug at her.

She snatched it from his hand and dropped it, spilling its contents over the concrete floor. 'Whoops, sorry about that,' she remarked. 'Now I'll have some without the… whatever was in that.'

'Clever,' Artimus said, picking up the mug and taking it back to the office. Leaving the door open, he placed the now empty mug on the desk with the others, filled it from the jug, and then grabbed another, returning to the prisoner, taking a sip as he did. The entire time, her eyes followed him like a target-shooter trained on their kill.

'Happy?' he asked, giving her a sly grin.

She reached for the mug and, from between the bars, skolled its contents.

'Better?' Artimus asked, reaching for the mug.

She glared at him and dropped it.

'Do you treat all the people you meet this way?' he said.

'What do you think?' she replied, returning an equally sly but pained grin. 'Only the ones I intend to kill.'

'And how's that going for you?'

'If I don't succeed, they will only send another.'

'Who's they?'

Once more, she brushed aside Artimus's question, crossing her arms with that awkward sly grin still marring her face. But it was only short-lasting, as it faded, replaced by a seriousness he hadn't seen from her yet.

Artimus knew what that meant. 'Good stuff, hey?'

'What?'

'You didn't think I gave you just water, did you?'

'What have you done to me?' she demanded.

'I also like how it changes the flavour of the water. Makes it more palatable. Don't you think?'

'What poison is this?' she asked, grabbing hold of the bars of the cell for stability.

'Oh, don't worry,' he said with a broad grin. 'Unlike you, I don't kill by stealth. I want you alive, and that painkiller might actually do you some good. But after the amount you just drank, you won't remember any of this. Night night,' he said while he waved.

After the prisoner collapsed, Artimus returned to the offices, reclining with a satisfied groan behind the clean timber desk of the Officer-in-Charge. He removed the wrapped knife from his coat and set it down before picking up a report that had been left in the tray to read.

As he did, Hunter stomped in, garbed in his oddly silent metal armour, with Wistham trailing like a stray pup behind.

'Hunter. Good to see you,' Artimus said, setting aside the report.

'Get to the point, Wyrm.'

'I expect a little more—'

'What do you want?' Hunter said, his toneless orotund voice cutting Artimus off.

'Can you kill a boart by hand?'

'Is that a question or a challenge?'

'I have a prisoner that needs a drop-off somewhere between here and, I assume, the Garret mountains. It must appear as though she survived a boart attack and fought it off with this knife,' Artimus said, holding out the wrapped split blade weapon.

Hunter took the parcel, unwrapped it, and ran his dark eyes over the knife's sharp lines and sleek contours.

'Admiral,' Wistham interjected, 'but is this the way we are meant to deal with prisoners?'

Artimus glared at his lieutenant. 'When someone comes to kill you in your sleep, you tell me how you want to handle them. Until then, you leave this to me.'

'Aye, sir,' Wistham said, removing himself from the conversation and the room.

'I will do this if I can keep this after it's done,' Hunter said, pocketing the knife.

'The knife is hers. For this to look genuine, we need to make her think she killed it with that.'

'Then what's the payment?'

'A tendawn of dinners at The Boart's Head,' Artimus replied. 'If you keep your hands off the knife, I'll throw in drinks. Agreed?'

'For taking on a boart in knife combat? Four tendaws at the Rifle and Pistol, and I'll forget the insult.'

16 BONDED part 1

Four masked strangers wearing headlamps burst into my room, tear away the bedsheets and drag me from the depths of sleep. Before I can clear the fog from my mind, they yank a thick cowl over my head. The air is heavy, and the blackness suffocates—adrenaline kicks in, and with it, the desperate urge to fight.

Four against one—it barely seems fair. With a few carefully judged manoeuvres and accompanying grunts from my captors, I almost break free, but their grip is too strong.

The masked assailants carry me in silence up fifteen steps to a small room, presumably on the second floor, and dump me, still writhing, on a cold, hard metal chair.

Their grip loosens, and my wild punch lands with a satisfying humph. I only wish I knew where it hit.

The cowl comes off, and I'm blinded by their headlamps. They must think of me as some kind of wild animal, for they guard their retreat with pistols drawn. Then the door closes with a bang behind them, and I am alone.

As my vision adjusts to the dimmer light, there's nothing familiar about this tiny, stark room. Only a small table occupies a corner, laid out with a pile of clothes and a handwritten note.

'Your clothes, chosen by your guardian. Dress and return to the chair.'

A cendec later, and I find myself stuck with the most despicable person imaginable, cuffed together by a meta of thin metal chain. Alyx Blackthorn would be the last person I'd want to endure this test with, but here we are. It's only been five decs, and already her ghostly grey eyes glare with such intense animosity it's as though she intends to burn holes into my soul. The reverberating echo of the truck's engine fades between the mountains, leaving us without weapons or provisions deep in an unfamiliar stretch of new-growth forest, far from the Gord.

'It's your fault,' Alyx accuses, driving her fingers into the small muscles of my shoulder. 'If you hadn't been so nice to that unoppressed compliant thviet, we wouldn't be here.'

'What are you talking about?'

'Your girlfriend.' Alyx's jabs become short-distance Shitak'na-style punches.

'She's not—'

Alyx laughs over my words. 'Your girlfriend? Of course she is. It's blatantly obvious. We know how you defend her and act all sweet-like towards her. You're too nice, and it's sickening to watch.'

I return her retort with a stony glare. 'You think you're going to make me cry, is that it?'

'I'll make you cry at some point, even if I have to cut it out of you.'

'Okay, well, while you figure that out, how about we start by finding our way back?' I suggest brushing off her snide remark.

The next punch is hard enough to make me take a step back to keep balance.

'You're a smartarse,' she says. 'Let me make this clear. What *I* say goes. You do as I say, speak when I say. You don't even shak until I say. Got it?'

'Did you fall on your head getting out of the truck or something?'

She steps in closer. 'Watch ya mouth, or I'll do something about it.'

'Okay, Alyx, what *do you* want us to do?'

'Walk. Follow the track back to the Gord.'

'And what are we going to do for water?'

'Well, frak me a tomadai, look at you,' Alyx sneers. 'I said *I* give the orders, and *I* say we're walking.'

'If *you* insist. After two days without water, you and I *will* eventually die of thirst. With you wasting energy on all that hot air, flibberjabbing, I'm guessing it'll be you first, and I'm not dragging your dead arse around.'

'Flibberjabbing?' she remarks. 'Really? You're an idiot.' Then she lifts her cuffed wrist with the dangling chain. 'In case you haven't noticed, you're not going anywhere without me.'

Once again, I try to ignore Alyx and carry on. 'From my guess, we have a five day—'

'Your guess?' she interrupts. 'What makes you the expert around here?'

This is going to be a long five days.

I huff with exasperation at Alyx's arrogance. It's clear this isn't going to work very well. Whoever thought of putting Alyx and me together either has some sick sense of humour or really isn't intending on us surviving this test—if we don't kill each other first. 'Expert or not, *Alyx,* we need water so we don't die in a fraking hole chained together.'

'I told you to watch ya mouth. Consider it *my* rule number one,' she growls, turning her little power play into a staring competition.

Resisting the urge to snap Alyx's neck, I break my gaze and shift my attention to surveying the surrounding landscape instead.

'I thought so, you fraking tomadai wimp,' she says, slapping me across the face.

'Don't,' I reply in a calm tone.

'Get over it and find me water.' She yanks the chain across her body like a canis owner trying to get their animal to walk on a lead.

I ignore it and focus on the task at hand. 'First, I need to get my bearing. We don't want to walk the wrong way.'

At this altitude, forest and mountain tops flank the road, leaving the rising sun as my only reliable point of reference. 'The sun rises that way, and we travelled mostly west, judging from the sunlight shining through the back of the truck. The Gord is somewhere that way.' As though pointing calls upon the Progenitors, the clouds shift, exposing the hazy terraced mountain range in the distance.

But how to find the fastest route via a water source?

The valley dips away to the right, and I figure water travels downhill, so…

Alyx yanks on the chain again. 'Come on, lead the way, little tomadai. Let's see if you walk us off the edge of the world.'

From the angle of the sun, we must have hiked at least a cendec without talking again. Alyx drops herself in front of an exposed boulder, pulling me down with her. I take the moment of quiet to rest and watch the aves play in the sky until the sudden reverberation of Alyx bashing at the chain jolts me back to reality.

'What are you doing?' I ask.

'What does it look like I'm doing? *Idiot,*' Alyx snaps as she strikes at the chain close to her wrist with a fist-sized rock. 'I'm not going to spend however long dragging you around behind me.'

'Well, good luck with that.'

This time, the intensity of her glare somehow screams out 'silence', and she resumes bashing at the metal until the rock falls apart in her hand. 'Argh,' she growls, chucking the fragments away. From all that effort, the chain appears no worse for wear.

'Looks like you're stuck with me,' I chuckle.

'You're going to regret saying that.'

'How are you going to keep up your strength if you keep glaring at me like that?'

'You have no idea. If I should fall while this,' she snarls, holding up the chain, 'binds us, I'll blame you, and then I'll glare at you until the end and beyond. Move, this break is over.'

There is a list of more annoying people or things than Alyx. Number one… Instructor Blackthorn? Nope. Shaddix? Close, but no…

I wish I knew what Alyx's intention is here, but it's clear she's trying to make the journey as uncomfortable as possible, jerking on the chain and deliberately snagging it around random trees. The constant jarring of the cuff bruises and chafes my wrist, and though I hold on to the chain to limit its movement, my wrist is red-raw by day's end. Pain consumes my thoughts, and I've become more concerned about that than remembering which direction we're heading.

'Where are we?' Alyx accuses after we stop for the third time in as many decs. 'We're lost, aren't we?'

'Not lost, just directionally challenged.'

'Admit it, we're lost. You got us lost. It's all your fault because you took us this way instead of the road.'

While Alyx persists with her verbal assault, the wind changes direction, carrying a familiar sound. 'We've got no food and—'

'Shh. Quiet.'

'Excuse me?' she says, punching my already tender shoulder. 'We're going to die, and all you do—'

'Shut up!'

'—is get us lost.' She punches me again. 'And that's for talking over me.'

'Running water.'

'What? I don't hear running water.'

'Because you can't close your mouth.'

Alyx goes to strike me a third time, but I catch her fist, making her gasp.

'Close your mouth, Alyx. It's coming from that way.'

The patchwork forest of dead and regrowing trees gives way to a rock field covered by shale and the occasional boulder. We follow the sound of trickling water to a carpet of lush green grass extending from a hidden inlet. There, two full-leafed trees stand guard over a little oasis where flocks of brightly coloured aves frolic in a stream.

'It's beautiful,' I gasp, marvelling at the cascade of water seeping through a rock wall. It starts as a small trickle, splashing over dark green leaves the size of my head into puddle-sized pools before overflowing as a gushing waterfall into a larger pond. Delicate plants float on the pond's surface, and underneath, shoals of fingerling fish nibble at moss-covered rocks, darting to safety when I peer into the water. It's the cleanest, most pristine water I've ever seen.

Alyx kicks at a soft strip of grass beside a pool. 'This is where I'm sleeping tonight,' she says with smug satisfaction, 'how about you?'

'I'd think we have about two cendecs before—'

She faces me, tapping the side of my head. 'Rule two, I do the thinking.'

'And that's served us well so far…'

And then she slaps me. 'Rule one.'

To reduce the temptation to retaliate, I dig my free hand into my jacket pocket, where my fingers contact a woven strap. Feeling the weave texture between my fingertips helps to soothe my angst and fills me with renewed hope.

'Then you have seen the trampled grass and know what it means?' I challenge her, pointing at the ground by the water's edge.

Alyx shrugs, and her blank expression gives me the answer I expect.

'Boarts come to drink here.'

'So?' she huffs.

'So, if you're lying there when they come… you're the smart one, figure it out. Anyway, as I was about to say, we have about two cendecs before nightfall. In that time, we need to make weapons, gather firewood and find a safer place to sleep.'

'And where do you expect that to be?'

Great! Another person I have to school.

By the time we make spears out of saplings with tips of sharpened shale, the sun reaches the edge of the valley, threatening us with the night.

Alyx promptly tests hers out by throwing it in my direction. I can only hope she intended to miss, but my heart skips a beat anyhow.

She laughs, retrieving the spear from a nearby tree trunk. 'Damn, you're jumpy. That's why you're a timid little tomadai.'

'Why did you do that? What if you hit me?'

'I didn't hit you.'

'Seriously, we have to work together to survive. That's the point of this test.'

'The point of this test?' she scoffs. 'Pfft, I don't give a shak about the point of this test, and I don't trust anyone. You least of all.'

'Whatever. Just help collect some firewood.'

After more arguments, we catch some fish and gather edible plants and fungi for dinner, along with enough timber from our surroundings to make a small fire.

With the base set, Alyx settles back against a boulder and chuckles. 'My work is done,' she says with a smug expression. 'Your turn now. I wanna see how you're gunna start that.'

The fact she thinks this will be an arduous task gives me a pang of satisfaction as I pull the fire bracelet from its place of concealment. Alyx sits up and watches with a raised eyebrow while I strike the ends twice, shooting forth sparks into the kindling and igniting the fire.

'Now isn't that a thing? How is it you've got that?' Alyx asks.

I shrug.

'No matter,' she says, snatching it from my hands. 'Always wanted a fire bracelet, but difficult to get from what Mother says.'

'It's mine,' I yell, trying to snatch it back. 'Sera gave it to me for my namedawn.'

'Don't care. It's mine now,' she says, dropping it into her pocket. 'Who's Sera? Don't answer. I don't care about that either. Fix my spear while you're at it.'

The sun sheds its final beams of light over the forest, and we seek a suitable tree to hold us both for the night. Climbing a tree without equipment is difficult, but climbing while chained to another contemptuous person is damn near impossible. It takes some time, but we manage it without a rope, and rubbing my aching shoulder, I prepare for a hard night's sleep.

In the early dawn of the second day, we drink our fill of the freshwater and trudge on, spears in hand, toward the sunrise.

As the day progresses, mountainous landscapes flatten out into dead forests, highlighted with random patches of green. None of it, however, provides a sufficient source of drinking water, leaving us parched and sluggish. Alyx lacks her usual energy, only tugging the chain a few times before giving up. At least she's more compliant, follows directions and doesn't complain while I dirty my hands foraging for something edible for dinner.

By day's end, we've said little to each other, only looking forward to relaxing our weary limbs.

Night creeps in, casting a darkening shadow over the forest like a blanket being drawn across the sky. It forces us to abandon our search for more food and water and find another tree for the night. There, we share the meagre collection of gritty, uncooked vegetables, and I endure Alyx's futile complaints about how tasteless they are. Eventually, she gives up, and I relish in the soothing sounds of the forest.

'Did you hear that?' Alyx asks, suddenly breaking the silence.

'What?'

'I thought I heard people talking.'

The cool breeze shifts, carrying the laughter and raised voices of people amusing themselves in the distance.

'Raiders,' Alyx says. 'Gotta be. And they're bound to have some food and water.'

'Water, maybe, but food—ahh…'

'Don't care. I'm thirsty.' She dismounts the tree and drags me along.

Nursing the chain to reduce its noise, I follow her footsteps toward the raiders gathered around their roaring fire. Judging by how this lot is carrying on, stumbling around, spilling their drinks and shouting their stories of might and conquest, it becomes apparent stealth may have been unnecessary.

Scattered around the camp are packs haphazardly strewn, with bedrolls dumped in random locations and a canvas sheet flapping between two trees as though only half erected.

In some strange way, I envy those raiders, cavorting like they don't have a care in the world. Here I am, chained to a psychopathic nimwit, who would sooner cross a room full of venomous snacas to put a knife through me than say a kind word.

'Come on.' Alyx tugs at the chain. 'We can steal some water while they're not look'n.'

We have to find it first.

Like a compliant little canis pup, Alyx drags me along, shuffling closer to the camp, hoping her single-minded decision doesn't get us captured.

'I'm surprised I heard the seven of them before I could smell them,' Alyx whispers, waving her free hand in front of her nose.

'Seven? No, there'll be eight. Look for the last—'

A figure lurches out of the darkness, startling us, and I yank hard on the chain to silence the rattle against the ground. Alyx loses balance and falls to her hands.

'Quiet,' I whisper into her ear. Even in the dark, I know she's giving me that icy glare she does so well.

Holding my breath, I raise my spear, its tip hovering chest height to the man who's unaware of its presence.

He's gotta be twice my size and reeks of truck fuel and the garbage chute back home. He stops at a log just beyond the end of my shale-tipped spear and, swaying, fumbles with something in the front of his pants.

Panicked, I thrust my weapon upward and into his ribcage. He lets out a haunting gasp and snatches the wooden shaft from my hands, tearing it from his chest. If he hadn't seen me before, he has now.

Fury glistening in his eyes, he stumbles forward and raises the spear.

Fearing he'll use it on me, my muscles seize up. The raider sways as though drunk, then drops the spear and falls to his knees, clutching at the bleeding wound in his chest. His breath wheezes and his leathery face contorts in obvious pain. He tries to call out…

Alyx kicks him in the head—I hadn't even noticed her stand—and he falls to the dirt.

He lies there, gasping like a fish out of water.

In a moment of mercy, I draw a crude, handmade knife from his belt. 'May you find more peace on the other side than you did in life,' I whisper to him as I push his knife deep into his chest.

The raider's eyes widen, and with one final exhale, death claims him.

'Why were you so nice to him?' Alyx asks, unimpressed as she pats the body down. She takes his pistol and belt and fastens them around her waist.

'Everyone deserves kindness, even raiders.'

'Ugh, puke,' Alyx says, thrusting the shaft of her spear into my hand. 'Here, I'm done with this shak.'

'Hey, D'Tauro,' a voice yells from the campfire. 'Stop bendn' them small trees, or done you caught your coq in your pants again.'

The rest of the raiders crack up with laughter.

That lot are tanked.

'We need to move,' I stress. 'As soon as they find D'Tauro here, there going to come looking for us. I want to be gone when that happens.'

'No,' Alyx says with a stubborn finality. 'That's a perfect camping spot. It has shelter and resources.'

'And raiders, eight of them, well, seven now. I don't know about you, but I'm not keen on going up against seven armed raiders.'

'Don't worry,' Alyx says, cocking the pistol. 'I have this, and we've already knocked over one. Don't be such a wimp. Sometimes you have to take risks to get what you want.'

'Right, I prefer the options that keep me alive. And this, Alyx,' I say, pointing to the camp, 'is suicide.'

'Yoy, D'Tauro,' the same voice yells from the camp. 'Yo still there?'

They snigger again.

Alyx glares at me with a wicked grin, then lifts her head towards the camp. 'Ahh, yup,' she says in a deep, loud voice.

'What d'you do that for?' I hiss.

She returns an indifferent shrug.

The other raiders grab their weapons and disperse into the night.

'Shak!' I swear, and we run, keen to put as much distance between them and us before poor old D'Tauro's friends discover his body.

From close behind comes a harrowing scream.

Too late.

'Found D'Tauro!' yells a woman in a shrill voice. 'He's dead!'

We barely have time to take cover behind a fallen tree when she yells out again. 'That way. I dun caught some'n move over there.'

'I can't throw left-handed,' I whisper-shout, passing the spear back to Alyx. 'You throw it.'

With a reluctant huff, she grabs it, whips her arm back and sends the spear hurtling through the night, like a silent missile piercing the female raider's rustic armour and sending her into a screaming fit.

Amid frenzied shouts and shrieks from the woman, we turn to make our escape. From out of the blackness, a hand grabs my arm, yanking me sideways and the unexpected change in direction pulls Alyx from her feet.

In the flickering light from the raiders' fire, my captor's grizzled, scar-ridden face is contorted in a grimace of rotting, clenched teeth. 'Gotcha little scrag,' he says, with breath more putrid than all of D'Tauro. 'You's gonna pay for whatcha done to D'Tauro and M'Shaksa.'

While he drags me toward the camp, Alyx frantically sifts through the knee-high grass. The chain snaps taut. I stifle a groan at the pain in my arm as Alyx is pulled along behind. She keeps to the shadows and out of the raider's sight.

'Oi, got 'er!' the raider announces, pulling me toward the circle of light.

It could have been the heavy beating of my heart against my ribs or a ground tremor, but then the vibrations underfoot continue to build.

The vibrations turn to rumbles, and the rumbling intensifies.

Possibly startled by the sudden seismic development, the raider loosens his grip on my arm and turns to face the noise. 'What's that–'

From the scrub, an enormous four-legged shadow with sharp, upward-pointing tusks barrels towards us, taking my captor clean off his feet and continuing unhindered like a battering ram past the fire.

Without hesitation, Alyx and I bolt for the nearest sturdiest tree, and with cooperation I didn't think we were capable of, scale it in a matter of midecs.

Now that two metas of tree trunk separate us from the ground, all we can do is watch five more shadowy figures charge in with their bloody intent.

In staggered succession, they flatten vegetation and stampede the camp. At least the raiders have lost interest in us now.

The wounded woman attempts to stand, and her screams turn from pain to terror.

Six muzzle flashes strobe through the trees, then five and four. The sounder of boarts makes light work of the raiders who, armed only with pistols and knives, don't stand a chance.

'That was brutal,' Alyx shrieks with delight as a young boart gores the last of the unfortunate raiders.

I turn on her with fury, not unlike the boarts'. 'That was too close. You almost got us killed!'

'But I didn't, did I? Besides, I'm not the one who got captured,' she accuses.

'You're the one with the pistol. You could have shot the guy.'

'*Had* a pistol. I dropped the fraking thing when you yanked my arm.'

'That wasn't my fault. It's just as well the boarts showed up. If it weren't for them, we would have been on the menu tonight.'

'You're seriously thanking the boarts?'

'Well, didn't you see how efficiently they slaughtered those raiders? You've got to admire that raw power,' I say, trying to diffuse the argument.

The way the animals carry on, with their snorts, scuffles and messy eating, there seems little difference between them and the raiders.

A smaller animal forced away from feeding approaches our tree, its beady eyes glaring up with the patience of a rock. It reminds me of my old friend Chompers, the outcast of the group. It stands guard at the base of our tree while its friends wreak havoc on the camp. At least he does until another comes bolting from the camp, squealing in panic and towing a flaming piece of canvas along behind.

The boart sounder scatters, and the forest has just fallen silent when Alyx moves forward and peers through the branches. 'I want to go down there,' she says impatiently.

'Why? Can't it wait until morning?'

'I want water and food, and the boarts have gone.'

'So do I, but down there, it's still dangerous. If the boarts come back, we,' I hold up the chain, 'are not fast enough to outrun them.'

'If you don't come, I'm going to drag you down,' Alyx threatens, and the moment she lowers herself off the branch, movement below has her scurrying back to safety. A large, boart-shaped shadow meanders past as if to remind us they're still watching.

'They're nocturnal and have much better eyesight than us in the dark,' I say, unimpressed Alyx needed reminding.

'Fine,' she huffs, settling herself back on the branch beside me. 'I don't want to go down just yet, anyway.'

I thought you'd change your mind.

Sleep doesn't come easy.

17 THE LOOMING STORM

'I'll have the Kah-Pow special thanks, Islay,' Sage said, handing back the menu to the server.

'Kah-Pow!' his daughter blurted, bouncing with delight on his lap. It was the name of the quaint café at which Sage, with his family, had stopped to spend breakfast. Little Averyx was happily playing with a menu and had become fascinated by its colourful cover, which had a big red splat and the word 'Kah-Pow!' plastered in its centre.

Islay laughed. 'Very good!'

Islay, the café's owner, was a delightfully perky, middle-aged woman whom, Sage mused, could never be unhappy. She always called him 'Ave'. Then again, she called everyone that.

'She's getting to become quite the avid reader, aren't you, Averyx?' Sage said, bouncing her on his knee.

Averyx giggled.

'How old are you now?' Islay asked.

'Four,' Averyx replied, holding up three stubby little fingers.

'We might need to work on your counting, though,' Sage said.

'Very good try, anyway. Can I get anything for you and the little one, Ave?' Islay said, directing the question to Jaylyn, seated across from Sage at the small, circular, reconstituted metal table.

Sage observed his wife cradling their youngest daughter Kiera while she perused the menu, admiring how the morning sunlight shone off her long, light brown hair, making it appear golden.

'I'll have the same,' she eventually said, handing the menu back to Islay. 'And a flat-white kahwah with sweetener, thanks.'

'Your usual, too, Ave?' she asked Sage.

He nodded. 'You know me so well,' Sage replied, earning him a speculative look from his wife.

'Part of the service, Ave.' She collected the menus and left Sage and his family to their own company once more.

'This is nice,' Jaylyn said, lifting her face to the warm sun. 'It's not often you get a day off to spend with us.'

Sage adjusted his scarf and rolled up the sleeves of his plain blue shirt to feel the sun's warmth on his skin. 'I know, but I'm here now.'

'You know, Jaxson,' Jaylyn said, projecting her voice to the man sitting at a neighbouring table. 'There's plenty of room here. Why don't you come sit with us?'

Jaxson glanced up. Like Sage, he was wearing casual clothes and a short-brimmed hat but still had the appearance of a canis ready to leap into action at any moment.

'Are you sure?' he directed the question to Sage.

'Of course, bro, plenty of room.' He pulled out a chair and allowed Jaxson to sit.

'Hey,' Averyx said to him as he sat.

'Hey, squirmy,' Jaxon replied, scruffing her shoulder-length blonde hair. 'You're growing up fast.'

'You're telling me,' Sage said. 'Just the other day, Kiera called me Dadda, and this one can write her name almost perfectly.'

'Ohh, that's awesome,' Jaxson said, earning him a grin from Averyx nearly as broad as her face. 'What's that?' Jaxson then asked, pointing to a folder Sage had hidden beneath a menu at the edge of the table.

'No, you didn't,' Jaylyn protested. 'It's your day off. No work. You promised.'

'I know,' he replied sullenly. 'There are just some things I have to keep an eye on.'

'You know, you need to relax,' she said, almost pleading. She was right, though. Sage was sitting stiffly in his chair and had not given himself time to just be in the moment. Jaylyn held out her hand, and with a sigh, he pulled out the black folder and passed it over. 'Enjoy your time with your family. Work can wait a day.'

While Averyx climbed back to her chair beside him, Sage's gaze drifted to the street. From his sunny position at their outside table, he could watch the people going about their business, disappearing into shops and side streets, carrying on with whatever errand had brought them there. It was a simple pleasure he used to enjoy. Lately, though, he'd been too preoccupied to bother.

'You know,' Sage said, after a while, 'there's a reason I just don't sit and watch anymore.'

'Why's that, babe?' Jaylyn asked with concern.

'It reminds me how fast things are changing.'

Just then, a woman and a boy aged about ten made a beeline for Sage. Under the table, Jaxson discretely covered his pistol with his hand but relaxed when she pulled out a camera.

The boy tugged at the woman's sleeve. 'See, I told you it was him.'

'Morn, Surprime, sir. Sorry to bother you, but would you mind if my son and I have a photo with you? We're big fans of yours.'

Sage glanced at his wife and Jaxson, then nodded. 'Not at all,' he replied, standing so the two could stand with him.

The woman handed Jaxson her camera and gave their biggest smiles for the picture.

'Thank you so much, Surprime. We will treasure this picture always.'

As the two walked away, the boy waved at him with a massive smile. Sage couldn't help but smile in return.

'Do you know who those people were?' he asked Jaxson as they disappeared down the street.

'No, I thought you did.'

Sage sighed again, and his smile vanished. 'See what I mean. Things are moving so fast. It feels like only yesterday, I was holding a newborn babe in my arms. So precious and small. Now, look at her. Averyx is always running around helping and looking after her baby sister. I can't keep up.'

Jaxson laughed. 'Don't be so hard on yourself, man. Look at them, they're fine. This is good. Progress is good. I'll tell you what, come over to my place tonight. I'm tapping my latest brew, and I could use the company. We can drink to progress and lost time together—with the wife's permission, of course.' That last bit, it appeared to Sage, Jaxson had added almost as an afterthought, giving Jaylyn a pleading look as though she were about to scold him for not asking her first.

Sage chuckled. 'I don't know.'

'C'mon, bro. It'll be great.'

'I have no issue with it,' Jaylyn said, putting Sage more at ease. 'Babe, all this time around us girls, I think you could use some male company. Just for the life of me, don't overdo it. The last thing we need is The Hope Chronicle headlining with; "Surprime felled by Jaxson's jungle juice".'

'Ha, ha,' Jaxson laughed. 'I prefer to call it "artisanal ale".' He leaned in closer to Sage with a cheeky smirk. 'I don't mean to brag, but I reckon I've got it. Between you and me, this could just be the best brew in Hope.'

'That says a lot after your last batch. That nearly blew my head clean off.'

'Even more reason to come test it with me.' He elbowed Sage in the ribs. 'What do you say?'

'Here we go, Ave,' Islay said, emerging by the table bearing plates of steaming food. 'Two Kah-Pow specials and kahwahs.'

The food looked wonderful, but it was the delectable aroma of kahwah that filled Sage's senses. He lifted the cup, ready to take a sip, when a slow-moving truck rumbled along the street before him, the enormous sign running down its side catching his attention. It read:

Gigantic moon-sized event
Starts in 5 days
Gathering in Sempro Park, fifty decs before sunset
Sponsored by LunaTec.

'Did you see that?' Sage asked no one in particular.

'What's a "moon-sized" event?' Jaylyn asked.

'I don't know,' Sage replied, 'but I have to find out. I'm sorry, Islay, but can I please have this to go?'

'But Sage…?' Jaylyn pleaded.

Clutching his boxed breakfast, Sage hurried after the truck.

He entered Sempro Park to find the truck parked on the grass. Despite his purpose, he briefly paid his respects to the life-sized bronze statue of Gaius, then continued toward the two men standing on the back of a flatbed truck who were busily unloading scaffolding onto the manicured lawn.

'Ahh, excuse me,' Sage called out as he stormed towards them, cringing at the tyre tracks in the otherwise perfect turf.

The two wore jumpsuits emblazoned with LT logos on their backs. Surprime or not, it didn't matter. They finished up what they were doing and tossed a heavy timber plank onto the grass before facing Sage.

Eyes blazing, Sage yelled at the men. 'What's going on here?'

'What do you mean by that, then?' one man responded.

'This!' Sage stabbed a finger at the truck, scaffold and the damaged lawn. He'd almost forgotten he was holding his kahwah with that hand, and it sloshed all over the place as he gesticulated.

'Look, mate, we were told to come to this park, put the stage together and come back, that's all.' He then pulled a card from his breast pocket, leaned over and placed it on top of the box in Sage's hand. 'Any questions, speak to them.'

'Hey!' Sage retorted. 'Just who do you think you're talking to?'

'Don't care, mate. We're on the clock.' He pointed at the card he'd given Sage. 'Take it up with them.'

The second worker looked at the first, and they promptly went back to what they were doing, ignoring the enraged Surprime.

Conrad startled as Sage thundered through the door. 'Isn't this your day off?' he asked cautiously.

Sage grumbled, 'Nice of you to notice. Contact LunaTec. I need Cristal here and call a ministerial meeting. I'll be in my office, eating my cold breakfast.'

Four days later, the ministry assembled in the chambers, all verbalising their thoughts on the happenings in Sempro Park.

Orian entered the hall and took her seat at the head of the room. 'Surprime Solon, it seems we're missing Ms Spriggs and Defence Minister Wyrm.'

'Esteemed Chairperson Gracyn,' Conrad replied, standing in the wings. 'The Admirable Minister Wyrm and guest, Attaché Spriggs, have been called and should be with us shortly. The Admirable Minister Kinton, however, sends his apologies. Aside from him, we have a full house.'

The room fell silent when the door burst open, and Artimus stormed in, dropping into his chair. Cristal slipped in through the gap behind him, reading papers in her grip, and meandered to her seat. Orian glared at her while she tapped the sheets together on the large table and dropped them into a folio, then, as though unperturbed by the whole ministry waiting for her, took her seat.

Sage stood, adjusted his red ministerial robes and spoke up. 'Four days ago, I was happily enjoying breakfast with my family when a truck filled with scaffolding passed me by. I found it in Sempro Park, where it had destroyed a garden bed and the manicured lawn. It appears they were erecting a stage of some sort. You wouldn't happen to know anything about that, would you, Ms Spriggs?'

'Ah, well,' Cristal replied, 'LunaTec has a thing on tomorrow, and we would like everyone to attend.'

'I can see that,' Sage said dryly. 'I called you here four days ago to explain yourself.'

'We've been busy,' she shrugged. 'As you can understand.'

'That is not the situation at hand,' Sage retorted. 'Please tell us why there is now a stage in the middle of the Gaius Sempro memorial park.'

'LunaTec will pay for the damages,' she replied unapologetically.

'The funds aren't the issue here,' Sage yelled, a little more forcefully than he'd intended, and he could only imagine his face was turning as red as his robes. 'You can't just host an event anywhere you wish. There are protocols.'

'Like what?' Cristal asked.

'Conrad, would you please?' Sage said, directing the attention of the room to his very nervous assistant.

Conrad cleared his throat and recited notes from the paper in his hands. 'Events are not permitted on public land without; lodgement of form one-two-seven F: *intent to use public property for event*, form one-two-seven G: *intent to host on public property*, form number—'

Before he could finish, Cristal removed a stack of papers from her folio and slapped them on the table in front of Conrad, making the young man jump. 'We trust you'll find these sufficient,' Cristal said with a smirk. 'LunaTec will abide by your requirements, however bureaucratic they may be. The event must, and will, go on.'

'Yet you chose not to discuss this with us first?' Sage said.

'No, why should we?'

'Because this is a matter of public interest, that's why. What's this all about anyway, and why the secrecy? Tell us, Ms Spriggs, what's so important LunaTec feels it necessary to violate our sacred memorial park?'

Cristal crossed her arms and appeared to choose her next words carefully. 'That is a matter of confidence. Besides, where's the fun in that?' she winked at Sage as if to tease him. She must already suspect how furious this whole situation had made him. For four days, Sage had tried every avenue to get in touch with LunaTec, and for four long nights, Sage tossed and turned, worried that LunaTec was planning something horrible. Now, she sat across from him, smiling sweetly as though it were nothing, and he'd called the meeting to discuss the weather.

'If you must know, Surprime,' she sighed, 'it will free up much-needed space in the LunaTec facility. The Gaius Sempro memorial park is in the ideal location. It has the necessary space and plenty of prime vantage spots. Rest assured, LunaTec promises something spectacular. Consider it a gift to the people of Hope for their graciousness and courtesy. No doubt it will boost morale and prove even through funding and supply cuts, going against the contract signed by Gaius's hand eight cycles ago, LunaTec is still operational.'

Sage stood. 'The Hope government cannot sustain the resources LunaTec has increasingly been demanding. But we're not here to defend Hope or its people. We're here to find out what LunaTec is planning.'

'LunaTec regrets any damage caused to Hope public property and has already agreed to recompense you for that. The hospital repairs are nearing completion, are they not? As for the information you seek, we cannot provide further details at this time.'

'Why did I expect you to say that?' Sage raged, trying and failing to maintain his calm. 'Over the cycles, you have been the envoy between Hope and LunaTec, but I still think you haven't been as forthcoming with information as you could be. You disappear for nearly two whole treys—this is the first we've even seen of you lately. You refuse our contact, deflect our questions and no longer attend ministry meetings.' He slammed his palms on the table. 'It's about time you come clean with us. What have you been up to? What are you hiding?'

'Sorry you feel that way, Surprime,' she said, calmly collecting her belongings and rising from her seat, 'but work is work, and messages must be passed along. We must not delay, so, if you don't mind, the clock is ticking, and there is still much work to do.' And with no further comment, Cristal strode from the chambers, leaving Sage glaring at her like the monsoonal weather front that was brewing over Hope.

18 BONDED part 2

It's the third morning of our retched test, and I'm surprised I've made it this far. Whoever said throwing two enemies together to make them resolve their differences was a good idea has obviously never met Alyx. If it weren't for the dehydration, hunger and exhaustion, I'm fairly certain we would've killed each other by now. Thinking about that does nothing for my mood, and it seems I'm not the only one feeling the oppression. The aves aren't out singing their usual raucous wake-up tunes, and from the stifling humidity in the air, I think I know why. I take a quiet moment to lie on my branch with eyes closed to absorb the calmer sounds of the forest. Though the sun hasn't fully risen yet to distribute its warmth, my clothing clings to my skin with sticky discomfort—it's almost as if the air were any heavier, I'd be able to swim in it. The only consolation is the occasional cool breeze, which helps to relieve the stuffiness. A subtle wind change carries the unmistakable smell of petrichor blended with smoke from the smouldering campfire.

That confirms my suspicions. Things are going to get very damp. And soon.

When I open my eyes, gritty as they are, the sky is thick with billowing clouds, and the scant sunlight discolours the surrounding landscape an eerie yellow-grey.

I give Alyx a nudge.

She huffs. 'What?'

'I think we better find cover,' I say, my words coming out as a raspy crackle.

'Water,' she groans. 'Need water. Check the camp first.'

It's been more than a day since I've had something decent to drink, and now my mouth feels as though I've been chewing on dry bark. The moment I try to sit, a pounding headache almost has me lying back down. I have to agree, but judging by this humidity, we should be careful what we ask for.

The raider camp resembles a scene from one of those blood and gore features Sera likes to watch on the VT. Torn fabric, stray clothing, a few crude handmade weapons, and the occasional gnawed body part are strewn everywhere. Good thing I hadn't eaten; the gruesome sight would've turned most stomachs inside out.

Amongst the debris is a bloodied pistol with its belt and holster. It lies near where the canvas sheet used to be and the gored remains of a raider. Seems this guy learned the hard way pistols don't work on boarts. Before Alyx notices, I snatch up the weapon and tie it around my waist.

The smashed crates offer more interesting salvage; ammunition, green metal canteens filled with liquid, and packs of what looks like food.

Hopefully, it's edible, knowing what raiders like to eat. No matter how hungry I am, I'm not eating that.

With the imminent storm rolling in over the mountains, we collect a canteen each and as much of the food and pistol ammo as we can stuff into a canvas bag.

'That's it,' I say, preparing to leave. 'We're done here.'

'Not yet,' Alyx replies, taking a pistol from a dismembered corpse. Without so much as a warning, she yanks the chain, and me with it, over to a boulder.

'No,' I moan, 'not again.'

'You can't say you're enjoying this.'

'Of course, I'm not. But I don't think you get the point of this exercise.'

'Frak the exercise. I want out of this thing.'

'Be careful, though.'

'Oh, be careful, though,' Alyx mimics in a tone dripping with overly melodramatic sarcasm.

She cocks the weapon, but before I can take cover, the slug ricochets, and I swear it just misses my head.

'Fraking fraksticks, Alyx! That was close!'

'What the frak is this chain made of?' Alyx growls, lining it up for another shot.

'No!' I yell, snatching the weapon from her grasp. 'That nearly hit me.'

'Hey!' she yells back.

'Face it, we're stuck like this. Deal with it.'

She drags me to my feet and sticks her face up close to mine. 'I'll say when I'm done, and I say I'm not done. The sooner I can get this piece of fraking shak off my wrist and be free of you, the better.' She then snatches back the pistol and shoves it into her holster.

'Okay, but I don't want to stick around for that storm. If it's alright with you, I'd like to move on.'

'Fine,' she huffs. 'First, pass me that water.'

I pass over one of the green metal canteens from the bag and take one for myself. Unscrewing the lid, I raise the rim to my lips. Before I can take a sip, Alyx spits out her mouthful, spraying me with a pungent liquid.

'What the frak?' she coughs. 'Whatever that is, that's NOT water.'

Although the odour irritates my sinuses, curiosity gets the better of me. The moment it touches my tongue, it burns like nothing else.

'Gaw blithey,' I cough, choking on the acrid liquid. 'That smells worse than that truck fuel Miss Wolaver drank.'

'Bad, huh?' Alyx says, taking another swig.

'Bad? This stuff is putrid.' I lift the canteen to empty the contents, but Alyx snatches it from my hand.

'Uh uh,' she says. 'Waste not. You don't want it…' and she takes another mouthful, almost drowning herself, guzzling it down. 'Wow!' she coughs, spitting up most of it on the ground. 'That *is* vile!'

I grab the canteen back and tip the horrible substance out.

'Whatdidya do that for?' Alyx protests. 'I'm drinking that.'

'What, so I have to lug your drunken arse around? No thanks. We need water, not whatever stuff that is. I suggest we look for some. There's gotta be some around here somewhere.'

'What about that?' Alyx says, pointing at a bucket by a pile of shattered crates. Inside, a carcass of some unfortunate animal floats on the surface.

'Shak. What did they drink other than this stuff?'

The wind picks up, and the impending storm reasserts its presence. I shove an empty canteen into Alyx's hand. 'We'll just have to hope it rains enough to fill these bottles.'

Sure enough, as we make our way out from the raider camp, a heavy curtain of grey descends upon us and blots out the nearby mountains.

Heavy raindrops fall, assaulting our surroundings like slugs. With only dead trees and scant foliage, the landscape beyond the destroyed raider camp offers little protection from the storm. At least we have water. After lifting the empty canteens to the sky, they fill in decs. Without even needing to stop, we open our mouths to quench our thirst and press on through the deluge.

Pools of water soon coalesce into a thick, shallow river of mud that consumes our boots and threatens to wash us away. The torrent gathers speed and depth, pushing us and a stream of flotsam along. But with the thick mud resisting our retreat, every step is slow going, and my thighs burn with the effort of fighting.

The muddy water rises ever higher.

Alyx slogs along behind.

'We've got to get to higher ground!' I yell over the maddening noise.

'That tree,' Alyx shouts back, pointing at a dark, twisted object just visible in the greyout ahead.

'Go!' I yell, pushing harder towards the solitary tree.

Almost there… *one more step.* Reaching out for a branch, my hand swipes air…

The chain snaps taut, and the ground suddenly disappears. For a moment, I'm weightless. In a gushing torrent of muddy water, debris and flailing limbs, the ground plummets downwards, flushing us along with it. There's no choice but to close my eyes and ride this out like the toboggan outside of Curio, but a lot wetter and without the toboggan. Memories of Sera "looking after that stick" come to mind. I ball up tight, bracing for the inevitable impact.

With an abrupt jolt, the plunge stops.

Searing pain rips through my shoulder. I would scream, but the raging waterfall fills my mouth with mud and muffles the sound. Between the nausea and my feet dangling precariously, I dare not open my eyes or even move.

Something smacks into my face, and I tentatively lift a hand to find out what it is. Alyx—she seems unresponsive to my probing touch, but at least she's still with me. With only her waist and a dangling hand to go by, I can't tell if she's unconscious or worse.

The chain slips on whatever is holding us in place. Pangs of adrenaline course through my body again, and with an agonising groan, I grab hold of the pistol belt around Alyx's waist. It's only a matter of time before…

The raging waterfall consumes us again, flushing us down a near-vertical slope. Under other circumstances, it may be enjoyable, but sharp rocks, hidden tree roots and submerged debris pulverise my body like a meat tenderiser. Combined with the agonising pain in my shoulder, it makes this a torturous ride.

Finally, the embankment slopes outwards, the ground softens, and we splash down into a deep pool. Our situation suddenly becomes so much worse.

After all these cycles, it's only now I regret having never learned to swim. I can shoot a slug with frightening accuracy at seven hundred metas. I can kill a person with a single strike, and I can survive for days in conditions like this with nothing but the clothes on my back, but here I am, drowning in a temporary body of water on the flats just outside of home.

Disorientation adds to the agony as I flail about in the murky floodwater.

Which way is up? I can't touch the bottom. Where is the bottom?

Kicking frantically at the stirred-up muck, I push toward the direction I hope is the surface while fighting against the chain pulling me under.

With a desperate gasp, I breach the surface.

It's so hard to breathe. Why can't I breathe?

The pelting rain splashing on the water's surface makes it near impossible to breathe, and it leaves me gasping. Fortunately, a dead snag pokes out of the water, and I grab hold of it for dear life. It gives me time to think and a chance to finally catch a breath.

Where's Alyx?

If I'm going to survive this, I need to reach her soon.

Something bobs in the water not far away, and as it drifts closer, I recognise its gaian form. Alyx lies facedown and is still not moving.

Her deadweight pulls me down like an anchor. Somehow, I've got to get us both to the bank before we drown. I grab hold of the chain and, conjuring all my strength, reel her in. Once she's within range, I turn her face up. With reluctance, I let go of my little refuge, clutch Alyx by her pistol belt and squint through the deluge to find the bank. Then, kicking my legs like I'd seen athletes do on the VT, try to swim for it.

Horribly exhausted, my muscles scream for relief. With another gulp of muddy water, my lungs burn from the resulting spluttering fits. I know the bank is close, but right now, with a mental fog verging on hypoxic blackout, it could be a million decametas away.

Almost there. Just a bit further.

One more reach. Another mouthful of choking water.

I'm not going to make it.

My head goes under.

Just when I think that's it, my knees hit something squishy.

Whatever it is, I can keep my head above water, and that fills me with instant relief. It takes a few attempts before I'm able to get a purchase on the soft ground, but I can stand and, with my good arm, drag Alyx up out of the water.

Her face is pale, her lips are blue, and she isn't breathing.

I never understood why an assassin would need to know resuscitation. Still, my only hope of getting home now rests on my ability to remember the technique.

Pump and breathe. Pump and breathe.

Lying as she is, Alyx no longer seems that threatening. After all the grief she has put me through, half of me wants to give up now. The other half—the better half—urges me to continue.

One more breath and Alyx splutters to life, coughing up water and clutching her chest.

'Are you okay?' I shout over the rain, extending my hand in an offer of support, but she slaps it away.

'Frak off,' she growls between coughs. 'What the frak? Why do you care?'

'Why are you always such a…? You drowned you ungrateful piece of shak. I just saved your life.'

'What? Is that why my chest hurts?'

'Yes. I only asked if you were okay because a midec ago, you weren't breathing. The least you could do is say thank you.'

That shut her up. It's not like Alyx to be lost for words, but I can tell from her frown and the way she opened and quickly closed her mouth, the reality she almost died has sunk in. I can only imagine what she's thinking right now as she wraps her arms around her knees and sits glaring at the flooded flats with a hazed expression. 'Thank you,' she says after a while, just loud enough to be audible over the rain.

'Damn straight,' I mutter, cradling my shoulder. Never have I experienced this much pain in all my life.

'What's wrong with you?' she asks, motioning with her chin.

'It's okay, I'll manage,' I wince.

'And it looks like you're doing that just fine too,' she says sarcastically, shuffling closer, and it's obvious my attempts to conceal the pain are transparent.

'If you must know then, it's my shoulder. I think it's dislocated.'

'Let me look at it,' she says, struggling to her knees, but I brush her off. The last thing I want right now is for her to touch me.

'No, I'm fine,' I insist, lifting my arm to dismiss her, but the shooting pain makes me yelp in agony.

'It's dislocated alright. I can fix that.'

'Don't touch me! Knowing you, I think I'll put up with the pain.'

'Suffer in your own time,' she says, reaching for my injured shoulder. 'I told you I can fix it, and I will.'

'You can fix this?'

'Yes,' she says, 'but if you want to be a baby, you can cry about it later.'

'Alright, fine.'

'Don't you go thinking this means we're friends. You go all gooey on me, and I'll dislocate it again.'

'Whatever just do it,' I concede and allow her to do what she needs to do. Even tearing my arm off seems better than how it's feeling right now.

'Sit still,' she says, sliding my jacket off my shoulder. As Alyx works, I'm surprised at the deftness of her touch. She massages the tender muscles with a gentle but firm hand until the pain subsides and the shoulder pops back into place.

'Done. How's that?' she asks.

Tentatively, I try rotating my shoulder a few times. It's tender, but nowhere near like it was before. 'Better. How d'you know how to do that?'

'How d'you know resuscitation?'

'Sera…'

'Yeah, well, you're not the only one who got taught "other useful skills". Mother taught me more than just combat, you know. I've dislocated joints often enough. She showed me how to reset them.'

'You call your guardian, Mother?'

'You don't? Anyway, use that belt to strap your arm. It's still going to hurt.'

'Thank—'

'There you go, being all fraking nice again. Don't be like that all the time.'

And just when I thought we were getting on like civilised people.

I give an audible groan. 'Why do you have to be such a…?'

'Bikkja? Go ahead, say it,' she yells. 'I want you to say it.'

'Why?'

'Do it. See if I fraking care. You don't know me, and I don't want to know you. This test is stupid. We're supposed to not trust each other. Yet, here they go, chaining us together like fraking convicts and leaving us out in this Progenitor-forsaken forest to die. Us? It doesn't make any fraking sense!'

'This isn't a test of trust, Alyx. It's a test of respect. To respect the things that threaten to drag us down. Just like instructor Blackthorn said, once we learn to respect one another, we are more likely to help each other and survive.'

'Well, that's just stupid fraking logic,' she retorts.

'She's *your* guardian.'

'And I'll tell her that too.'

'I'm sure you will,' I say, trying to imagine how that conversation would go down. 'Anyway, it doesn't matter. We're here now. No point crying about it. We just have to get it done.'

'Ugh,' Alyx huffs.

'Did you know our guardians were tethered together during their test?'

'So?' she yells as the torrential rain dials back, like a tap being turned off. 'Should I care?'

'Just thought you might want to know.'

Visibility returns, and the sun, almost forgotten, peeks from behind the clouds, releasing a bridge of multicoloured light extending in an arc towards the horizon. At its eastern end is our destination, Garret Gord.

'Oh, wow!' I exclaim, marvelling at the coloured display in the sky. 'I've never seen a waterarch like that before.'

'So,' Alyx says, 'where's the road?'

'Um, I think it's beneath that,' I point at the temporary lake stretching as far as it is wide, standing between us and home. Its shimmering surface covers the entire flats with no apparent means of getting around.

'Then how do we get home?' Alyx asks.

'It would appear we don't. At least not today. Here's hoping, by the morning, the water will have receded, and we'll be able to walk across.'

Alyx huffs again. 'The morning it is, then. I'm starving. Have we got any food left?'

'Oh, shak, where's the bag?' I swear, looking around for the bag we'd collected from the raider camp with the canteens and other items we'd collected. Seems it's become a casualty of the waterslide, and I'm getting a sick sense of history repeating.

Alyx glares at me, but her expression seems less harsh this time. Either I've become accustomed to it, or she's become accustomed to me.

'It's probably somewhere at the bottom of that,' I say, pointing at the lake. 'My pistol's gone too.'

'Shak,' she curses. After a moment, she reaches into a trouser pocket and pulls out a couple of sodden brown packets. 'Will these do?'

'What's that?' I ask, taking one from her. 'They look like protein bars. Where'd you get these?'

'The raider camp, duh.'

'Aren't you full of surprises?'

'Still doesn't make us friends, but it sure beats going to bed hearing your stomach gurgling.'

'Well, with any luck, you won't have to do that for much longer. The sooner we can get out of here, the better it'll be for both of us.'

Evening descends quickly, and after eating the soggy but edible food, we do our best to make our little island as comfortable as possible.

As I lie in my bed of heaped-up leaves, looking up at the twinkling stars in the now clear sky, a small but intense light streaks skyward from somewhere beyond the mountains.

'Did you see that?' I ask, pointing at the receding fireball rumbling upwards.

Alyx props herself up on an elbow to look at it. 'What the frak is that?'

'Dunno,' I reply, squinting to focus my vision, but it just looks like a fast-moving, yellow blur. 'Maybe it came from Hope?'

'Hope what?'

'It's a place. Apparently, a bunch of people live there. It's somewhere over that mountain range.'

'And you know that how?'

'I just do.'

'Whatever,' she snaps, lying back down. 'Now shut up. I want to sleep.'

'Suits me,' I mumble, rolling over and watching the streak ascend until it disappears to join the stars beyond the blue-black veil. I'd never really thought about what lay beyond that veil. I'd always imagined that's where the Progenitors lived, or at least went all those cycles ago when they disappeared. It's that last thought that sends me off into a deep but fitful sleep filled with fireballs and Progenitors. At least, in my dreams, there's no pain.

19 THE MAIN EVENT

Five days came and went painfully slowly for Artimus Wyrm. While most anticipated LunaTec's mysterious spectacle with delight and excitement, Artimus, who had been sequestered at the last moment to supervise LunaTec's preparations, had all but lost the last of what little enthusiasm he had. With the murder investigation finally making progress, overseeing security plans and managing crowd control with LunaTec's incorrigible event planner was the last thing Artimus wanted to be doing. Although he may have been physically present, in his mind, he was somewhere else, eagerly awaiting word on Hunter's progress.

The only thing keeping him from blowing the whole thing off was his need to discover what LunaTec were up to, why the secrecy and why he, of all people, had been kept in the dark about the providence of this so-called 'moon-sized event.' So, there he was, standing under a temporary marquee erected in the centre of Sempro Park, watching workers set up sound and lighting equipment. His demeanour soured as the rain set in, drenching everything in a sheet of water and turning the park into a soggy quagmire.

'There's the matter of crowd overflow from the park,' the event planner droned on while Artimus pretended to pay attention. 'If you look at these figures and compare it to the map...'

'Look,' Artimus said, his gruff appearance making the scrawny woman flinch as though he were going to pick her up and throw her. 'I don't care what you do. Don't bother me with these tedious details. Get to the point or get out of my face.'

'But sir—'

'Right,' Artimus said absentmindedly, his attention drifting to the happenings behind the stage. There, Cristal was conversing with a man Artimus had never seen before—a man who, by comparison, made himself feel tiny. This very tall, well-defined individual wore a huge oilskin coat and carried himself as though everything else was insignificant. He towered over Cristal's slender frame, appearing to be delivering instructions.

'Excuse me, work beckons,' Artimus said, pulling up the hood on his weatherproof coat and plunging into the rain, leaving the planner spluttering.

Cristal was focused on a clipboard, which she handed to the goliath of a man when Artimus approached.

'We carry on as planned.' His resonant voice carried through the rain as he walked away to talk with someone else.

'Minister,' she said, not bothering to introduce her friend.

'Who is that?' Artimus asked.

'Nobody you should concern yourself with. We are just about done here.'

'Are you really going to proceed with all this rain?'

'LunaTec's meteorologists aren't concerned. These types of storms rarely last long, and Hope is built on good soil. By this evening, everything should be good to go.'

'So, you're still not going to tell me what this is all about, then?' Artimus probed, expecting Cristal to at least tell him something.

'If the Surprime doesn't know all the details, what makes you think LunaTec will supply you with the information?'

'I'm head of security for this little shindig,' Artimus protested. 'If not courtesy, then how about, because it's my fraking job?'

'Relax, Minister. The event planner has all the details. Everything's under control,' Cristal said.

'Oh, for fraks sake,' Artimus swore. 'Last time someone said that the world ended…'

'Admiral…' an urgent voice came from behind, and Artimus lost interest in Cristal's void-filled answers.

A flustered HomeGuard soldier sprinted towards him with the unmistakable, armoured man, striding like an unstoppable machine behind.

'Apologies, sir, I couldn't stop him,' the officer protested.

'I would have liked to have seen you try,' Artimus mocked, comparing the immense size difference between the officer and Hunter—still, Artimus mused, that was nothing compared to Cristal's unnamed colleague. 'Dismissed, Cadet.'

With a puzzled look, the young soldier left Artimus with Hunter to return to his post across the sodden field. 'We're not done yet,' he said to Cristal, who shrugged and promptly went back to her own work.

'Here, I thought you'd forgotten about me.' Artimus said with a dry tone.

'I never forget,' Hunter replied as Artimus escorted him back to the marquee's shelter and out of earshot of potential eavesdroppers. 'You hired me to tail the mark. I did.'

The event planner had moved on elsewhere, leaving the marquee empty, and the rain created the perfect sound mask. Unfortunately, it also meant Artimus and Hunter had to speak over the rain to hear one another. 'And where did she lead you?' Artimus shouted.

'The Garret Mountains.'

Artimus's eyes widened with surprise. 'So there *is* something up there?'

'Something enough. Map?'

Artimus groaned inwardly at Hunter's often primitive grasp of conventional communication and stepped over to a portable table lined with sodden papers. He delaminated a map from the wad depicting Hope and the surrounding area, including a high terrain region marked as the Garret mountains.

'There,' Hunter pointed. 'There's a fortification on Lower-Garret.'

Artimus considered the map more closely. 'A fortification? And you're sure she went in there?'

Hunter nodded.

'That's Garret Flats. There's a small lake up there, but what else could there be that requires fortification? A hidden base, perhaps?'

Hunter grunted. 'Hidden, hardly. It's a box of wood posts with toy soldiers at the entrance,' Hunter said in his usual emotionless drone.

'Toy soldiers, huh? Can you describe them?'

'Brown, grey, white fatigues, with rifles and pistols. No obvious military training. Gotta be ex-raiders.'

'Do you want to take a breath?' Artimus said, half mocking the stone-faced man after hearing more than he usually does from him. 'I've seen a few "soldiers" matching that description recently at The Boart's Head. Ex-raiders, you say?'

Hunter grunted. 'A blind old man could get past them,' he said with a deadpan expression.

'Did you just make a joke?' Artimus said in astonishment. 'I didn't think you were capable of such a thing. Not anymore.'

Hunter blinked.

'Anyway,' Artimus said. 'So, we have a hidden fort patrolled by ex-raiders or a bunch of recruited incompetents. Interesting. And how long ago was this?'

'Three days. You have your information. The contract is complete.'

Artimus glared at him. Hunter didn't shift.

'What do you want now?' Artimus asked. 'It's so hard to read what you're thinking. Is it breaking any scientific laws for you to smile?' He paused, trying to read the block of stone of a man. 'Oh, that's right, I'll talk to the publican at The Rifle and Pistol. You sure you want that place? It's a little upmarket. Why not The Boart's Head? That's more your style.'

Hunter raised his finger at the admiral. 'Deal's a deal.'

The Boart's Head at the edge of town wasn't the most upmarket of establishments. Timber walls and thick post beams supporting high shelves filled with pre-war trinkets and technology nicely complemented mismatched furniture that looked as though it had been rescued from a junk heap. Combined with its constant smell of stale ale, sticky floorboards and atmospheric haze from the kitchen, Artimus described it as 'eclectic'. Despite its rough reputation, many gravitated there, for it served as a good, dark place to get a cold drink, an edible bite and some peace and quiet.

By the time Artimus arrived, the sky had darkened, and the usual evening chill had set in. Dressed in civilian clothing, he swaggered in, removed his weather coat and took a seat at the darker end of the L-shaped bar, taking care to leave a space between himself and two people wearing uniforms Hunter had described. He discreetly tried to listen in on their conversation. It didn't help that every time a patron opened the door, the sound of loud music echoed in from a distance, reminding Artimus there were other places he should be.

From the collection of empty tankards lined up on the tacky, wooden surface in front of them, the two uniformed men had been there a while and were already well and truly enjoying themselves on the establishment's weak but cheap house brew.

Artimus ordered a tankard for himself from the wiry bartender and moved in closer to listen.

'… her arse was so tight, ohh, I could've just bounc'd off of it,' the scruffy, blonde-haired one was saying, using broad hand movements to illustrate his lascivious description. 'I'd 've tapp'd that all night long. Just last tendawn, I'd three guardians and two day guards crawl bow-legg'd from me place.'

'Nasty,' his darker, brawnier companion said. 'Guardians, really? They let *you* frak them? Wow. That's bold. Which ones?'

'Dunno their names, but one of 'ems got a cane. Don't let that fool ya. She could turn a man's innards out wit' 'er pelvis alone. Man, she's wild.'

While the stranger continued his explicit description of his antics, Artimus cringed, trying to picture it in his mind. Even he had no idea how some of it was physically possible and figured the guy was not only 'punching above his weight' but also grossly exaggerating.

'I don't believe you,' the loudmouth's partner said, openly laughing in his companion's face, then taking another swig from his tankard.

'Why not?' the loudmouth boaster protested. 'It's true. I swears.'

'But *you*? What about the Patriarch? Does he know this shak is goin' down?'

'Whaddya think, Slugs? Ya think I'm that stupid? No, the frak he does not, and he ain't gonna know either. Ya say this to anyone, and I'll cut ya fat throat, ya got it?'

Artimus chuckled.

'Oi, scarface,' the boastful man shouted at Artimus, 'this is a private conversation. Butt out.'

Artimus chuckled again. 'And this is a public bar. The way you two were talking, I thought your conversation was public, too. If you want to have a private conversation, I suggest you tone it down.'

The larger of the two—Slugs—growled, edging toward Artimus as though he were ready to start something.

'I bet folks just go crazy over a uniform like that?' Artimus said casually but holding his tankard with a light grip, so he could 'use it' if necessary. Then the brawny man's boastful but level-headed companion stuck out his arm, and Slugs sat back down.

'Yer,' the blonde guy replied, 'wouldn't ya like to know.'

'I would, actually,' Artimus said, feigning interest.

'Alright, *friend*. Buy us a round. We'll tell you a story or two.'

The woman tending the bar kept an eye on the patrons in the establishment while Artimus flicked her three fingers for drinks. She responded as though she had left her enthusiasm at home.

'The name's Buck,' the blonde man said. 'An' this is Slugs. You're?'

'Crius,' Artimus replied without flinching.

'You local, Crius?' Buck said.

'Something like that. You?'

The two men sniggered. 'Something like that.'

'So, Crius,' Buck said, 'what happen'd to ya face? Half it's all rippled and shak.'

Artimus shifted uncomfortably on his stool, letting the comment slide. 'I'm not here to talk about that. Tell me your stories.'

Three metal tankards landed on the bar, spilling their foaming heads over the tacky surface. Artimus pulled out a handful of coins, slapped three down on the bar and pushed them over in payment.

Buck grinned broadly, reaching for a fresh tankard. 'Why so curious about the uniform?' he asked, taking a deep swig. 'Lookin' for some action? Cos, I can totally get why.'

'Maybe,' Artimus said.

'I hear some people dig scars,' Slugs added with a wink. 'And with a face like that… I'm sure you'd get plenty of takers.'

Artimus glared but kept his composure.

'Well, Crius,' Buck said, leaning in so close Artimus could smell the ale on his breath. 'Ya could join that lame HomeGuard, and be a pussy or ya could join us at the Gord, up in them mountains and babysit a bunch of kick-arse femmes. I hear they're looking for fresh meat—I mean recruits.'

To save Buck from a serious broken teeth problem, Artimus gripped his tankard hard until his knuckles went white and then chugged down its contents. *Ugh,* he groaned inwardly at the horridly bland flavour of the clearly watered-down ale. With mock satisfaction, he let out an 'AHHHH!' slamming the now empty, malformed vessel on the bar and wiping the foam from his upper lip.

Slugs and Buck reeled, picked up their drinks and exchanged glances before following Artimus to the bottom of their tankards.

Three more drinks replaced the empties.

'Tell me about these guardians then?' Artimus asked.

Several tankards later, Artimus's head swam. He'd lost count of the number of drinks he'd consumed. Buck and Slugs were just about passed out on the bar and having extracted more than he needed to know from the two inebriated Garret Gord guards, Artimus drained the contents of his last tankard. Then everything inside The Boart's Head shook, almost like the time the hospital had its unplanned redesign, shaking paraphernalia from the shelves and sending them crashing to the floor.

The door flung open, and someone yelled, 'everyone quick. LunaTec just shot something into the sky!'

Artimus grabbed his coat and stumbled from the bar. Outside, a thunderous roar emanated from LunaTec's mountain complex as a plume of flame, presumably from a rocket, streaked up and into the night sky. He held his hand up against the intense torch lighting the darkness, burning higher and higher. Below, four barely visible intense lines of light seemed to push the object through the clouds and into the upper atmosphere.

20 HOMECOMING

Sleeping on the ground feels strange for many reasons; well, not sleeping in a tree, period, but the terrain is soaking wet, and with my arm strapped tightly to my side, it makes for an uncomfortable rest. That night, I dreamt about Sera, impaled on a stick, floating on a raft in the middle of a giant, fast-flowing river. I'm clinging to the side, being dragged by the current over rapids and sharp rocks while a wave the size of a mountain pursues us. Seems I have a knack for getting us into trouble, even in my dreams.

'Jayne!' my dream yells.

'What?' Did I dream that or speak it aloud?

'Ready to go?'

I open my eyes to that early morning, where the landscape is in greyscale. 'Bit early. You want to go now?'

'That's a feral hike.' Alyx points her chin at the soggy flats. 'I'm not staying out here one midec longer than I have to.'

'Give me a moment, then. I need to get my head together first.'

Pools of remnant floodwater still cover the deeper parts of the flats, though it appears from the grasses swaying in the subtle breeze, most of the water has subsided. At least the area seems passable now. 'Let's aim for that rocky outcrop,' I suggest, pointing toward a hazy grey-brown area somewhere on the opposite side of the vast expanse of bog. 'It's the narrowest section and shouldn't take us too long to reach.'

'Okay, but we need to stop there to rest for a bit,' Alyx says, pointing at a small island somewhere in the middle. 'I don't think we'll make it all in one go.'

As we step out onto the flats, the ground is squishy underfoot, but it seems firm enough to hold our weight. We wade into the ankle-depth water with trepidation, dragging our feet low and testing the ground before stepping forward.

A few paces in, Alyx's foot disappears, and she sinks waist-deep into the mud, yanking the chain down with her. It jerks painfully at my strapped arm, and I almost go down too, but thankfully maintain balance enough to avoid joining her.

The surface of the hidden hole in which she is sinking looks just like the ground surrounding it, only it bobs and ripples when Alyx moves, sucking her in deeper.

'Jayne!' she cries, 'I'm sinking.'

'Stop flailing and give me your hand,' I yell back, crouching low and reaching out to her with my free arm.

Alyx reaches out, and our fingertips almost connect. I edge closer, taking utmost care not to fall into the floating death trap, but I can't reach far enough.

Readjusting my footing, I sit on the firmer ground to distribute my weight and rest my legs on either side of Alyx to give her something to hold onto. At least that stops her from sinking further.

'I can't move,' she complains. 'I'm stuck!'

'Hold still. Pass me your arms,' I shout, and with a howl, partly from the exertion and partly from the pain, I lean back to pull. Despite our attempts, the bog still won't let go.

'Stop, stop, STOP!' I cry after Alyx's counterweight almost pulls me in with her. 'My legs are sinking. They go under, and we're both sunk.'

'So how…?' Alyx says, her face filled with panic as the consuming mud rises to her chest.

'Can you move at all?'

'I'm not sure I want to.'

Our situation seems impossible. Of all the times I've been out with Sera, even with bloodthirsty raiders and boarts chasing us, this situation is way worse. Scouring my thoughts for solutions, I remember something Sera once said after she'd sent me to the box; *'When you can learn to channel your emotional energy, you have the power to overcome anything.'*

When she said it, it just sounded like Sera's usual cryptic gibberish—a convoluted way of instructing me how to defeat a larger opponent.

But how do you do that when your opponent is mud?

And then it clicks.

'Alyx, you need to relax,' I tell her calmly, hoping against hope I'm not about to make the situation worse. 'Close your eyes if you have to, but you can't fight it.'

From Alyx's puzzled look, she isn't convinced.

'Are you fraking kidding me?' she swears, shifting her grip on my thighs. The mud is slippery, and each time she wriggles, it creeps up ever higher.

'Do you see any other options?' I insist. 'You haven't got time to argue. You have to trust me.'

The instant I say the forbidden word, Alyx glares at me as though I'd gravely insulted her. Cycles of rule four being drilled into us, trust is not something taken or given lightly. And here, I've just given Alyx no choice but to break that rule.

'You frakin' what?' she hisses. 'I don't trust you. I never will. Don't ever say that to me again!'

'Alyx, look around you,' I snap back, and I'm losing my patience. Every midec Alyx hesitates, she sinks deeper, and my plan along with her. If I can't get her to follow a simple instruction, there's no way either of us are getting out of here alive. 'How do you suppose you're going to get out of this, huh? This petty—whatever it is—isn't going to save us. I'll chew off my own arm before I allow you to take me down with you. So, either shut up and listen or sink. Your choice.'

Alyx hesitates, and I can almost see cogs whirring in her mind. Animosity aside, she seems to surrender to the idea and, with obvious reluctance, relaxes the muscles in her arms.

'Now take three deep breaths,' I instruct.

Surprisingly, she follows without question. The effect is instantaneous—she stops sinking. Now all I have to do is get her to remain still. For that, I have to distract her.

'Do you have a visiontube?' I ask.

'What?' She says, opening her eyes to give me one of her famous glares.

'Just focus on my voice,' I try to assure her. 'It'll help you relax.'

She mutters a sceptical, 'uh-huh.'

'Alyx, just do it.'

'Yes, I have a VT,' she huffs. 'What's that got to do with—'

'Great. What's your favourite show?'

'Jayne, we don't have time for this. I'm sinking in an abominable bog, and all you can think about is your damn visiontube.'

'Answer the question.'

She sighs again. 'I do like *The Legion,*' she replies after thinking about it for a moment. 'But…?'

'Okay, close your eyes and wrap your arms around me. Picture yourself as a contestant on the show.'

Alyx closes her eyes, then cautiously reaches forward and clutches hold of my body.

'You're nimble on your feet,' I continue, 'effortlessly navigating the course with your team around you. Fresh with the thrill of winning a major challenge, you've come to the semi-final.'

While I tell the story, Alyx relaxes, and gradually, I lean back to pull her out.

'Picture yourself at the starting line. You leap the first wall and take to the climbing ropes. They're high, but you're strong, fast, and scramble up them like a genet.'

'Damn right,' Alyx grins.

I continue pulling. 'You come to the overhead climb. It's an intricate, moving contraption, but you've trained for this—you know your abilities. One leap and you clutch hold of the bar. Bar after twisted bar, you make your way across to the other side.'

Alyx relaxes more.

I keep pulling. 'Next obstacle is the ice plunge. It's steep and freezing cold, but your team is there beckoning you on. You scramble over the obstacles and make it to the other side with only midecs to spare on the clock. Your teammate reaches forward, grabs you under the arm and pulls you to safety.'

And, like a stopper from a bottle, Alyx slides free. Together, we collapse in a muddy heap on sturdier ground.

My stomach rumbles, and my head spins from the exertion, reminding me the only thing I've eaten recently were Alyx's pilfered rations.

At least Alyx is out of immediate danger.

By now, my shoulder burns like a boart has tried to gnaw it off, and I lie waiting for my head to stop spinning.

Alyx climbs to her feet, shaking off the mud dropping in clumps from her body. 'That's it!' she rages. 'I've had it with this chain, I've had it with this test, and I've had it with you! Four days I've had to endure this shak. I've had it. *If* we survive this, I never want to see your fraking face again!'

'The feeling's mutual,' I grumble as I sit and watch with amusement while she throws her little tantrum. 'Do you honestly think I'm enjoying this? You know, this entire time, you've been less than civil. Things would have been a lot easier if you weren't such a coq.'

'Oh, so you think this is *my* fault?' Alyx snaps back. 'You think I'm the one who got us in that bog, is that it?'

'Did I say that? No. But I got you out, didn't I? And that's not the only time I saved your ungrateful arse.'

'Ungrateful? You wanna talk about gratitude? *You* should be *grateful* I didn't decide to cut off your arm and go on my own,' Alyx snaps.

'Charming, Alyx. Like you'd get very far, anyway. How long would you have lasted without my help, I wonder?'

'Alright then, *Miss Ingenuity*, get us out of this mess.'

'Okay,' I say sarcastically. 'Since you asked, I have an idea.'

'You fraking what?'

'Have you got a knife?'

She stares at me with a look of incredulity, and with all the melodrama I expect of Alyx, she reaches into her boot and pulls out a big-bladed hunting knife.

'This do?' She presents it with a smug grin.

'What the?' I exclaim, glaring at it. 'You've had that there this whole time?'

'Yeah, so?'

'Well, at least that's something we didn't lose in the flood. Now can you follow instructions…?'

Alyx retorts with her usual nasty glare and is about to hand me the knife, but I glance down at my strapped arm. 'Ugh, huh. You've got to do this.'

'Okay,' she says, complete with attitude. 'What have I got to do?'

'Cut branches off those saplings,' I instruct her, pointing at a patch of green shoots poking up out of the mud at the bog's edge. 'We need as much of the younger, more fibrous parts as we can get.'

Alyx follows the instructions without too much drama, and after she's cut off enough branches, I demonstrate the weaving technique. Soon, we have four club-shaped shoes, and I can only hope if they're good enough for snow, they should work on thick, peat-covered mud too.

Alyx affixes long grass straps to tie them to our boots. They're not as sturdy as the ones Sera made, but with any luck, they should get us across.

'This better work,' Alyx says, trying out the shoes.

'Just go slow and steady and watch out for holes like the one you fell into. We'll be fine.'

One by one, we cautiously step out onto the bog, and it quickly becomes apparent that although the mud sticks to them, the roughly constructed shoes work almost as well as they did on snow.

It's slow going and takes most of the day to get across, stopping at Alyx's island for rest and repairs before moving on. The moment we step off the other side onto more solid ground, we collapse in fits of exhilaration and exhaustion-fuelled laughter.

I can't believe it worked, and while I still can't figure out how, we managed to survive.

'Look,' Alyx shouts, breaking me from my reverie. She points out two tiny figures emerging from the mist in the distance, almost where we were washed down the mountain.

As we strip off our constructed shoes, we watch with anticipation as the pair enter the bog. When it would appear they've seen us, they hasten their pace, picking their way with carefully placed steps. They seem to be doing fine—until they vanish.

That could have been us.

'Show's over,' Alyx says when they don't re-emerge. 'Let's go home.'

With reluctance, I pull my eyes away, and all I can think about now is Ilona. I can't imagine how she's managing with this or who she's been saddled with. I can only hope for her sake they're more cooperative than Alyx has been and that, in the name of the Progenitors, she wasn't one of the girls whose fate was sealed by the bog.

21 HANGOVER

Sitting in his ministerial office with the curtains drawn, Artimus nursed his throbbing head in one hand and a large tin mug of kahwah in the other. Only his lamp pulled down close to his desk provided lighting in the otherwise darkened room.

He took a sip of his drink, remembering how much he disliked the taste of kahwah—but knew it was good for hangovers—and examined the map on the desk before him.

So, that's where you're hiding? He thought to himself as he drew a circle with his red-tipped scribe around the flat mountain peak depicting Garret Gord.

If those idiot guards had any truth to their bragging, it shouldn't be too hard to find you.

The only problem now was how he was going to get there. Sitting beside the map was a report that had come in that morning. It stated that due to the recent downpour, the Rika river had burst its banks and had washed away the roads leading out of Hope. The city's engineers estimate it'll take days, even tendaws, to clear a path through, and that's just the roads they knew of. He moaned at the thought of yet another obstacle hampering his attempts to apprehend Gaius's killer.

'Big man!' Sage said, unexpectedly barging through Artimus's door in an explosive burst of energy, seeming oblivious to the admiral's current delicate state. It was the last thing he needed. 'You see the launch last night?'

'What do you think?' Artimus groaned, screwing up his face.

'The pre-show live music, skyfire and the fly-by of wingcraft, then the launch—it was spectacular. LunaTec really do know how to put on a spectacle.'

'You'll excuse me for being rude,' Artimus replied dryly. 'But I don't care.'

'And how's that different from normal?'

'*Some of us* had to work.'

'Work? You were supposed to be overseeing security at the event, but I don't recall seeing you there.'

Artimus groaned again.

'What was that monstrosity all about anyway?'

'You didn't know?'

'I knew as much as Spriggs knows how to speak truthfully. Which is about as much as Hunter knows how to speak at all. I lost interest around the same time as my boots filled with water.'

'Right, so you saw nothing then?'

'That's what I said.'

'It was a test launch for one of their rockets.'

Artimus involuntarily raised an eyebrow. 'Rockets? Since when does LunaTec have working rockets?'

'Since about yesterday, apparently. That piqued your interest now, didn't it?'

'Sage,' Artimus growled, trying to conceal that that little nugget of information had indeed piqued his interest. For the longest while, Artimus had been invested in space exploration, and his involvement in the fact was something he kept a closely guarded secret. Before the war, Artimus personally led the SGA military's covert space program but had since lost contact. He hadn't thought about it until now, hoping LunaTec would eventually provide the means to re-establish communication with his personnel—that's if they still existed. But to think LunaTec had been developing their own space-bound propulsion technology, even with the limited resources they apparently had, it gave him reason to be anxious. He groaned inwardly, careful not to let Sage see his concern. 'That's another problem I don't have time to deal with right now. In case you haven't noticed, I've got more pressing matters on my plate. I'll deal with LunaTec another time.'

'Man, is it stuffy in here?' Sage said, changing subjects, strutting behind Artimus, and throwing open the curtains and window, flooding the room with bright light.

Artimus hissed.

'There's something different about you this morn, Artimus,' he said. He was way too chirpy for Artimus's liking. 'I can't quite put my finger on it.'

Normally, Artimus could stomach Sage's overtly optimistic attitude, but this morning, it grated on his nerves like fingernails down a chalkboard. 'I'll ask you politely to not talk so loud.'

Sage moved in a little closer to take a whiff. 'Okay. Is it just me, or are you looking a bit greener than usual? For a start, you hate kahwah. Second, you smell like you bathed in Jaxson's keg. And it's not like you to be out of uniform.'

'At least I'm punctual.'

'Rough night?'

Artimus took another sip and then threw the remainder of his drink, mug included, out the open window. 'You could say that. On the upside, I've had a breakthrough on Gaius's case.'

'You have? And it involved ale?'

'The things I do for this job.'

'Last I checked, your position description said nothing about torturing your liver.'

Artimus sat back, crossing his arms. 'Commitment to the cause is a necessary evil, Sage. Anyway, I know where to find the killer. Do you want to know where?'

Sage shrugged. 'I respect the old man, but when is a case too stale for you?'

'In my eyes, it's not stale,' Artimus retorted. 'Do you want to know or not?'

'Alright, where?'

Artimus stabbed a finger at the map.

'The Garret mountains?' Sage asked, leaning over to see where Artimus was pointing.

'The place is called Garret Gord. According to Hunter, it's a hidden fort. And, you'll love this, it's a training complex for female assassins.'

'Right,' Sage snorted derisively. '*Female* assassins? Are you sure you didn't dream that? Or did your tin can friend tell you this?'

'Hunter played his part. But that last bit, about it being a training facility, I got that by, well, other means. You'd be surprised by the information you can get out of dimwits when you stroke their fragile egos and lubricate them with enough cheap ale.'

'Seems you lubricated yourself in the process,' Sage joked.

Artimus shrugged. 'The only problem now is how I'm going to get up there. My scouts reliably inform me the storm washed out the roads. We need Tryce to pull her finger out and get construction crews out there ASAP.'

'Wait a midec,' Sage said. 'If what you're saying about it being an assassin training camp is true, you're not going up there alone. Even when the roads are clear. I'm coming with you.'

'Respectfully, no,' Artimus said, looking Sage straight in the eye. 'It's a vespa nest. I'm not leading you, the Surprime, in there. Besides, this is *my* mission. HomeGuard *will* take care of it.'

Sage motioned to protest, but Artimus shut him down. 'Don't worry, though,' he added with a smirk. 'I'll find Gaius's killer, then finally, we'll be able to put the lid back on this box, once and for all. Oh, and Sage, when you leave, grab me some of that nice soup of the day, will you?'

22 INITIATION

Excerpt from Book of the Progenitors:

They called her Tide, the Progenitor of water and abundance. For untold cycles, her home had been a place called 'The Oasis', a lush, green paradise of fertile land and water of the purest kind. Those who shared The Oasis took her presence for granted and never gave back, insisting The Oasis was theirs to do with as they pleased. This made Tide angry, and she left.

The Oasis became barren. Crops faltered, then died. The people became concerned, wondering where Tide had gone and whether she would return, even blaming her for taking the water spirit with her. For ten cycles, they searched, but she was nowhere to be found. As the cycles passed and the surrounding desert consumed The Oasis, the people's food reserves withered, and so too did the people, leaving them to believe they had all but been abandoned.

Just when the people prepared to leave their homes, Tide returned. Bedraggled and weary, they looked upon their deity with mixed anger and relief. She simply raised her palms to the air and said, 'Fear not my people, for I have returned. I come bearing hope.' Then from her hands, poured forth water like the people had not seen in many cycles. She filled the lakes and the streams, the plants regrew, and the land became lush once more.

But Tide was not done. Struck with awe, the people listened as she stood before them and made her declaration. 'Though I may help you this day, the fate of this world is bound to you. This is a lesson I cannot teach. You allowed greed and gluttony to take hold and forgot that abundance is not guaranteed. Care for this world as I have, and abundance will be yours. Pillage it, and only ever take, and it will wither and die. Heed my warnings, else all my teachings will have been in vain.'

Eight cycles, I've lived at Garret Gord, and for eight cycles, I've studied hard, survived the rigorous training regimen, and endured tests that stretched my physical endurance, survival skills and combat capabilities to their very limits. Today is unlike any other day, for today, I face the final test: initiation.

With barely a cloud in the deep blue sky, Aster shines unhindered over the Gord. It's a stark contrast to the latest string of monsoonal downpours that flooded us and the rest of Jorth. But today, the fresh warm air kisses my face and toys with my ceremonial blue robes, and I am grateful for the reprieve. Perhaps it's a good omen. Who knows?

Sera, dressed in regal, black and gold-edged robes, provides silent escort to the other side of the Field, through the urban simulation, obstacle course and beyond the tree line, to the far end of the firing range; a place I've never been before. It's a long, anxious walk, causing what breakfast I could eat to churn over in my stomach like I've swallowed a pair of scrapping rodentia.

In quiet retrospection, I review the memories of my experiences here. It seems like only yesterday I stepped out of the back of that truck and learned rule four for the first time. Back then, everything was an ugly shade of grey and brown. Now, green grass has replaced the permafrost, the landscape is filled with vibrant colours of every shade and aves twitter in the trees, swooping from lush branches to catch insects. Even wearing a breathing mask is all but a memory, one I hope future generations won't ever have to endure.

Beyond a hedge wall of wild shrubs, the ground slopes lower towards the imposing fortified perimeter fence that towers overhead like a dense forest of branchless trees. At the lowest point of the dip, another hooded figure wearing robes similar to Sera's stands waiting beside what I can only describe as a metal door to some kind of concealed bunker. Ancient Progenitor-era runes are engraved into the strange door and its trapezoidal-shaped stone arch, but without any signs of degradation or rust, anyone would think they could have been built here this morning.

'Instructor Blackthorn,' I acknowledge when she pulls back her hood.

'Good morn, Jayne, Seraphin,' she gives a polite reply.

Sera also pulls back her hood, and the two guardians grasp each other by the forearm in greeting. 'Good morn, Vina.'

'Instructor Blackthorn,' Sera says, 'will read you the rite. This is as far as I go.'

Blackthorn lifts an aged copy of the *Book of the Progenitors,* opens it by a scarlet ribbon marking the page, and begins the recitation in an officious tone.

'Mighty Progenitors, wisdom everlasting,
We beseech thee.
Shall ye find thine tribute worthy,
Humble be thy plea.
May Aster shine to light thy journey,
Provide strength to shield from evil,
Where thy shall protect, may Gaia provide,
For once thy stone is cast,
And offered thyself as tribute,
Thare shall be no return.'

She pauses for a moment and looks up from the page. 'Guardian Seraphin MonLantry,' she addresses Sera directly, 'you have brought forth this Initiate to take the Rite of Passage. Do you declare that she is ready? That she has the knowledge, wisdom, skill and worth to face the final challenge and emerge victorious?'

'Yes, she does,' Sera replies, glancing in my direction so that I may catch the smile flash on her face.

Blackthorn turns to me. 'Initiate Ten, step forward and state your name.'

'Jayne Doe,' I reply.

Blackthorn acknowledges my response with a nod and continues. 'Jayne Doe, you have excelled in coming this far, demonstrating skills that will serve you well. Standing here this day, we give thanks to the mighty Progenitors for their blessing, guidance and strength. For it is here, during the Rite of Passage, your worth, mental aptitude and resolve will be tested. Succeed, and you, initiate Jayne Doe, will be indoctrinated into the Hildr operative guild's elite ranks. Do you accept this challenge?'

'Yes, but what will happen if I fail?'

'You won't come out,' Blackthorn replies with a blunt tone.

The weight of those words drops like a boulder delivered personally from Codan.

Sera reaches over and pulls me into a big hug. 'It's okay, Jayne,' she whispers into my ear. 'I have every confidence in you. Just remember what I said. Remember your studies, and you will succeed.'

Blackthorn presses on. 'Initiate Jayne Doe. Are you ready to accept your fate?'

What is *my worth? What's behind the door to warrant this kind of formality? I don't know.*

'I guess so, yes,' I reply nervously.

Blackthorn repeats herself. 'Initiate, are you ready to accept your fate?'

'Yes. Yes, I am.' This time I hope to sound a little more confident even though my heart is racing a million beats a midec, and I'm on the verge of passing out.

I have no idea why I'm so nervous. Surely, this can't be any worse than what I've endured already?

'Very well. Before you commence, we beseech the mighty Progenitors once more. Bow your head for the Rite Sanctification.'

Bowing my head, Blackthorn places a hand on my shoulder and reads from the book again.

'May Gotthard bestow upon you the confidence and skill to dominate any situation,
Xisnys, courage and constitution of will to persevere and never falter,
Codan, strength and fortitude to defeat any foe,
Martok, charisma and guile to rise to any challenge,
Tide, integrity and calm to choose the right path,
Aster, intelligence and wisdom to solve any problem,
And Anima, good health and synchronicity of body, mind and spirit to endure and recover swiftly.
So shall it be.'

'So shall it be,' I repeat, lifting my head. Blackthorn closes the book with a thud and tucks it under an arm. 'Weapons, tools and aids of any kind are prohibited inside the chamber,' she says. 'You must rely on your memory and skills alone. Remove your robes and shoes and present them to your guardian.'

Without my robes, in the shadow of this recess, the chilly morning breeze bites right through my flimsy, blue, loose-fitting clothing—a stark reminder the cold isn't done yet. Blackthorn pats me down to ensure I'm not concealing anything, then steps back and, with a theatrical wave of her hand, says, 'Guardian, open the chamber door.'

'See you on the other side,' Sera says, stepping forward to wave her hand over the centre of the door.

In response, the big metallic-looking door emits a whirring sound that radiates from within. And then, the panels separate at various odd angles, receding into the frame to reveal an unlit passageway.

'Progenitors be with you, Jayne,' Blackthorn says with an air of sincerity as I step barefoot over the threshold into the black.

Once I'm inside, the door closes behind, entombing me in total darkness.

It's just me now. If I'm going to find a way out, I first need to find the damn light switch.

The first thing I notice is the air. Though I have no idea how old this place is, I would expect it to be dank or stale. But it's fresh, probably cleaner than outside.

How can that be?

I step forward with trepidation on the smooth, stone floor. It illuminates underfoot, emitting a soft radiance that gradually brightens to the whitest hue I'd ever seen. As the trail of luminescent paving stones brightens, more of the passageway reveals itself, leading to another trapezoidal door several metas ahead, similar in architecture to the one I just passed through.

In parallel to the illuminated path, running at the base of the chamber's sloped walls are two black strips that seem to absorb all light, making them appear as dark as the passage was before the floor lit up.

The surface of the black strips ripple like the wind across a lake, but there is no wind here and the way the substance moves, it appears to be much thicker than water. These eerie black moats ignite in blue flame with a subtle whoosh, gently warming the air, adding brighter illumination to the corridor and highlighting the intricate decorations adorning its walls.

How I hadn't noticed the decorations before, I'll never know. Beautifully carved, gold-accented white frescos of the Progenitors line the walls' length. There's Xisnys breathing fire, dressed in her shining scaled dragon armour; Codan, all bulk and rippling muscles, holding a boulder aloft; and Gotthard, attired in long flowing robes, wielding lightning from his fingertips. Like everything else in this place, the likenesses of these mighty Antecedents bares no age.

The multi-dimensional images on the walls become easier to inspect in the brighter light, as though the air itself is illuminating them. They're so engaging and visually stunning that the images seem to leap off the walls. By the time I reach the doorway at the other end of the short corridor, perspiration beads on my forehead and runs down my back, and I have no idea how much time has passed. But there's still another wall, and I yearn to read it to uncover how the story ends. This heat, however, is oppressive, and I must move on.

As Sera did, I wave my hand in front of the door's centre, expecting it to open. It doesn't. I even try touching the door in various places and hitting it a few times. Despite all my efforts, it doesn't budge.

The door is intricate, that's for sure. I only wish I'd spent more time examining it than the frescos around the walls. So, while I bake in my own skin with salty sweat stinging my eyes, I frantically search for clues.

Inscribed around the trapezoidal frame are a set of runes from the ancient Gaia'Tan language. I've seen them before—if only I could recall their meaning.

Touch the hjatra and touch the key. That's what the phrase says.

'What is hjatra again, and what key? What key?' I say out loud in frustration. 'There is no key in here, and I was told I had everything I needed. Hjatra?'

By now, the room is stifling; it has to be near boiling in here, and I can't stop for the mesmerising story on the walls. With great effort, I resist their temptation and fix my eyes on the floor, following the glowing white path back to the entry again, scanning for something like a key while I struggle with the heat to remember my ancient languages. *There's no key here. Think!*

'Heart. Hjatra—touch the heart, touch the key. My heart?'

Staring at the door from afar, the only unique stone is a V-shaped stone set into the loadstone above the alcove spanning the top of the opening.

Approaching the door again with eyes fixed on it to keep me focused, I place a hand on my chest and leap for what must be the keystone with the other, slapping it with my fingertips.

'Ouch,' I groan from the pain in my still sore shoulder.

The door doesn't budge.

Damn, it's hot in here.

'Why is the door so high?' I shout, wiping sweat from my brow.

I change arms for the next jump, and this time, part of my palm touches the stone, but the passage remains sealed. 'What? Are you faulty?' I scream.

Placing my right hand on the centre of the door to steady myself, I leap once more. With a slap, my entire left palm touches the keystone, and I find myself sprawled onto the floor of the next room.

Fresh air envelopes me, and I lie for a moment on the cool stone floor to soothe my overheated body.

The realisation dawns.

Of course! Hjatra doesn't mean my *heart. It means the heart of the door. How could I be so stupid?*

Compared to the corridor, this room is chilly, and at approximately four by seven metas, by my guess, it's much larger. It's just as ornate, though. The most prominent feature here is a rectangular green marbled slab of stone positioned in the centre of the room. What's peculiar about this stone slab is it's floating, as if by magic, about a meta above my head.

I spend a good couple of decs examining the mysterious, gravity-defying stone slab. It doesn't move when I use it to stand, and when I'd had enough waving my arms around it to find out how it stays there, my attention falls to the detailed paintings adorning its surface. Unlike the previous room, I'm not mesmerised by them. Seems forces are going on here I'm not meant to understand, and quite frankly, I'm happy leaving it that way. Here, the images depict people holding fish, flowers and various other items, with some holding hands. And in its centre is a gold-rimmed, black chalice, sitting on a gold plinth.

Like the substance in the moat, the black cup doesn't reflect any light, making it hard to focus on its form. If it weren't for the gold rim, it would appear as though it were a flat silhouette. Beneath the gold rim are two tiny horizontal wavy lines also painted in gold.

Lifting it from its plinth, I marvel at its apparent lack of dimension, wondering what I'm supposed to do with it. As if by design, the sound of trickling water etches its way into my consciousness.

A fountain. I must have been too fixated on the table and the cup to hear it before.

The fountain is an intricate sculpture of the Progenitor Tide. With long flowing hair and clothing, her angelic likeness protrudes from one wall, pouring water from her upright palms into a fluted pool below.

Painted on the backs of each of her hands are the two wavy lines from the cup. The water flowing from her hands is so pure it's like crystal, allowing the brightly coloured mosaic fishes swimming near the bottom of the pool to be clearly visible.

When I wave a hand under the stream, the water passes straight through, like it's an apparition, and it's the same with the contents of the pool. The fish seem unfazed by this, though, even letting me touch them as they playfully swim by.

'If you're real, why isn't the water?'

Adorning the opposite wall is another sculpture of a Progenitor, although it's difficult to make out who this one's supposed to be. The statue's face is distorted, as though in motion, almost like the sculptor didn't know what to carve. The likeness holds an empty stone cup in clasped hands, not unlike the one I'm holding, and is bending over as though about to drink.

This room is some kind of puzzle, but how I'm supposed to solve it isn't abundantly clear.

Looking back at the people painted on the levitating table, it appears their poses form runes that repeat around its surface.

Those many nights spent reading over Gaia'Tan texts and learning passages from the *Book of the Progenitors* instead of watching *The Unattached* with Sera may not have been worthless after all. After translating the writing, six discrete words stand out:

Drink, Cup, Truth, Quench, Thirst, Deceit

'So, to drink from the cup of truth, first quench the thirst of deceit.'

What's that supposed to mean?

'The statue doesn't have a face. Who are you supposed to be?'

Martok was the only Progenitor who didn't have a distinct description. After all, he was the master of disguise. Seeing no one ever knew what he truly looked like, maybe this is him?

He did have one discerning feature, though—his lizard-shaped pendant. It's always depicted in images of him, and sure enough, there, carved around the neck of this statue, is a lizard-shaped pendant.

'So, you *are* Martok.'

Quench the thirst of deceit.

'Deception must be thirsty work. You thirsty, Martok?'

I must be losing it, as I'm now talking to statues. I wonder if insanity is part of the test?

Brushing the thought aside, I return to examining the cup. It's lighter than it looks, and with the wavy lines under its rim matching the lines on the fountain, that has to be a connection.

I hold it under the fountain, and to my surprise, it fills. The pristine water looks refreshing, and I certainly can use a drink, but the moment the cup touches my lips, it's empty.

Well, that settles that. I'm not meant to drink the water.

I refill the cup and return to Martok's chalice to pour it in. Though it's similar in shape to the one I'm holding, it's much larger, and so it only fills halfway.

With the water level falling short of the statue's mouth, I return to the fountain for another cupful.

But not everything in this place is as it seems.

Sure enough, as soon as I pour in the second cup, the water rapidly drains away, leaving Martok's chalice empty again.

Nothing else happens.

Did it work? Now what am I supposed to do?

I resume searching the room for more clues.

Between the levitating table, Tide's fountain and Martok's statue, all refusing to offer further help, I slump to the floor facing the corridor.

That's when my eyes fall to the cup between my knees.

Its form is still deceiving, but as I angle it towards the light, a thin band in a lighter shade of black is visible on its inner surface. It's so subtle, I almost missed it.

Beneath it, painted in the same lighter shade, is a glyph similar to the one in gold at the rim, only it's a single vertical wavy line.

That can't just be for decoration. What does that mean?

I'd already found the dual wavy lines printed on the back of Tide's hands, and I know I'd seen the single vertical glyph before, but where? Was it part of my studies, or is it somewhere here? It seems so long ago since I last saw that symbol.

Where was that?

'There's nothing else in this room. It's got to be in the corridor.'

I'm reluctant to return to that oven-like passageway, where the story on the walls doom to entrap me forever, but it seems I have no other option.

As I cross the room and enter the hallway, my eyes fix on the frescoed walls.

A loud clatter startles me from the Progenitor dream world, and I realise the cup had slipped from my grasp.

Somehow, as it hit the floor, it's remained intact, but thankfully the noise was enough to break the fresco-induced trance. 'Oh shak,' I cry as the cup rolls towards the flaming moat. It begins to sink into the thick, black substance, and that's when I notice it. Just above the flames, printed on the wall, is the black mark of the single vertical wavy line.

So, that's where I'd seen it.

Without thinking, I snatch the cup from the fire, and the moment my hand touches the flame, there's no pain or burning. Instead, a chill runs up my arm as though I'd dipped it in ice. It's just the illusion of heat, like deceit and truth.

Dunking the cup in the black liquid, I fill it to the line marked inside, then return to Martok. At this point, I can't be sure if this stuff is supposed to go into Martok's cup, but I pour it in anyway. I guess I'm about to find out. Now for the water.

The first cup of water pours in without an issue and returning with the second, I stand before Martok's statue, hesitant.

'Now, Martok,' I say, holding the second cupful. 'Let's see if you're thirsty. I know I am. Here goes nothing.'

Holding my breath with anticipation, I gradually pour the water into Martok's chalice.

Unlike last time, the water level rises until it overflows into the statue's mouth.

'And that's how you quench the thirst of deceit. So, what now, Martok?'

Scanning the room to see what's changed, my attention is drawn back to the levitating table.

A circle of white light now illuminates the plinth where the cup once sat, and the painted rune for 'home' is glowing.

Upon returning to the table, I set the cup down on its plinth in the circle of light.

Like magic, the cup half fills with a cloudy brown liquid, and the rune for 'drink' illuminates on its surface.

I'm thirsty, but I'm not that thirsty to drink a mysterious, opaque liquid that seems to have materialised out of thin air.

But, seeing as this is what the task calls for, I take the chalice and lift it to my lips.

It both looks and tastes like muddy water, and after draining the cup, my tongue tingles and goes numb.

Whatever that was, it wasn't water.

The moment I set the chalice back down, I'm crossing a threshold and stepping out onto a wide verandah through a blue front door. From the sun's low position in the sky, it's creeping toward evening, and the cool afternoon breeze tingles my skin. I inhale the crisp air laced with the sweet aroma of fresh-cut grass and gaze out towards the green-topped mountain range in the distance. I know this place—it's my childhood home in Pluvale, Nusmore, and it's just as I remember it. With its white rendered walls, polished timber deck and green and white painted railings and balustrade, it's a normal family home, like all the other houses lined up along the quaint suburban street. My teenage neighbour, Amity, is sitting in the basket-weave chair by the steps, quietly reading her book. Strangely, I recall her being much older, but looking at her now, with her long coppery-brown hair and thick-rimmed glasses framing her soft, youthful face, she's no older than I am. She occasionally glances up over the pages to watch a seven-cycle-old girl with shoulder-length fiery red hair in animal print overalls doing cartwheels and handstands on the lawn.

On any other day, this could have been just an ordinary, lazy afternoon—two girls enjoying the ambience of a pleasant sunset. But I know what this is, and it sends an icy shiver down my spine as the familiar scene plays out in full vivid detail. Even though it was ten cycles ago, the horror of knowing what happens next still fills me with terror. Bile rises in the back of my throat and sets my heart racing. Before my mind can associate the memory with the scene, an intense, searing light blots out the sky like an exploding sun. The two girls freeze, and I watch helplessly as the ensuing cloud inferno blows them past me through the open front door.

Amity lies horribly burned and blinded on the floor, her scorched and blackened arms clambering aimlessly for help. Her milky-white eyes stare up at me as though piercing into my soul, trying to judge what kind of person I am. Though I may have learned to overcome my fear, reliving it now, even older as I am, it's still as debilitating as it was when I was that scared little girl. Torn between rendering aid and seeking the safety of the space under her bed, my younger self tears off down the hall. All I want to do is follow.

I'm a coward; that's what I am.

The realisation hits me harder than the searing heat threatening to melt the skin from my bones.

I force myself to glance at Amity one last time, to commit her face to memory, burned as it is. Suddenly, her face briefly flickers to Sera's, making my heart skip a beat and sending a pang of adrenaline flooding through my body.

Slowly, I kneel beside her and reach out to take her hand, but just like the water in Tide's magic fountain, my hand passes straight through.

This isn't real. It can't be real. Then why *does it feel real?*

Kneeling there, the hollow, sour feeling of guilt wrestles with my paralysing fear, and I'm gripped with indecision. The world is disintegrating around me, and yet I can't leave Amity—she's still alive and dying right in front of me. When I was seven, I didn't understand. I knew nothing of the delicate balance of life and death. I knew nothing at all. Even now, having lived through cycles of survival training and having countless close encounters with death, I'm still afraid.

I'm still afraid of monsters.

I don't know why I wish to save Amity so much. Perhaps it's because I'm supposed to be strong, stronger than her. Perhaps, in some weird way, saving her is saving part of myself. I don't know. All I know is there's nothing I can do, and it leaves me feeling as helpless as I was when I was that scared little child. I couldn't help her then, and I can't help her now. The impossibility of it all drowns me in anguish, and my eyes brim with tears.

But if I run, it'll only prove that I am a coward and what good is a coward if I am to be what I'm supposed to be? I can't even say the word. Maybe I am a coward?

The roof collapses, and that makes my decision for me. Forced to leave Amity lying there in the rubble, I pursue my younger self to safety.

I'm running, but a force holds me back as though I'm caught in time. All around, the house is flying apart in excruciatingly slow motion; the roof, walls and furniture, everything disintegrates while I run towards the place where my room used to be. When

I reach the door, it burns away, leaving my wall-less bedroom and crumpled bed covered in bricks, surrounded by an endless field of flames and smoke.

Hiding beneath the bed, pinned in place and terrified beyond comprehension, is the little girl I barely recognise. The extreme fear in her blackened, tear-streaked face is hauntingly familiar, and it causes the same fear—fear I thought I'd long since chased away, to re-emerge.

'Don't be scared,' I say, as much for her benefit as it is for mine. I reach out my hand to her just as Lou did all those cycles ago. 'I'm here to help you.'

The smoke thickens, and my younger self retreats inside her dirty top. Everything disappears into a swirling cloud of grey.

A seven-cycle-old girl with long curly red hair emerges from the choking haze—her playful laughter echoing around the void behind her like ghosts on the wind.

I barely remember Ester. It's been so long since I'd seen her, but her appearance is instantly reassuring.

The thick, choking smoke disperses, and I'm cowering beneath the wire-frame cot in Gotthard while Ester sits cross-legged on the floor, enticing me to go hunt monsters. Before I can answer, a young spectre separates from my body, and the two sister-like girls run off down a corridor.

I give chase, hoping to catch them, but the children are faster. We round a corner into a shower of water where a giant of a man with pitch-black hair and sharp facial features is snatching Ester from her feet and carrying her away. Both my younger self and I yell out, but it's no use. Ester is gone. Desperate to know where, I leave my childhood self behind to pursue them through the door.

The instant I run through, I'm outside and surrounded by grimy snow, crates and garbage. It's the raiders' camp Sera and I found on our first camping trip together. There's the wretched cage, and beyond that, the frozen lake. The camp is deserted, save a few raggedly dressed figures in the cage. I edge closer and shudder, recognising the captives. Huddled and shivering behind the bars are Mum and Dad. They're wearing the same clothes I last saw them in, only they're filthy and tattered, and in Mum's arms is a bundle wrapped in a rotting blanket. The bundle cries like a newborn baby.

'I'll get you out,' I yell, searching for a means to open the cage.

'It's okay, Jayne,' my mother says in a gentle voice. 'You can't help us. You can only help yourself. Save yourself.'

From the bushes, two sets of angry yellow eyes appear.

Boarts!

From the other direction, six raiders emerge brandishing crude axes and knives dripping with blood.

I'm flanked.

'Run!' Dad says with urgency. 'Leave us and run, Jayne. Don't look back.'

'I can't just leave you,' I cry, grabbing onto the rusted bars as though shaking them will somehow break them free.

Mum reaches forward with a gentle hand and grasps mine. Even in the cold, her touch is warm and comforting. 'It's okay, my darling Jayne. We still love you. We will always love you. Remember that. Now, go!'

I stare at their grubby, sullen faces, their soft and loving expressions juxtaposed against the brutality of the cold and insipid cage in which they are trapped.

The boarts and raiders draw nearer.

'Go!' they insist, one last time, and with eyes darting between the cage and the encroaching danger. I have no choice but to leave.

'I love you, Mum, I love you, Dad. I miss you so much,' I cry, fighting back more tears. Then turning, I run in the only direction available, across the frozen lake. I've done this before. I just need to lower my centre of balance.

But it's not like before. Try as I might run, I may as well be wading through thick mud.

Behind, the cage bursts into flames. The last I see of my family are their haunting figures engulfed in flame, waving goodbye.

I fight to move faster across the lake with every fibre of my being, but that sticky resistance slows my progress.

A deep reverberating groan echoes underfoot, rippling outwards across the ice.

Without warning, there's an almighty crack, and the lake's surface gives way, plunging me into the freezing water.

Flailing in desperation to keep my head above the surface, my muscles cramp, and my lungs burn. Then, for a fleeting moment, strong, familiar arms embrace me. There's the splashing of a waterfall, a powerful rush of attraction, then the water disappears, and I'm falling, frictionless, down and down, deeper and down through engulfing blackness.

The darkness is reminiscent of the time in the box. Without control, helpless and alone, I close my eyes and surrender to the inevitable. When it seems it would go on forever, it abruptly ends, and I tumble out onto what feels like a concrete floor.

Opening my eyes, there is very little visible except the outlines of a few boxes. The air is musty and filled with dust. It's my and Ilona's secret room.

Behind a box in the corner, away from the door, is the familiar blue glow of a bioluminescent lamp. I move towards it and set myself down.

There's a gentle tap on my shoulder, and Ilona is sitting at my side, just visible in the low light. Her long fine dark hair frames her slender, soft face. She smiles and caresses my cheek with a tender touch.

'I was wondering when you would come,' she says, leaning in close.

'I came as soon as I could. Have you been here long?'

'I've always been here,' she replies, resting her head on my shoulder.

The sweet fragrance of Ilona's hair fills my heart with delight and washes all fear away. She takes my head between her hands, and our lips connect. For a moment of passion, all the horrors disappear, and I'm at peace again. With the soft touch of her lips, the taste of her tongue and the warmth of her embrace, I close my eyes and drink it all in. If only this moment could last forever.

But like all the other scenes from my tormented past, when I open my eyes, Ilona is gone.

'You pathetic bikkja,' Alyx snaps, sitting too close for comfort with nothing but that forsaken meta length of chain separating us. She's wearing the same dirty clothes we wore at the end of our test and stares me up and down with all the repugnance I expect, showing off that glare she does so well. 'Sneaking around having forbidden romantic interludes, I always knew you were weak and wretched.'

I leap to my feet in defiance, ready to fight and glance down to see what she's staring at. I'm naked.

Alyx disappears, then re-appears, standing behind me. 'It is with great honour you have been brought here and taught its secrets as we have,' she says. 'But that doesn't grant you automatic privilege to its benefits. You need to earn those and prove you are worthy. I can see how that may be a challenge for you.' The peculiar words may have come from Alyx's mouth, but they are not hers.

Then whose are they?

'I am who I am,' I reply, 'and I am here because I have no choice. That doesn't mean I don't want to succeed.'

'Then prove it.'

A table appears a few steps away, covered with a crisp white cloth. Laid out on it is an assortment of weapons; a pistol, throwing knives, a rifle and Sera's lost knife. To my relief, I'm wearing clothes again.

'You are better than this,' Ilona pleads, now standing where Alyx had been. 'Stay true to yourself. You don't need to prove anything to anyone.'

Then Alyx materialises behind Ilona, holding her hunting knife to Ilona's throat.

I glance at the replica of Sera's knife on the table—*it can't be the real one*—and up at Alyx.

'Do what you came here to do,' Alyx says.

'Do what?'

'Prove yourself worthy. Kill them.'

She points with her knife at something in the shadows. A bright light shines down on a chair where a dark figure dressed all in black sits restrained. Their bowed head is cowled, so I can't see their face.

'I can't do that,' I protest. 'I don't even know who they are.'

'You can, and you will,' Alyx chides. 'And if you need motivation…' she raises the knife to Ilona's throat again, 'this should motivate you.'

'No,' I yell, 'leave her out of this.'

Conflicted between the captive stranger and Ilona, my eyes dart between the two. Ilona holds her head high against Alyx's blade while drops of her blood glisten on its surface as it presses into her flesh.

'Don't you dare hurt her!' I scream.

'Then do it. Kill your target. Prove yourself.'

Panic wells inside as my love for Ilona battles with my moral conscience.

'This isn't real,' I yell. 'None of it is real. This is just a figment of my imagination. You're messing with my mind.'

'Is it?' Alyx says, appearing at my side and swipes her blade across my forearm.

It hurts, and blood seeps from the wound, proving whatever this is, it's not imaginary.

'Real enough for you?'

What is this?

Alyx shimmers away, and a cloud from the dark forms itself into the Patriarch. He stands behind Ilona with the knife to her throat, grabs a fistful of her hair and yanks her head backwards. She stares up at him with a blank expression as he bends down and forcefully plants a kiss on her lips. Seeing him do that and knowing what he's already done to her makes me seethe with rage, and I clench my fists, trying to keep my anger contained. I reach for the knife on the table and prepare to use it on him.

'You're angry,' he says, with eyes still fixed on Ilona, whose expression hasn't changed. 'That's good. Use that.' He then pushes her to the floor, forcing her to kneel at his feet.

'Number Ten,' he demands, keeping the knife in view while directing his attention at me. 'Tell me, what is rule number one?'

'Protect and obey the Patriarch and the chain of command,' I reply, the words rolling off my tongue by rote.

'And who am I?' he says.

'The Patriarch, our father and saviour.' Again, the words roll out, but I feel no connection to them.

'And the mission?'

'The mission is key. No compromises.'

'Good, Number Ten, you are hereby ordered by your Patriarch to terminate your subject. You will comply. Fail to do so, and you will fail this test. You will be deemed unworthy, and Number Twenty-eight's life will be forfeit in your subject's stead as substitute for your non-compliance.'

White knuckled, I grip the opaline handle of the knife harder as though to crush it, glaring at him with fury.

'I am not your enemy, Number Ten,' he says calmly, gesturing to the cowled figure restrained in the chair. 'But they are. Kill them!'

He turns the knife in the palm of his hand, placing its point to Ilona's chest.

They are not real; nobody here is real. I try to convince myself. But I can't watch Ilona, real or not, be murdered.

Disconnected from my own thoughts, the knife swings in my hand. I level the intricately etched blade and charge at the cowled figure, thrusting the weapon forward. With the force of my momentum, I ram it into the victim's chest. The sturdy chair holds them firm while the blade slides into their body as though through butter.

They didn't even mutter a word.

In response to my actions, the Patriarch drops his knife beside Ilona with a wicked smile. 'Congratulations, Number Ten. You have successfully completed the Rite of Passage. Welcome to Hildr.'

And like that, he and Ilona are gone.

Having completed my initiation, I should be pleased. But this challenge has left me disturbed and empty. Beside me, the stranger's cowled body remains slumped in the chair with the knife protruding from their chest.

Who did I just kill? I need to know.

With trembling hands, I remove the cowl and look upon my victim's face.

Ginger locks cascade down a pale face with lifeless green eyes. To my horror, I'm looking at a familiar face, a face I see in the mirror every day.

I have just killed myself.

After that, it may as well have been me, for the experience has left me dead inside like a rotten nut.

I'm not a coward. I'm something much worse.

I couldn't save Amity, and I couldn't save those captives in the cage. Even when I could help, like with Sera, things turned out bad. She can't work because of me, and it's all my fault. *What use am I?* If this initiation has taught me anything, it's that I have no agency—that I'm nothing but an unwitting participant in someone else's twisted nightmare. The life I'm living is not my own, like a puppet, dancing to someone else's tune, living out the motions set for me by someone else. And all I can do is play along. At this crushing realisation, my knees give way, and I collapse to the floor, sobbing uncontrollably.

Is that it? Is that what they want from me, an empty husk of a person feeble of mind enough to comply implicitly to their whims? Do they just expect me to stand there and watch while the world burns? How could this even be right? Nothing seems right anymore.

All light fades from the room, and I am consumed by total darkness that seems to creep into my very soul. It's cold and oppressing, and with nothing of comfort left to cling to, I lift my knees to my chest and hug them.

Tears stream down my face but detached even from my own body, I don't feel them. I can't feel anything anymore.

In the distance, a tiny speck of light appears, growing more prominent.

I wipe my face and clamber to my feet. Step after stumbling step, I stagger towards the light, shielding my eyes from the blinding whiteness. As soon as I emerge from the tunnel, I am swarmed by hooded figures wearing surgical gowns and masks.

The world spins, and then there is nothing.

23 FUN AND GAMES

Disinfectant.

Why do I smell disinfectant?

The room is dark, save for only a portable lamp in a close corner emitting just enough light to illuminate the bed, some medical equipment, and a shadowy figure slumped in a nearby chair.

Medical. Why am I in medical?

Assorted tubes and wires connect me to various machines and equipment, reminding me of the time I saw Sera after the accident.

But if I'm here, what happened to me?

I try to think back, but I can't recall being hurt even in that horrible dream. At least not badly enough to warrant me being here.

Everything is blurry. Blinking a few times, I try to clear the fog.

Maybe I hit my head?

The shadowy figure moves closer, its form morphing into a person as they lean over the bed.

'Hi Jayne,' says Sera's soft, melodious voice.

'Sera?' I ask, groggily trying to sit up. Searing pain rips through my pelvis, and I fall back to the pillows.

'Ow,' Sera winces, placing a hand on my shoulder. 'Try not to move. You might burst your stitches.'

'Stitches? What stitches?' I lift the sheet to reveal a bloodied patch covering my lower abdomen from hip to hip. 'What the frak?'

'It's okay,' Sera replies, 'you were injured. They patched you up.'

Sera just lied. She's told little lies before but never like this. *Why would she do that?*

What could have happened during the test that caused me to be injured *down there*? I turn over my arm to inspect where I remember Alyx slashing me, but there's not even a scratch.

Was it real? What was *real?*

'Injured? But how?' I ask.

Sera purses her lips and strokes my hair in a show of comfort. 'You will be fine. I am so proud of you for completing the Rite of Passage. You performed better than any of us had hoped. In fact, from what I have been told, you are the only one who has ever walked out of there. Not even I managed that.'

'What about Ilona?'

'Who?'

'Ilona, I saw her.'

Sera pulls the chair closer, resting her arms on the bed with her hands cupping mine. 'What you saw in there is for you and *only* you,' she says in her soothing voice. 'There was nobody else there. If you saw anyone, it was only a figment of your imagination. Now rest. There will be plenty of time to talk later.'

She smiles and then kisses me on the cheek. 'Ilona is fine,' she whispers into my ear so that no one else can overhear. 'She made it out, too. Now rest.'

'How's patient Jayne doing?' a familiar voice asks as Doctor Davi appears at the foot of the bed, holding a clipboard. 'Any nausea? Pain?'

'Only when I move,' I reply.

'That's to be expected,' she says, fiddling with the bottle of clear fluid hanging on a pole beside the bed. 'I've given you something for the pain, which will help you sleep.' She then turns to Sera. 'She'll be fine. I just want to keep her a little longer for observation. Another day should do it, and then she's all yours.'

The days draw by. I would like to go outside, but the rain has been relentless. Sera tells me that since the downpour that nearly drowned Alyx and I, all access to the Gord has been cut. So, even if I wanted to leave, I couldn't. It's given me time to catch up with the diary, though, watch some of Sera's terrible shows and read something for pleasure now that I don't have to study. It's strange not having to nurse the daily scrape or bruise, but the wound across my pelvis still causes concern as it takes its time to heal.

Sera says I should relish the moment and relax, for as soon as I'm inducted into 'the Guild,' I'll be busier than a tomadai in mating season.

By the end of the fourth tendawn, I have returned to light training and become proficient at pocketball.

'Looks like you're almost back to your usual self,' Sera says as I lean over the table in one of our regular games.

'Yeah, I'm feeling much better. But I still can't for the life of me recall how this happened. Red ball, corner pocket,' I announce, aligning my stick for a tricky shot.

'Nice one,' Sera compliments when the ball drops into the intended pocket. 'It's about time you heard this, anyway. You deserve to know the truth before someone else tells you.'

I rest the end of the stick on the floor and look at her, confused. 'Truth? What truth?'

'This may come as a shock to you, but you weren't injured.'

'No shak, Sera. I already knew that. But why? What *really* happened?'

'You had surgery.'

'I figured that too. But what for? Am I sick?'

'How about you come to the table, and we talk there?'

'No, I want to hear this now. What are you talking about?'

She sighs. 'Part of being who and what we are… comes with certain… sacrifices.'

Sera's eyes dart around the room, and she shifts her weight in discomfort, looking as though she'd rather be somewhere else. 'What I mean to say is,' she explains, carefully choosing her words, 'we are not normal people. And, as such, we cannot do normal things… like, have children.'

'Ah…' I stammer. 'Are you saying what I think you're saying?'

'They have sterilised you, Jayne.' She says the words as though emotionally disconnected from them. 'So have we all.'

I can't help but stare at her with incredulity, wringing the stick in my hands. 'What? You're serious?'

'I am sorry, Jayne. But yes, I am serious. All assets your age undergo the procedure before entering active duty. It is Hildr policy.'

That knot of anger wells in the pit of my stomach. 'Asset? Is that all I am to them? To you? An Asset? Well, that's not *my* policy. Nobody asked me!'

'No, that is because they do not give us a choice. As I said, it is part of who we are.'

'You sound like you're okay with that. For fraks sake, Sera. I can't believe you're justifying this!'

'I am not justifying it. I have just accepted it is what it is. Believe me, I am as much displeased with this as you…'

'My arse it is!' I yell. 'I never wanted this. It's my body and my life. What right do they have messing with me like this?'

'I know it upsets you, Jayne. It upset me when I went through this. The difference between you and me is, I have had time to accept it. That it is just the way it is. And after some time, you will accept it too.'

Just when I thought I was starting to get any sort of control over my life, I'm struck with this. Compounded with the treacherous tests, the maddening mind games and the Patriarch's insipid rules, I doubt I will ever just 'accept it', no matter what Sera says.

'Think about it,' she continues. 'Can you imagine falling pregnant and having to raise a child in these conditions? We do not know one day to the next where we will be or what we will be doing. This is dangerous work. We cannot expose a baby to this.'

'You did, with me, didn't you?'

'That is different. You were eight, and I was never pregnant.'

'And I bet you never wanted to be either.'

'Jayne, you know that is not true. You are the closest—'

'Sera, I don't know what's true anymore. Can you honestly tell me that when you came to Gotthard and told me you were taking me to someplace better, *this* is what you meant? You knew all along this is what I would have to go through, and you still think this is *better? Well, is it?'*

'It's better than dying of fixo in your sleep.'

'Gotthard may have sucked, and I was miserable there, but at least they never pretended the place was better than what it actually was.'

'I have said it before, and I will say it again. I have never lied to you, Jayne—not about this. I did not choose you just because some stranger told me to find you. I chose you because I truly believed you were the right choice. Was I wrong?'

'Yes, Sera. You *are* wrong.' I snap at her, and I don't think I've ever been this furious with her in all my life. Sera and I have had our arguments before, but this, this is something different, like it's been brewing for some time. And while I know she's done her best to support me, I still can't help shaking the notion that even after everything that's happened—everything they've done to her and me—she's been complicit. 'All of this fraking shak is wrong. You bring me here under false pretences and raise me to be an assassin, which you don't bother telling me until after you start the training, then you put me through all this mental and physical boartcrud. I mean, you force me to endure the progenitor-forsaken wilds chained to a psychopath with a death wish who nearly rips off my arm. You force me to relive all my lifelong horrors, and now you allow them to cut me open and take away my life-born right to have a family? What the frak am I to you?'

'It's not like that.'

'Then what is it, Sera? Tell me? And no more lies!'

Sera blinks at me in shock. 'I see… but if you want to talk about lies when were you planning to tell me about your relationship with Ilona? You think I did not know about that?'

'Why would I tell you about that? You don't even want me to have friends. "Don't trust anyone," that's rule number four, isn't it? Well, I'm sick of these stupid rules, and I'm tired of your double standards. I won't be anyone's puppet. Leave me alone!'

'Jayne…'

'No! I've had it with this place, and I've had it with you!' Before Sera can say another word, I snap the stick over my knee, throw the pieces to the ground and, grabbing my coat from the couch, storm out of the apartment.

There, in the dark hallway, I slump to the floor, tears openly streaming down my face.

I can't believe Sera, of all people, would allow them to do this to me.

Menacing thoughts fuel the bilious churning in my stomach. Sera's apathy leaves me consumed by rage. 'How dare she do this to me!' I scream in my mind, fists balled so tight, they've gone white. I thought Sera was different, but tonight she's demonstrated she's no different to all the others. It's obvious I can't trust her. The only person I believe I can trust is locked away inside the room next door. Oh, so I want to take Ilona and run away just as she wanted to do all those cycles ago. I'm filled with so much furious energy I could just about punch the wall until I bore a way out of this compound. But then, where would we go?

With only the invisible storm clouds looming over my head, I sit on the cold concrete floor, arms crossed, staring at Ilona's door.

How I want to see her, have her hold me in her arms again and console my rage.

Mustering up the courage, I pull myself off the floor and knock our secret pattern. Without waiting for a response, I climb into the ventilation duct and head for our secret room.

In the dim blue light of the lamp, the silence is deafening.

I hope she heard my signal.

For what seems like a lifetime, I wait with self-pity as my only companion. Preoccupied with the chaos, I almost miss Ilona quietly slipping out of the vent.

'You came!' I exclaim, throwing my arms around her when she settles on the floor at my side. Before she can utter a word, I grab her head between my hands and plant a kiss on her tender lips. How I missed the sweet taste of her.

Ilona reciprocates, pulling me closer. Beyond this room, with her holding me tight and her lips locked with mine—*this is real, right?*—nothing else matters. But just like all moments of pleasure, it doesn't last, and when she pulls away, her sullen expression is not what I expect.

'What's wrong?' I ask. 'You look sad.'

She bites her lip in the cute way she does when thinking. 'I…' she stammers. 'I… don't think we can do this anymore.'

The pain returns, and it sinks to the pit of my stomach where it was before Ilona arrived.

'Why?'

'Tomorrow's graduation,' Ilona says. 'After that, who knows?'

'That shouldn't stop us from seeing each other, surely?'

'I just don't think it's going to work out,' she says with glistening eyes. 'Don't get me wrong, Jayne, I care for you deeply, but it's become too risky now.' She reaches forward to cup my tear-streaked face in her hands. 'Don't be sad, though. We still have here and now.'

I nod, allowing her soft touch to soothe me. Then, out of nowhere, she leans forward and whispers in my ear. 'Let me show you something.' Her hands move towards the buttons of her top, and slowly, she peels the fabric away, revealing a black lacy bra. Nestled between her petite breasts is a marbled black and white pendant on a gold chain.

'What's that?' I ask, clasping it between my fingers.

She glances down at it. 'Oh, that,' she says with indifference. 'That's just something my father gave me before he left.'

'And the old man and Shaddix, they let you keep it?'

'I dunno. I guess so,' she shrugs, softly plucking it from my hands. 'Anyway, that's not what I wanted to show you. Say, Jayne, do you trust me?'

It's as if Ilona is reading my thoughts, but I never expected her to call me on it. I bashfully brush a stray lock of hair over my ear and nod my reply.

'Then take your top off,' she says.

After a moment of hesitation, I pull my light, flowing blouse over my head, revealing a more utilitarian, skin-coloured bra of my own. Sitting there half naked with Ilona looking at me, my hands instinctually move to cover my modesty.

Ilona smiles. 'It's okay. You have a lovely body. Be proud of it.'

'I don't know about that.'

'Do you remember our Shitak'na training? Of course you would. It was Sera's class. Anyway, she told us to be one with ourselves—to flow like water. If it helps, close your eyes and allow yourself to flow like water. I promise I won't hurt you.'

In that moment, I am awash with unfamiliar emotions. As much as I want to trust Ilona, my conditioning screams at me otherwise. While I contemplate whether to submit, the soft touch of her hand on my shoulder brings me back into the room. There's nothing I can't handle. I've already proven that. Ilona has already trusted me on many occasions, so there's no reason not to trust her now. Besides, rule four is only there to keep us apart. Knowing that I banish it from all thought and allow Ilona to gently lower me to the floor.

With my heart pounding like a drum in my ears, she slips off my pants and then drops her skirt. Her lacy black under-knickers match her bra, and I'm acutely aware mine don't. But that thought doesn't last long the instant she leans over and nibbles my neck.

It tickles.

Nobody has ever done that to me before.

'Relax,' Ilona whispers in my ear, running a hand down my belly. 'Don't think about it. Just follow your feelings. You can always say stop if you want.'

'Keep going,' I mutter breathlessly.

Her fingers linger on the fresh scar at my pelvis, and it tickles as she runs a finger along it. 'You have one of those too.'

'Ah-huh,' I sigh. 'I don't want to talk about it.'

'Me neither. But it doesn't mean we can't have a bit of fun,' she smiles a cheeky smile. 'Would you like to know what *that* feels like?'

'Hmm,' I mumble, focusing on the strange feelings building inside.

Her hand drifts lower, below the band of my under-knickers…

Muffled voices and the musical jingling of keys in the corridor outside shatter the moment.

'The lamp,' I gasp, grabbing it just in time as a key grinds into the lock and the door groans open.

Two silhouettes fill the doorway and their conversation, now intelligible, continues.

'… I have to do something, Vina. *MonLantry* has already caused me enough strife.'

'But Patriarch, Seraphin has also done a lot for this establishment. We can't be talking about retirement!'

'I've made my decision,' the Patriarch-shaped silhouette says, flicking on the light switch. Ilona and I duck deeper behind the crates, peering at the adults through a gap. 'Now where is that?' Elihus says, glancing around the room.

'When was the last time you came in here?' Blackthorn coughs, swiping swirling dust away from her face. 'Had I known, I would have brought my old mask and a duster.'

'Ah, there it is,' he says to the sound of rattling bottles.

Shuffling footsteps head towards the door. Elihus reaches for the handle, and I breathe a quiet sigh of relief.

'Okay, you can come out now,' he says, stopping in the doorway. 'I know you're in here.'

24 GRADUATION

Dressed in nothing but our undergarments, Ilona and I glare at each other in horror, realising the vent cover is still open.

'I said get out here,' the Patriarch growls. 'That's an order!'

Knowing we can't keep our ruse any longer, we emerge from our hiding spot, covering as much bare skin as we can.

Blackthorn looks stunned. 'How did you know they were in here?'

'Something's been stealing my prized malt. And I'm certain rodentia don't drink.'

'You two,' Blackthorn barks. 'Patriarch's office. Now!'

Grabbing our clothes, we file out of the storeroom.

'Fetch their Guardians,' he orders Blackthorn.

'Yes, sir,' she says, rushing off, leaving Elihus to herd us to his office at the end of the long hallway.

The door closes, and he eyes us up and down with a sadistic grin. Though we clutch our clothes close to our bodies, we may as well be naked.

'Under different circumstances, I may have found this intriguing,' he says, brushing the back of his hand across Ilona's face. Slowly, his wandering hands move down her neck and chest to her hands, where he forces them down until she drops her clothes on the floor. 'Although I must say, I'm very disappointed you didn't invite me.'

She shies away from his gaze.

'Unfortunately, there are witnesses, and I must adhere to code. This… fling, or whatever you want to call it, is over. There's also the matter of my stolen malt. Fifty cycles, that's how old that is. What's in that storeroom is all that's left. I hope you enjoyed it. Because when I'm done with you, it may be the last thing you taste.'

Ilona is visibly trembling now, desperately trying not to make eye contact with him.

When the old man turns to face me, he tries the same intimidation tactics, but I stand with defiance like I've seen Sera do with him before.

'MonLantry's girl,' he says with that same slimy look. 'It has been some time since I've seen you in here, has it not?'

When I don't reply, he steps forward and shouts in my face. 'I asked you a question, girl!'

His unexpected change in demeanour startles me.

'Are you simple? Answer me!'

'Yes, sir,' I reply, eyes fixed forward.

'Good, you can speak. You're quite the looker too, I must say,' he says, slapping away my clutch of clothing. I can feel him undressing me with his beady little eyes. It makes my skin crawl. 'Kiss her.'

The order catches me by surprise.

'You heard me,' he demands, continuing to gawk, 'I said, kiss her. And do it like you mean it.'

Hesitantly, we turn to each other, and I gaze into Ilona's fear-filled, almost black eyes. The last thing I wanted was to be ordered by the Patriarch to kiss her in front of him for his sick entertainment.

'I don't have all day,' he shouts, making us both flinch. 'DO IT!'

We move closer and are about to touch lips when the door bursts open. Blackthorn strides in, followed by Shaddix and Sera trailing behind. Finding us bosom to bosom, the three stare at us with condemnation plastered all over their faces. All of a sudden, the room feels claustrophobic, compounding the uncomfortable tension. At least we don't have to follow the Patriarch's last order.

Shaddix marches straight up to Ilona, hand ready to slap her. Without thinking, I move to block it, and her guardian turns livid, backhanding me in the side of the face.

'How dare you,' she scowls, grabbing Ilona and pulling her aside. 'Pick up your clothes, you dirty little bikkja.'

'Stop!' Sera yells. 'Stop it.'

I'm not concerned by the sting from the backhand, only Sera's deathly cold stare.

'What is the meaning of this?' the Patriarch howls.

'I'm deeply sorry, Patriarch,' Shaddix grovels. 'I shall ensure this does not happen again. Ilona will be punished at once.'

'I would expect nothing less,' the Patriarch says with a sneer. 'By all rights, they should be banished for their indiscretions and blatant insubordination, and you along with them. But alas, that would be a terrible waste. I must say, this disappoints me greatly. The conduct exhibited tonight is not what I would expect of my best and brightest.'

'Please don't banish us,' Ilona pleads. 'We were just fooling around.'

'Fooling around! Is that what you call it?' he shouts.

'It is my fault,' Sera says, stepping forward, deliberately placing herself between Elihus and me. 'I was careless and failed to see this coming. Please do not punish the girls on account of my mistake. They are young and do not know what they are doing, and I take full responsibility for their actions. If you are going to punish anyone, punish me.'

'No!' I protest. 'Please, don't do that.'

The Patriarch pushes past Shaddix and clutches Sera by the jaw, tilting her head to gaze into her brown eyes. It surprises me how calm she remains, like a rock.

'Seraphin MonLantry,' he growls, speaking her name as though having eaten something sour. 'How is it that every time there's trouble, you are somehow at the centre of it?'

Just like that time I'd seen Sera through the vent, she doesn't utter a word, expertly holding her ground with that cool defiance I one day hope to master myself.

'Do you know how long it has been since this facility received orders from our superiors?' the Patriarch growls, flecks of spittle showering Sera's face. 'Five cycles. That's how long. How does an establishment like this survive on one mission every five cycles? I must confess, I was elated at the prospect of reactivation. I even assigned my best asset, thinking you would do us proud.' His face contorts into a vicious scowl as he squeezes Sera's cheeks harder. Despite his fingers digging into her skin, her expression still doesn't change. 'But then you had to go and screw it up, and now we haven't so much as received a single scrap of paper since. And now this! MonLantry, you are a disgrace.'

His hand whips from her jaw, leaving red score marks where each finger had been.

How can Sera remain so calm?

'Hold her,' he then orders the other guardians, and I'm struck with a pang of gut-wrenching fear. They each grab one of Sera's arms, gripping her tight, while he saunters over to collect a pair of black leather gloves and the sinister black cane with the shiny brass fist from the wall by the window.

Casually, he puts on the gloves. 'Have I told you the tale of the ursus wrangler?' he says, pausing as though expecting an answer. 'No? It's very fascinating how they train their animals. You see, ursus live in tight-knit family units where the cubs learn respect from their parents. Ursus wranglers have found the best way to teach young cubs respect is to let the parents serve as an example. They beat…' he raises the stick and slams the fist end into Sera's belly. With a grunt, she doubles over.

'No!' I cry, leaping to Sera's defence, but Ilona steps in to seize my arm.

Elihus glares at me as he raises the stick again. 'They beat the parents…' he growls, smacking Sera across the face, '… into submission.' He then strikes her a third time. Blood streams from a fresh gash across her forehead, but not once did she struggle or resist.

Fight back.

'It's the only way the cubs learn who is in charge,' he concludes, setting down the stick with a smug look of satisfaction. He removes his gloves while Sera, with her face bleeding, remains restrained in the arms of the other guardians.

'I am Patriarch, and this is MY house,' he declares to the room, his voice reverberating in my chest. 'Let this be a lesson to you all. In my house, order, discipline and respect for me and my vision exceed all else. Without order, there is chaos, and I will NOT have chaos reign in my house. We have but five rules, and I expect them to be followed without question. Violation of these rules is insubordination, and insubordination will be punished with pain. You dare disrespect *me* in *my* house; you will pay the price. Do I make myself clear?'

'Yes, Patriarch,' we all say in unison, and then he turns to me.

'I am the alpha; you are insignificant,' he says, flicking his hand towards the guardians and the door. 'Throw MonLantry in the box! Now, get out of my sight.'

The night is near freezing, and I can't bring myself to stay in the warm apartment while Sera faces hypothermia sitting out in that cold, dark pit alone, especially not after what she did for me. I gather my bedroll, a spare warm blanket and a flask of hot stew I'd prepared for dinner and carry it up top.

A solo silver moon casts dappled light over the Field as I slink past the dozing guard, across the frost-covered grass clearing to where chairs and a stage have already been set up for tomorrow's ceremony. Approaching the box, I duck behind its far side, out of sight.

'Sera,' I whisper into the slot, unrolling the bedroll.

'Jayne?' comes a weak reply. 'What are you doing here?' From the warbling sound of her voice, she's freezing.

'I've come to see you. I've brought you something to eat and a blanket. It should help, but that's the best I could do.'

'Thank you,' she says as I pass the items through to her. 'That is very thoughtful. But you should not have come. What if someone sees you?'

'I don't care,' I say, probably with a bit more directness than intended. Of course, I meant it, even if it would compromise my graduation if I got caught. But after what I've already been through, there's nothing more the Patriarch could do to me that could make things any worse. 'What *he* did to you was—*I can't even think of a word strong enough*—wrong. So, frak the rules.'

She coughs something that sounds like a reserved chortle. 'After that little speech earlier, I am surprised to hear *you* say that. But I will not have you compromising yourself on my behalf, especially not now that you have come this far.'

'Sera, I said I don't care. That should be me in the box, not you.'

'I made my choice. I stand by it.'

'But why? Why did you do that?'

'I made a promise to you that I would protect you. I mean that.'

'Even if I deliberately broke the rules? I mean I…'

'Yes,' she cuts me off as if anticipating what I was going to say next. 'Even because of that. I don't expect you to understand. Just know that I do.'

Everything's so raw; the gruelling training, the insane tests, and the sterilisation, I often forget Sera's gone through it all before. That realisation gives me pause, and it leaves me staring through the dark gap in the box in awe. A gleam of moonlight reflecting in her eyes is all I can see of her. I wish more than anything to be having this conversation back in the warmth of our apartment. Thanks to me, we're not.

'I'm so sorry, Sera,' I babble as my emotions boil to the surface.

'Sorry for everything. I never meant to hurt you or get you dragged into this mess. I didn't want you to end up in the box for me and…'

'It is okay, Jayne,' she says. 'If I had this moment over again, I would not change a thing. I know you are angry. You have every right to be. Believe me when I tell you I understand your frustration at feeling you have no control over your life. I mean, look at where I am.'

'So, are you angry with me for breaking the rules? I mean, I am the reason you're here.'

Sera chuckles. 'Of course, I am angry, but not at you. I am here because I chose to take your place, remember? And secondly, those are the rules of a stupid misogynistic bigot.'

'I can't believe you just said that,' I snort at Sera's lewd description of Elihus. Considering how revered she'd held him before now, it seemed particularly odd coming from her. I opted not to press further. 'So… how long have you known about Ilona and me?'

'A while now. I tried to tell you to be careful, but… this is not an "I told you so" speech. You deserve to be happy, and if you find that with Ilona, then… Unfortunately, we do not live in a place that is open to these things, so you have to be discreet. As I said, respect may be expected, but trust; that is yours alone to hand out. If you find someone who improves your world, take them, grab hold of them with both hands, and fight to keep them safe. Just be prepared to accept the consequences if you are wrong.'

'Like you?'

She sighs. 'Yes. Like me. I have made enough mistakes for a lifetime. All I wish for you is to learn from my mistakes so you do not repeat them.'

'I can't make any promises,' I say in earnest. 'What makes you think I can?'

'You are young. You have your entire life ahead of you.'

'Funny you should say that,' I scoff, thinking about how I've been unable to avoid trouble so far. After all, it was my doing that put Sera here in the first place. 'How much of a life do you honestly think I will have? Judging from my encounters with the Patriarch, I'm not in his good graces. And by the sound of it, I'm expendable too.'

'No, Jayne. You are not expendable,' she says, and I only wish I could see her face. 'Far from it, in fact. It is a bit more complicated than that. And I promise I will tell you everything you want to know when I am out of here. You deserve that. Suffice to say, there is much more at stake here than the petty whims of that incorrigible old man.'

'The Patriarch? I'm surprised to hear you say that.'

'It is true. I cannot have that sadistic monster hurt you like he has the others.'

'You've never said that about him before. Why now?'

She sighs. 'Test someone's resolve, and they will show their true colours. Either that or I was too blind to see it before now.' Sera hesitates for a moment, and I can almost hear the thoughts whirring around in her head. 'I am ashamed to say it has taken me all this time to realise the truth.'

'What's that?'

'That I made a terrible mistake,' she confesses in a deeply repentant tone. 'I had all but accepted he had our best interests—the world's best interests—at heart. I believed he was acting according to our mission directive, but now I see that could not have been further from the truth. All those cycles ago, when I told you why I brought you here, and you started questioning things, you were right to do that. I was wrong to say otherwise. You have no idea how sorry I am about that.'

Sera's words hit me like a punch to the guts. As much as I'm pleased to hear her say these things, it terrifies me to think the lines between right and wrong could have become so blurry. My thoughts drift back to the conversation cycles ago when Sera told me she'd killed an innocent man on the Patriarch's orders. It was our first real argument, and I knew I was petulant back then, but to hear Sera confess that I may have been right all along, raises more questions than it answers. 'As you said, you were just doing your job, weren't you?'

'Yes, but that doesn't make it right.'

'I thought you said we had to trust our superiors knew what they were doing.'

'I did—until the Gaius Sempro mission. That really showed me something was off,' she explains. 'That was a tumbling rock in a much larger avalanche, I think and helped put everything else into perspective. But it was you, Jayne, who helped me see the error. Once again, you proved yourself more capable and free-thinking than I had ever expected. Had you not asked those questions, I do not think I ever would have realised what Elihus was doing. I cannot believe I have been so stupid.'

'I don't think you're stupid, Sera. I would never say that.'

'You are kind, but what person, if not stupid, follows someone blindly off a cliff and expects not to fall?'

'A person who has spent their entire life being told what to believe by the establishment so convincingly, it has become the very foundation of their belief system,' I speculate. 'That's what this is, isn't it?'

'That may be true, Jayne, but we cannot afford to talk this way. We are but leaves caught in the wind. Best not whip that wind up into a storm. At least, not now.'

Just when I think we're making progress, she retracts again, as though her programming automatically kicked in, preventing her from expressing her true feelings. Even though it frustrates me, it makes sense. 'I guess you're right,' I concede with a resolute sigh.

'There is one good thing that has come out of all this,' she says in a brighter tone.

'What's that?'

'You,' she says, reaching a hand through the slot to touch my arm. 'I do not know what I would have done without you. I must confess, when I was told I would have a child, I was not happy about that. In my line of work, I am conditioned to fight, not raise children. But when you came into my life, the way you carried yourself when I first met you in Gotthard, your independence and sense of integrity, you reminded me of the person I used to be. You impressed me then and every day since. You are not a contract to me, Jayne. You are my daughter, I love you, and I could not be happier with you in my life.'

'I… don't know what to say,' I stammer. Maybe it's because of all that's happened lately or that Sera's in the box, but hearing her say those words spark something within me, and the tears spill over. It's not like she hasn't said anything like that to me before, but now, it feels more sincere, more genuine. Looking back on our cycles together, I'd become complacent, failing to see that I had Sera despite the horridness happening all around me. Stalwart, dependable, always caring Sera. Each time I got hurt, she was there to patch me up. Each time I got into trouble, she put me right. And each time I needed help, she was there, either with a compassionate ear, an inspirational word or something to guide me to get me through. I'm ashamed to think I could have ever doubted her.

'I'm sorry, Sera,' I say, wiping away the tears that flow openly. 'Sorry for not listening to you.'

'Oh, but you did. You listened, alright. I am the one who should've been taking my own advice.'

'As you said, we are but leaves in the wind,' I mimic her words.

'Jayne, you are a beautifully strong, intelligent, and capable young woman, so full of spirit. You prove that to me every day. Never have I doubted my decision to choose you as my daughter. And as hard as it is to believe, there is good to be done here. We need you more than you can ever know. Just promise me, you will never let anyone try to change this about you. Not me, not Ilona, and certainly not Elihus. You must decide for yourself who you really are. That is what you have control over.'

'I wish I knew how.' But something else bothers me. With graduation tomorrow, and the Patriarch certain to act on his threat to punish me, I can't think what lies ahead. 'So, what are we going to do now? We can't stay here, surely?'

'As I also said,' she says, retracting her hand. 'There are motions at play that are of far more importance than you understand. For now, you must stay here and keep out of trouble. You have come this far. You must see this through.'

'What about you?'

'Me? Jayne, this is my home. I am not going anywhere. Whatever lies ahead for me, I will accept it here.'

'Even retirement?'

'Retirement?' she asks with a startled voice. 'Who said anything about that?'

'The Patriarch. I overheard him talking to Blackthorn about it. What does that mean?'

'Don't worry about that,' she says, trying to sound reassuring, but I can tell from the concern in her voice she's not convinced. 'We must focus on you. That is all that matters now.'

I wish I could not worry about it. Everything Ilona had been telling me makes sense now. Sera had been true to her word. She'd been shielding me from the horrible realities of this place. But to do that, she had borne the brunt of it herself. It was unfair, and I knew it. My only consolation is it has given me a unique perspective of how the Patriarch's deep indoctrination works. The rules, the pompous posturing, the threats and intimidation, and the initiation rituals; it was all part of his elaborate scheme to build and maintain a harem of women duty-bound to protect and serve only him. And Sera was only just becoming aware of it.

'Thank you, Sera. For everything. So… what will happen to me after tomorrow?'

'You will be inducted into the Guild and given your first mission, probably.'

'And what will you do?'

'There are plenty of other things going on in this world. Do not worry about me. I think I might try becoming a chef after all.'

Sera and I spent the night talking; about her life before the war, those she loved and lost, and what it was like being an asset in the Hildr Guild. We laughed and cried. It's almost as if her being in the box has brought us closer, and somehow, we managed to forget the reason they had put her there, even if it was just for a little while. Before we know it, the sun cracks above the horizon, and I'm rushing off so as not to get caught in the brightening light. As I collect my belongings and pack them into my shoulder bag to head back towards the apartments, an enormous winged craft, like a giant black ave, soars overhead and disappears somewhere beyond the shooting range.

Curiosity gets the better of me, and I rush to find out what it is, just as a black-cloaked figure slips between an entrance hut and the mess hall.

Slipping around behind the mess, I catch the stranger with their back to me, observing the vessel landing. The collar of their long, form-fitting black coat is raised to conceal their face, but something about them feels familiar. Perhaps it's the tufts of ginger hair protruding beneath their short-brimmed leather hat, the way they move, or the way they turn away when I approach—*I know this person.*

'Lou Tenant Doe!' I shout as the realisation dawns. The woman freezes in place, and a shiver runs down my spine. Maybe it's the excitement of finally seeing the person who saved my life all those cycles ago, who I'd never thought I'd meet again? But seeing her standing there like an enigma stirs something in me I struggle to describe.

She slowly turns to face me. 'Hello, Jayne.'

The next words tumble out involuntarily. 'What are you doing here? Where have you been? Did you come to see me graduate? Maybe I can introduce you to Sera…'

'Whoa, Jayne,' Lou pulls back. 'Slow down. One thing at a time.'

'Sorry, I just wasn't expecting you to be here. It's been a long time. It's good to see you. Why didn't you visit?'

'I wanted to, believe me, I did, but I couldn't.'

'Why?'

'I wish I could tell you that. But I'm here now.'

'So, you *did* come for my graduation?'

'Not exactly. I've come to see you, though. But no one else can know I'm here. Do you understand?'

'Can I at least introduce you to Sera later? I'm sure she'd love to meet you.'

'Okay, why not,' she says, pulling out a slip of paper from her coat pocket. 'Later.'

'Then, why *are* you here?'

'This is for you,' she says, handing the paper to me.

The aged, folded slip of paper is delicate at the creases, and inside, scrawled in black ink, it reads;

The Dragon is Awake. The Phoenix has Risen.
Don't Burn the Ashes.

'I know this, but it's wrong. It's "The Fenix has Risen". The ship is called the Fenix.'

'No, Jayne, it's right.'

'No, I'm sure it's Fenix. I must have read that book like a hundred times. It's definitely the Fenix.'

'And who do you think wrote that book?' she asks, lifting her chin to look right at me with those emerald eyes.

'You wrote *"Beyond the Horizon"*?'

With a sly smirk on her oval face, she nods. *I know that smirk; it looks just like…*

Shrugging off the bizarre thought, I'm more interested in discussing the book. 'So, if you're the author, you've gotta tell me how it ends. I lost the only copy I had, and it was missing the ending. Please tell me what happens to Ajee Yond?'

'That's *not* the point of the story,' she says bluntly.

'What? Why?'

'I can't tell you that. But what I can tell you is that message was written for you.'

'Me? But I don't even know what it means?'

'You will. For now, I will tell you one thing. The Dragon *IS* awake and needs you. Don't bother looking, or your search will be in vain. You will know when the time comes, the Dragon will find you, and you can't hesitate in your decision. That is all I can say.'

'I, um, what? That doesn't make any sense.'

'I know, it won't. But it will, in time.'

'How d'you…?'

The question lingers like a snowflake in the air. All she needs to do is stand there with that eerily familiar smirk on her face and allow my mind to catch up. For her build, height, and even her fair skin and slight freckles, it's as though I'm looking into a mirror. Either she's my much older identical twin, or…

'Remember that time when you were on your first camping trip with Sera,' she says, 'and you lit that bonfire to allow those people in the cage to pass to Gaia with dignity? You wanted to burn the whole world down. You were so angry at what had happened to them.'

'Wow!' I say, cupping a hand to my mouth in astonishment. 'How do you…? No one but Sera and I know about that.'

'Or last night, you stayed with Sera, and she told you about Loriana. How you cried when she said what she'd been ordered to do. It made you think about how you would feel if that were Ilona.'

'No. That's impossible.' I remember the incidents so vividly, I can almost feel the mix of emotions building within me. But, it's strange that even though she says the words, they seem foreign in her mouth, as though she's disconnected from them.

'Those two moments have shaped me into becoming the person I am—the person *you* will become.'

'Me? Are you saying…?'

'Yes.'

'Frak. You're serious?'

'Yes.'

'What the? But how?'

'I can't say. Just know it's true.' *Trust me,* she adds, using the secret hand signals only Ilona and I are supposed to know.

Trust isn't a sign we use often, so for her to know it leaves me stunned. 'So…You really *are* me?'

She nods with a smirk.

'Let me get this straight. All this time, I've been thinking your name was Lou Tenant Doe, but it's actually Lieutenant Jayne Doe?' We both chuckle at that with hauntingly similar mannerisms, confirming what she's said to be true.

'Yes.'

'Wow. Fraking fraksticks,' we both say at the same time and break out into hushed laughter.

'That said, we are still different. A lot has happened since I stood where you are now. A lot I'm afraid you're going to have to experience for yourself.'

'That's… insane,' I gasp in awe. *I still can't believe I'm talking to myself—my older self. How can this be?*

'Oh, and Jayne,' she says with a little more seriousness. 'This is important, you need to keep your diary. Carry it with you always. You cannot know how vital it is.'

'Okay. Why?'

'Just do it.'

'Alright,' I reply with a dubious shrug, not really sure why my scribblings could be important to anyone but myself. 'I'll do that… Anything else?'

'I should go,' she says abruptly, turning to leave.

'But I have so many questions,' I protest. 'There's still so much I need to know.'

'I know you do. But I can't stay,' she says sadly. 'Just remember the message and the diary. And Jayne, give Mum a hug for me.'

'But Jayne, can't you stay?' I ask, and it seems weird calling to my own reflection.

'No, sorry.'

And then she's gone.

At five, the sun, having reached its zenith, fills the cloudless day with warmth. Dressed in the blue ceremonial robe from the Rite and black skin-tight clothing under that, I wander over to the Field. Already, a crowd of guardians and graduates, as well as a few other unrecognisable faces, gather.

Shaddix and Ilona stand to one side, away from everyone else.

They don't appear to be talking. Ilona lifts her head and gives me a look of recognition but turns away just as quickly. Not quick enough, it seems, as Shaddix grips Ilona's face and, from her expression, reprimands her.

Half of me wants to slap the shak out of that decrepit old bovis, but the other part listens to Sera's words still reverberating in my mind, and I proceed toward the rows of chairs set up in front of the stage instead.

Nineteen; that's how many chairs are positioned in the front row of the small crowd. One for each of the eighteen other students who stand with their guardians. Nineteen out of thirty—sixty-three per cent—that's all that passed? Aside from those two in the bog, whom I know their fate, what happened to those who aren't here today? I shudder to think.

Cane in hand, Sera hobbles—more so than usual—from the apartments. She looks as prim as always, clean and refreshed in a new embroidered blue dress, similar in design to the one she wore the day she picked me up from Gotthard.

Without hesitation, I race over to greet her and throw my arms around her in excitement. 'Mum! You made it!'

She stops and wraps her arms around me in return. 'Mum?' she asks with surprise, and I'm sure I catch a tear in the corner of her eye.

'I thought it appropriate, don't you think?' I reply with a broad smile.

'It is nice. I like it. Now how about escorting me to my chair, daughter?'

Settling Sera in her assigned seat in the second row, I glance over toward the Patriarch, standing by the stage. With him is an enormous, dark-haired man that towers over the old man like a giant. Something about him is familiar.

'Who's that?' I ask Sera, gesturing discretely toward him.

'Oh, Progenitors!' she says, wide-eyed. 'He has come.'

'Who?'

'Commander.'

At the mention of the name, memories of the giant in the sodden hallway at Gotthard return, and I instantly remember who the man is. 'He's the one who took Ester from me.'

'Sorry?' Sera says, and I realise I said that last part out loud.

'He's the one who took my friend Ester from Gotthard,' I say just loud enough for Sera to hear. 'Who is he? And if he's here, where's Ester? Could she have been one of the ones…' I couldn't bring myself to finish that sentence, knowing if I learned Ester had been one of the first to perish here, I'd be unable to live with myself.

'I don't know about your friend, but Commander is our leader.'

'But I thought…'

'Elihus may be the Patriarch, but he only runs this place. Commander is the one who's really in charge.'

'So that's who the Patriarch was referring to when he said something about receiving orders from a superior?'

'Yes. Both he and Elihus established Garret Gord. Elihus took care of administrative matters while Commander trained us. Before your cohort, we didn't have guardians. So, he did that himself.'

'He trained you?'

'Yes. Everything you learned about combat and defence came from him.'

'So, all that talk about Elihus being a visionary? What was that all about?'

'That is the story Elihus likes to tell to make himself look bigger. It may be true, in part, but our mission directive comes from Commander himself.'

'If he's so important, why haven't we seen him until now?'

'I do not know. For reasons I was never told, he left. Nobody has seen him since. Why he has come back now, I can only guess…'

'What?'

'It is nothing.'

'Sisters,' Trainer Blackthorn announces from the stage. 'Please take your seats.'

I climb back to my allocated place in front of Sera and sit wearing my sincerest look of interest while churning about what Commander's appearance may mean. Perhaps he's here to see his second cohort graduate, but something tells me it's more than that, and I realise Garret Gord's secrets are unending.

'It is with great honour I officially open the graduation ceremony of Hildr cohort Beta of Garret Gord,' Blackthorn says after the crowd chatter dies down. 'To deliver the opening remarks, I welcome our father, founder and saviour, his graciousness, the Patriarch, Elihus Kinton!'

Dressed in his customary pristine white suit, complete with long flowing sleeves, the Patriarch rises from his seat at the side of the stage and steps up to the podium.

'Guardians. Graduates,' he announces, arms outstretched aloft. 'Today is a truly remarkable day. Under the ever-watchful eyes of the Progenitors, we witness the dawning of a new chapter for Garret Gord. For today is the day nineteen girls become women, and women become titans.'

The gathered crowd applauses, and then with a gesture from the Patriarch, the crowd falls silent.

'You are here,' he continues, 'because you have earned the right and have proven yourselves worthy. Nine cycles ago, thirty girls came to me. Each one timid, weak and pathetic. But after cycles of training, discipline and transformation, nineteen have emerged victorious. Today, we induct those nineteen into the illustrious ranks of the Hildr Guild. I know each and every one of you will serve me, your Patriarch, with all your heart, mind, body and soul. I demand honour, respect and stalwart devotion. You will follow orders without question, act with the precision of a surgeon, and call upon your strength and commitment to do me and my House proud.'

He steps back, and the crowd applauds once more. Sera and I glance at each other and join them more out of obligation than actual sentiment; the Patriarch's speech did nothing to inspire me. So, I sit in my chair, enduring the tedious ceremony like everyone else.

Read out in order of our assigned numbers are the names of the nineteen graduates, each one rising to approach the stage and receive their accolade; a ceremonial gold ring delivered with Patriarch pomp.

'Alyx, daughter of Blackthorn,' Blackthorn calls out, and Alyx rises from her seat. I drift off into my own world.

'Jayne, daughter of MonLantry…'

Distracted, I barely hear my name being called. Sera gives me a poke, and I stand to ascend the stage. The Patriarch presents the ceremonial ring, which he places on my index finger without so much as a feigned smile. The expression is more akin to an ursus wrangler collaring an animal he's just tamed.

From the stage, I look out across the small gathered crowd. Sera claps, wearing a smile larger than any I had seen on her face before. But that's not what catches my attention.

There's a commotion at the gates. Three trucks painted green and black, like Fenton's, barrel their way through the entrance. The guards on duty make a feeble attempt to stop them but surrender when twenty soldiers swarm from the trucks with rifles and pistols drawn.

The vehicles continue toward the gathered crowd, followed by the soldiers on foot.

A large man with a scarred face slides from the lead truck's front passenger seat and, with two of his men following, searches through the disturbed crowd.

'Artimus, what is the meaning of this?' Elihus cries out from the stage.

'HomeGuard business, Elihus. Stay out of this,' the burly man—Artimus—yells back in a deep, raspy voice.

The Patriarch climbs down into the crowd. 'I will do no such thing.'

'That's her,' Artimus yells, pointing toward Sera. 'Seize her!'

Two soldiers descend on Sera and immobilise her like a pair of genets pouncing on their prey. She tries fending them off, but even with her skills, it's to little avail.

'Seraphin MonLantry, you're quite the tough person to find,' Artimus says.

'Unhand her,' Elihus bellows, but Artimus ignores him.

'I've been searching for you for more cycles than I care to mention. And to think you were here all along. No matter. Seraphin MonLantry, you are hereby under arrest for the assassination of Gaius Sempro!'

Oh no!

'You can't just charge in here and harass my people,' the Patriarch protests, looking like a frail old man compared to Artimus, with his muscular bulk.

'Elihus, I don't care if she's "your people" or not, she's a wanted murderer, and she will return to Hope where she will stand trial for Gaius's murder.'

'On what grounds?'

Artimus reaches into a pocket to produce a long, smooth green and white object. The look on Sera's face says it all; it's part of the handle of her lost knife.

'On the grounds she's guilty,' Artimus replies, tossing it at her. 'You're lucky I'm not arresting you as well, *Minister*, for aiding and abetting her. So, stand back and let me do my job.'

The large, scarred man reaches forward and grabs Sera's arm.

'No, leave Sera alone,' I yell from the stage, but Artimus ignores me and stands to block my view.

'I told you to unhand her,' Elihus growls, clutching Sera's other arm. Between them, a strange tug-of-war breaks out.

Elihus steps to one side to pull Sera closer to him, but then she doubles over, falling in deadweight to her knees between the grasp of both men.

It all plays out in slow-motion to the crack of a target rifle in the distance. Sera's head drops as a crimson stain seeps through the delicate blue fabric of her dress.

With screams of horror, I dodge the frenzied people running in random directions to make my way to her. The distance between the stage and Sera dissolves before I know I'm running.

By the time I push through the crowd to reach Sera, she lays there on her back with her mouth open in a pained gasp, her eyes darting all around. They lock on mine, and in that instant, I know.

'MEDIC!' I yell in desperation while using my hands to plug the gaping wound in her chest. Despite my efforts to stem the flow, her warm blood pulsates between my fingers.

For that moment, it's just Sera and me; the rest of the world fades into the background.

'Hang on, Sera,' I cry. 'Please hang on.'

Her hand touches my glistening cheek while the other grips my hand. 'I am sorry, Jayne,' she croaks, coughing up a mouthful of blood. There's so much blood.

The monster from my childhood returns, and I can't breathe, squeezing at my chest like a vice. I grip Sera tighter. 'No, don't talk like that. We've been through this before, and we've made it out. You can do it again. After all this time, I finally have a mother again. I have *you*. You can't leave me. Not now.'

Tears stream down my cheeks as Sera's breathing labours beneath my hands.

'I love you, Jayne,' she whispers with a fading voice.

'No, Mum. No! I love you…'

For the briefest of moments, her pale face cracks into a smile. Then, as though it's the only thing she's been waiting for, her hand drops, and that effervescent sparkle vanishes from her eyes.

She's gone.

25 BURN NOTICE

Elihus took solace in his office, leaned back in his comfortable chair, and relished in the silence. Despite the peace, his mind reeled. 'How is Artimus still alive?'

He opened the locked bottom drawer of his desk for his bottle of malt and groaned at how little remained. Frustrated, he stormed to the door where the scruffy guard, Buck, stood sentry outside.

'You!' he shouted at the burly guard. 'Bring me DelTasker.' He then strode off down the hallway.

Returning to his office moments later, holding a fresh bottle of malt, Elihus found a handsome-looking brunette sitting on the opposite side of his desk. Despite the massive purple bruise above her left eye, she sat with arms crossed and back straight, not even bothering to look at him as he entered.

Elihus opened the bottle without saying a word, poured a nip into his glass, and locked the bottle away. Taking a sip of the smooth amber liquid, he sat back in his chair and considered the woman with a steely glare. 'What happened to you, my dear?'

'Nothing I couldn't handle, sir.'

'No matter. You carried out your duties with exemplary efficiency. I would have preferred you waited until I was out of the vicinity, but I cannot fault a job well done.'

'Your order is my duty, sir,' she said without any change in expression whatsoever.

'There is, however, the matter of our unexpected visitor.'

'Sir?'

'Artimus Wyrm,' Elihus snapped. 'Tell me, Asset, how is it that man still draws breath?'

'I don't understand, sir.'

'Your mission was to dispatch him in Hope, was it not?'

'Affirmative, sir.'

'Then how is it he showed up here very much alive?'

'I do not know, sir.'

'You don't know or won't say?'

'I do not know, sir. I am certain I completed the mission, yet I have no memory of it.'

'You can't remember?' Elihus leaned forward, set his glass to one side, clasped his hands on his desk, and glared at the woman more intently. 'Curious. A person such as Artimus Wyrm is hardly forgettable.'

'All I remember is receiving my orders and going to Hope. Next thing, I awaken injured and lying beside a slain boart with the bloodied knife in my hand. I remember nothing else. Under oath of the Progenitors, I swear that is the truth.'

'You dare blaspheme in my House?'

Her lips thinned, but she remained silent.

'You still haven't answered my question,' Elihus roared, slamming his fists on the desk with a loud thump. 'How is it that you allowed Artimus Wyrm to turn up here?'

The seasoned 'resilience under duress' instructor remained silent and unfazed by his outburst. It infuriated him even more that she refused to show any sign of intimidation.

'This has put me in a very difficult situation,' he continued. 'What do you think is going to happen when Artimus returns to Hope and fronts the ministry? He has a crazy story of catching a murderer he's been hunting for the last four cycles, but she's killed in his hands by a target shooter on my property. Care to explain that?'

'Sir, I cannot,' she said with a blank expression. 'As far as I am concerned, I carried out my orders.'

'Incorrect!' he spat. 'You failed to kill Artimus Wyrm. That means you have failed your orders, and in so doing, you have failed me. You of all people should know the penalty for failure.'

DelTasker's voice faltered, and it gave him a slight glimmer he was finally getting to her. 'But you wouldn't—'

'This is my house. I would think by now, you know exactly what I will and will not do. Or perhaps MonLantry's failures were not a strong enough example for you?'

'You cannot be seriously comparing me to her?' DelTasker protested, and it seemed her 'impenetrable' façade was beginning to crack.

'Why not? At least she produced a viable asset.'

'A viable asset, sir?' she said, with the semblance of a sneer. 'Then where is she?'

'More to the point, where's yours?'

Once again, she chose silence as her answer, her face as blank as an empty page.

Elihus scoffed. 'Viable indeed. Your asset couldn't even survive the first five cycles. Since then, you have been nothing but a drain on my resources. Tell me, Asset, why should you not deserve the same punishment?'

'Sir, I apologise. I can make amends. Give me another chance, and I assure you, Artimus Wyrm will not escape this time.'

'Too late. It's already taken care of.'

'By whom?' she said with a raised eyebrow.

'That's none of your concern. It's out of your hands now.'

She held her head high in defiance, seeming to realise her fate had already been decided the moment she stepped into his office. 'Then what can I do?'

'You, DelTasker, have done more than enough. Consider this your notice of retirement. You have one day to get your affairs in order. Now get out of my office.'

From her neutral expression, Elihus couldn't tell what was going through her mind. She had been so well trained in maintaining composure under duress, he'd appointed her to instruct it. But he could hazard a guess. None ever took notice of retirement well.

Under Elihus's unwavering gaze, she slowly stood.

Then she sprung at him with a knife seeming to materialise in her hand.

Without flinching, Elihus reacted. A single slug from the smoking pistol in his own hand dropped the enraged assassin mid-flight, sprawling her across his neat desk with a bloody hole marring the flawless pale skin between her lifeless eyes.

The guard burst into the room with his pistol drawn.

'Clean this up,' Elihus instructed him as he rose from his chair, emptied his glass, and left.

Buck wasn't the only one who had heard the shot. Within moments, Blackthorn was at his door. She took one look at the body sprawled across his desk and sighed.

'DelTasker?' she asked.

'Tell me you have good news,' Elihus grumbled, pushing past her.

Blackthorn followed him into the hallway. 'We're still searching,' she said, maintaining her calm. 'But we will find her. There are only a few places she can go.'

'See that you do. I'm fast running out of assets.'

'Was that necessary?' she asked, gesturing back toward his office.

'Do not question me!' he snapped. 'Just focus on finding the girl.'

'Of course, sir.'

'It's bad enough Commander returns out of the aether making demands. Now I have to deal with a fugitive. This is a catastrophe.'

'What did Commander want exactly?'

Elihus gave her a sideward glare. He never appreciated being questioned but answered her anyway.

'His daughter.'

'And what do you plan to do?'

'I have the matter in hand. And Blackthorn. I am not above retiring anyone else who displeases me. If you cannot complete your mission, I will see that someone else does.'

26 REVENGE

There's something about this place. Maybe it's the crude name or the graphic image of a decapitated boart's head on the sign overhead. Nonetheless, having searched half a cendec for a cheap meal, it's the hand-scrawled writing on the A-frame sign outside that draws me in.

The Boart's Head stew and ale 3ħ

The timber floor is sticky underfoot, and the place reeks of stale ale and other things, but the thick smoke haze and irregular lighting makes it the perfect place to blend in.

A few intoxicated patrons gather between the door, a scattering of tables, and the L-shaped bar. They seem just as liberal with their drinks as they are with their boisterous conversation.

Besides the collective by the door, only one other person, seemingly in a depressive state that mirrors my own, nurses their drink in one of the gloomy booths lining the walls. The whites of their sullen eyes follow me as I make my way through the rabble, past them to the darkened end of the bar. I take a seat by the wall, and they return to their quiet, melancholic reverie.

Perhaps they're waiting for someone?

Here, from my vantage point in the shadows, I can survey the bar without attracting further attention. At least 'creepy old mate' with his starey glare has lost interest for now.

It's only been a day since graduation, and the memory of Sera being shot dead in front of me is still very raw on my nerves. After the chaos that ensued, I didn't care about the consequences. And with Ilona no longer able to return my affections, nothing holds me to Garret Gord anymore. So, I hitched a ride in an unsuspecting HomeGuard truck and came to Hope seeking revenge.

I had hoped drowning my sorrows would numb the pain, but with only a handful of coins I'd managed to pickpocket from a passer-by, all I can afford is the cheap swill they call ale. What I wouldn't do to get some of that malt the Patriarch savours so much.

The Patriarch—now that's a man I wouldn't mind seeing his blood on the end of my blade. But it's the man called Artimus Wyrm whose blood I seek. Picturing his twisted face in my mind sets my blood boiling. He came to Garret Gord with the express intent of hunting Sera and seeking vengeance for the death of Gaius Sempro. If it wasn't for him, she would still be alive. Somehow, a target shooter misfired. It's the only plausible explanation for how she's dead and that horrid, disfigured man still lives. I slam three coins on the bar and signal to the server, an older, grizzled-looking woman, for the special. She takes them and disappears, returning a dec later with a steaming bowl of stew and a small tankard of ale. This swill will have to do.

A slender man, overdressed for this sort of establishment, barges through the front door and stands at the threshold wearing the cheesiest grin. The rabble cheer at him, raising their tankards in toast and yelling 'skaal', while the person in the booth fidgets uncomfortably, seemingly unimpressed by the joviality disturbing their sour mood. From behind, a comparatively small individual wearing a thick grey coat and hat pushes past the well-dressed man. They swiftly juggle something small from their hand into their coat pocket before approaching the bar. Sitting a stool away, with their arms crossed on the bar top, they take off their hat…

'Ilona?' I say with genuine surprise.

'Hi Jayne,' she says, staring down at a spot in front of her. 'It's a good idea we talk like we don't know each other. How much for that?' She nudges an elbow at my bowl.

'Three hopemarks. And I don't think anyone will care in here.'

She feels around in her coat pocket and pulls out three coins for the yawning bar attendant.

'What are you doing here?' I ask, grateful for the company but also suspicious of her motives. *Did she come here for me or because she was ordered to?*

'I came looking for you, silly?'

'Why?'

'Because I saw what happened.'

'I see.' Suddenly, the contents of my bowl seem more inviting. Thankfully, Ilona's meal arrives, and she turns her attention to blowing on a steaming spoonful of the rough-tasting stew.

‘What is this stuff?’ she asks after tasting it.

‘Boart stew, I think the sign said. Horrid, isn’t it?’

‘Nah,’ she says, scooping up another mouthful. ‘After cycles of Shaddix’s cooking, this is amazing.’

‘You can have the rest of mine as well,’ I say, pushing my bowl towards her. She snatches it up and clutches it like she’s been starving. I return to surveying the room. ‘Aside from Creepy-starey guy over there, I think we should be okay.’

‘They’re good. They’re not interested in us,’ Ilona says between scoopfuls of stew.

‘Why are you really here?’ I ask.

Before Ilona can answer, the well-dressed man shouts in alarm. ‘Hey, my money’s missing!’

Creepy-starey guy skolls his drink and yells out, ‘I’ll teach you fur sleeping with me sister,’ before charging the group. He collides with Well-dressed man and the two break out into a scuffle. Cheers of ‘hit ‘em again’ and ‘get ‘em Landen’ erupt from the crowd as tables, drinks, and fists go flying.

‘OUTSIDE!’ the bar attendant bellows, ‘before I call the ‘Guard.’

As if someone flicked a switch, the rabble stops and clears out of the bar, leaving Ilona and me as the only remaining patrons.

I push another coin over to the bar attendant for a second drink. ‘You know how to kill a mood,’ I say in jest.

‘I ain’t takin’ that,’ she nods at the coin. ‘Finish ya drinks and be on ya way. Bar’s closed.’

‘What?’ I protest, ‘but we weren’t part of that.’

‘Don’t care,’ she says. ‘I can’t take no trouble. The ‘Guard’ve already supplied enough justice this tendawn. Once a brawl starts, that’s it. Now finish up ‘n get out.’

‘Where to? We don’t have a place to stay?’

‘Don’t care ‘bout that neither. Not my problem.’

‘Please,’ Ilona interrupts, ‘we just need somewhere to stay, that’s all. Do you know of a place? We don’t have many coins left, and we—’

‘There’s a place round the corner,’ the bartender replies with a softer tone. ‘They have a few of the old huts left for a mark or two a night. They’re rough but comfortable. Now finish ya meals and be on ya way.’

The bartender was right; the tiny single-room hut is rough, with its crude furniture, empty kitchen and an ancient oil heater that doesn't seem to warm the room.

Ilona wanders around the dark hut with a bio-lamp. 'This was the Administrator's place? For one Hopemark, what do you suppose the other rooms are like compared to this?' She sits the lamp on the small circular dining table and turns the brightness up, illuminating the table and surrounds.

'I don't imagine it being much better than this.'

'I can't believe they used to live like this,' Ilona agrees.

We stare at each other in the blue-ish light, and it reminds me of the storeroom.

'So…' we both say in chorus.

'You go first,' Ilona says.

'No, you.'

Ilona scratches her head and sits at the table. 'I'm not supposed to reveal details of missions, you know that. Standard protocol.'

'So you *are* here on a mission?'

'Crud,' she says, realising her error.

'Screw standard protocol. It's me. Or…are you here to kill me?'

Ilona snorts. 'You? Frak no. I came here to find you, not kill you. Why would you even think that?'

'I dunno, I'm just a little on edge, I guess. But you *are* here to kill someone, right?'

'Um…'

'Ilona?'

'I'm sorry, Jayne. I just can't.'

'Okay, what if I told you I came here to kill Artimus Wyrm?'

'Who?'

'You remember the guy who crashed our graduation?'

'The guy with the weird, burnt face?' Ilona asks.

'Yep, that's him,' I reply with a scowl. 'Well…'

'So, you want to kill the guy who crashed our graduation? Why?'

'He didn't just crash our graduation, Ilona. He killed Sera. I'm going to make him pay for that.'

'Ah,' she says, sitting back in her chair. 'I didn't know that. Are you sure?'

'Yes, Ilona,' I shout, unintentionally raising my voice at her. 'Had he not been there, Sera would still be alive.'

'Hmm,' she says, biting her tongue.

I quickly move to put the subject back on track. 'So, you know mine. Who's your mark?'

'Nobody,' she says with a cheeky grin.

'But you just said...?'

She leans forward and pecks me on the lips. 'I felt like doing that,' she chuckles. 'You're so cute when you're serious.'

'Ilona, this *is* serious. Can we focus?'

'Okay, if you insist.'

'So, are you going to tell me who your mark is or not?'

'Artimus Wyrm,' she replies, fidgeting with her guild ring.

'Wyrm's your mark?' I ask in disbelief.

Ilona nods.

'You mean to tell me you've been sitting there all this time listening to me rabble on about Artimus Wyrm, and he's been your contract all along?'

'Yes, but that's why I didn't say anything. I knew you'd be upset.'

'Upset? Confused, maybe, but I'm not upset. Why would the Patriarch give you the contract?'

'Well, he wants you back and figured he could kill two aves with...well, that's not the right phrase...make efficient use of my time here...that's better. It would seem the Patriarch wasn't impressed with the gatecrasher either. Why did you leave?'

'I wasn't going to wait for permission. I saw my opportunity and took it.'

'The Patriarch was furious when you ran away. You could have waited. I'm sure he would have assigned the mission to you, eventually.'

'I doubt it, and frankly, I don't care. Sera's dead. I'm going to make sure the person responsible pays. The Patriarch may have sent you to do it, but *I'm* doing this no matter what. I would prefer to do it with you. So, do you want to?'

'Want to what?' she asks.

'Help me? I hear he's a pretty tricky target. One of the Alphas tried, or so I'm told. She ended up being fed to a boart.'

'Brutal.'

'So, are we going to team up or not?'

She flashes another one of those cheeky smiles. 'Of course, silly. I'll help you.'

'Perfect. One way or another, I *will* see Artimus Wyrm dead for what he did to Sera. Mark my words.'

'Good,' she says, shuffling her chair closer. 'I've already scoped out his movements…'

27 SOLON VOW

'It's a school,' Elihus protested, 'and a reform school for young women at that. I was put in charge of it long before the war. I should not need to justify it to you.'

Sage sat crossed-armed at his desk, considering the wiry old man with a stern glare. 'And yet you didn't care to tell me about it?'

'I didn't think I had to,' Elihus shrugged. 'It has nothing to do with you or Hope. Besides, it isn't professional to mix business interests. You have my assurance this will have no impact on my capacity to perform as both Minister and Principal.'

'And what of your responsibilities to Hope? For the last six tendaws, you've been absent. What am I to do when you're not here?'

'With all due respect, Surprime, that's your responsibility, not mine.'

Sage's scowl deepened the furrow in his brow. 'I need to know where my ministers are when they don't show up for meetings.'

Elihus scoffed. 'We only have one school in Hope with but a handful of students.'

Sage didn't take his eyes off his minister, holding the room in uncomfortable silence, before asking, 'What did you say the place is called?'

Before Elihus could answer, Conrad shouted from the antechamber, interrupting their conversation. 'You can't go in there, Minister Wyrm, he's already—'

The door to Sage's office burst open, and in stormed Artimus, red-faced and seething.

'Don't trust this man, Sage!' he roared, jabbing a pointed finger at Elihus.

'Artimus,' Sage said, 'please join us.'

'Whatever he's selling, don't buy it.'

Sage shot him a puzzled look. 'Okay, well, Elihus was just telling me about the reform school he's set up for—'

'Skip the rehashed sales pitch,' Artimus spat. 'It's lies. All lies. I was there, and I saw it for myself. Whatever it is, it's *not* a school. I can't put my finger on it, but there's something not right about the place, and this man knows why.'

'Some bold claims there, *Minister*,' Elihus countered. 'For your information, it is a premier institution where we teach languages, mathematics, sciences, history—all the necessary life skills required to produce graduates of the highest order—'

'Highest order? Where are the buildings? Where are the students? I saw no evidence of a school. All I saw was a fort guarded by heavily armed wannabes playing soldier.'

'What would you know about schools and education?' Elihus retorted. 'I bet the last school you went to was whatever run-down derelict of a public institution that *educated* you—'

'Careful,' Artimus warned, looming over Elihus, who didn't seem too perturbed by the brutish man overshadowing him.

'Pfft, no,' Elihus said, waving a limp hand in the Admiral's direction. 'You know nothing of education, let alone the intricacies involved in teaching the next generation how to survive in this world.'

'Then care to tell me why you were protecting a fugitive?'

Sage raised an eyebrow at that but let the two continue their squabble uninterrupted.

'Are you referring to my poor teacher you had killed?' Elihus accused.

'*I* had killed?' Artimus objected angrily. 'Speak for yourself. No, Elihus, that was a take-down, and you know it.'

At that point, Sage's intrigue had reached its peak. This conversation had taken a dangerous turn, and it was time he stepped in. 'What are you two talking about?' he said.

'Surprime,' Elihus shouted, somehow managing to speak over Artimus's booming voice, effectively blocking the Admiral's retort, 'this man stormed my school with the express intent of harassing one of my teachers. He assaults her, and the next thing she ends up dead with a hole in her chest.'

'How do you suppose I did that?' Artimus growled. 'No, Sage, from that range, that was a highly trained target-shooter. That aside, why would I kill someone I wanted to talk to? It seems more likely *he* had her killed.'

Elihus threw his hands in the air. 'This is preposterous! Only HomeGuard have target-shooters that are that well trained. Besides, why would I have one of my best teachers killed?'

'You tell me, Elihus. Sage, I had her in my hands—the woman who murdered Gaius—but now all I have is a corpse. Thanks to Pops here, I can't put a corpse on trial.'

'Are you sure she was the one, Artimus?' Sage asked.

'I'd bet my reputation on it. She gave herself away when I presented her with the knife. Hunter verified her body. Oh, and Sage, the place is called Garret Gord.'

'Garret Gord?' Sage mused, mulling the information over in his mind. He recalled this coming up in a ministerial meeting where Elihus had apportioned funds under a mysterious purchase order issued with the letters GG. Now, it was starting to make sense. 'GG? Grade Gratuity my backside! Elihus, explain!'

Elihus spluttered. 'I'll never!'

'There's more,' Artimus said. 'At this "school" of his, Elihus is called 'Patriarch'. Sound familiar?'

As Sage raised a brow in surprise, Artimus continued. 'I told you I'd get to the bottom of it, although I still don't know how a schoolteacher came to be an assassin. I'm afraid now that our prime suspect is dead, we won't likely find out. It seems our boy Elihus here has been busy covering up MonLantry's tracks. I want to know why.'

'Elihus, did you have anything to do with Gaius's murder?' Sage asked, not wanting to avoid the issue any further.

'No, of course not!' Elihus protested indignantly. 'How was I to know all about Seraphin's extracurricular activities? Furthermore, I resent the insinuation that I, of all people, would do such a heinous thing.'

Despite Elihus's answer, Sage continued his line of questioning, feeling the tension in the room rise with his blood pressure. 'Has Hope been supplying funds and resources to your little side enterprise?'

Elihus glared at him wide-eyed. 'This is absurd. Ridiculous, even. I will not sit here and allow this pistol nut to sully my name. I am a seasoned representative of the people, someone who has been a respectable member of the government for longer than you've been able to grow facial hair. How dare you take his word over mine!'

Sage leaned forward, staring at Elihus with such intensity he shifted with discomfort in his chair. 'I only asked a simple question, but considering your defensive attitude, I'm more inclined to go with Artimus on this. You have a choice, Elihus,' he paused, contemplating his next words carefully.

Elihus sat stone-faced, his left eyelid twitching involuntarily under the questioning, providing Sage with all the confirmation he needed.

'You can resume your position as education minister and continue to serve Hope.' Sage held a hand up to quell the enraged Artimus. '*Or*, you can relinquish your position and go back to your school in the mountains. Either way, you can't have both.'

Elihus scowled at the ultimatum. 'Can I think about it?'

'Take as long as you need. But if you step beyond the boundaries of Hope, I'll take it you've made your decision and move to elect your replacement.'

'Come on, Sage,' Elihus implored, 'this is hardly reasonable. Whatever happened to the friendly and amenable Sage we all know and respect?'

'He died alongside Gaius with a knife in his chest four cycles ago.'

'Alright,' Elihus said, rising from his seat. 'If this must be. You know where to find me.'

After the confrontation with Elihus, the day had dragged on, forcing Sage to think of the new developments surrounding his education minister instead of other pressing matters. It was with somewhat of a relief a knock came at the door. Artimus entered to say it was time to leave, taking a moment to reassure Sage the matter with Elihus was nothing for him to worry about.

They exited through the town hall's main doors and stopped at the top step like a pair of tomadai caught in a vehicle's headlights.

A reception of waiting media had gathered at the steps and surged on the two politicians the moment they appeared, firing pointed questions about Elihus and his alleged resignation.

Sage only wanted to get home to be with his family. He raised his hand to shield his eyes from the flashing lights, scanning the sea of reporters for Jaxson and his means of escape.

Beside him, Artimus stared into the cameras with a stony expression as though willing them to explode. 'No comment.'

Just visible beyond the media lights in the early night, Sage's car waited. He watched with relief as the crowd parted to make way for Jaxson as his burly bodyguard and friend pushed his way through the mass of bodies towards him.

'Sage,' Artimus said, pulling him closer to speak in private. 'I'm taking a staff car and heading to one of my outposts to look into something. I'll be back tomorrow.'

Jaxson broke through to the head of the crowd and ascended the stairs to make room for Sage.

'Surprime! Surely, you have something to say to the public?' one reporter forcefully shouted over the noise of other questions.

Sage straightened his shoulders and faced them. 'Minister Kinton hasn't resigned or been stood down,' he said. 'But, I'm sorry, I'm unable to comment any further. The matter's still in Minister Kinton's hands. That's all I can say. Now, if you'll please excuse me, I'm off to see my wife.'

'Thank you, Artimus,' Sage said, turning to his defence minister and patting him on the shoulder in a show of gratitude for his presence. Artimus gave him a wry smile in return, then he and Jaxson disappeared into the consuming mob, leaving Artimus to find his own way out.

28 THE ROCK AND THE HARD PLACE

Dimly lit streets and buildings whiz past as the truck's engine screams out its top speed.

Earlier that evening, Ilona had barged into our little hut, telling me to grab my gear as our time to act was now.

With a surge of adrenaline, I happily abandoned my cup of tei and chased her out the door.

I still have no idea where she got the truck from, but the poor delivery driver hadn't expected to take a nap so soon. We'd hefted his heavy body into the seat between us, then Ilona threw me the keys and told me I'd be driving.

'I've just seen him,' Ilona yells out. 'Keep going, two more intersections…one…turn.'

Tyres groan and screech into the corner as I grip the steering wheel firm, hoping the truck stays upright. It bounces and slides around the corner on two wheels, and when the tyres plant firm on the road again, I floor the accelerator.

Headlights cross the road in front, and I brace for impact.

The whole scene plays out in vivid, slow motion. The smaller, dark-coloured car passes through where our headlights should be. Both vehicles embrace in a shrieking, cacophonous dance before separating in their own spin and finally coming to rest.

Aside from the hissing and the tick, tick, tick of the smashed radiator, the only other sound is the incessant ringing in my ears. Dazed by the collision, my head spins, and I fight to keep conscious.

Fibrous material, glass and metal are scattered all over the place. Part of it seems to have come from the truck's windscreen, which now lays like a glittering sheet across the road.

Ilona's out of the cabin before I can shake off the shock and is peering through the windows of the other mangled vehicle.

Ignoring the ringing in my ears, I unclip my safety belt, drag the unfortunate delivery driver behind the wheel and climb out. My legs, wobbly from the impact, almost collapse the moment my feet touch the ground, and I cling to the door for support.

The crash aftermath is like a war scene. Strewn wreckage and a trail of leaking fuel lead from the smaller black car whose unfortunate driver, slumped in a bloodied heap, already appears dead. Its front end is impaled on the corner of a concrete building, and it teeters precariously over a brick-edged garden bed.

As I make my way over to Ilona, she fervently bashes at the rear passenger side window with a hefty chunk of concrete.

Something's not right.

Through the cracked front passenger window, I can just make out the shapes of two affluent-looking men in the back seats.

Ilona throws the concrete block at the window again and screams in frustration when it doesn't break.

Suddenly the black car's front end ignites, and I'm forced back by the whoosh of searing hot flame.

The fire quickly engulfs the bonnet, and the trail of fuel leading from the car ignites, burning its way towards the truck.

'Hurry,' I yell.

Ilona grunts, picks up the brick, and throws it again. Stress fractures spread in the glass as throw after throw, she heaves her weight behind the slab.

'It's not breaking,' she howls, picking it up and throwing it once more. 'I can't break this wretched glass!'

'It's compo-graphene,' I yell back, keeping my eye on the creeping flame. 'Keep going. It'll break. Come on, we're running out of time,' I shout nervously as the fire licks at the underside of the truck's cabin.

With Ilona's next throw, the glass cracks and the block wedges in the window. She removes it to reveal a hole big enough to see through.

Sitting unconscious in the back seat is a well-dressed, sandy blonde-haired man and a similarly aged, ochre-tanned man who, from his uniform, appears to be a high-ranking member of the Surprime guard. Neither are Artimus Wyrm.

'Ilona! Stop!'

She ignores me and continues to raise the concrete block above her head.

'STOP!' I shout again. 'That's not him. That's not our mark.'

The Surprime guard stirs, groggily opening his eyes to witness Ilona hurl the block again.

Ilona pulls her weapon from the caved-in window and turns on me with a vicious scowl. With the flickering flame reflecting in her deep, almost black irises, her expression is one I have never seen on her before. 'No,' she says with a voice cold and dripping with vehemence. 'He's mine.' She then hauls the chunk directly at the blonde man again.

'Sage!' the guard yells as the block smashes its way through, catching the blonde man in the side of his head.

The guard glares at us with mixed shock and anger and fumbles for something in his jacket pocket. Ilona reaches for another block.

Between the guard and the burning truck, our time has run out.

'No!' I yell, grabbing Ilona's hand and dragging her from the scene. 'We're done here.'

Moments later, an explosion rips through the quiet street a block behind us, lighting up the night.

29 LOVE AND DEATH

Thanks to the money we gained from the unfortunate delivery driver, we seek refuge in a stylish hotel in the centre of town. It means we no longer have to put up with that cold, bug-ridden shack. Still filled with the euphoric rush from the adrenaline, my heart feels like it's racing a million beats a dec. And looking out the hotel room's expansive two-storey window, an orange haze casts silhouettes of the buildings from where we'd just come.

As the door to our lavish room clicks shut, I can't help but marvel at the large pillow-covered bed in its centre. Regrettably, it only serves as a momentary distraction before I spin on my heel and face Ilona.

'What was that?' I yell at her. She frustratingly doesn't seem in the least bit fazed by what's just transpired.

She drops her gear by the door and casually starts undressing. 'What was what?'

'Back there, what was that?' I drop my gear by hers and try not to let her derail me. 'That wasn't our mark.'

'No, Jayne,' she says in a level tone. '*We* never had a mark. That was *my* mark.'

I glare at her, aghast. 'What? Yours? What do you mean?'

'Those were my orders, not yours.'

'But you said… why didn't you tell me?'

'Because the old man ordered me not to.'

'What? Why?'

'Jayne, why do you think?'

Conceding she has a point, I give an indignant huff. Had I known, I probably would have been furious we were wasting our time on someone who's not Artimus Wyrm. 'Who was that guy, anyway?'

'Do you really want to know?' she asks.

'Yes, I do.'

She strips down and stands unabashed in her matching lacy black undergarments, like a woman from *The Unattached*. Then, as though the name means nothing to her, she says, 'Sage Solon.'

That name sounds familiar. 'The SURPRIME!' I yell when it hits me. 'We just killed the Surprime?'

'Shh,' Ilona hushes. 'Keep your voice down.' She snatches open the door to check the hallway, then closes it again. 'Yes, the Surprime. That's why I couldn't tell you.'

'Shak,' I swear, pacing the room. 'But why?'

'I don't know. It's not our place to question orders. You know that.'

'So, what now? I guess this means our other job is off?' I grumble, making it clear I'm not impressed.

'No. Just after tonight, I think we'll have to lie low for a while. Maybe even go back and wait for stuff to blow over.'

'That's just it. Stuff doesn't just "blow over".'

'Sure it does,' Ilona says, shrugging, then disappears into the adjacent bathroom.

'Artimus waited four cycles to catch Sera,' I say, but from the running water, I know she wouldn't have heard it.

Alone, thoughts churn through my mind like dark storm clouds.

I can't believe Ilona lied to me.

We killed the Surprime. But why?

How am I going to get Artimus Wyrm now?

While I strip out of my dirty clothes, I try to distract myself, but thoughts, worse thoughts, come flooding back; Sera dying in my arms, those two men stuck in the burning car, and Ilona hacking at that window with a wild ferocity I'd only ever seen in a boart. Confounded by what-ifs and an ever-growing cloud of doubt, I sit on the end of the bed wearing only my undergarments and fall into a deepening melancholic haze, wondering how I allowed things to get to this.

Ilona emerges from the bathroom wrapped in a fluffy white towel, her long black hair tied up and a serene smile on her radiant face as if somehow everything isn't quite so bad.

'What's wrong?' she asks, ambivalent, and I get the sense the gravity of what we'd done hasn't dawned on her yet.

'Artimus Wyrm,' I reply sourly.

'What about him?'

'He came for Sera because she assassinated Gaius Sempro.'

'Gaius Sempro? Who's that? Oh, you mean the guy whose hut we stayed in last night, that Gaius Sempro?'

'Yes, well, back then, he was the administrator and, according to what I've heard, the beloved founder of Hope. Had he survived, he would've become Surprime. He was a pretty big deal.'

'Oh,' Ilona says, showing some semblance of understanding.

'Yeah, oh.'

'But, if he was so beloved, why would anyone want him dead—or that Solon guy for that matter? Seems someone doesn't like Surprimes.'

'Ilona!'

'So what?' she shrugs with indifference.

'So… you're the one who killed him,' I try to explain. 'If they're already pissed about Gaius. What do you think they're going to do now that Sage has been assassinated too?'

She stares at me with a blank expression. 'But we set it up as an accident.'

'If the Surprime guard have half the intelligence of those dimwits they call guards at the Gord, they'll see right through that. It was only enough to give us time to get away.'

'I hadn't thought of that.'

And, there it is, now she gets it. But why isn't she showing any remorse?

'Ilona, I just lost Sera. I can't bear—' At that moment, my eyes involuntarily well with tears, and all the emotions come crashing down like bricks on the front of that car. 'I just can't shake the feeling we've made a terrible mistake.'

'What mistake? You mean by fulfilling my contract?'

'That's cold, Ilona. Haven't you thought of the consequences now he's dead? I can't believe you're being so casual about this.'

Ilona sits on the bed and shuffles in close.

'You shouldn't be concerned about that. All I did was my job. If anyone should be questioning my actions, it's the ones who sent me.'

'I don't know, Ilona. It feels… wrong.'

'Okay, put it this way. We are weapons, like a knife or a pistol. Does a pistol second guess its role in killing someone? Of course, it doesn't. Like that pistol, we do what we're ordered. That's all.'

'Yes, but pistols don't have conscious thought.'

'We did nothing wrong,' she insists, rubbing my shoulders.

Whether it's the tiredness or my present mental state, I don't know, but at that moment, memories of my last conversation with Sera overwhelm me, and I break down.

There's an awkward silence, and even with Ilona sitting right here, I can't shake it.

Clasping one of my hands in hers, she allows the silence to linger while those mystical, colour-changing eyes of hers, now blue, lock gaze with mine. It's as though she's peering directly into my soul and reaching out with hers to pull me from the depths of despair.

'Jayne,' she says, delicately brushing a strand of hair from my eyes. 'You are the strongest, most sweetest and loveliest person I know. Don't let worry wrinkle that cute face of yours.'

If only to conceal the warm flush rising from my chest into my cheeks, I manage a smile. Embarrassed, I look down and find myself gazing into Ilona's lap.

'Do you remember that time when we met,' she says, 'and I asked you where you were from?'

'Yeah. I answered you, then asked the same, but you didn't want to say. You kinda went quiet and strange.'

She chuckles, and now we're both gazing at her lap. 'I know,' she replies. 'I didn't mean that. I was… jealous of you. Until then, I'd never been outside the Gord, let alone with anyone else. When you told me about your life before that place, I was sad because that place has been my life.'

'So, you weren't adopted?'

'No, I was born there.'

'Does that mean Shaddix—?'

'No. Martok no. She's not my mother, not even half the woman my mum was. My mother died when I was young.'

'And your father?'

She sighs, and I feel I've hit a nerve.

'I don't know what happened to him. He disappeared when I was four, so I barely remember him. All I know is he joined the military—he became a commander or something like that. Anyway, I haven't seen or heard from him since.'

Her comment makes me think of the giant man called Commander, who'd turned up to our graduation. Could that be him? Without wanting to stress Ilona, I shelve the thought. 'I'm so sorry, Ilona. I didn't know.'

'I don't even have the pendant he gave me anymore,' she says, touching the bare patch on her chest where it should be.

'What? What happened to it?'

'The Patriarch confiscated it. He said I didn't deserve it and that he needed to hold onto it for "safekeeping." Anyway, it's okay,' she shrugs. 'It's not like it meant anything. Father was barely ever around, so how could I miss him? Mum pretty much raised me on her own. The hardest part was losing her. I still remember her with her long golden hair and deep blue eyes. I wish I had hair like hers. This,' she says, tugging at her hair like it's a dirty rag attached to her scalp, 'apparently, I inherited from father.'

'But I love your hair,' I protest, pulling her hair tie out and combing my fingers through her long silky smooth black locks. 'I wish I had hair like yours. And your eyes, I don't know how you do it, but they keep changing colour.'

'They do?'

'You didn't know that?'

'No,' she says, brushing aside her momentary unease. 'Mother was soft and gentle, and she cared for me like Sera cared for you. We would go on trips into the forest and soak up the beauty. You wouldn't believe what it was like back then. There was so much vibrance and life. Flowers of every colour imaginable and the aves, they were everywhere. I loved how the soft grass felt underfoot and its sweet perfume in the air. There was this one place she took me where there was a waterfall concealed in a nook of rock. We'd take off our clothes, and she'd teach me how to swim. But then the war happened, and she was gone. I cried for tendaws afterwards. Shaddix took me in and told me to stop being a baby. And that was it. You know the rest. I've tried to hold on to these memories, but over the cycles, they've faded like old photos. It's been so long since I've even spoken about them.'

'I don't know what to say. You've had a pretty traumatic childhood. I'm not surprised you acted the way you did towards me.'

'And I am so sorry about that, Jayne. Really, I am.'

'Why does Shaddix treat you the way she does?'

'I don't know, and I really don't care. Since meeting you, I've realised life still has things worth having in it. That night in the forest, when you saved me from those raiders, the berries and myself, I would have died not even knowing or caring that someone like you was out there. Since my mother died, I've been treated like a worthless wretch. When I'm with you, gazing into those beautiful green eyes of yours, none of that matters. I feel the world is complete, and everything is alright.'

'You're no worthless wretch, Ilona…'

Leaning in closer, she gently cups my cheek in her hand, and as she gazes at me, I stop talking and feel the need to copy. Her flawless face draws nearer. She teases with her linger, a peck of anticipation, driving me crazy until finally, she presses her supple lips against mine, and we kiss.

As our lips lock, I realise this kiss is nothing like the cheeky stolen kisses we shared in our secret room. This is more intense, more soulful. Ilona wraps her arms around me, and I close my eyes, allowing my other senses to take in the moment; the sweet taste of her tongue, the delicate floral scent of her hair and the soft smoothness of her skin against mine—it sets my body to tremble.

Cheek to cheek, Ilona whispers in my ear. 'I want you.'

'Uh-huh,' I utter as a rush of excitement leaves me breathless.

She releases her towel, and it falls to the floor, revealing her beautifully lascivious body.

Gazing upon the smooth curves of her petite, athletic figure with her perky breasts and soft, golden tanned skin in the low lamplight, she is breathtakingly beautiful. But in this simple act, I know Ilona is revealing more to me than just her body.

It's impossible to believe this is the meek girl I met cycles ago who came so close to throwing her life away. Since then, we have shared experiences, fears, hopes and dreams, despite an establishment forbidding such things. Without Ilona, I doubt I would be here either, so for her to share the most intimate part of herself with me is more than I could ever wish for.

I only hope I'm worth it.

'Remember that last time in the storeroom?' she asks, positioning a pillow for me on the bed. 'Well, I've never done this willingly. But with you, it's different. Jayne, I want you to feel me, and I want to know what it feels like to be with you.'

Hearing those words, my heart pounds furiously in my chest, more so than it ever had during any of my tests. I'm surprised Ilona can't hear it.

Her hand lightly rests on my shoulder. 'Remember what I said before?' she says soothingly. 'Let it flow like water and relax. You're safe with me.'

Biting my lip, I position myself on the bed, and she slides in beside me, placing a hand on my belly. The gentle touch of her fingertips on my bare skin tickles, making parts of me pulsate as though my heart pounding wasn't enough. With Ilona lying naked at my side and the knowledge we're alone with only our inhibitions holding us back, I let go of my fear.

'I think we can do away with these,' she says, tugging at my undergarments.

Paralysed with emotion, I close my eyes again and beckon Ilona to continue. She presses her body against mine and softly nibbles at my neck. 'I promise I'll be gentle,' she whispers into my ear as her hand slips between my thighs.

Never have I allowed anyone to get this close, to touch me like this, or make me feel the way Ilona is making me feel. And as our bodies intertwine, I lose myself in her. Everything else that consumed my thoughts no longer matters—I'm in love, and for the first time, someone loves me back.

30 REPERCUSSIONS

A middle-aged woman with silvery-grey hair pulled into a tight bun brings over two menus as we select a table inside a quaint café across the road from our hotel. Her name badge reads 'Islay'.

'Good morn,' she says. 'Are we arriving or leaving?'

'Sorry?' I ask, glancing around. Aside from an elderly man sitting at the bar with a newspaper and sipping on a steaming cup of black liquid, the place is empty.

'Your bags?'

'Oh, just passing through.'

'Right, well, I hope you've enjoyed your time here. Can I start you off with a tei or kahwah?'

'Kahwah?' I ask, 'what's that?'

'Ah,' she replies, bemused, 'it's like tei, only it's not tei.'

'Right, ahh…' I say, perusing the menu. 'I'll have a tei, and the dawn stack, thanks.'

'And you, ave?'

Ilona purses her lips, then hands back the menu and smiles. 'I'll try the kahwah, and I'll have the dawn stack too, thanks.'

As Islay walks away with the menus, Ilona leans over the table with her head between her elbows, bearing the largest grin I think I've ever seen on her. The warm golden light streams through the window making her onyx black hair glow. 'Last night was incredible,' she says, her magical eyes iridescent blue.

'Yeah, it was, wasn't it?' I sigh, chuckling to myself.

'What's funny?'

'Ah, nothing. Just something Sera said.'

'Sera? What did she say?'

I chuckle again. 'This one morning, Sera had a "guy visitor" who she sent streaking naked through our apartment. Anyway, we got talking about sex, and she said something like, "one day, you'll understand". I guess I do, now.'

Ilona strokes a strand of hair from my face. 'I'm really sorry about what happened to her, Jayne.'

'Yeah, me too,' I reply sullenly. Having Ilona here to help share my burden helps a lot. But, each time I think of Sera, it's as if a giant chasm has opened in my heart, and I'll fall right into it. Last night, Ilona proved to me that despite my grief for Sera, I can still be happy, and it helped me forget about my worldly troubles, even if it was for just that moment. 'Thank you, Ilona.' I say, placing my hand on hers.

'For what?'

'For everything.'

She leans in and kisses me. 'No thank you necessary. You've given me all the thanks I need,' she says, the cheeky grin returning.

'Alright, lovelies,' Islay says, returning with a tray carrying our food and drinks and setting them down on the table between us. Ilona considers the dark brown liquid with trepidation as though it'll leap out and bite her, then takes one sip and spits it back into the cup. 'Ugh, that's… horrible.'

'You're braver than me,' I chuckle.

Islay giggles then passes Ilona a paper cloth before placing a small jug of milk and a pot of a crystalline substance on the table. 'Try it with some of this,' she suggests.

Ilona scoops in four spoonfuls of the crystalline stuff and stirs in the jug's entire contents, then takes another sip. 'Ah, that's better.'

'Oh, no!' says the man at the bar, and I'm struck with a pang of anxiety.

'What is it, Bronal?' Islay asks, turning to him.

'Oh no, oh no, oh no,' he moans, lifting up the paper. 'It's the Surprime.'

'What about him?'

'He's dead!'

'What? Excuse me, aves,' Islay says, rushing to look over the old man's shoulder to get a glimpse of the headline.

'Killed in a car accident, it says,' Bronal adds.

'Oh, no…' Islay cries, her eyes wide with disbelief. 'His poor family.'

'Excuse me?' Ilona asks, 'but what's happened?'

'It's the Surprime, ave. He's been killed in a car accident. He has a wife and two children. Oh, they must be heartbroken.'

'He was a good man,' Bronal says. 'A great man. Like Gaius before him. Seems the Progenitors don't want us to have good people leading this place.'

Ilona and I exchange troubled looks.

'It's a terrible shame…' Islay's words drift off into a muffle as two trucks pull up outside our hotel. A contingent of heavily armed HomeGuard soldiers climb out and storm the building.

I tap out a message to Ilona with our secret hand signals, '*we have to go*.'

'Shak,' she whispers back.

Leaving our uneaten breakfast behind, we grab our belongings and are out the door before anyone can notice we're gone.

The newspapers may have reported the Surprime's death as an accident, but from the looks of those troops swarming the hotel, someone knows it wasn't. I can't be sure how they know who they're searching for, but remembering the stark terror in the Surprime guard's eyes, I can hazard a guess. Ilona and I do our best to blend in, falling in step with the general foot traffic. Once we're out of sight, we break into a run, following the main road out of Hope.

'I should have killed that guy,' Ilona huffs as she jogs beside me.

'It wouldn't have mattered. They would've figured it out, eventually.'

'How do you know?' she snaps. 'That fire should've taken care of it. Unless that guard somehow survived. If he did, he's seen our faces. Stands to reason he's the one whose sent those soldiers after us.'

Having run far enough, I slow to a walk. 'You don't know that. It could've been someone else.'

A few strides ahead, Ilona also stops and turns to me with a pained expression. 'I still should have killed him.'

I grab her by the arm and try to reason with her, but she seems intent on blaming herself. 'We may be… who we are, but that doesn't mean we have to kill everyone we come across. Our only obligation is our mark. Unless you can tell me otherwise, that man wasn't your mark.'

'I disagree,' she protests. 'Our job is to make the kill smooth and clean. Get in, get out, that's it. If that means collateral damage, then so be it.'

'Alright. Put it this way, then. That guy was drawing his pistol. If we'd spent any more time there, you would've been shot, or we both would've been caught up in the explosion. We're lucky I got us out of there when I did.'

From the way she's biting her lip, what I've said seems to be sinking in, but she's still not happy about it.

'I just don't like leaving loose ends.'

'Ilona, I love you, but you have some really twisted ideals.'

Here, in the older outskirts of town, the buildings are more dilapidated and spread out, forming the remnants of a shantytown of smaller shacks like the one in which we stayed. Constructed of junk, each one appears derelict, reclaimed by vegetation. It's a wonder anyone could have lived here.

Beads of perspiration roll down my back, and I remove my jacket to cool down. While we stop to catch our breath, I take a quiet moment to survey the surroundings, breathe in the warm fresh scented air, and listen to the aves chirp in the surrounding trees; a welcome relief from the town's sterile concrete.

Despite the signs of nature recovering, evidence of destruction remains in the burned trees and rusted husks of vehicles scattered around, forming unlikely homes for saplings springing up to fill in the desolation.

The two of us trudge further out-of-town, shadowing the main road towards the Rika River, keeping out of sight from the lookouts.

A large brown, grey and white object emerges in a clearing just visible through a gap in the new growth.

Ilona lifts a hand to shade her eyes from the sun strobing through the trees. 'Is that what I think it is?'

'Looks like it.' The object becomes recognisable as a Garret Gord truck. Two guards stand at ease ahead of it, holding rifles with the muzzles pointing down, while another sits behind the wheel.

I halt to scope the situation, but impulsively, Ilona pushes on into the clearing.

'Ilona, no!'

The crack of a gunshot rings out, shattering the peace. Ilona drops like a felled tree, and I dive for cover behind a nearby boulder.

Alerted to our presence, the two guards leap into the scrub in their hunt, flanking my position like a pair of predatory animals hungry for my blood.

'Yoo-hoo, Jayne,' a familiar voice bellows from the direction of the vehicle.

Alyx?

'Come out,' she yells, 'I know you're there. No use hiding. I'll find you eventually, you cowardly tomadai.'

Ilona still hasn't moved. Why isn't she moving?

As much as I would like to focus on Ilona, the stomping of the guards closing in on my position draws my attention to more pressing matters. Muscle memory brings back the full gravitas of my situation as I recognise the balance and weight of a throwing knife in my hand.

Cool and gritty to the touch, dirt dries the sweat from my palms against the steel, and with a firm flick of the wrist, it sails through the air with deadly accuracy, embedding in one of the guard's throats.

His demise draws the attention of the others, and they respond with a volley of slugs splintering trees and trimming the shrubs surrounding where I crawl for the downed man.

Writhing and gurgling, he clutches at the knife protruding from his neck while he struggles to stop me from stealing the pistol from his belt. But his weakening strength is no match for mine. Movement of something charging across the clearing from behind presses urgency. Loosening the pistol free from its holster, two shots ring out.

My heart stops.

From beneath the charging guard's hat, a rivulet of bright red seeps out and down his forehead, his sardonic grin frozen across his face as he collapses mid-leap before me.

But it seems the dead man is a better shot than I thought, for a mild burning sensation niggles at my arm. Looking down, his slug has grazed me and has left a finger-sized hole in my shirt, where blood now stains the fabric.

The gurgling guard continues to writhe beside me.

'I'll make this easy for you,' I say, squeezing a round off into his head without remorse, reclaiming my blade and scurrying for the nearby boulder, dodging slugs trying to cut me down.

'Watcha up to, Jayne?' Alyx taunts when the shooting stops.

Once again, Alyx and her last remaining guard fade out at the edges of my perception, for in the intervening space, Ilona still lies motionless, concealed in the long grass. She's all I can think about. She lies with her back to me, and I can't be sure if she's dead or alive. A pang of guilt rips through my gut as I desperately want to go to her aid, but with Alyx hunting me for some reason, all I can do is remain here. None of this makes any sense.

Though only a few steps separate us, that open space may as well be filled with venomous snacas. Even with the boulder blocking my view, I can sense Alyx's pistol trained on me, watching and patiently waiting for me to make my next move. She may only have a pistol, but she's as good a shot as I am, and that's all she needs to take me down.

But why is she attacking us? Aren't we supposed to be on the same side?

I push the thoughts aside, knowing my survival depends on me keeping my head, and turn my attention to surveying the clearing instead. It's about thirty metas across, surrounded by foliage and at its edge, just off to the right of the truck, is the rusted-out husk of a car—it's the perfect place for an ambush.

'Ilona!' I yell desperately for a response. 'Ilona, are you okay? Please respond!'

The guard shifts position. From between the grasses and the protection of my boulder, I set my sights on him. The single shot sends both him and Alyx scarpering for cover.

'You little shak,' she curses from her new hiding place behind the rusted car.

The idiot guard crouches behind the truck's furthest front wheel, clutching at a freshly bloodstained shirtsleeve.

I knew I hit him.

A shot ricochets off my rock, and while he reloads, my third round hits him directly between the eyes.

And then it's just Alyx and me. 'Seems like you're all out of friends, Alyx.'

A gunshot echoes through the clearing, passing too close for comfort and embedding in the tree trunk behind me.

'Speak for yourself, bikkja,' she yells back. 'Tell me, how well do you really know that scrag girlfriend of yours?'

'Leave Ilona out of this.'

'Oh, she's in it, alright. Did she tell you the real reason she's here?'

'That's not going to work.'

'No?' Alyx shouts, firing a few more slugs off in my direction. 'They sent her to bring you back.'

'I already knew that. But why are *you* here?'

She laughs. 'Are you stupid? I thought that was pretty clear. As for Ilona, nobody said you had to be brought back alive.'

'Liar!'

'*I'm* a liar?' Alyx laughs again. 'She's the one leading you around. Let me guess, she lured you out here so she could frak you?'

Focus, Jayne. She's just trying to goad you.

'I take it from your silence, she did,' Alyx laughs again. 'No, it seems your little squeeze has me beat there. She betrayed you, and you can't even see it. It's so cruel and ironic, it's hilarious! It's a shame I have to kill you both.'

'Not if I have anything to say about it,' I yell, standing to leave my cover and fire across the clearing at the rusted hulk until the weapon clicks empty.

'You think you're lucky enough to survive the next dec?' Alyx yells out, standing and taking aim.

'Do you think I care?'

'You won't when I put you down.'

'Are you that cowardice you need a pistol?' I shout, throwing my useless weapon away.

In front of her right eye, outlined by the metal frame, the blackness of the barrel observes me with a deadly glare.

Click.

Her death stare is nothing more than an empty threat now, but Alyx doesn't react to the impotence of the weapon, instead following me with it as I turn my back on her to rush to Ilona.

I don't care what Alyx says. I try to reassure myself. *Ilona didn't come here to kill me. She couldn't have.*

As I kneel at Ilona's side, her face is pale, and her bloodied hands clutch at a wound in her chest.

'Come on, Jayne, your move,' Alyx taunts from across the clearing. 'Whatcha gonna do now, huh? Or are you too afraid to challenge me?'

Ilona's breath comes in ragged gasps, and the scene is all too familiar. It was only days ago that I lost Sera like this, and the fear of losing Ilona as well is paralysing.

Stifling tears, I drop my backpack beside her and break out the medkit to pack the wound.

There's so much blood.

Ilona lifts a feeble hand, and I grab hold as though it's the only thing that matters in the world.

'Jayne…' she gurgles, trying to speak, but coughs up blood instead.

'It'll be alright,' I say, caressing her hand and applying pressure to the wound. 'Just hang in there.'

Though I desire more than anything for that to be true, I know the words are more for my own comfort than hers.

Alyx drifts closer until she's standing above us and chuckles. 'Oops. Seems I've put a hole in this little sexcapade. How does it feel to finally realise you're not as good as you think you are?'

'What's your problem, Alyx?' I say calmly, trying to ignore her taunts and focus on Ilona.

'My problem? My problem is dirty little treasonous traitors like you, with your repugnant little relationship. It makes me want to vomit.'

'Back off, Alyx,' I snap.

'I'll back off when I've finished my mission.'

'What mission? I thought we'd resolved this?'

'You're talking about that little jaunt in the forest?' Alyx chuckles, arms crossed and looming over me like a dark cloud. 'Are you kidding? We resolved nothing.'

'But you'd be dead if it weren't for me.'

'Correction, *we* would be dead if it weren't for *us*. You still don't get it, do you? That wasn't about cooperation, you naïve little thviet. It was about survival. Plain and simple. We are what they've trained us to be—killers. Nothing more.'

Ilona coughs again, and I grip her hand tighter.

'No, Alyx,' I snap at her through gritted teeth. 'You're a pawn, an expendable object brainwashed into believing a perverted old man's lies. He doesn't care about you. He doesn't care about any of us. The only difference between you and me is that I've realised this.'

It's obvious Alyx is trying to disempower me. Every moment I spend deflecting her insults, the less I spend on what really matters. Ignoring Alyx, I return my attention to Ilona, cradling her shivering body in my arms.

Ilona stares at me with grey eyes like pools of molten silver. 'It doesn't hurt,' she says. Despite her words, the pain shows, and I apply firmer pressure to stem the flow of blood that refuses to stay in her body.

'Don't you dare go anywhere, Ilona,' I plead. 'Hold still, I'll get you out of this.'

'This is very touching,' Alyx mocks. 'But I want to get this over with now.'

'Don't,' Ilona cries, her tears joining mine. 'Don't… leave me.' She grips my hand tighter, nowhere near as firm as I know it can be. 'It's better this way. I'll be free. He can't touch me anymore.'

'But I can't either. Don't you see, you can't go—you're the only person in my life now.'

'You've always been the stronger one, Jayne. You don't need anyone.'

'I can't…' I cry, pressing my cheek to Ilona's to conceal my emotions.

'I never said…' she whispers with laboured breath in my ear, '… never said love.'

Holding her close for comfort, I place a tender kiss on her cheek and smooth her fine dark hair. It still smells the same as it did last night.

'Enough,' Alyx snaps, kicking me in the side. 'The sooner you realise love is nothing but a useless emotion, the better. It makes you weak. Let me demonstrate.' She draws a long hunting knife from a sheath on her calf and a glint of steel sweeps overhead.

'Go. Destroy her… for me,' Ilona croaks.

Divided by conflict, I stare into Ilona's glistening eyes. Part of me wants to fight Alyx and put her out of the way. The other part—the larger part—wants to stay with my Ilona. 'You've been the best part of my life,' I reply, kissing her on the forehead and drawing my short blade from my pack.

Ilona mouths the words, 'Go. Be free.'

Alyx flashes a sinister smile and sweeps her knife in an X pattern across her body—she always favours theatrics over form.

She lunges forward three times with the same movement, forcing me back each time. Parrying her third attempt, my pommel lands hard on her forearm, her grip wavers, and her knife drops to the ground.

Weaponless, Alyx glares at me, eyeing off her blade, then turns to her fists, throwing a series of jabs and blocks against my knife offence.

She overextends too much on her left.

She strikes out with a punch. My grip encloses her outstretched fist, and with a spin, I draw her into a guillotine choke.

With a grunt, I pull her to the ground and tighten my grip. Reminiscent of the choke-lock Sera demonstrated on me cycles ago, I hold Alyx firm.

I don't know why I feared her hatred all this time—it only took two midecs to put her down.

Colour drains from her face, and she appears to be succumbing. Her grip loosens, and she stops struggling. My gaze momentarily shifts to Ilona, and I long to be by her side.

You can't die alone.

Suddenly, I'm engulfed in searing pain radiating from my right ear. Blood streams from the fresh wound and down my neck, forcing my hold on Alyx to waver. She scrambles free, responding with a swift kick to the head that drops me to the dirt.

Alyx crawls away, visibly groggy from almost losing consciousness.

I almost had her.

While she figuratively licks her wounds, I lift a hand to inspect my ear. Part of it seems to be missing, and it only serves to fuel my anger.

Then Alyx launches, brandishing her bloodied blade. Clambering to my feet, I again raise my knife to meet her attack.

Despite my attempt to block her vicious downward strike, its sheer force casts the knife from my grip, leaving her blade to cleave a deep gash across my forearm. It stabs into my sternum, and I let out a breathless gasp from the sharp pain.

Wrestling with all my strength, I clasp Alyx's wrist to stop her from driving the blade in further. With only the knife's length between us, we lock eyes in a contemptuous, unblinking game of intimidation.

'Face it, you've never been able to beat me,' she snarls, forcing me backward. 'You're weak.'

I don't know how she can talk when all I can do is groan under the strain of her weight.

She pushes me back another step until my foot hits a rock, and I can't retreat any further. 'I've always been faster and stronger. You can't beat me.'

There's a wild ferocity in Alyx's eyes I just don't understand. There's no logic to her attacks, just raw emotion. I drop my gaze and allow Alyx to think I'm faltering. With all her force directed one way, I twist sideways away from the blade and headbutt her as she fumbles forward.

The blade slides past my chest, slicing my shirt, while Alyx, clutching her bloodied nose, is sent reeling.

'Yeah, but I use my head,' I retort, recovering my footing.

When she regains her composure, the scowl on her blood-smeared face is something I'd expect from a monstrous beast. She may have perfected the scowl, but this is fury personified, and with that, she launches at me again, knife outstretched.

Either this time I'm quicker, or Alyx's raw emotion is compromising her form, for it only takes a single shoulder jab to disable her arm. She drops the knife again to clutch at her incapacitated limb.

With the two knives now lying in the dirt nearby, I pick them up and clutch them in either hand.

'Come on, coward,' Alyx spits, circling me and rubbing the feeling back into her arm. 'You don't need those. Fight me like a warrior.'

'So, now you want a fair fight?' I yell, throwing the weapons into the nearest tree.

The instant the last blade leaves my hand, Alyx charges.

It is not about a person's strength, or speed or skill. It is about how they use it that matters.

While the moment plays out seemingly in slow motion, Sera's words resonate in my mind as though spoken by Sera herself.

Your strength comes from up here, not your muscles.

I take the Shihung'na rock stance…

If you use that wisely, you can rise to any challenge.

…and bury my shoulder into Alyx's gut. In a single fluid motion, she launches over my back.

And with a solid thump, she hits the ground.

As exhaustion and nausea threaten unconsciousness upon me, I collapse, barely able to move. While lying there, watching the hazy light play tricks on my vision, the world seems to have lost its colour. It takes a moment to realise Alyx isn't standing over me or throwing taunts anymore. I wonder what's become of her. When I turn to see where she's landed, she's lying face up in the grass, uncharacteristically quiet and unmoving.

Stifling a groan, I drag myself towards her, where her pale face gazes up at the sky with fear-filled eyes. Despite my weight pinning her arms in place, she doesn't struggle. Then I feel behind her head. There, her neck rests against a rock, slicked with a viscous film of fresh blood. 'I think your neck's broken,' I say in a voice as cold as ice. 'I *should* kill you now, but this is no longer fair combat. This is the least you deserve after what you've done.'

Alyx growls, but the vehemence of her aggression is lacking. 'What I've done? You and that little tramp of yours are the traitors. I'm only following orders. You should be the one lying here, not me.'

'But I'm not. I have no compassion left for you. Goodbye, Alyx.' Without a second glance, I leave her in that paralysed state and crawl over to Ilona's side.

'You can't leave me like this,' Alyx cries out. 'I can't move. Please help me. If you won't help me, kill me!'

Alyx may as well be pleading to thin air, for I've banished her from all conscious thought. While I collapse on the ground beside Ilona, all hope evaporates. She gazes up at the cloudless midday sky with a glazed film across her unblinking silver eyes.

'Ilona,' I cry, stroking her soft face. 'I've returned for you. Please say something, Ilona.'

I reach for her hand, but she doesn't grip back. I shout her name, shake her, do everything I can to rouse her, but she doesn't even blink. I lean over her chest to listen for a heartbeat.

Ilona is gone.

My entire body aches as I lay beside her, scoop her up and lovingly cradle her in my arms as though doing so would return me to this morning when we just lay there and held each other tight.

'I'm sorry I couldn't be with you, my love, but I took care of Alyx like you asked.' Rivers of tears openly stream down my cheeks while I clutch her lifeless body to mine.

Just when I think things are looking up and I'm starting to take control of my own life, I'm thrust back into that pit of despair, deeper than I'd ever been before. Too exhausted to fight any longer or even care, I lie there and willingly accept the inevitable.

Everything goes white.

Aves chirping in the distance brings my consciousness back to reality, and all I want to do is yell at them for being so boisterous. Maybe they're here to guide Ilona into the next life, a happier life that's free from this painful existence. By now, Ilona's pale skin has cooled, and with reluctance, I struggle to my feet, unsure of how long I'd been lying there.

I can't leave her here. But where can I take her?

Water trickling from somewhere beyond the clearing answers my unspoken question. Still in agony, I labour to lift Ilona's stiffening body and carry her down a rough trodden path towards the sound.

As I fight through the scrub, the river emerges into view. Part of it forks off into a brook, pooling into a serene little pond shadowed by a large tree anchored on a grassy slope. Had Ilona still been with me, she would have loved it as well.

I can't imagine a more serene location for resting.

Using my knife to dig a shallow grave, I solemnly lower Ilona into her final resting place, close her eyes and fold her arms over her chest.

'My sweetheart, Ilona,' I say, gently kissing her forehead. 'I know you couldn't say you loved me, I understand. But I know you shared our love. You proved that to me last night. Until another life, I will always love you.'

With the stark realisation this is the last time I will ever see her again, I kiss her goodbye and drape my coat over her face.

A new tear wells for every handful of dirt and every rock I place to cover her.

Shadows elongate as the afternoon drags on, and I pry myself away from the rock I scratched an 'I' into, marking her grave. Despite my physical pain, it's the pain in my heart that wounds me the most. It's almost as though it's being gouged out. I haven't cried this much since I was seven, hiding in terror under my bed. With both Ilona and Sera gone, I'm alone again.

I could have died right there and then. If a sounder of boarts charge, or raiders attack, or more bombs explode to burn the sky, I wouldn't have cared.

But I'm not trained for sorrow and self-pity. I'm trained to fight. And fight is what I'll do.

The bombs all those cycles ago stripped me of my family. And now that both Sera and Ilona have been murdered, and the Patriarch with his guild of assassins out for my blood, too; I've survived this far; I won't let them have it. They're all responsible for killing everyone I loved. Garret Gord didn't save me. It destroyed me.

'I hate you, Lou Tenant Doe! I hate you!' I scream out, knowing she can't hear me. 'My life is nothing, thanks to you.'

All that's left now is revenge.

31 BURN THE SKY

NC11

Time; it's a fickle thing. It only seems like a cendec ago I was waking to the sun streaming in through the hotel window, warming my face whilst I nestled in Ilona's arms. But then again, it also seems like a distant memory. For now, I hide, waiting in Alyx's truck in the darkened scrub off the road. The clock on the dashboard clicks over to midnight—the first dec of New Calendar eleven. Time to move.

With nothing but my throwing knives, pistol and a formidable determination, I leave the truck and hike towards the place that was my life for over nine cycles.

Fog fills the basin between my position and the Gord, giving off that awed, creepy feeling that prickles the hair on the back of your neck. It's just like I remember the day I arrived. Seems appropriate, given my present mood. Strolling through the open gates, the guards congregate in their small brick hut, too preoccupied with toting their drinks and laughing at whatever is funny to them to notice me pass.

The midnight sky is mostly clear, allowing Jorth's dual moons to cast dappled shadows across the open compound, illuminating the entry buildings leading down to the apartments like little white marshmallows. The last time I saw both moons risen at once was the night in the forest when I first met Ilona. Normally, I would marvel at the sight, but seeing them now only fills me with grief. And with their brighter light, it makes it harder to remain in the shadows. By now, everyone will be asleep, but I know I'm no longer welcome here, so I move stealthily, taking care to not draw any unwanted attention. Once inside the apartment, I silently close the heavy door.

So many cycles living here, I'd become accustomed to coming home and finding the delectable aroma of Sera's cooking filling the room or seeing her sitting on the couch, content watching her shows. The scene that faces me now is a stark contrast. Now, with only the diffused light streaming through the skylights, it's dark, the air is dank and musty, and most of Sera's prized pot plants are dead or missing. The place feels much bigger than I remember, but then there are a lot of empty spaces where furniture once stood—even the green couch is gone. Seems they weren't expecting me to return either—they've even taken the medkit from the bathroom.

Standing there at the bathroom mirror, I pull back my matted, shoulder-length hair to consider my reflection. The person staring back resembles a victim from a horror story. My hair and clothes are covered in dried blood, the top of my right ear is missing, and there's an accompanying slice across my cheek that looks like it might need stitches. Though I try to clean the wounds the best I can, I can't do much else without the proper medical supplies. Aside from extensive bruising and the gash on my forearm, externally, everything else looks superficial. It still hurts to move, though. If I'm going to have any hope of surviving tonight, I'll need something for the pain.

My bedroom almost resembles my childhood room back in Nusmore. All that remains of its ransacked contents is a kicked-over chair, which I use to collect my diary; thankfully, it still remains in its hiding place in the ceiling. Stuffing it into my backpack, I move on to Sera's room to see if there's anything else left of value.

This is the first time I've set foot in her room, and it's as empty as mine, with only a few of her older dresses and torn pieces of paper strewn about the floor. The paper is from Sera's treasured history folio. It seems someone found it and took a disliking to it, except for the leather cover, which is nowhere to be found. Sera dedicated much of her adult life to compiling that folio. It would be a shame to see it all go to waste. As I collect the papers, the headline of a newspaper clipping stands out. Dated 105 Centraal 1938, I straighten it out and lift it to the light.

Sovereignty claim responsibility for research facility attack. Project director suicides.

Extremist group, the Sovereignty have claimed responsibility for the mysterious explosion that destroyed a Cedrean megloinium research facility in what has been described as a terrorist attack, after the words "The reckoning is coming… Jorth must be cleansed" were found spray-painted on the building's walls. Witnesses also report suspected Sovereignty heavyweight, Siegfried Leaton, may have been the mastermind behind the plot. He and his two accomplices were allegedly seen fleeing the scene prior to the attack that claimed over 200 lives. Sovereignty devotees have long heralded the return of the Gaia'Ta to Jorth. They have been responsible for several attacks on government facilities in recent treys. To date, Leaton and his accomplices remain at large.

In a surprise twist, the project director of the Cedrean research facility Loriana Marquess was found dead last night in her home in Mon Loq, following reports she'd gone missing. First thought killed in the explosion, authorities now confirm she had taken her own life after a glass laced with strychnine and a handwritten suicide note were found in her home. Authorities now turn their search to Marquess's young daughter, whose whereabouts remain unknown.

My eyes widen as the enormity of this little newspaper clipping hit me. Sera had told me she'd been the one responsible for Loriana Marquess's death, but what did she have to do with this Sovereignty? Was she part of a terrorist organisation that aimed to cleanse Jorth? And why? What does it mean they "heralded the return of the Gaia'Ta?". Who was this Siegfried Leaton, and was Sera one of his accomplices?

So many questions. And no time for answers.

I stuff the pages into my backpack and continue searching the room, hoping that by busying myself with other matters, I can forget, even for a while, about Sera and that I may have become inducted into a terrorist organisation bent on destroying the world.

After searching for some time, it seems they've taken my little single-shot, wrist-mounted pistol too—I can't imagine why; I may have fixed it, but it's still virtually useless. Then, with great reluctance, I pry myself away from the apartment and watch its heavy door close for the last time.

Ilona's apartment haunts me as I hurry past. I almost expect to see the startlingly beautiful, colour-changing eyes staring through the gap in the door, and it causes me to misstep.

Forcing the thought aside, I head up the stairwell and along the darkened corridor towards a familiar section of the compound, divided by two large, swing-hinged doors. Above, polished metallic letters spell out *MEDICAL*.

I may have been here many times before, but on this occasion, it feels uncannily reminiscent of that first day I visited Sera. Only night lights illuminate the corridor, whereas the unoccupied wards remain silent in the dark.

I'm not visiting the wards this time.

Wrestling the memories from my focus, I dart between shadows, scanning each room for what I came here to find.

At the very end of the corridor, stored inside a locked, unmarked room, are rows of glass cabinets containing an assortment of medications. Switching on a cabinet light, its doors pry open with a little encouragement. Before pocketing a bottle labelled 'for treatment of severe pain', I swallow two tablets.

'Whose there?' a familiar but shaky voice enquires from behind. Still dressed in her white coat, Doctor Davi stands there in a circle of light, looking like she hasn't slept in treys. 'Jayne? Is that you?' she asks, stepping into the tiny room. 'But I thought you ran away?'

Caught by surprise and without knowing what to say, I open my mouth to offer a lame excuse, but Davi cuts me off. 'Oh, my! What happened to you? Don't answer that. I don't want to know.'

'Doctor, I don't want to cause trouble. I just needed something for the pain—'

'You're going to need more than that, my dear,' she says, removing another bottle from the cabinet. 'Those nasty gashes on your face and arm are going to need treatment.'

'I haven't got time—'

The doctor gently takes my arm. 'Come over here. Let me take a look at you.'

Though I resist, the doctor's kind manner is comforting, and she escorts me to an examination room to tend to my wounds.

'This is going to hurt, I'm sorry,' she says, threading a surgical needle with suture twine.

'I'll be fine,' I say, wincing at the pain while she dabs a soft antiseptic swab across the wound on my cheek.

'What I don't understand is,' Davi asks while she works, 'why didn't you come to see me? You know you don't need to sneak in here and steal anything.'

'I didn't think you would help me.'

She pauses for a moment in surprise. 'Why?'

'You don't know?' I ask, suddenly realising she may not be aware of what has transpired over the last few days.

'I'm a doctor,' she says, with a touch of petulance. 'I swore an oath to help people. It's what I do. Now, I understand they don't tell me much of what goes on around here, and I don't like to ask questions. I just patch you up and send you out. That's my job.'

'Then it's probably best you don't know.'

'I don't want to know then if you don't want to tell me.'

I sigh, building the courage to tell her. 'They killed Sera and Ilona.'

'They what?' she says, eyes wide with shock. It occurs to me the good doctor must not have even seen Sera after the incident. 'They wouldn't. Would they?'

'They have. And now they're trying to kill me.'

Her eyes brim with tears. 'I can't believe it. Why would they do that?'

'I don't know. I can only assume the Patriarch's gone mad, and he's killing everyone who's crossed him. I guess I'm at the top of his list now.'

'Oh dear,' she sighs, shakily tying off the last stitch and placing a patch over the wound. She then moves her attention to my arm. 'Are you sure it was the Patriarch?' she asks after a while.

'As certain as I'm sitting here. He threatened Sera with retirement.'

'I don't know what that means.'

'It means execution, Doctor. It's his solution to solving problems. Ilona and I were ambushed on our way back here. That's why I look like this.'

'Are you sure it was them who killed Ilona?' she asked, and I could clearly see the terror in her eyes. She knew something but quickly pretended she didn't.

'Yes, I was there. They sent Alyx to kill us. I fought her off but I wasn't able to save Ilona. Why?'

'Never mind,' she said, shaking her head. 'As I said, I don't like to ask questions. It's none of my business,' she added dismissively. 'I know some of what goes on around here by what injuries I have to patch up, but I learned a long time ago to keep my nose out of things. I much prefer it that way.' She neatly ties off the bandage around my arm and pushes her metal tray of tools away. 'Well, I'm done here. They'll need to come out in a few days, but something tells me you're not going to be around for that.'

'No,' I shrug. 'And come to think of it, neither should you.'

She shakes her head vigorously in disbelief, possibly fearful that the comfortable position she's held for so long is starting to crumble around her. I don't blame her. Not even I could resist the Patriarch's hold over me. Who knows what the doctor has had to endure? 'Oh, no Jayne. I can't do that. I'm needed here.'

'Doctor,' I reply with a level tone, 'they don't need you. They don't deserve you. You're a good person, and good people don't belong here.'

Raising her hands in refusal, she shakes her head again. 'That's very sweet of you, dear, but I can't just leave. This is my home.'

'It *was* my home, too. But that was before they executed Sera, made me a mark and ransacked my home. When you see what they're capable of, you'll see this is not home. It's a prison.'

She pats me on the knee, and while I know she's trying to be comforting, I can tell my words are starting to resonate, even if she doesn't want to believe them. 'It's late, dear. I don't suppose this can wait 'til morning?'

I grab her hand. 'No. Believe me, you don't want to be here come morning.'

'Why? What's going on?' she asks, considering me with a worried expression.

'I'm sorry, I don't have time to explain. I've been here too long already. Please, Doctor, you have to believe me. It's too dangerous for you to stay here.'

My comment seems to make her uncomfortable, for she shuffles a little further away. 'Jayne, you're frightening me.'

'You have to leave, now.'

She tries to interject, but I cut her off. 'Just listen. Meet me at the truck yard at 2:20 sharp. Bring only what you can fit into a small bag—close personal effects you can't part with, that sort of thing, and Hope money if you have any. Wear dark colours. And don't let anyone see you, you understand?'

The doctor responds with a wary nod. 'So, you're not going to tell me what this is all about?'

'I will when we're both safe.'

'Safe?'

'Please, Doctor. Just do it. I'll see you at 2:20. If I'm not there, take a truck and leave for Hope. Don't look back. Okay?'

She hesitates, and I can see she's wracked by indecision.

'Alright,' she says, placing the bottle she took from the cabinet in the palm of my hand. 'Take two of these; it'll stop that getting infected.' And without another word, she gets up and hurries away.

There's no turning back now. I'm committed. Grabbing my bag, I run towards the compound entrance of the medical wing. Just before reaching the surface, I pry open a vent cover in the stairwell and climb inside. While I crawl along the memorised labyrinth of ducts, it's as though traversing a corridor I'd walked a million times before.

This duct leads to the armoury, a veritable treasure trove of armour, weapons and ammunition. Normally sealed by a large metal gate with a solid lock, it seems no one thought to secure it from above. I slip inside the weapon-lined room and instantly feel like a kid given free rein of the sweet shop in Hope. With no time to lose, I shove whatever I can reach into my bag, including a rare repeating pistol to replace the simple one I'd stolen from the guard, along with a few boxes of rounds. Then, wrapping a belt of smoke grenades around my torso, I begin stuffing the rest into large field operation bags.

It's a waste if I leave all these other weapons here.

In decs, I've broken the lock on the gate and am quietly loading the armoury's entire contents into the back of a truck. When I'm done, my watch reads *1:01*. I set its timer for the same time as sunrise; *2:30*, and with the two remaining bags, I climb back into the vent.

Crawling through the air ducts with two heavy bags is tiresome work, let alone with stitches and bruises all over, but as I move from room to room, the bags get lighter.

1:90.

By the time I reach the solitary room at the far end of the long vent, my last bag is almost empty. Unlike before, the light to the Patriarch's office is out. I can't say I'm not disappointed, but I'm not leaving without paying it one last visit. Setting the bag aside in the duct, I slip through the vent and slide down the bookcase. Both moons, one just slightly smaller and offset from the other, are framed in the narrow, elongated window on the far wall like a painting, streaming their combined luminescence into the room. The strange items in here make the room feel like I've crashed some kind of blackout party. It sends a cold shiver down my spine, and I flick on the desk lamp.

The instant the room illuminates, I'm surrounded by creepy stone busts that seem like they're following me around with their stony glare.

And then I see it. Draped around the neck of one of the busts depicting a balding, moustachioed man is a gold pendant featuring a marbled black and white stone. It's the pendant Ilona wore. The one she said the Patriarch had confiscated.

I'll take this back, thank you.

Holding it in my hand, there are markings inside I hadn't seen when Ilona was wearing it. They appear to be runes, like the ones inscribed around the room where I performed my final initiation. But these, I don't recognise.

I wonder what they mean.

I slip the pendant around my neck, rummage through the drawers for anything of interest, grabbing an unopened bottle of malt, and finish what I came here to do.

2:00. Time to go.

I pay the room good riddance and climb back into the vent.

Emerging from the vent into the corridor outside the second-floor staircase, who should appear from the shadows but Shaddix; the very picture of indignation personified, flanked by two burly guards.

'I thought I heard something thumping around in there,' she says, glaring at me like she's talking to vermin she's caught in a trap. 'Didn't expect it to be you. Where's Ilona?'

'Not here,' I reply, cautiously pulling my backpack over my shoulder.

'That's a shame.' She yanks an emergency alarm on the wall, and I scarper for the stairs.

'You better run,' she yells from behind as I take the corner. A guard stands on the stairs blocking my retreat. With little effort, I throw him like garbage over my shoulder and send him barreling into two of his colleagues below. Unclipping a stun grenade from my belt, it bounces down the stairs, and I dive for the next landing. The flash, smoke and deafening bang fills the stairway, and I scramble with my ears ringing toward the exit.

The big metal door leading out into the compound is all that stands between me and freedom. What lies beyond it, I don't know. So many times have I been through it, it's hard to believe this will be the last I do so.

Its hinges give off an uncomfortable squeal as I open it wide enough to peer through. Despite the alarm, it's eerily silent. The Field is empty, and the three parked trucks form silhouettes against the open gate in the early morning light. At least the lazy guards are preoccupied with other things now and have left the guardhouse empty. I squeeze through just as torchlight flashes around a corner, and I duck into a darkened alcove to avoid being seen.

2:22.

Stopping at the ventilation hut, I unclip the smoke grenades from my belt, wedge them in the grill in front of the fans and tug out the pins. A plume of green smoke bellows into the underground complex, drawn in by the air intake.

With a long, anxious breath, I prepare myself and make a break for the trucks.

'There she is!' A voice yells from behind. A cursory backward glance, and there's a contingent of guards in pursuit. I slip behind the building as a smattering of slugs pepper the concrete, grab the repeater pistol, and lay down cover fire.

As I bolt for the truck loaded with gear, a darkened figure hides there.

She waited?

'Doctor,' I yell above the gunshots ringing out through the dawn, 'get in!' Together we jump inside. Closing the heavy doors, I start the ignition to the dinging of slugs hitting metal.

2:27.

The gearbox grinds as I wrench the truck into gear, and not wanting to stick around a midec longer, I floor it out the gate in a plume of dust.

I don't care how; I just have to put enough distance between us and that place. Not uttering a word, Doctor Davi clings to the passenger seat like it's the only thing keeping her in the vehicle.

The truck screams down the steep road. In my rear-vision mirror, another set of headlights reveals a truck in pursuit.

2:30.

A violent rumble, like a Jorth tremor, shakes the ground, sending vibrations through the truck, making it difficult to keep to the rough, steeply descending track. An almighty crack rips through the air and a monstrous fireball, visible in the mirrors, rises from the complex, turning the early morning sky from night to day.

As much as I wish to witness it, I concentrate on the road and push the pedal further.

A visual compression wave clears the sky before an enormous dust cloud blots out the light. Glancing behind, from the heart of the Gord, a fountain of dirt, concrete, and steel erupts like a volcano spewing forth its contents and raining a deadly hail of debris. Somehow the massive chunks miss the two trucks as they pummel the road.

Like a hungry monster, the rapidly expanding dust descends the mountain at a terrifying pace, encroaching the rear of our pursuant, consuming them.

Still hungry, the voracious dust cloud laps at our side mirrors, and with my foot cramming the pedal against the firewall, I will the truck to go faster. The road begins its ascent, and as though the monstrous cloud has reached the end of its leash, it falters then dissipates. We emerge above it into a gloriously clear dawn sky.

The road levels out, and the doctor looks deathly pale.

'Pull over, pull over!' she yells, and just as we come to a stop, she jumps out and promptly vomits.

At the top of the rise, we are awarded a perfect view overlooking the valley toward the Gord. While the good doctor empties her stomach, I climb out to watch the dust settle.

As though the Progenitors approve my actions, the sun peeks over the horizon, turning the sky burnt orange, welcoming the new cycle and revealing a formidable gouge where Garret Gord once was.

Eleven cycles ago, I witnessed the sky burn. And it terrified me. Today, I do so again, only this time, I'm not cowering in fear beneath my bed. For unlike before, when I was a trapped and helpless child, I stand here now with the breeze on my face and nothing holding me back. Now, I am free.

While I stand there, watching the sun glisten over the ruins of what used to be my home, Doctor Davi shuffles to my side, wiping her mouth with a sleeve.

‘Please talk to me, Doctor,’ I say, not taking my eyes from my handiwork. ‘Are you alright?’

‘What just happened?’ she mutters, her brow creased with worry.

‘What needed to happen.’

She gazes up at me with fear-filled eyes, and I can understand how terrifying this would be to her. ‘We have to go back!’

‘Go back? Where? There’s nothing to go back to.’

‘I can’t…’ she stammers. ‘Is that your doing?’

‘What if I said it was?’

Disbelief replaces her fear, and she takes a step back. ‘I can’t believe… All those people…’

‘People who would kill you in an instant without any remorse,’ I cut in, knowing it won’t ease her concern, but I’m not asking for forgiveness. ‘I get that this will be difficult for you to understand, but Garret Gord is an abomination. It had to be destroyed.’

‘And what about me? I’m part of Garret Gord. Are you going to kill me too?’

‘I wouldn’t have spared you if I thought you were,’ I reply, turning to her. Colour has returned to her face, but she still looks shaken, like a helpless tomadai that’s just escaped an ursus. The light wind whips her long blonde hair, and I can’t imagine a person such as her living in a place like that. ‘You are not a destroyer of worlds.’

‘I don’t know what that means…’ she sighs.

It prompts me to finally ask the question that’s been bothering me since meeting her. I’m also hoping it will distract her enough to help her calm down. ‘How did you end up at Garret Gord? I mean, you just don’t seem like the kind of person they’d recruit.’

‘Because I’m not cold and vicious?’ she snaps.

‘I’m sorry, that came out wrong. What I meant to say is, how did you get your job? You’re a kind and gentle person. That’s rare around here.’

‘Thank you, dear,’ she replies with a wry smile. ‘Since you asked, my parents were close friends of Elihus. I studied medicine, and when I finished my internment, he recruited me here.’ From the way she says that she seems ashamed, and I can’t tell if it’s because having any connection to that man would be offensive or that she never really earned her post.

She continues, ‘He told me all these wonderful stories of how great life would be working on top of a mountain. But all I ever did was stay underground. Things were always too dangerous for me up top.'

'So, you never saw what was out here?'

'Every now and then, I would go for short walks around the compound, but I would never venture far. Even before the war, I never really left those gates.'

'I take it you understand what I mean when I say that place was an abomination.'

She looks up at me with glistening eyes. 'They banished her,' she then says, seemingly out of nowhere.

'What? Banished who?'

'Dagley,' she replies, and the tears stream openly down her cheeks. 'The HomeGuard medic. I was ordered not to say anything, but they banished her to the forest. They as good as killed her.'

'I see,' I reply, remembering with fondness the brawny but gentle woman who saved Sera and me all those cycles ago. She, Captain Fenton and their whole team just disappeared as though they never even existed, and it always pained me that I hadn't found out why. Learning this only makes my actions more justified. 'So, you know what I mean when I say they're monsters.'

'But what right do you have doing that?' she says, gesturing towards the smoking mountain. 'Doesn't that make you no different to them?'

'I'm what they made me. What *HE* made me. Still, I'm nothing like them.'

'Could've fooled me. Look at what you did!'

'Don't blame the pistol; blame the person who wields it. *THEY* set me on this path.'

'But the rules?'

'The rules,' I scoff, 'are a lie. Intended for the benefit of only one person. The orders that came from that place only made the world better for him. I have followed the aftermath of those orders, and nothing good ever came from them. Not for Sera, not for Ilona, and certainly not for me.'

Davi glares at me.

'Look, I don't expect you to understand,' I say gently. 'Perhaps, someday you will. I've given you freedom. At least be satisfied with that.'

'Free?' she retorts, waving a hand at the surrounding forest. 'You call this free? Jayne, we're in the middle of nowhere!'

'I'm heading to Hope. They're used to taking in people like us, and I know they could use decent professionals like you. There, you'll be respected and be able to do the good work you do, surrounded by others who appreciate you.'

'I don't know, Jayne. After what I've done?'

'Can't be any worse than what I've done. You'll do well to come with me. I'm offering you a second chance if you want it. It beats staying here.'

She hesitates, caught in her indecision, and I don't blame her. Were I in her shoes, I probably would have this conflict too.

'How on Jorth did it get to this?' she says after a while.

'You don't want to know about my life, Doctor,' I say, walking back to the truck. 'But I've just given you back yours.'

32 ORIAN'S MALADY

Orian watched with a soft, sympathetic expression as Jaylyn stood frozen in the doorway of the Surprime's office, her eyes swollen red from crying. Trembling, she stepped inside and glanced up at the long red woollen coat still hanging from its rack. It was as though it had only just been hung there. The tears came again. With a shaky hand, she reached out to take it and hold it against her cheek. 'It still carries the scent of him,' she sobbed, burying her face in the fabric.

It had been three days since Jaylyn had received the devastating news her husband—the Surprime—had perished in a fiery car crash. While Artimus was out of town, his HomeGuard investigators were busy piecing together what had happened. So far, they'd concluded it was an accident. A drunken delivery driver had collided with his vehicle head-on, but everything about that story didn't seem right. It was Orian who chose to break the news to Jaylyn, refusing to leave the grieving widow's side while she dealt with the tragedy, even offering to personally escort her to Sage's offices to retrieve his belongings.

'I'm sorry, Orian,' Jaylyn sniffled, brushing a stray tear from her cheek with the back of a hand. 'You don't want to see this.'

'It's alright,' Orian replied gently, entering the room. 'Take your time.'

She glanced around at all the peculiar artifacts Sage had lining the shelves, running her hand along the shelf and picking up a broken mug that said, 'World's best da.' It brought a tear to her eye, thinking of Sage's two girls having to live without their father. 'Do you want some help?' she said, putting it back down.

Jaylyn shook her head. 'Thank you, but no. I'd imagine you'd have more important things to do.'

'More important than this? No, it's not a problem at all, hun. Anything you need, just ask.'

Jaylyn grinned, but only for a moment. 'You know, I just can't believe he's gone,' she said, gripping the coat tighter. 'Every time I close my eyes, he's there.'

Orian closed the door and moved closer, placing a hand on her friend's back for comfort. 'I know.'

'You know, my father gave him this,' Jaylyn said wistfully. 'Ever since that day, he admired Sage—the idiot who risked his life for a stupid animal. Dad never suspected I'd end up being the one to marry him.'

Jaylyn turned from Orian to wipe away her tears with a sleeve. 'I'm sorry, I'm sure you don't want to hear this.'

'No, it's fine. It's really quite endearing.'

Jaylyn smiled at that, seemingly glad to reminisce of happier times to a willing ear. 'I still remember the night he took me up to the overlook. It was cold, and I'd forgotten to bring my coat, so he took this off and put it around me. I couldn't believe I was with Sage Solon, wearing his famous red coat.' She sniffled and continued. 'The overlook was his favourite place in Hope, where he could watch over the entire town. That night, he laid out a blanket, and in front of all Hope, we consummated our love. Afterwards, we just lay there in each other's arms, watching the lights and the darkened figures scurrying below, silently going about their own business, never knowing we were there. It was magical. That was the night he proposed to me.'

'Oh, Jaylyn,' Orian sighed, 'that's beautiful. I never took Sage as the romantic type.'

Jaylyn hung her head. 'I couldn't believe someone like him could go for a person like me,' she said, sobbing openly. 'I miss him so much.'

Orian pulled her into a hug. 'It's okay. You'll get through this. I promise you will.'

All of a sudden, the door burst open, startling the two women.

'Ah, you're here,' Elihus announced, complete with ostentatious entrance.

'What do you want, Elihus?' Orian said, still clutching Sage's grieving widow in her arms.

'I'm looking for Martell. Is he about?'

'No, why?'

'Nothing with which you need concern yourself, madam Surprime.' He said the last bit with a slow drawl, as though he was still becoming accustomed to the feel of it in his mouth. 'Say, as the late Surprime's *provisional* replacement, when will you be taking residence in this office?'

'I'm not,' Orian replied.

'Oh? You're just going to leave it sitting vacant then?'

'That's what I said, Elihus.'

'Why?'

'I have my reasons, not that it's any of your business.'

'Right, well,' he said, stepping forward to touch Jaylyn's face, but Orian turned her back, stepping between him and Jaylyn to block his reach. Elihus retracted his hand. 'Cheer up, dear. It's been what, a few days? You'll get over it. You can always come to me if you want anything.'

'I think she'll be fine, thank you, Elihus.'

'Good. Good, well, then let me know when Martell shows up. I must speak with him as a matter of urgency.' He turned and, with a flare of his coattails, left.

Orian scowled. 'Now *that* is a vile man.'

The days following the Surprime's unexpected death had been among the hardest of Orian's career. Not just because it was Sage, but because, as his replacement, Hope turned to her for strength and guidance. She considered her elevation to Virtuous Surprime a bittersweet appointment. Not only did she respect Sage as a colleague and close friend, but Orian now appreciated how he must have felt when he took the role under similar circumstances. It was this thought that gave her strength.

The afternoon air was cooling rapidly, and Orian pulled her thick purple loaghtan cowl tighter around her neck. It also helped to conceal the fact she was crying.

First Gaius and now Sage. *What's happening to Hope*? Orian thought as she stood by the gravesite in the older parts of town where Sage was laid to rest beside Gaius and Rika; the three vanguards of Hope returned to Jorth where they may finally rest.

An intimate group of Sage's family and friends had gathered with her to say their farewells in a small memorial service in his honour. Jaylyn, dressed in a long, deep red cloak reminiscent of her husband's symbolic coat, stood stalwart before them with a sheet of paper in hand, her face flushed from crying as she prepared to deliver the eulogy.

To Orian's astute eye, she looked almost on the verge of collapse under the crowd's weighty glare, so she moved in closer to support her friend. Jaylyn returned the gesture with a pained smile and lifted her head to address the small crowd.

'Family, friends, good people of Hope,' she began in her piping voice, replicating the way Sage often started his speeches. 'I am heartened by your presence here today, as I'm sure Sage would have been, too. Eight cycles ago, I met Sage whilst the town took shelter in a concrete bunker. It's hard to believe so much has changed since then. He was elected to Surprime, helped Hope grow into the town it is today, and he, for some reason, married me and fathered two beautiful daughters. He made good on his promise to make Hope a better version of itself. And I know he would have continued to do so...'

She stopped momentarily to choke back the tears brimming in her eyes. Orian placed an arm around her to help give her strength. Jaylyn took a steady breath and continued.

'Most of you would find this as no surprise when I say Sage was one of the most loving, dedicated and personable people you could meet. He never expected to become Surprime, but I couldn't be prouder to be there with him when he did. This was a man who would never turn someone away when they needed something or had a question to ask.

'Sage was charismatic—he may not have been good at formal speeches, but he always knew how to put people at ease. Like the time during our first date when instead of waiting patiently for me to arrive, like a normal person, I found him, standing, foot up on a chair, five people deep, entertaining an entire restaurant with one of his crazy stories.

'I walk in, wondering what the ruckus is all about, and suddenly, I hear a shout, "BANG! And his eyebrows were gone". And there he was, right in the centre of the laughing crowd who were hanging on his every word.' She gave a slight chuckle at that but then resumed her sobriety and carried on.

'I still to this day thank the Progenitors for bringing us together. Though our time with you was short, the girls and I will forever cherish every midec we had you in our lives. Sage, my love, I miss you and love you with all my heart. May your spirit find everlasting peace and rest forever now in the arms of our mothers and fathers.'

Cupping her face in her hands, Jaylyn stepped back and allowed Orian to guide her to where Abril waited with young Kiera and Averyx. There was not a dry eye among them. The moment Orian looked upon the children, her heart sank for them, especially Averyx. At five cycles, she would just be old enough to comprehend what had happened to her father, and to think of a child having to experience such loss so young was heartbreaking.

As the crowd dissipated, Orian caught Conrad striding towards her. He'd been at the ceremony but had been called aside by a HomeGuard officer who she noticed passed him a slip of paper. The shock on his face said it all—whatever was on the piece of paper had him concerned, and after he handed it to her, she instantly saw why. It was a flyer containing a black and white image of Sage as a Cedreau target shooter with the words, 'Sage Solon; the Cedrean Traitor' emblazoned across the top.

'There's more,' Conrad whispered, trying not to attract unwanted attention. She apologised to Jaylyn and the others and allowed him to direct her—escorted by a contingent of Surprime guards—to the town hall steps. There, a small but angry group of people had gathered, all waving the incriminating flyers while Elihus Kinton, dressed all in white, spoke to them like a preacher from the top step.

'This,' he was saying, waving the flyer in his outstretched hands, 'is an indictment of trust—the very fabric upon which Hope was constructed. I assure you, I am as shocked as you all are to learn we entrusted Hope to a war criminal. This cannot stand. You have my assurances that I will make this right.'

As if he'd only just noticed her presence, Elihus then turned to Orian, the crowd following his gaze with scorn in their eyes.

'Madam Surprime…' he said, 'what have you to say about these shocking revelations?'

'What revelations?' she said, 'all I see is unsubstantiated slander. What is your issue with Sage? What's going on here?'

'Haven't you heard? Sage was a traitorous Cedrean war criminal.'

She stepped up to Elihus and spoke in a low voice. 'No, this is the first I've heard of this. But these are rumours; that's all this is.'

He turned to the crowd to voice his response so they could hear. 'No, my dear Madam Surprime, this is not just an unsubstantiated rumour. My office has looked into it. I assure you, this photograph is real. The people deserve to know the truth!'

'But your office is the Ministry of Education. Since when do you "look into" anything?'

'Only when it deserves to be heard.'

'Be that as it may, this is hardly the time. Not only is this disrespectful, but do you want to incite an insurrection?'

'That is up to you, my dear.'

'Can we at least discuss this?'

'The lady Surprime wishes to discuss this,' Elihus announced. 'Whatever she has to say in defence of that treasonous rodentia, she can say in front of her people. Let them judge for themselves.'

Orian stood stunned. 'I will have to look into this,' she said, trying to sound calm and in control. She had certainly not seen this coming. 'This is beyond my knowledge, but I will get to the bottom of it, I promise. Please, go home. This is not the Hope way.'

As her guards led her and Conrad away, the angry voices calling out venom-filled taunts behind her cut into her heart like a knife, but she kept on walking. Whatever Elihus was trying to do, she had to put a stop to it, and fast.

Clutching her aching head, Orian thought her day couldn't get any worse until she pushed open the door to her office and found a dishevelled-looking Artimus seated in the guest chair at her desk. Though he was wearing a suit and tie, it looked as though he'd slept in them.

Orian knew the moment she saw him, this discussion wasn't going to go well. They'd had their differences before, but she'd never had to deal with him like this, and from the expression he was giving her, he didn't much care for it either.

'The prodigal Admiral returns,' she said, stepping behind her desk.

'What did I miss?' Artimus slurred.

'Everything,' Orian replied in a curt tone. 'Are you drunk?'

Artimus shrugged. 'I had a few ales.'

'Smells like you drank the whole bar,' Orian scoffed, glaring at him like a mother scalding a delinquent child. 'Artimus, you go missing for days on end, and on the days you do decide to show up, you do so drunk and unruly. Explain yourself.'

'I don't need to explain myself to you,' he spat an indignant reply.

She ignored his insolence. 'Yes, you do. In case you've forgotten, I am Surprime now, and that makes me your superior officer.'

'Very good for you, Orian, but I don't recognise your authority.'

'I'm sorry you feel that way. Be that as it may, Sage elected me as his vice. Now that he's not here, that makes me Surprime. Like it or not, that's the way things are. For goodness sake, Artimus. You're a minister of Hope. Act like it.'

'So? You expect me to do as you say, is that it?'

'Artimus, I expect you to do your job. You're the leader of HomeGuard, are you not? Start by finding out who killed Sage.'

'How do I know it wasn't you?'

'Be serious,' Orian stated, crossing her arms.

'Alright,' Artimus said, fidgeting like a child. 'He was killed in a car crash. Case closed.'

Orian placed her hands on the desk and leaned forward to glare at him. 'If you believe that, you're more stupid than I thought.'

'What do you think I've been doing, Orian?' Artimus retorted, lounging in his chair, arms crossed. 'Sitting at the Boart's Head drowning my sorrows?'

She dismissed his rude behaviour and took her seat. 'That'd be my first guess, yes. He was your friend, wasn't he? Show him some respect. Better still, show up for his memorial!'

'Don't you think I wanted to be there?' Artimus said, raising his voice. Now he was the one on the defensive. 'I did. You should know some things take precedence. But since you asked, I was following a lead.'

'To the bottom of an ale keg?'

'For Martok's sake. I don't... in case you haven't noticed, the cemetery is filling with Surprimes. We're fast running out of space.'

'I've noticed,' she said dryly and wasn't too impressed where Artimus was going with this.

'You should. If this trend continues, you're next.'

'Artimus, is that a threat?'

'No, Orian, it's a warning. And judging by that crowd out there, it's not far off. There's a cancer in this town, and I'm going to find it. When I do, I will cut it out and ensure it never grows back. You understand?'

'I—'

'Good. That's why I'm declaring martial law. Effective immediately.' The tone of his voice, no longer marred by any signs of his intoxication, left no room for argument. Orian knew he was alluding to something, but she could never have guessed it would be this, and from the way he said it, he meant every word. Still, she wasn't going to allow him to take control. Not while she still held office.

'You what? The heck you are!'

'Orian, if you know what's best for you, stay out of it. I don't interfere with your work. Keep out of mine.'

'Absolutely not,' Orian said, leaning in to glare at him again. Even from her side of the desk, she could smell the ale on his breath. 'I will not have your crony heavyweights roughing up my citizens. By all means, hunt your assassin. But find another way to do it.'

'It's your funeral,' he said, then stormed out.

'Gah,' she growled as he left, just as Jaylyn and Abril walked in. To her surprise, Jaxson came in with them. He still wore bandages on his arms from his miraculous escape. Orian still didn't know how he managed to survive but was grateful she only had to bury one close friend and not two.

'Trouble?' Abril asked, glancing back at the Admiral.

'Artimus being Artimus,' Orian sighed. 'No, actually, this is Artimus being worse than his usual self. I have no idea what's gotten into him, but that man does not have a good track record of making smart decisions when he's like this. And believe me, that's worrying.'

'Should we be concerned?' Jaxson asked.

'No, I think he's just taking exception to me now being his boss, and he doesn't like it. Say Jaxson, how are you doing? I wasn't expecting to see you. Were you at the memorial?'

'I'm fine,' he replied. 'A sounder of boarts couldn't keep me away. I just hung out at the back.'

'You could have joined us,' Abril said, giving him a gentle nudge.

'Thanks, but… I was okay where I was. I almost followed you.'

'About that,' Abril said, 'I'm sure you've seen the commotion out front.'

'Yes. What the heck is that all about?' Abril asked.

'This,' Orian replied, sliding the flyer across the desk. 'I'm so sorry, Jaylyn. But I'll get to the bottom of this.'

The sombre-faced brunette warily picked up the piece of paper and instantly cupped a hand to her face to stifle a gasp. 'W..w..w..

what is this?' she stammered, allowing Jaxson to take the page from her grasp.

'Elihus!' He swore. 'That rotting son of a boart.'

'Can someone please tell me what's going on?' Abril protested, glaring at the page in Jaxson's hand.

It was Orian who answered. 'Someone—I suspect Elihus—has come across information claiming Sage is, or was, in the Cedrean military. Judging from that picture, a target shooter. They're claiming he's some kind of traitorous war criminal.'

'Is it true?' Abril asked.

'I don't care if it's true,' Orian snapped. 'It's an unsubstantiated slanderous rumour, and I'm putting a stop to it.'

'He's trying to pull dirt on Sage. That's what it sounds like,' Abril retorted.

'That's exactly what he's trying to do,' Jaylyn piped up. 'But it isn't going to work.'

Abril was livid now. 'Isn't going to work? He just accused Sage—your husband—of being a traitor. Right now, there's an angry mob of people outside who seem to believe it too.'

'That's because it is true,' Jaylyn replied flatly.

'What?' Abril exclaimed.

'Whatever happened to "what's passed is past"?' Jaylyn shrugged, dismissing Abril's outburst.

'Of course, there's that,' Abril retracted. 'But if Sage never spoke about his past, how do you know?'

'What does it matter, anyway? We all did what we had to do during the war. But that's not who we are now. I don't care about who Sage was. He could have launched the bombs for all I care. I only care about who he became. And so should all of you.'

'Jaylyn, none of us are thinking ill of him, nor will we ever,' Orian said. 'Nothing that wretch of a man can say will change that. Believe me, we all know better than to let that man drag Sage down like that.'

'Exactly!' Abril added. 'I was just asking how you knew, that was all.'

'I *was* married to him,' Jaylyn replied. 'There's little we kept from each other. Besides, I found him one night sitting in his office, looking upset. As soon as I entered, he tossed something into the fireplace. Later he told me what it was. Artimus had uncovered a dossier on him during his investigations. I won't say what it contained, but let's just say it wasn't something Sage wanted keeping. I don't know how Elihus found out, but it's troubling that he would do such a thing as this.'

'Why's it such an issue? Jaxson asked. 'Who cares? Nobody here even thinks about that stuff anymore, surely?'

'Say that to the angry mob out front,' Abril said dryly.

Orian cut in. 'Some people still like to remember the faction rifts and will try to re-open them any chance they get,' she replied casually. 'Seems Elihus is trying to stir trouble for some reason. Perhaps he's preying on my Skoycan heritage. If he can move a wedge between Sage and I, it could disempower me.'

'Oh, why would he do that?' Abril said.

Orian sighed. 'I wish I knew. To make matters worse, Artimus wants to declare martial law.'

Everyone gasped.

'He what?' Jaxson said.

'Between that,' Orian said, 'Elihus trying to incite an insurrection and Niklas likely to follow him, I'm afraid I'm losing control of my ministry. If I can't have their support, how can I effectively govern Hope?'

'You have our support, Orian,' Abril said. 'Garan and me will follow you to the ends of Jorth if we must.'

'That's very kind of you, Abril. I appreciate that, but if Artimus is right about one thing, insurrection festers like cancer. If this continues, and I lose confidence with the other ministers, this government will fall. I'm going to have to hold an election. There's no other way.'

33 TREASON AND PLOT

'Xanthe Zurole here in the bustling tally room where results are steadily coming in for what is already promising to be a nail-biting election.' The static-filled colour image of a slender, green-haired woman sharpened on the visiontube. She held a large microphone and was dressed as though attending a ball, her bright green frilled dress the same shade as her hair. 'We've had an extraordinary turnout today,' she continued in her perky, sing-song voice. 'With a record number of votes, it could be some time before we'll be able to confirm the victor. So, sit back, grab a cup of kahwah or something more exciting and join us for your exclusive coverage of the Hope Surprime election, Tenebrosity, NC11.'

Orian paced back and forth across the floor of the old community hall like a caged genet, wringing her hands while her electoral team gathered with anticipation in front of the VT.

The scene on the screen changed to earlier recorded footage of Orian standing before Gaius's statue in Sempro Memorial Park, addressing her supporters. Dressed in a simple but elegant deep purple pantsuit, with her long braided grey hair draped over a shoulder, Orian spoke of how she intended to further Gaius's vision for Hope, just as her beloved predecessor, Sage, had done. 'Hope prospered under their leadership,' she said, gesturing to the buildings surrounding her. 'What once was a mere refugee camp is now a thriving town, and I was there every step of the way. I strive to carry on their legacy. To deliver better services for Hope and seek partnership and trade with other communities so that we may continue to prosper.'

The scene then changed to Elihus, also at Sempro Park, wearing his customary flowing white outfit, and standing before a swelling crowd. 'Why should we continue to follow a course that was established when we were nothing more than a refugee camp?'

he announced, the crowd hanging on his every word. 'For Hope to achieve its full potential, we need more than just antiquated policies and fluffy rhetoric. Hope must strengthen our connection with LunaTec. Together we will create a stronger, more united Hope. Only my leadership will guarantee that.'

'With about sixty per cent of the votes counted,' Xanthe said as the image returned to her. 'Here are the current results. The polled favourite and incumbent, Orian Gracyn, stands at 1502 votes. Niklas Martel at 301 and a surprising contender, Elihus Kinton, 1535. There are still more votes to count, so we'll resume with the program as "The Melted Asteroids" play their new song—'

'This's absurd,' Jaylyn said, muting the VT in disgust and rising from her chair to approach the nervous Surprime. 'I still don't understand why you called this election. You were the Vice. I think Sage would have wanted you to continue on without all this.'

'I couldn't have taken up the mantle without making it official,' Orian humbly replied. 'It's the right thing to do.'

'It doesn't make any sense. How can Kinton have more votes than you?' Abril protested.

'It's still early yet,' Orian said with optimism. 'Anything can happen at this point.'

'Well, it's a surprise that Kinton's received any votes at all, let alone more than half of what's been counted so far,' Abril scoffed.

'Maybe I'm not doing as good a job as I thought,' Orian said ruefully. 'If you'll excuse me. I think I need some fresh air.'

Jaxson moved to escort her, and the two exited the doors into the quiet, lamplit street.

'This could be the last time I walk these streets as Surprime,' Orian told him despondently. 'But that's not what frightens me. I'm afraid if Hope elects Elihus, I don't know what will become of us. Have I really done that poor of a job?'

'You want me to speak freely?' he asked, a little surprised by her candidness.

'Of course. That's why I asked.'

'Then no, I don't think you've done a poor job. And, if it makes you feel any better, Sage went through this as well, if I recall. The difference is, he had you to help him. I doubt he could have done as well without you by his side. If you don't mind me saying so.'

'That's very kind of you, Jaxson, but I don't need your piety.'

'I'm just telling the truth.'

They strolled in silence through the business quarter past shops closed for the night, Orian deep in thought with Jaxson ambling along beside. Her mind turned to him, and she realised she'd been a bit harsh. She hadn't spoken to him much since the incident, not even learning the circumstances that led to his escape. Most just assumed Jaxson was a sturdy fellow capable of handling himself. But since that night, she'd observed a change in him.

'I'm sorry, Jaxson,' she said eventually. 'That wasn't fair. I've just got a bit on my mind.'

'It's my job,' he shrugged. 'And as your personal guard, I've been around you long enough to understand.'

'I've been meaning to ask,' she said, stopping to turn to him. Even in the darkness, she was certain the creases in his brow were deeper, and his usual jovial personality, which was so apparent around Sage, was lacking. 'How are you doing?'

'Me?' he said, seemingly taken aback by her question. 'I'm fine. Why do people keep asking me that?'

'You just seem more reserved, more absent. I know you've been through a lot lately. I just want to make sure you're alright.'

'Don't worry about me, ma'am,' he said, looking everywhere else but at her. No matter how long they'd known each other, she couldn't seem to rid him of that habit.

She involuntarily compressed her lips. 'Please don't call me that archaic title, Jaxson. You should know by now you can call me Orian.'

'Sorry… Orian.'

'See, that's what I'm talking about. Something's been awry with you lately, and it's got me a little concerned.'

'Don't be. It will not affect my work.'

'That's not what I mean.'

Just then, two men stumbled out of a dark alleyway. By their looks, they were intoxicated, and their sudden appearance made Orian take a cautious step backward. Jaxson positioned himself between her and them, resting his hand on the pistol at his hip. The men took one look at him, then her, and gave them a wide berth. When Jaxson turned back to her, he wore a sombre expression on his dark, charmingly handsome face. 'If you really want to know, I… I'm still…' he sighed, and she could tell there was something he wanted to get off his chest, but it wasn't quite coming out. 'I'm still in pain. Burns take time to heal.'

'I understand. And how are you doing emotionally? Sage was like a brother to you, wasn't he?'

'Ahh, if you don't mind, ma'... Orian, I'd like to talk about something else...'

By the time Jaxson pushed open the doors to the hall again, twenty decs had passed. The moment Orian crossed the threshold, Xanthe's musical voice was holding the room silent. '... finished counting, and the final numbers are; for the sitting incumbent, Orian Gracyn, 2553, Niklas Martell, 612 and Elihus Kinton with 2558. And with that, we have a new Virtuous Surprime. What a surprise! Who would have—'

Jaylyn lurched at the visiontube, turning it off the moment she saw Orian standing at the door.

'That can't be!' Abril said, outraged. 'How is it we've lost by five votes? This doesn't make sense.'

'It stinks; that's what this is,' Jaylyn added. 'I can't stand the thought of that... tyrant usurping Orian's right. Not after what he's done.'

'It's not my right, though. It's up to the people, and it seems they're not happy with my performance,' Orian said, trying to sound calmer than she felt.

'That's not true,' Abril said. 'That can't be true.'

A knock at the door startled everyone, and it was Abril who answered it.

'It's for you, Orian,' she called as a man handed her a single piece of paper, then left.

Orian stepped forward and took the paper from her.

When she read it, she could not conceal her apprehension.

'What is it?' Abril asked.

'It's from Elihus. He wants to see me tomorrow.'

Orian ascended the stairs to the Town Hall with trepidation and proceeded inside towards the Surprime's offices.

As soon as she stepped in the doorway to the antechamber, Conrad met her with sincere sympathy. 'I'm so sorry, Orian. Whatever happens, you have my support.'

'Thank you, Conrad,' she replied, then knocked on the big wooden door.

Normally, that door wasn't closed. Sage preferred an open-door policy, but that policy had obviously changed.

'Enter!' called a rough voice from within.

Orian pushed open the door.

Elihus lounged behind the large timber desk. Looking around at the expensive paintings on the walls, sculptures, polished timber furniture and carpets, she couldn't believe the office was already furnished with his own garish belongings. 'How did you…?' Orian said.

'Sit,' Elihus ordered, not looking up from something he was reading.

Orian straightened her skirt and sat in the tiny wooden chair opposing him at the desk—the comfortable guest chair had also been replaced.

After a while, Elihus looked up, set down his papers, removed his spectacles and considered her with scorn suitable for a wretch. 'This is going to go one of two ways,' he said, clasping his hands on the desk in front of him. 'You will either tender your resignation and publicly denounce your position, declaring you have been under a lot of strain and, for that reason, have decided to step down and quit politics. Or, I will depose you publicly, and you can kiss any shred of dignity you may have left goodbye. Either way, you will be leaving this government. It's your choice as to the manner in which that happens. I must caution you, though. Should you choose the latter, I will have no choice but to depose the others as well. Their shame will be yours.'

Orian scowled at him with shock. 'But why?'

'Why? Because Ms Gracyn, I don't tolerate insurrection—your word, not mine. Anyone who would strive to undermine my authority is not welcome in my ministry. From the very moment I met you, you made it perfectly clear where you stood. If I cannot have your loyalty, I cannot have you in my government. Is that clear?'

'Perfectly.'

'Good.'

'That's it, then. You're deposing me based on an interaction we had cycles ago? Sage at least gave you the courtesy of a dignified choice.'

'I'm not Sage, am I?' He raised his chin and shouted at the door. 'Conrad!'

The young assistant entered with his head slightly bowed.

'Call a press conference. One cendec from now.' Elihus ordered, not taking his eyes off Orian. '*Ms* Gracyn has an announcement to make.'

Conrad nodded ruefully. 'Yes, Surprime.'

As he left, Elihus smirked. 'That should be long enough for you to decide.'

Orian stepped up to the podium outside the ministerial chambers. A large crowd of townsfolk and media had gathered on the lawn below. Despite her purpose, she stood resolute, refusing to show any sign of emotion that could give Elihus the satisfaction of knowing he had defeated her more than just stripping her of her title. He stood behind her, flanked by Artimus and Niklas, who were clearly there to ensure she did as ordered. And as she announced her resignation, the onlookers gasped with disbelief, turning to each other to mutter under their breaths. Between her statements, she caught the crowd's objections, and it gave her some relief knowing some still supported her. She knew she had made the right decision.

At the conclusion of her brief speech, Orian bowed her head and descended the steps no longer as a minister of Hope but as Ms Orian Gracyn.

Abril and Garan stood in the front row, their expressions of shock mixing with the crowds. Some gave her congratulations, others commiserations, while the media wanted to grill her for answers. Exhausted and consumed by emotion, she wasn't fit to answer any of them, instead forcing her way through the throng just to escape. She barely noticed Abril and Garan at her side. They had pushed their way through the wall of media to rescue her, almost causing a few of them to trip over their tripods as Garan shoved them out of her way.

Faintly, she could hear Elihus making his declarations behind her. Words like 'coalition', 'unification' and 'potential' drifted to her ears—words that meant nothing to Orian. She knew he was just saying these things because that's what the crowd wanted to hear. But that didn't matter anymore. It was no longer her problem. Hope had spoken, and she had lost.

Far enough away from prying ears and eyes, Abril stopped her and pulled her into a hug. Orian had to conjure every part of herself to not break down in tears.

'It'll be alright,' Abril said softly.

Orian wished she could believe that, but for the moment, she was just happy to have Abril there.

'What are we going to do now?' she asked after letting Orian go.

'I haven't the faintest of ideas,' Orian replied earnestly. It was the first time since the war she could recall ever feeling this helpless. She wiped a hand across her eyes, raised her chin and spoke with as much compulsion as she could muster. 'Gather the others. Have them meet me at the old council backup meeting place in one cendec. I'll have something by then.'

∞

Jaxson stepped up to the doorway of Gaius's old hut. From the outside, the roughly constructed shack was just the way he remembered it, but as he reached out to take the handle, the door opened, and a dishevelled-looking Orian met him. He'd never seen her looking like this. As he stepped inside, the place was fully furnished, and judging by the simple elegance of the items; the small bookcase along the wall filled with novels, the neatly made bed at the back and the simple cookware in the kitchen, these were Orian's belongings—her life laid bare before him.

'Are you *living* here?' he asked, trying not to pay too much attention to the personal items surrounding him. Orian just replied with a reserved sigh.

'No!' Jaxson blurted almost involuntarily. 'Absolutely not!'

'Jaxson,' she said, calmly trying to reassure him. 'It's okay.'

'Orian, no, it's not okay. This is not how you treat a former Surprime. We have to go back there and demand…'

'No,' she said, touching his arm. 'We mustn't cause a scene. This is fine. I'm fine.'

'But…'

'This is better than the alternative.'

'Alternative? Orian, did he *threaten* to banish you?'

She gave a solemn nod.

'That son of a boart!' he raged and was about to turn on his heel to storm out the door when she caught his arm.

'No,' she implored. 'Please, don't. If you make an issue out of this, it'll only make matters worse.'

'Worse? Orian, the moment you left, Elihus demoted all the women in the ministry to menial, clerical positions, stripping them of their government entitlements. Indira resigned, and Abril and Alessandra are now nothing more than office staff.'

'I… what about Garan?' she asked with a deeply concerned expression.

'He's fine. You know Garan; unassuming and non-combative. He kept his position, but Elihus is watching him closely.'

'I'm sorry. There's nothing I can do. There's nothing I could have done. I failed. Besides, I'm comfortable here.'

At that moment, as though summoned, Abril and Garan filed through the door, followed by Jaylyn with her children and Lexi, dressed in casual clothes. They all looked as shocked by Orian's new living arrangements as Jaxson was.

'What's going on here?' Lexi asked, glancing around the room.

'Elihus,' Jaxson scorned. 'This is the price he's put on Orian's right to stay in Hope.'

'He *exiled* you?' she said with incredulity.

'Not quite. It was either this or leave Hope.'

'So,' Abril piped up, 'far enough away to keep you out of sight, but close enough to keep you under his thumb, is that it? He may as well put a leash on you and parade you around like some kind of trained pet. This is an outrage!'

'I know what you're all thinking, but we can't. Not now. I thank you for your concern for my well-being, but I really am fine here. I'll make do. Look, I want to thank you all for coming. I'm sure after what just happened, you have a lot of questions.'

Abril took a seat beside Jaylyn to help her with her youngest. 'No kidding,' she replied. 'What in the Progenitors' names is going on?'

Orian sighed. 'This may not come as a surprise to most of you, but my resignation wasn't… willing.'

'I knew it!' Abril said.

The others gave equally scornful remarks.

'Elihus insisted I resign in order to protect you,' Orian continued. 'He threatened to depose us all if I didn't comply.'

'Well, he did that anyway,' Abril said. 'Right after the speeches ended, he pulled me, Alessandra and Indira into his office and demoted us.'

'I know. Jaxson told me. I am sorry.'

'Not as sorry as I am!' Abril spat. 'I'll show that scumbag where he can stick his secretarial position.'

'Abril, I know you're angry, but we have to be smart about this. Anyway, so now you know the truth.'

'That slimy son of a boart,' Garan cursed. 'He didn' even leave your corpse to cool before buryin' you.'

That comment earned him a nudge in the ribs from his wife. 'Garan!' Abril chided him. 'Don't be so vulgar in front of Jaylyn and the children. Sorry sweetheart.'

Jaylyn cracked a smile. 'No, it's okay. In a crude, roundabout way, he's right. Elihus has done nothing for this town. He just comes in here, manipulates and schemes and somehow gets what he wants. Sage was going to have him stood down. I can only assume that's the reason he…' she couldn't finish the sentence.

Abril patted her back for support. 'How that man won this election, I'll never know.'

'He didn't,' Jaxson said, stepping up to the table. 'Well, not legitimately.'

Orian gestured for him to sit.

He waved his hand at the chair, preferring to stand. 'Elihus won the election because it was rigged.'

'What?' Abril gasped again. 'Are you sure?'

'Why does that not surprise me?' Orian said, dumbfounded. 'But how do you know? Do you have proof?'

'I have a mate in the electoral office. He found this.' Jaxson produced a slip of paper and handed it to Orian.'

'This is a page from the electoral register,' she said, examining it. 'What about it?'

'Look at the names,' he said, pointing out the underlined names with his index finger.

BELZAIRE, Edsel
SEMPRO, Gaius
SEMPRO, Rika

'Don't get me wrong,' Garan said, leaning across the page to get a better look. 'I loved Gaius, but I don't think he's eligible to vote.'

'And Bronal Belzaire,' Lexi said, also examining the list. 'His name's not underlined, but he passed a trey ago.'

'Oh, no, Bronal!' Abril cried. 'He died? I didn't know that.'

'Anyway, they're Hope residents alright,' Jaxson said, returning the conversation to point. 'Just on this single page of 216 names, there are at least seventy who are deceased. Last I checked, the deceased can't vote. More than enough to swing the count in Kinton's favour.'

Orian frowned. 'So, he cheated?'

'That's what it looks like,' Jaxson said.

'I hate to be saying this,' Orian said hesitantly, 'but does Artimus know, and is this enough proof?'

'No, and no,' Jaxson replied. 'Shortly after I got this, Elihus had the register destroyed. This is the only remaining page. Besides, without being able to match votes to names, there's no way of proving who did it without incriminating Orian.'

'How do you mean? Surely this proves the election was rigged?' Abril protested.

'Yes, but it doesn't prove by whom,' Jaxson replied. 'If we accuse Elihus of cheating with this, he'd be just as inclined to turn it back on Orian. After all, Gaius's name is on the list. He'd be more likely to vote for Orian than Elihus, wouldn't you say?'

'I see,' Abril said. 'This sucks. He cheated, but we've got nothing to prove it!'

'As for Artimus,' Jaxson continued. 'He's gone off-kilter. Even if I could present him with solid evidence that could prove Elihus's guilt, he'd likely just ignore it, and that's if I can find him first.'

'Well, that settles it then.' Orian said.

'Settles what?' Jaxson said.

Orian slid the paper back to him. 'Elihus Kinton is a scoundrel, and Artimus is, well, being Artimus. We can't trust either of them. That leaves us in a very untenable position.'

'Then what do we do?' Abril asked.

'I don't know yet,' Orian replied calmly. 'Thanks to you, Jaxson, we already know what happened to Sage was no accident, and now this. It shows Elihus is dangerous, but we're on our own without a reliable means of exposing him. He may be the Surprime now, but that does not mean we will willingly surrender our town and our freedoms to him.'

Abril fumed. 'We can't just sit here and take this. It's wrong!'

Garan gently placed an arm around his seething wife. 'Calm down, dear. We all feel that way. I'm sure we'll come up with somethin'.'

'Mark my words, Abril,' Orian said, partly to quell her own anger as much as Abril's. 'That man will not be allowed to get away with tyranny. Not if *we* can help it. With your support, all of you, we shall return Hope to the people.'

'But how?' Garan asked, scratching at his mop of blonde hair. 'Elihus has all the power and resources. What can we do?'

'I'm still working on that.'

'Anyways, whatever you come up with, you have our full support, Orian. Anythin' you need, we got your back,' Garan said.

'Absolutely,' Abril added, 'you've done so much for this town, and for us, it's high time we returned the favour. What he did to you was… heinous.'

Jaylyn shifted Averyx on her lap, the five-cycle-old nestled quietly in her arms. 'Us too. Sage would be grateful for everything you've done.'

'We all are. And I'll stand by you as always,' Jaxson said, adding his sentiment to the groups. 'I may be responsible for defending the Surprime, but it's the position I protect. Sage is the rightful holder of that position.' He cleared his throat and continued. 'But after he was taken from us, and you, Orian, unceremoniously torn down as you were, I don't hold as much interest in the post anymore. I know where my allegiances lie, and that's with Hope, not a tyrant. If I can, I'll make sure justice is done. Something is very wrong here, and we need to make it right.'

'Hear hear!' they all said in unison.

'Thank you,' Orian said, on the verge of tears. 'Thank you so very much, all of you. This means a great deal. I don't know what to call this. Treason seems too harsh a word. So let's, for now, call it a gathering of old friends. I don't yet have a plan, and I'm not sure where this path will take us, so for now, please keep your heads down and try to keep out of trouble. You are all better to stay where you are. You just need to avoid drawing unwanted attention. There's no telling what he'd do if he found out what we're up to.

In the meantime, we'll continue these little gatherings. We can talk like we did in the old days, and together, we'll get through this.'

Abril touched her shoulder, smiling, and Orian glanced down at Jaylyn's youngest, cradled in her arms.

'If not for us,' Orian added, with fondness sparkling in her eyes, 'for them. At least Sage lives on in them.'

Jaxson had to concede the little girl did indeed resemble her father.

They all exchanged hugs and, one by one, discretely exited the little hut until Orian, Jaxson and Lexi remained behind.

'Is there something going on between you two?' Orian said. 'Not that it's any business of mine, but you two seem to be spending a bit of time together.'

They glanced at each other and gave an awkward chuckle.

'Ahh,' Jaxson stammered, scratching the back of his neck.

But it was Lexi who stepped forward to reply. 'Orian, there's something you should know…'

34 COMMAND AND CONTROL

NC12

'Load balancing capacitors are not charging evenly, Quinn,' Ester said, turning to her dishevelled-looking uncle, who paced around her now vacant office. She pointed at the large, computerised console where its green screen flashed a message. 'Tests have also failed on the laser outputs.'

'Say whaa...?' Quinn said, striding over to look at the error. Upon seeing the message, he ran his hands through his unruly mop of blonde hair in frustration. 'Oh, yer well, it's difficult to calibrate the megloinium output with this simple tech. Of all the things we find in the ruins of society, we happen across a kahwah machine factory. Ten thousand pristine kahwah machines, but not a single laboratory with one flipping laser calibrator. Do you know how hard it is to calibrate that stuff? Everything...'

Ester stopped listening to Quinn's rantings and returned her attention to the only significant item remaining in her office—the console. She compared the printed digits on its screen with those scribbled in the notebook she held. Sifting through days' worth of orbit projections, fuel consumption calculations, and other random scribblings, she then reached for a folder stacked atop the console to recheck a number and corrected it.

Quinn finished his complaints just as Ester turned to face him, sliding her workings over. 'I know exactly what you mean, but if you look at these calculations,' she said, running a finger over a hand-drawn diagram of a flight trajectory covered in complex mathematical equations, 'we'll fall short of the correct elliptical orbit. If one of the modules doesn't make it, the entire mission fails.'

He glanced with a blank expression at the workings on the page. 'That doesn't make sense.'

'Here, see?' Ester pointed at an equation on her notepad. 'The calculations are correct. They work out the same, every time.'

'Oh, righto. I don't know how I didn't see that the first time or the second time.'

Ester glared at him and was about to respond when he continued. 'It's no use pointing at something yellow if the person you're talking to can't see the colour. I might be an engineer, but that squiggly blandang is beyond my knowledge. I have some capacitors and lasers to inspect before I pack up my lab. I still have to organise transport for the tri-helium super-fluidic quantum singularity displacement drive.'

Ester stared at him, open-mouthed. 'That *what*?'

'The big metal cylinder?' he prompted.

'Oh. My. Progenitors,' she groaned, shaking her head in dismay. 'You're such a…' she trailed off, searching for a suitable insult but couldn't find one.

'Or you can call it the Quinn Drive if you like,' he added with one of his cheesy grins.

'You wish. Does that mean it works?'

'It does, now,' he said, leaning on the console. 'It doesn't disassemble hospitals anymore if that's what you're asking.'

'That's good. The last thing we need is for it to disassemble our ship while we're in it.' She set the notebook down in her lap and considered him. He always looked scruffy, but at least he didn't look perpetually tired and frazzled like he used to. He'd spent so long working on the big cylinder, she almost expected to never see it properly working. Still, despite all the cendecs she assisted Quinn with it, all she knew about it was that Commander had retrieved it from a crashed ship back in 01. That was before her time. Since then, Quinn had been busily working on it, tearing his hair out in the process. When they finally did turn it on, gravity went haywire. Now, two cycles later, it's apparently working, and Commander's ordered everything to be packed up. That couldn't be a coincidence. 'What is that thing anyway... really?'

Quinn scratched his head for a moment, presumably wondering if he should answer. 'It's a quantum skipdrive.'

Ester blinked at him as though she should know what that meant.

'Right,' he said, correctly reading her expression. 'I guess you can stump me with fancy equations, but I can stump you with this. It's just like the old sci-fi stories. You use it to instantly transport yourself from one place to another.'

'Transport? So, why did it redecorate the hospital?'

'Because I had the quantum stasis reversed,' he said, then proceeded to explain with hand gestures. 'It took something that fell within its quantum field and relocated it here instead of relocating us there.'

'Right. Then, is it supposed to invert gravity like that? That seems like a pretty serious occupational hazard,' she said, absently tugging at her locket, not needing to remember the pain of breaking her ribs. It felt like the room had tipped 90 degrees and dumped her out, right on top of Cristal, who had, for some reason, fared better than she had.

'I've fixed that,' Quinn said.

'Good. Because if you hadn't, and we had to use that thing again, I don't want to be anywhere near it.'

'Point taken, but don't worry your pretty head. Your Uncle Quinn has it all sorted.'

She gave him a dubious look. 'How'd you figure that?'

'With great difficulty. That, and I'm awesome.' He grinned again.

Ester groaned. 'Commander gave you the schematics, didn't he?'

'I'll neither confirm nor deny that,' Quinn replied dismissively, suddenly avoiding eye contact. He then puffed out his chest and flicked back his head in a manner remarkably similar to a male ave posturing to a female. 'I *am* a genius, you know.'

'Well, don't forget who helped, *genius*.' She picked up the notebook to continue working. 'Anyway, while you load the quantum...'

'Quinn Drive,' he supplied with another one of his cheesy grins.

'Whatever. Anyway, while you do that, I'll load these figures into the console and run a simulation to be sure. After that, we should be good to go...'

'So, you knew about it as well?' Cristal exclaimed, bursting into the room.

Both Ester and Quinn stopped what they were doing, their attention now drawn to the door where Cristal stood, eyes wild and hands on hips, looking as though she was just about ready to tear them apart.

'Knew about what?' Quinn asked innocently. That didn't improve Cristal's mood.

'Don't be dense, Quinn. This!' She waved her hand at the room, pointing at the bare walls and floor where Ester's desk and equipment used to be.

'Oh, you mean that,' he said, shrugging at Ester. 'We're mostly packed and ready for the big move.'

Cristal huffed and stormed from the room.

'What's up with her?' Ester asked.

∞

Cristal charged down the corridor into Commander's office, startling the department heads who were making their tendaw reports. Fafnir sat behind his spartan desk, where he had orderly stacks of folios lined up as though he'd used an accurate measure to square them in place.

Aside from the desk, that was all the furniture that now filled the room, making it feel even more expansive than it was before. At least Cristal knew the reason for this. The scorch marks marring the walls remained as a stark reminder. Fafnir was normally a reserved man, devoid of emotion. A cycle ago, she delivered the message that Artimus had found the person responsible for Gaius Sempro's murder and had revealed the existence of a secret facility up in the Garret Mountains. It was destroyed three days later. Cristal saw first-hand just what kind of temper Fafnir had when he'd taken his fury out on his office. It was like someone had rigged it with explosives and set them to detonate. Few dared to approach him after that. Not even Cristal felt bold enough to ask the reason for his outburst, but she knew it had something to do with that facility.

'Out!' she shouted, pointing at the door. 'Everybody out!'

As the others glanced at Commander, he approved the request with a nod, then directed his attention to Cristal. 'Explain this intrusion, Cristal.'

'Oh, sorry about ruining things and upsetting your life by changing things on you,' Cristal accused curtly, promptly shutting the door after the last of the department heads had left.

'You are more emotional today,' he asked in an offhand manner. He had a habit of doing that. 'Are you nearing menstruation?'

Cristal scowled at him, her face searing red. 'What does that have to do with leaving Jorth?'

He clasped his hands on the desk in front of him and sat back, his expression unchanging. 'Yes. We are leaving Jorth.'

'And when were you planning on making that fact known?'

'Department heads have been advised. I have granted approval for subordinates to be informed. Departure procedures have commenced.'

'In case you haven't noticed, only one person is dealing with the PR in Hope, and there is no department head. When were you planning on telling us?'

'Cristal,' he said calmly. 'Is there a problem?'

'Of course there's a problem,' she snapped. 'You make plans to leave this planet and not even mention it to your partner?'

'Is that what this outburst is about?'

'What do you think?'

He pursed his lips and leaned back in his chair, placing his thick arms on the armrests in the manner he did when he was about to deliver a lecture. 'I may allow you to share my bed and offer you certain... liberties, but do not forget your place. You are still a member of my personnel, and we still follow military protocols. I expect you to respect the chain of command. Your position does not mean that I must communicate everything to you directly.'

She stood tall, trying not to let the hurt show. It infuriated her that after all this time and the progress she'd made with him, even so far as mothering his child, he still kept her at arm's length. 'You think this is about position?' she accused. 'What about Ragnar? Did you think about him?'

'Of course,' he replied simply. 'This is all for him.'

'And still, you didn't care to consult his mother?' she yelled, stepping up to the desk and locking eyes with him.

'I am his father. I know what is best for him.'

'What's best for him?' she yelled, her voice raising an octave. 'What's best for him is a stable home environment and a place to grow up. What he needs is here on Jorth!'

The way he lounged in his chair with a neutral expression on his immaculately chiselled face, it was as though her yelling amused him, and it only infuriated her more.

'What he *needs,*' he said, leaning forward and staring at her with his dark, bespeckled eyes, 'is to be with his people, learn his heritage and become who he is meant to be.'

She crossed her arms indignantly. '*His people!* What are you talking about? *We're* his people.'

'No,' he said, calmly but firmly. 'His people transcended this planet two thousand cycles ago.'

She blinked at him, confounded. 'That makes absolutely no sense.'

He shook his head. 'Cristal, I thought you were smarter than this. Surely you would have figured it out by now.'

'Figured out what?'

He smiled, and it still felt unnatural even though he only did it around her. 'That I am not Gaian. I am Gaia'Ta.'

'Gaia'Ta?' she gasped, a shiver running down her spine like someone had poured ice water down her back. That was certainly not where she expected this conversation to be heading. She wasn't even sure to believe what she was hearing. Fafnir may have his secrets, but he hadn't lied to her before. Not like this. She knew about the Gaia'Ta from the stories she'd been told as a child, but that was all. Then she recalled the thin blue wires she'd seen running beneath his skin. This close to him, she could just make them out now, crisscrossing beneath the thinner skin of his hand. She remembered having read somewhere in the legends of how the Gaia'Ta bore augments that allowed them to do their 'magic'; magic she didn't believe in. 'Gaia'Ta,' she repeated, eyes wide with awe. 'As in *Progenitor*?'

He gave a wry grin. 'Not exactly. The Mighty Seven may have been Progenitors, and we inherited their advancements, but that is not who we are. To your kind, the differentiation is minor and therefore a common misconception.'

'But the Gaia'Ta? That's impossible! They died out.'

'Not yet. Not if I can help it,' he said. As he spoke, he turned to the safe in the cabinet behind his desk, unlocked it, retrieved a vial of the swirling black metallic substance and inserted it into an injector. 'Thanks to the Progenitors, much of our genetic heritage still remains on this planet.'

Cristal found herself both intrigued and wary, remembering the sickness she'd suffered after he'd given her just a small dose of that stuff. 'So why leave?'

Fafnir rolled up his sleeve, exposing his thick muscular forearm—and more of those blue wires—and pressed the injector against his skin, repeatedly clenching his fist until the vial was empty. 'My work can no longer be done here.'

When he'd placed the spent injector on the desk, he gazed at Cristal, and for a moment, his eyes went inky black. A grin spread across his face as his eyes returned to normal, and besides a few dark speckles, there was no evidence of what had transpired.

'What work?'

From the pile of papers before him, he picked up a sheet and stood, joining Cristal on the other side of the desk. He pinched a page corner between his thumb and forefinger, and she marvelled at a spark that flashed between them, igniting the paper.

Another one of those smirks appeared on his otherwise stonelike face. He then scooped the flame off the page with one hand and held it burning micrometas above his outstretched palm. Cristal watched with amazement as it danced along with the rolling motion of his fingers.

'Oh, that's a neat trick,' she said, reaching out to touch the apparent illusion, then snatched her hand away just as quick, wide-eyed in disbelief. 'It's... real.'

He rolled the flame over his hand and moulded it between his palms. Rolling it as though it were a snowball. Its size grew, and the fire licked at the air between his fingers, hungry for more fuel. Then, with a flick of his wrist, he lobbed the fireball over her shoulder into a wastepaper bin sitting by the wall. With a whoosh, the few scrunched-up balls of paper within disintegrated into ash.

'How did you?' she gasped.

He responded only with silence and that unusual but reserved grin.

'You really are Gaia'Ta?'

He nodded.

'And that means?'

'Our son is Gaia'Ta as well.'

'He can do that?' she asked, pointing at the smoking wastepaper bin.

'It is more complicated than that. This planet doesn't have the resources he needs.'

'Is that why we're leaving?'

Fafnir set the burnt page down and cupped her face gently with a cool hand. After what she'd just witnessed, she expected his hand to be hot or burned, but all she felt was the warm softness of his skin against hers. 'Do you remember what I said when we left the Watchtower?'

'Of course,' she nodded, trying to subdue the heart flutters, making her breathless. 'You said that one day, from the ashes, a great empire will rise again.'

He smiled. 'Do you believe that?'

'Yes.'

'And you remember Garret Gord?'

'Yes,' she replied dubiously. Conscious of the last time she'd mentioned those words to him. Only then he'd sent her from the room. At least now she could see why and where the scorch marks had come from. She swallowed. 'That was the name of the training facility up in the mountains. It was for female assassins, wasn't it? But it was destroyed.'

'Yes, it was. But they were not assassins. They were Gaia'Tan warriors. My daughter was among them.'

Cristal gasped. 'So that's why? Wait. You have a daughter?'

'Had.' For the first time, she saw pain in his eyes. Deep, enduring pain.

She took a step back. 'Sorry... didn't know.'

'I've come to terms with it,' he said. 'I built Garret Gord to preserve my people; to produce strong Gaia'Tan women. Strong in every sense. I fathered one of them. Her name was Ilona.'

'Ilona.' She repeated the name almost whimsically.

'Her mother died when she was young. I left her to train with the others. I intended to collect her before our departure, but I was betrayed.'

'Betrayed?' She intended to ask by whom, but the pain in his eyes stifled her. She'd never seen him like this before. This was unchartered territory, and the fact that he was opening up to her left her wondering if she should comfort him or keep her distance. At first, she thought he had been keeping her out, and probably he was, but now that she knew this, all manner of questions flooded her mind. 'That facility was yours?'

He nodded.

Then something else occurred to her, and she had to know. 'Does that mean...' she hesitated, not knowing how to ask. 'Were you the one who ordered Gaius's death?'

She may have gone too far. His answer was crisp and clinical. 'In the grand scheme, sacrifices are necessary.'

She took a step back, shocked. Speechless, her head reeled.

'Understand, there was no animosity intended toward him. The mission is key, that's all. He was a threat that needed to be neutralised. One life to save thousands.'

'But...' she was almost on the verge of tears now. She barely knew Gaius, but for Fafnir to kill him in cold blood like she'd witnessed with the Watchtower crew was unthinkable.

'Cristal,' he said, closing the distance that had opened between them. 'Everything I've done, I've done to see my mission complete. That's all that matters. I've sacrificed more than you'll ever know. You are not expected to understand, not right now. But one day, you will. I've chosen you because I know your mind is open. You gave me Ragnar. Right now, we must focus on the future. And now, with Garret Gord gone. With Ilona gone, there's nothing left for us here. We *must* protect Ragnar. He's the mission now. We must move forward.'

'Mission? Forward?'

His gaze momentarily lifted toward the ceiling. 'Do not worry,' he said in the calm voice he reserved only for her. 'The matter's in hand. Forget about all of this. You will continue your duties in Hope. You will tell them nothing of this and what we are doing here. When we are ready, pack only essential items for yourself and Ragnar. Destroy the rest. Understood?'

He lifted a hand and gently stroked her cheek. She closed her eyes, relishing in the feel of his skin against hers. No matter what he had done, he was the father of her child, and she still loved him.

'Yes,' she said, almost trembling. Learning who he was, *what* he was, made her head swim. She was conflicted. On the one hand, she had always known there was something extraordinary about him, something no one else could see. On the other, he was a ruthless killer, just as Lexi had said. But to her, all that seemed insignificant. Who was she to deny the will of a god? Perhaps his reasons were justified. One thing was clear, he was Gaia'Ta, a real-life, living legend. And she'd born a child with him. That realisation alone gave her solace. The outburst. The requirement to leave Jorth. It all started to make sense. Where before she felt on the outer, she now glowed with the knowledge Fafnir had entrusted her with much more than anyone else. And that made her swell with pride. As she gazed upon him; a Gaia'Ta, *her* Gaia'Ta, it filled her with purpose; his purpose, and in her mind, it was enough to absolve him of everything else.

'From the ashes of this world, the Gaia'Ta *will* rise again,' he said, his face close enough to kiss her. 'Trust in me, and we will complete that mission. By my side, you will have the best vantage point in the galaxy.'

35 JAYNE

Gotta love the smell of stale ale in the evening. I never used to, but after a full cycle working as a delivery driver, servicing all the pubs in town, I've grown accustomed to it. After my demolition of Garret Gord, I'd gone to Hope and, as luck would have it, found a reasonable-paying job. Of course, I'd have to credit Ilona for that. Seems Gerriott—the guy who owned the delivery service that employed our poor delivery driver who wasn't supposed to die in a fiery car crash—had trouble finding a replacement. He saw my arrival as timely and employed me on the spot, especially given I came with my own truck. Thankfully, he never asked where I got it. And after stashing its contents in a safe place just outside of Hope, I got straight to work.

Graylianne, the proprietor of this particular establishment, has come to know me as a regular. Every evening after unloading the last of my deliveries, I retire to my usual two-person booth in the darkened corner of The Boart's Head for an ale and a bite to eat. After my first visit, I'm surprised I found myself back in here. After all, I'd need much more than a cycle, and a cycle's worth of ale, to dull the raw nerves that still prevent me from sitting at the end of the bar where Ilona once sat. So, I sit facing the door, watching the people come and go while drowning my sorrows.

Without warning, a pair of HomeGuard officers storm into the pub and arrest a neatly dressed man sitting at a table with his friends. They beat him with their nightsticks, and when he's bloodied and no longer squirming, they drag him out the door.

The place settles down quickly afterwards like it's a common occurrence, and that's what strikes me as disturbing. Where Hope was once a happy-go-lucky sort of place, it's become dark, as though an oppressive, ever-present storm cloud has set in. I see it in the forlorn faces of the people filling this marginal space. And it's not just because of this place, it's everywhere. Five of my usual delivery locations just up and cancelled this tendawn alone. If it weren't for Graylianne, I'm sure there won't be much for me to do soon.

Sauntering over with a steaming bowl and a frothing tankard, Graylianne sets them down at my small table. 'Hard day, luv?' she asks, obviously noticing my sour mood. It seems to be catching.

'Something like that. What was that all about?'

She leans in close to speak in a low voice. 'The Surprime's declared that all people of Lafir heritage are illegals. They're being arrested and banished from town.'

'They're what?' I exclaim.

'Keep ya voice down,' she hisses, glancing around the room to ensure nobody heard. 'Ya dun wanna attract that kinda attention.'

She's got a point. Though I was raised at Garret Gord, I was born in Nusmore—Lafir territory. I'd like to see them try to drag me out like that, but I still wouldn't want to test it. Since Elihus took the position of Surprime, this place has become reminiscent of Garret Gord, cold and inhospitable. Even the thought of his name sets bile rising to the back of my throat. My jaw involuntarily clenches, and I have to will the thought from my mind, else I might do something I'll later regret. Graylianne must have sensed my unease, for she shoots me a wary look as if to say, 'don't do anything stupid.' For some reason, she's started looking out for me. I have no idea why. Glancing down at my bowl, I opt for a change of subject. 'Boart stew again?'

'Yep. But I think ya'll like this one,' she says with a curious smile. 'Chef's changed the recipe.'

The dark brown slop pushes around the bowl. There are chunks in it this time; meat and vegetables, by the looks of it, it's richer, and the thicker texture drips slower from the spoon.

'Not bad,' I say after tasting a mouthful. 'Either Chef *is* getting better, or I'm getting the taste for it. What's changed?'

She gives a slight chuckle. 'He tried some of those spices ya done recommended.'

'Oh, right. Good. Needs more salt, though.'

'I'll let 'im know,' she says with a smile. 'Maybe I should put ya on as a chef. Delivery drivin' just don't seem ya callin'.'

'No, it's not.' I shrug. 'But then again, neither's cooking. There are too many knives in a kitchen.'

'Fair, but ya don't strike me as the clumsy type.'

'Hmm, I'm not usually, no,' I reply with a smirk. 'Besides, I prefer being outdoors, moving around, and all that. If I spend too long indoors, I get restless.'

She pushes the mug closer to me. 'Fair nuff. Well, ya keep those suggestions comin', luv. Now that Chef's food's edible, I think we'll be gettin' a few more customers pretty well soon. And I canna tell ya just how good that'll be. Things are startin' to look a little bleak.'

'I've noticed. What's going on?'

'Well,' she says, discretely glancing around, then takes the seat across from me. 'Aside from the arrests, taxes, rate increases, ya name it. That new Surprimes' gone and done it. Since he got in, he's gone and put in all these new charges but then went and cut the CI.'

'The what?'

'Ya know? The CI—Citizen's Income?'

'Nope, never heard of it.'

'Right,' she says. 'Ya are new, ain't ya? Anyways, it's a base income all Hope citizens get to help pay for essentials, like food, clothes and a place to live. Well, we did before that Surprime Kinton done cut it the first thing he got in. Since then, people ain't been comin' here for social no more. They be comin' for food though, which may just save me hide. Between us and the co-op, we've gotta be the cheapest place to get a feed in town right now. But if things continue like this, I'll be lucky if I don't join 'em.'

'Oh.'

'Yeah, oh. You just make sure ya hold onto that job of yours, missy,' she says, reaching out to tap my hand. 'It may just save ya.'

'Thanks for the advice.'

A man crosses the floor to the bar, and Graylianne stands, smoothing her apron as she does. 'Anyways, ya don't want me whining at ya as ya eat ya dinner.'

'Before you go, what else can you tell me about the Surprime?'

'I dunno, luv. He comes in here every once in a while, but other than that, nothin'.'

'Right. Thanks, Graylianne.'

'No worries, luv. Oh, and let me know if ya wanna a top-up. Next one's on the house. After that little cooking tip, ya earned it.'

While I wallow in the darkness, finishing my stew and ale, watching the crowd grow, the door bursts open, and two overly dressed men in fancy tailored suits and shiny shoes stand in the doorway like they own the place. The most ostentatious of the pair seems to almost prance as he crosses the room—if it weren't for the drunken swagger. 'Ale,' he declares, slapping a hand on the bar.

Graylianne doesn't seem to care what sorts saunter into her bar so long as they drink, eat and are reasonably well behaved. As the pompous man waits, he leans on the bar, swaying. His neckless partner, whom I presume is his bodyguard by his burly stature, oddly formal attire, and the appearance of a stick shoved in dark places, skulks around behind. The man seems to have noticed me watching and winks. Stifling a groan, I promptly return to my meal.

But you know what they say about canis—DO NOT make eye contact. And just like a canis, the man, drink in hand, swaggers over and presents his ruffled, half-unbuttoned shirt in my face. The stench of ale on his breath is sickening. 'Ohh,' he slurs, leering at me with a look akin to a child with a shiny object. 'What have we here, then? Aren't you a pretty thing?'

Hoping this unctuous creep gets the point, I lift my mug, take a swig, and return to my meal.

'I've never seen you around here before, baby. But I'd like to see more. How about it? Maybe later?' He chuckles at his innuendo as if it were so witty, only he could've come up with it.

Just trying to ignore him grates on my nerves, and I sit on my left hand to resist the urge to use it to better demonstrate my displeasure.

A shadow covers my food. 'Boss arksed you a question.'

So the man muscle speaks?

Mr Creepy Ale-breath waves him away. 'S'alright. The lady and I are having a con…verrr…ssation.'

Some conversation.

'You shore you done want no help, boss?' the neckless, man-shaped rock says.

'I said back up, Creatch,' Mr Creepy says, turning on his companion with a touch of unnecessary aggression. 'Give the lady some space.'

'Creatch,' I snigger with ale almost coming out of my nose, glancing up only to consider the burly bodyguard. 'Is that a disease or a name?'

Where have I heard that name before?

The big man scowls at me before plodding back to the bar.

Mr Creepy Ale-breath continues, leaning in closer. 'Are you new here? You look new. Do you know who I am?'

'No.'

'No, you're not new, or no, you don't know who I am?'

'Pick one.'

'Hmm, interesting. Quiet *and* feisty. I like that. Anyway, the name's Voltaire. Voltaire Catlow.'

He puffs out his chest as though that's supposed to be attractive, and when he sees my expression doesn't change, he sits on the other chair and grabs my wrist, stopping me from lifting my drink.

'Don't do that,' I warn him, taking back my hand with a steely glare. *You really want to do this, buddy?*

'Oh, what beautiful green eyes you have. Like sparkling emeralds. And that red hair. I bet you'd be a firecracker in bed. You know, I'm the head of a very successful company. Perhaps you've heard of me; OrbEn Enterprises?'

'Is that supposed to mean something?'

'Well, it does to most women. They swoon over me.'

'I'm not most women.'

'That's understandable. You haven't felt me yet.'

Creepy Ale-Breath reaches out a hand to touch my face.

And that's your second mistake.

Grabbing his wrist, he giggles with delight. But his drunken humour fades into a whimper under the force of my grip. Sobriety replaces that oily grin running across his face as I wrench at his arm, his body whips forward, and his forehead slams on the tabletop.

He recoils.

Dazed and disoriented, his vacant stare slips, and he drops face-first into the remainder of my stew.

Before I can get out of the booth, Creatch stomps over from the bar with his augured punch hanging out like a clothesline.

With a simple block and jab to the throat, he stumbles back, coughing and clutching his neck, giving me time to stand.

Chubby face still crimson, he shuffles his feet, ready to charge again.

'Wait!' I yell, palms forward, giving him pause. 'You do this, I warn you, you'll be joining your friend. Is that how you want this to go?'

This time, his vicious snigger is even less intelligible as he lumbers forward, driving his fist at me like a battering ram.

Effortlessly, I deflect his attack. He strikes the wall with a sickening crunch, collapsing in an unconscious heap in the booth where I'd been sitting. If I didn't know any better, they'd just be a pair of drunkards, passed out together.

'Well, you felt me now,' I utter, dusting my hands off on my pants. 'I hope you liked it as much as I did.'

Everybody in the establishment stares at me in deathly silence. *And here, I thought brawls were a common thing.*

'Well, shak,' I curse under my breath, looking upon the two inert figures now occupying the messy booth. 'Sorry, Graylianne.'

Her response rings in the dead air. 'You definitely missed your callin', luv.'

'Um…'

'S'right, luv. That rodentia had it comin'. Never knew ya could do that, though. Gotta figure out how I'm to explain this to the 'Guard.'

'Tell them they slipped.'

A slow clap punctuates Graylianne's nervous laugh as a man with a dark complexion in a tidy, officious, red-piped uniform pushes through the stunned crowd.

I've seen this guy before, too.

'That's amazing,' the man congratulates me, leaning against the bar beyond arms' reach. 'Couldn't have happened to a more smimy orifice.' He then turns to Graylianne. 'I'll take two of what she's drinking.'

'You want some of that too?' I reply, gesturing to the booth.

'Oh, no,' he chuckles, his hands raised in supplication. 'I just admire art when I see it. And that…' he gestures at the two inert men, 'is what I call art. Very impressive.'

I smirk, and conversation in the room returns to the same volume it was before.

'I'm Jaxson,' the man says, extending his hand. I can't help but notice what looks like burn marks on his palm.

Two tankards replace his coins.

With that, I grab my things and turn towards the door. 'I'm leaving.'

He moves to block my path…

∞

'Jayne, please stay,' Jaxson said, hoping that using her name would be enough to get her attention. But it only made her eyes burn with a more fervent ferocity. And with that deep furrowed brow, fixed shoulders and curiously muscular arms gripping a shoulder bag as though it were a bludgeon, it was enough to convince Jaxson intercepting her like that wasn't such a wise move. Without saying another word, she sidestepped him and was gone.

'Leave her,' a woman's voice said from somewhere behind. The voice sounded familiar, and as Jaxson turned, he had to do a double-take.

'Didn't you just…?' he stammered, his sight falling on the voice's owner emerging from the dark booths on the other side of the room to join him at the bar. With her shoulder-length red hair, startling green eyes and attractive features, she was the spitting image of the woman who'd just left. If it weren't for her more sophisticated clothes and slightly more advanced age, Jaxson would have sworn she *was* the same person.

'Yes and no,' she said, taking the stool beside him. 'It's… complicated. Was this drink for me?'

'Go ahead,' he replied, flippantly gesturing at the tankard. 'Are you a sister, or twin, or…?'

'Not quite.'

'But you *do* know her?'

'Oh yes,' The strange woman said, taking a sip of her drink. 'But it's best you just leave her be. Safer that way.'

Jaxson rubbed his hands uneasily. 'For whom? Her or me?'

'See what she did here? You figure it out.'

'Really?' Jaxson gave her an indignant look. 'I think I can handle myself.'

'You think? Want to make a wager on that? I bet Creatch and Voltaire thought they could too, but…' she chuckled and mumbled something Jaxson couldn't quite hear.

He scratched the back of his neck. 'Umm… Who are you?'

'Lou.'

'Lou, I'm—'

'Jaxson Yanez, I know who you are. You're the Surprime's guard.' She took another sip from the tankard. 'So, what brings you to a dive like this, Jaxson?'

'Questions.'

'What sort of questions?'

'Questions meant for her. But, I guess that'll have to wait,' Jaxson replied, lifting the other tankard, and took a sip.

'I see.'

'Gaw,' he said, scrunching up his face in disgust. 'That's repulsive. How can people drink that?'

She gave a delicate chuckle. 'I don't think it's that bad.'

'Oh, it's bad. This tastes like the contents of a urinal. If you think it's alright, you've probably not tasted better.'

Graylianne shot him a sideways look while she busied herself serving another patron. He set the tankard down and pushed it to one side.

'So, you're not a regular here then?'

'How'd you guess?'

She smirked. 'How should I put this? I know what you're after, Jaxson. But it's not going to go the way you want it to.'

'Now, what do you mean by that?'

'She's… delicate. If you pursue her now, she'll disappear, and you'll never find the answers you're looking for.'

He lowered his voice. 'How'd you? What are you talking about?'

She leaned in and spoke in a voice matching his discreet tone. 'You're looking for the person who killed Sage Solon, right?'

Like a switch, his mind turned from the conversation to the events of that nightmarish night. Everyone had said it was a freak accident, but he knew better. After awakening in the smashed car to the taste of blood in his mouth and the acrid smell of fuel and burning rubber, he watched helplessly as a concrete slab penetrated the passenger side window and struck Sage in the head.

In his dazed state, there was nothing he could do. But remembered two hazy shadows against a backdrop of fire and a woman's voice crying out, 'No!' It was a scene that played in his mind like an ever-repeating horror show. And now, he was sure he knew who the owner of that voice was.

'It was an accident,' he lied, the words spilling out automatically.

'Is that the lie you tell yourself to make yourself feel better, or the one you perpetuate to tow the party line?'

'What do you want from me?' he said, turning to face her. 'To admit I was there to protect him and I did nothing, or to torture me about the fact. I know you were there. I remember your voice. The only thing I can't reason is why?'

'The person you saw was Jayne, and she's the one who can answer your questions.'

'Right.' He grabbed the tankard and took another gulp, hoping it would taste better if it didn't touch the sides. 'If that wasn't you, how do you know this?'

'I just do. I can't explain it. Listen, she can and will help you uncover the answers you've been looking for. But it's important you keep your distance. She knows you're after her, and if you press too hard, she *will* disappear, and you *will* lose the only chance you have to redeem yourself.'

'I'm not after redemption. I want to put things right.'

'Then you will do as I ask. I know you have no reason to trust me, but you know it's true. Trust that.'

He laughed another nervous laugh. 'It must be the ale talking. I don't know what's true anymore. This isn't making any sense. Why are you telling me this?'

She moved in closer, dazzling him with her mesmerising green eyes, among her other endearing qualities. 'Because you and I want the same thing. You *know* what I mean.'

'If you really want what I want, why come here? And now? And how do I know this is not some kind of setup?'

'Soon, that girl, Jayne, will take you to the person responsible for what happened to your Surprime. And at that moment, you will face a choice. You can either help her and bring the person responsible to justice, or you can resist and likely get you both killed. Now you and I both don't want the latter, and I *know* that's not going to happen. The reason I'm telling you this is because it's how you provide that help that matters.'

'What does that mean?'

'She doesn't know it yet, but she will need you. You will know when that happens, and when it does, you must give her this.'

Lou handed Jaxson a folded piece of paper; inside, it had an address scribbled down. He recognised it as someplace on the edge of town but didn't know where.

'What's this?'

'Hope's ticket to redemption. And yours. I can't tell you anything more. But when this all comes true, as I say, then I'll happily sit down over some mugs of better ale and explain it to you. That's a promise.'

'Why is it I always seem to get led astray by pretty women sprouting prophecy?' he said, jovially placing the slip of paper in a pocket. He took another swig of ale and shook his head. 'Nope, that's still foul. Okay. Say I believe you. What now?'

'We wait,' she replied, casually smiling. 'What do you mean, pretty women?'

'What?'

'You just said something about being led astray by pretty women. What did you mean by that?'

'Well…' he coughed nervously.

She leaned an elbow on the bar and glanced up at him with her piercing eyes. 'You find me attractive, do you?'

'That's the worst pickup line ever,' he joked. 'That, and the whole prophecy thing.'

'You think that's a pickup line?'

'Isn't it?'

36 MIDNIGHT ESCAPADES

Excerpt from Book of the Progenitors:

After the great war, the children of Jorth returned to their ancestral tribes to be with their loved ones, while the Gaian minions of the army of the damned either fled in defeat or surrendered.

For longer than memory did Gotthard and his kin fight for us, securing a major victory for all the people of the land.

We had come to learn of them as our protectors and saviours, mighty Progenitors. But even the mighty need to rest.

So it was that Gotthard the vanquisher, with Martok the deceiver, Xisnys the dragon and her beloved Codan, master of land and stone, marched those that remained of the vanquished north beyond the warm belt into the coldest of places; the Eir mountains. And there they vanished.

For cycles thereafter, brave adventurers and intrepid explorers vanished too, seeking for what had become of the eldest of the Mighty Seven.

Then it was that Lafir, the great explorer, took it upon himself to find what others had failed to find. On the night of the dark moons, with his band of brave assistants, they stopped in their tracks at the base of the Eir ranges, marvelling at the sight of prodigious fireballs shooting down the stars.

Jaxson's bedside clock clattered to the floor, waking him with a startle. Outside his tiny apartment, a monstrous rumble, accompanied by jarring ground tremors, intensified to a deafening crescendo, shaking the town from its peaceful slumber. He staggered out of bed and stumbled to the window, only to be blinded by an intense yellow light erupting from the Brimeuse mountains. He shielded his eyes from the magnificent fireball that lit up the valley like a second sun. Much like the LunaTec launch from one and a half cycles ago, it rocketed skyward, breaking in two with one half continuing its sojourn into space and the other, still red hot, falling back to Jorth. Now he understood just what Lafir mistook as shooting down stars all those eons ago when the Progenitors disappeared. Whatever LunaTec was doing, he didn't know, but he was certain no one else in Hope knew either.

As the light from the fading fireball diminished, Jaxson flicked on his bedside lamp.

There, curled up and sound asleep, was the woman he knew only as Lou.

If that is your real name, he thought, admiring the short mane of deep red hair cascading down the soft, pale skin of her neck. His gaze followed the smooth curves of her body, partially concealed beneath his bedsheets, to that peculiar dimple on her back, just above the hip, that marred her otherwise flawless skin.

The woman was certainly an enigma.

How did I end up with you? Jaxson pondered, grabbing his clothes from the floor. Even as he put them on, this is not how he imagined his night would end when he went to The Boart's Head. The evening had gone from interesting to strange to weirdly magnetic. At first, they just talked, but then as the night went on, his attraction to her grew, and the next thing he knew, they were shedding their clothes, and she was on top of him. He still couldn't quite figure out how that happened. Just thinking about it made him want to crawl back in beside her, but… 'Duty calls,' he said quietly, pulling on his shoes and hoping it wouldn't be the last time he saw her.

Rummaging in his pockets for his keys, his hand brushed paper—the note. Despite still being uncertain of her motives for giving him that, he decided to keep it there. Then, grabbing his coat, he turned off the light and, with a regretful backward glance, quietly left the room.

Half-distracted by the woman in his warm bed back in his apartment, he almost missed the bright headlights and deep rumble of a truck engine coming up from behind.

The driver's side window wound down, revealing Artimus behind the wheel.

'Artimus!' Jaxson said, surprised to see the admiral after such long absences.

'You going to stand there, or are you going to get in?' Artimus said in a more gruff-than-usual tone.

Jaxson snatched open the door. 'Where have you been? The whole town's been looking…'

'Buckle up.' Is all Artimus said.

It wasn't until they crossed the Rika bridge that Jaxson spoke again. 'Do you at least know what the frak is going on?'

'LunaTec are fleeing,' Artimus replied. 'We need to catch them before they do.'

'What? Why? Where would they even go?' Jaxson said, astonished.

'Off-world.'

'Huh?'

'Jaxson, come on,' Artimus growled, barely taking his eyes off the road. Trees whizzed past, crashing into the windscreen and the side of the truck, making Jaxson grab onto the dash and the bar above the door to steady himself.

'You didn't think that spectacle was all for our benefit?' Artimus continued. 'That was a charade masquerading as a test flight. They've built space-faring vessels, and they're using them to leave the planet. They have something I want, and they're not leaving with it.'

'And what would that be?'

'That's what we're going to find out,' Artimus said.

A second rocket launched into the moonless night sky, its magnificent plume of flame screaming into the atmosphere. For a moment, both men stared at it like bewildered children.

Then Artimus floored it.

By the fourth launch, they had made it to the LunaTec facility's main gates, choosing to ignore the brilliant fireworks displays in lieu of expediency.

Artimus mowed his truck through the wooden boom gate beside the oddly vacant guard post. They continued into the illuminated tunnel leading inside the mountain complex. It wasn't until they reached the cavernous garage and main reception they stopped.

To Jaxson's surprise, not a single LunaTec guard, staffer or official came to greet them. 'This is strange,' he said as they both climbed down.

Artimus grunted his reply.

Shortly after, several more HomeGuard trucks rolled into the gravelled area until twenty of Artimus's soldiers were lined up before them, waiting for orders.

'Pair up and spread out,' Artimus barked. 'If it moves, I want it brought back here. Report anything suspicious. Dismissed.'

The soldiers saluted and filed in through the door.

'A bunch of office workers and engineers won't take long to herd,' Artimus said arrogantly.

'Are you arresting these people?' Jaxson asked, puzzled at the excessive show of force directed toward a company that as yet had not caused any harm.

'Don't question me, Jaxson,' Artimus growled. 'You're here to observe. That's all. Leave us to do our job.'

'Whatever you say.' Jaxon shrugged, then followed the soldiers inside.

When he entered the spacious reception area, the scene resembled a bomb site. Everything behind the reception desk was smashed and burnt. It looked like the place had been looted, then vandalised with all the furniture piled up into smouldering heaps. There didn't appear to be anything of value remaining. Artimus followed in with an expression mixed with disbelief and concealed rage. His scarred face only amplified the severity of his temperament. 'Ah, shak,' he muttered. 'We're too late.'

As they passed from room to room through the haze-filled compound, every area, every room, and every workstation was the same as the first, littered with smashed equipment and charred debris. Not a single LunaTec person remained either. It seemed the only living things here now were Jaxson, Artimus and his troops, who continued to relay details of more empty rooms.

Eventually, they found their way to the remnants of a command centre. Beyond all the trash and left ajar was an enormously thick metal door, almost like a cube on hinges. It lured the two men, Artimus first followed by Jaxson, into the adjoining chamber.

In the colossal space, the cave roof disappeared to the starry night sky. The lack of lighting left parts of the cave in shadow, but it was enough to see by, and judging from the scorch marks on the concrete walls and floor, this was likely the point of departure. 'So, this is what they were doing,' Jaxson said. 'And to think they wanted to mine goethite. How stupid could we be?'

'What?' Artimus asked, also gazing up at the massive hole in the roof.

'When LunaTec first came to Hope, they said they wanted to mine the goethite from these caves. But that was obviously a lie. They traded food, medicine and supplies, but seeing this, I now understand why they wanted the caves so badly. What I don't get is, why keep it a secret?'

Jaxson's question was left hanging when at that moment, a young HomeGuard sergeant jogged in and approached the grizzly admiral. 'Sir,' she said, a little puffed. 'We've checked the complex. The whole place is deserted. But we did find something we think you'd want to see.'

Beside Jaxson, the Admiral tore his eyes away from the sight above to respond to his officer, allowing Jaxson to take in the room.

Approximately a hundred metas ahead stood a platform with tank tracks spanning a giant hole in the floor, both blackened with the same scorch marks he'd observed on the walls. He'd never before seen a vehicle that large. Its tracks pointed to five construction bays in a row, the first being much smaller than the others.

Four brick buildings the size of the old community hall were spaced out in 'corners' of the immense area. On the side of the closest building was a sign featuring large yellow writing which read;

"Warning LASER Radiation—looking into beam will cause permanent evaporation".

With Jaxson trailing along behind like a pet, Artimus followed the young sergeant through the meandering, warren-esque passageways toward a room deep in the bowels of the complex. The officer opened a door, revealing yet another room stripped bare but with a wall of windows overlooking a vast natural cavern. Scaffolding erected inside the cave beyond the windows suggested something large had been housed there. Whatever that could have been, Jaxson couldn't fathom.

Crossing the room to step out onto the metal walkway adjoining the building, Artimus muttered to himself. 'It was here.'

'What was here?' Jaxson asked, but the Admiral ignored him. He just stood on the platform, gazing around the cave.

'That's not the most impressive bit,' the Sergeant said, raising her torch to illuminate something at the rear of the cavern.

Jaxson squinted, and he could tell the Admiral standing beside him was doing the same, his head tilting so his good eye could focus on the jiggling circle of light.

Jaxson stepped up to the balustrade while the sergeant handed Artimus a pair of distance-looking glasses.

They gazed into the darkness where Jaxson could just make out the outline of an unnatural object.

'What can you see?' he enquired, trying to focus on the rear of the cave, but in the darkness, he couldn't quite determine what he was looking at. 'What is *that*?' he said, passing Artimus to descend the metal ladder to the cave floor.

Artimus followed. As they came closer, the object started to take shape, but it was the letters forming the words "emorial Hos" that caught Jaxson's attention. 'Well, I think we found the missing hospital wall,' he said dryly, kicking around some of the debris surrounding the segment of the brick wall.

'My thunderous backside, indeed!' Artimus swore. 'That bikkja lied straight to our faces! They knew this was here all along, yet they kept feeding us that drivel about residual nuclear radiation.'

'But how did it get here? It's not like you can just relocate the entire side of a building.'

'LunaTec found a way.'

'But why? What purpose would that serve? Do you think they were working on some kind of weapon?'

'Arrrgh!' Artimus screamed, kicking a loose brick with his boot and sending it flying off into the blackness.

'Sir,' the Sergeant said, almost trembling. 'There's more.'

'More?' he said, glaring at her. 'Where?'

'Not here.'

The sergeant led Jaxson and Artimus further into the complex. As she did, Jaxson couldn't believe how extensive the complex was. It almost seemed as if they walked any further, they'd end up back in Hope. Eventually, the corridors lightened up, with doors to rooms splitting off both sides. From what little remained of those rooms' contents, these were the sleeping quarters. It wasn't until they reached a solitary room at the far end Jaxson understood what drew the sergeant's attention. It wasn't like all the others, for it still had all its furniture intact, suggesting its occupant had been a young woman, and from the look of it, it was left as though she had just gone out for the day. As far as Jaxson could gather, they'd intended for it to be found this way.

Jaxson waited by the door while Artimus entered the room, sitting on the bed in its centre, brow furrowed deep in thought. It wasn't hard to imagine what he would be thinking as Jaxson gazed around the neat little room, wondering what sort of child would have grown up in an underground facility like this and, without having seen the stars, left to join them.

Then he remembered the young red-haired girl Cristal had brought with her occasionally to visit.

Tess, that was her name. Now that was a bright young girl.

He pondered over it while he examined the old toys and stuffed ursus, some even missing their sewn-on eyes, all lovingly lined up neat and tidy on shelves above an empty wooden desk. By the gap on the shelf, Jaxson guessed one of the soft toys had been taken.

Glancing down, a tattered piece of paper lay on the floor, resting behind the leg of the desk. Artimus must have seen it at the same time as he moved to shift the furniture, then returned to the bed to consider it.

It was then something happened Jaxson had not expected. Artimus started to sob. The ursus of a man had never done that before, and it was a haunting sound that chilled Jaxson to the bone. *What could have possibly elicited that sort of emotion from him?* Jaxson wondered as Artimus tilted the slip of paper in his hand. From that angle, Jaxson could only just make out that it was a discoloured photograph of a young girl holding a soft toy with another person standing behind her. But at that distance, he couldn't see their faces. Then his eyes followed Artimus's gaze toward the timber bedhead decorated with beautiful hand-drawn motifs of flowers and aves. It took a moment to see that between the artwork were letters making out a name.

That name was Ester.

37 TRUTH

This isn't where I imagined I'd be. Twelve cycles ago, I was a scared, lost seven-cycle-old little girl with nothing left in the world but the dirty, irradiated clothes on my back and a strong will to not die.

Hope has changed. Once, I would have given anything to come here. Now, all I can think about is what I'll do after I've finished my business with the place.

Since Elihus Kinton took power just over a cycle ago, Hope has been on a steady trajectory of decline. It's ever-present on the people's sullen faces and the boarded-up, graffiti-ridden shop fronts I pass every day on my way to work. It's as if a deep, corroding blight has set in, laying everything to waste.

Further along the street, a pair of HomeGuard officers beat into a man lying helpless on the pavement. On the wall above him, an unfinished slogan sprayed in red paint reads;

"Hope is a lie. Where is Ho".

Something tugs on my sleeve. "Scuse me, miss,' a woman's sullen voice says. 'My son and I are hungry. Could you spare a mark?' Sorrowful brown eyes lacking the healthy sparkle of life glance up from behind a veil of matted, long black hair. A skinny young boy, aged around seven, holds her hand. Seeing him standing there dressed in rags and staring at his holey shoes reminds me of what I must have looked like the day Lou rescued me from my destroyed home. The thought fills me with guilt, and so reaching deep into my pocket, I grab a handful of coins and place them in her cupped hands.

'Progenitors praise you, miss,' she says, and the two hurry up the street toward the co-op.

'It's the least I can do,' I mutter out of earshot.

An ear-splitting scream pierces the air, and I rush towards it. Outside the Kah-Pow café, a woman is being accosted by three brutes in HomeGuard uniforms. Two hold her by the arms while the other raises his night-stick, ready to strike. As I approach, the woman looks up between strands of blood-stained grey hair, and I gaze upon the tear and blood-streaked face of Islay, the café owner. One of her eyes is already swollen shut, and she's bleeding from a cut on her lip. Rage engulfs me, and the officer's nightstick is in my hand before he can comprehend what's going on. The three officers turn on me like rabid canis, leaving Islay to cower in the shelter of her shop entranceway.

'You should've kept your own business, missy,' one of them barks, lunging at me with his baton. Stepping sideways, the three surround me just inside my peripheral vision. 'You're going to hurt now.'

My feet slide into the Shihung'na rock stance as the same brute lunges again. Chucking the acquired baton at the man on my right, I throw the lunging man over my shoulder at the third. The three collapse simultaneously to the ground with a thud.

A quick check ensures they don't cause us any more trouble.

With the officers now prone on the pavement, I gesture to Islay.

She glares at me with terrified eyes.

'Islay,' I say, trying to keep my voice gentle and reassuring. 'Are you okay?'

She nods but retreats further into the doorway.

'Can you walk?'

She nods again.

'Good. Come with me. You'll be safe, but we have to go.'

After a moment of hesitation, she pushes away from the wall and shuffles closer, then tentatively side-stepping around the three HomeGuard soldiers, we take off down the street.

'How'd you do that?' she asks.

'It's a long story.'

Fortunately, the footpaths are mostly clear, which should be teeming with people at this time of day. I snatch open the door under a sign that says Gerriott's Delivery Service and gently usher Islay inside.

She collapses on a brown couch positioned by the door while I close the blinds, hoping we weren't followed.

'You're late,' a gruff voice grumbles from behind the counter. On most occasions, he greets me with some acetic quip about my tardiness. Seems today is no different.

'Fix your damn clock, Ger, you disgruntled old codger,' I say, glancing at my watch. 'My shift doesn't start for another three decs.'

He flicks through his morning newspaper. 'Nothin' wrong with me clock, you lazy young delinquent,' he retorts, barely glancing up from the page.

'Geez, Ger, you're slipping with the insults today. Is that really the best you can do? Anyway, in case you haven't noticed. We've got bigger problems.'

Ger pokes his head up from behind his counter to observe the waiting room – and Islay perched on the couch. I rush to the first aid kit and icebox to fetch treatment for Islay's face.

'Oh dear,' Ger says. 'Is that you, Islay?'

'Hello Ger,' Islay replies, still shaking from her ordeal.

'What was that all about?' I ask, handing her a glass of water and a bag filled with ice for her eye.

'I suppose you've heard about "The Purge",' she says, eyes fixed on the trembling glass in her hands.

'I heard there's been a decree branding all people of Lafian heritage illegals.'

'Yes, well, someone must've reported me because they came for me this morn. No questions, no warrant, no nothing. They just grabbed me, and…well…' she gestured toward herself and broke into tears. 'What am I going to do? I don't have anywhere to go.'

I glance over at Gerriott imploringly. Even though our personalities may be the polar opposite, I've found we work well together; he gives the orders, and I follow them. He's also a decent guy when he wants to be.

'I know someone who can help,' he says compassionately, smiling a gentle toothy grin at Islay. 'For the by, you can stay here.'

'Thank you,' Islay says, visibly relieved. She still looks shaken, but her shoulders have relaxed.

'But you, miss Jayne,' Ger says, turning to me with a sterner expression. 'No more bringin' back strays, you hear? I can help Islay here, but soon they'll come askin' questions.'

'Yes, Ger,' I reply.

'Now, shut your chopwagger, get changed and get going,' he says, dropping a clipboard onto the counter. 'Here's your manifest.'

'Will you be alright?' I ask Islay as I peruse today's list.

She nods, but it's Ger who responds. 'She'll be fine, but you won't be if you don't get your butt out there, now.'

'You're grumpier today. Didn't you get enough sleep last night, Ger?'

'I don't know how anyone could have gotten any sleep with that racket goin' on last night,' he growls.

I glance up at him over the top of the clipboard. 'Racket? What racket?'

He closes the paper and slides it over the counter.

In big, bold lettering across the page, the headline reads;

LunaTec Vanishes

'What?' I splutter.

He chuckles. 'Me thoughts exactly. With them gone and all these businesses shuttin' up shop, it's any wonder we'll still be in business. Oh, and this came for you.' He slides a sealed envelope across the counter.

On its front is my name written in neat, flowing handwriting.

'Oi,' Ger barks while I examine the letter. 'Time waits for no loafin'. These packages won't deliver themselves. And you be softly out there. People are, well, touchy. You hear? Now scrat!'

'Anyone would think you actually care,' I call as I grab my gear and head for the bathroom to get changed into my uniform. After loading the truck, I haul myself into the driver's seat. The unopened letter sits on the passenger seat where I threw it, beckoning me to open it.

Snatching it up, I tear open the seal:

Jayne,

I haven't much time.

If you're reading this, LunaTec has succeeded, and I'm now headed towards the asteroid belt.

This will be my last report for some time. I will try to maintain contact through the comms relay I stashed in the old complex, but that will depend on whether you can get it working. I'll continue to monitor the channel, just in case.

I still don't know why we left and what his plans are, but I intend to find out.

All I've been able to glean so far is they're planning some sort of big top-secret construction project code-named Phoenix. Commander is tight-lipped about it, even to Aunt Cristal, so finding out anything is going to be tricky.

Anyway, I guess it's grace even for now.

Stay safe down there.

Love Ester.

What the? Is that the same Ester I knew? That's a name I haven't come across in a very long time. Why's she writing to me now? This letter makes no sense.

Confused, I stash the letter in my pocket and set out for my route.

I don't know what it is, but as I pass the Sempro Memorial Gardens on the way to my first stop, I have the urge to pull over. I can't seem to get Islay out of my mind. As I pull up to the kerb, a life-sized brown metal statue of a man on a tall stone plinth towers over a lush green square filled with flower gardens and officious-looking people scurrying here and there. Even though I pass this way nearly every day along my routes, this is the first time I've stopped. A metal plaque affixed to the white stone plinth reads;

GAIUS SEMPRO
FOUNDER AND FATHER OF HOPE

FROM HIS VISION, THERE IS HOPE

Humble in appearance, the man's likeness stands tall, with head held high, arms by his side and one foot raised on a step. Even through it all, the weathered face is clean-shaven and smiling, as though considering everyone entering the park like a proud father would consider his children. *How is it that Sera came to be the one who ended his life*? She had said it was a grave mistake and didn't want me to do the same. After learning about the man who founded Hope, and the respect people had for him, I've come to believe she was right.

I wonder if Sage Solon was the same. Perhaps *I am* destined to make the same mistakes after all.

The soft crunch of footsteps on grass and movement in my peripheral vision alerts me to the familiar figure of a man in a red-piped Surprime Guard uniform carrying a bag over one shoulder.

'Are you following me?' I ask in a curt tone, not bothering to turn my head.

'Would it surprise you to learn I'm not?' he replies, stepping up to admire the statue as well but still keeping his distance.

'Yes, actually. Why do you always seem to appear where I am?'

'I come here regularly to pay my respects.' He looks up at the statue with admiration gleaming in his earnest brown eyes. Then they narrow, he rubs his hands together, and it's all seriousness again. 'Question is, why are you here?'

'You knew him?' I ask, gesturing with my chin.

'Yes. Most of us original Hope residents knew him. But unlike them, he was family to me. He was the gentlest, most considerate, and compassionate man you could ever meet.'

Hearing him say that, confirming everything Sera feared, the guilt strikes me like a knife to the gut, leaving me listless. All I can offer is weak sympathy in return. 'I'm sorry for your loss.'

'And I'm sorry for yours.'

'Excuse me?' I say, turning to face him.

He takes half a step back, and his mouth turns up at the edges into a knowing grin, but I can't quite decipher why. 'Your sister told me. About your mother.'

'My sister?'

'Yes, *your sister.* Lou?'

Lou? Who's Lou? Oh… 'Ah, yes, my sister.' *How has he met her?* 'I haven't seen her in a while. You know her?'

'Yes.'

There it is again, that smile. What is he getting at? 'Hmm.' Something about that look gives me the distinct impression 'Lou' and Jaxson have some sort of connection, and I think I'm starting to see why. Something is intriguing about him; those boyishly charming features, his dark brown eyes, and smooth, thick jaw. My experience with men so far has been limited—if you can call ex-raiders men. Just being in his presence should give me the jitters, especially given I'd tried to kill him. Not explicitly—there's no escaping the fact those burns on his hands were partly my doing. But for reasons I can't explain, this man, Jaxson, is different.

I miss Ilona so much. She would know what to do.

He begins patting himself down and carefully checking in his pockets. 'Wait, there's something…'

'Why do you work for him?' I blurt, eyeing over the uniform.

He stops. 'Why do you drive a delivery truck?' he asks bluntly. 'It's a job. Nothing more.'

'I should go.'

'Jayne, wait.'

I want to leave, but I'm also curious to know what he has to say.

'I apologise for yesterday,' he says with sincerity. 'That was stupid of me. I just wanted to talk to you, that's all.'

My anxiety gets the better of me, and I decide I've been standing there long enough. 'I'm not much of a talker,' I say, turning to leave. Sooner or later, he's going to realise I was one of the ones who killed his charge. And when that happens, that charming visage will dissolve in an instant, and the reason for him sporting that uniform will become crystal clear. I only hope that when that happens, Elihus dies first.

∞

Jaxson watched as the strange woman that looked and acted just like Lou walked away. There was an inexplicable feeling about her he couldn't put his finger on. Like a song for which he couldn't quite remember the name. He tried to deliver the message but couldn't find the paper.

Perhaps I left it in my other pants? Jaxson thought.

A soft voice called Jaxson's name, and Orian drifted from the shadows, wearing a hooded grey cloak pulled up to conceal her identity.

'Who was that?' she asked.

'Remember that woman I told you about?'

'The one from the incident?'

'Her.'

'I see,' Orian mused. 'And what was her business here?'

'I have no idea,' Jaxson shrugged. 'I suspect she didn't know either. Seems Gaius is still working his magic, moving us like pieces on a board.'

She chuckled and then was serious again. 'Any progress?'

'None whatsoever.'

'Not even a little?'

'No. And I don't think there will be either. But there may still be hope. I'm working on it.'

'I still think we need to involve the others,' Orian insisted.

'No,' Jaxson said, 'Certainly not. You heard what Lexi said. We can't risk it.'

'And LunaTec?'

'I went with Artimus to the Brimuse caves last night. They've cleared out.'

'Cleared out?' she said with a raised eyebrow. 'What do you mean?'

'Exactly what it means. They've cleared out completely. There's nothing left except for a few smashed bits and pieces. Seems they've left the planet.'

'But how? Where did they go?'

'No idea. All I know is those were space-bound launches, and they took everything of value with them.'

'Is that what you were up to, Cristal?' Orian murmured.

'We searched as much of the complex as we could. Whatever they didn't take, they destroyed. We did find an old comms relay, but it's beyond my skill to fix, and this, in one of the offices.' He pulled the bag from his back and lowered the sides to reveal a stained timber box with charred sides about the size of two house bricks with a keypad attached. 'This was hidden away under a destroyed desk. I suspect they may have missed it.'

'Goodness,' Orian said with a look of surprise. 'I haven't seen one of these in a very long time, and I'd never thought I'd see one again. And you said they just left this behind?'

'Yes. What is it?'

'It's a cypher cryptex. Or rather, one-half of an encrypted communications transmission device. This is the transmitter. The other half, the receiver, is a ticker tape box that prints encoded messages.'

'So, someone's been sending encoded messages from LunaTec, to where, and why?'

'In order to answer that, we'll need to have this analysed,' she replied. 'If we can decipher the code, it might tell us where the other end is.'

'I can now see why you'd think it strange they left this behind,' Jaxson said. 'Where it was, it's as if someone meant for it to be found.'

'That is very odd indeed.'

Jaxson passed the bag to Orian. 'And the comms relay?'

'I'll get one of the techs to examine that, too,' she said. 'Maybe they can get it working. If they can, it'll be our best clue to finding out where LunaTec went and what they're up to. Anything else?'

'Yes, we found out what happened to the hospital and—you're going to love this—Artimus has gone missing again.'

'Okay, one thing at a time. What about the hospital?'

'It seems LunaTec were doing some sort of strange experiment. We found the missing wall embedded in a cave deep inside the LunaTec complex.'

She turned to him, head cocked with a dubious expression. 'How did you know it was the Hospital?'

'I think the words "emoral Hos" written in big letters were the giveaway.'

'I see. I'm not even going to ask how it got there. And Artimus?'

'He found something in there that sent him, well, boart-rage crazy. And it wasn't the Hospital. I've never seen him like that before.'

'I have,' Orian sighed, clearly concerned. 'And I hoped I wouldn't ever see him like that again. What happened?'

'I'm not entirely sure, but does the name Ester mean anything to you?'

Orian gasped. 'Are you sure it was *that* name?'

'I'm certain. It was scribed into a bedhead inside a bedroom that hadn't been ransacked.'

'Then I can understand his reaction. Ester or Ester Megin-Wyrm was, or is, his daughter.'

'Oh, shak.'

'Megin was his wife's pre-marital name. She and Ester supposedly died fourteen cycles ago in the Hillfar bombings. When that happened, well, that was the last time he went "boart-rage crazy", as you say. What happened after that is inexplicable. If his daughter really is still alive, he's going to stop at nothing until he finds her. How could I be so stupid?'

'Stupid? You? Why?'

'I met her a few times when Cristal brought her to the ministry sessions.'

'Tess,' Jaxson said, recalling the name she'd gone by whilst she'd visited Hope. 'I know. But I didn't know she was Artimus's daughter.'

'It makes sense.'

'Shakking bricks! And he didn't know, either?'

Orian shook her head. 'LunaTec had her right under his nose in plain sight the whole time, and he never saw it.'

'And his wife? Could she still be alive too?'

'I don't really remember her, but it's possible.' Orian paused as though deep in thought. Then she looked up at Jaxson with an even more concerned expression. 'Artimus's absences are causing other problems. My agents inform me that whilst he's been away, Elihus has seized control of his troops. He's granted them unlimited authority over civil control so they can carry out his Purge orders. They've gone rogue.'

'I'm aware,' Jaxson said with a sigh. 'There's only so much I can do. The Surprime Guard are loyal to me but only so long as my orders do not conflict with Elihus's. Soon he will suspect me, and I'm afraid when that happens, I'll lose any leverage I have.' Jaxson still couldn't believe how they had been duped. He glanced at his wristwatch. The sun was getting higher. It meant time to go to work.

'It's okay, Jaxson,' she said, gathering up the bag. 'You've done well. This…' she shook the bag, 'has given us a valuable lead. Watch out for Artimus. If he is, as you say, he's extremely volatile and dangerous.'

He gave a reserved nod, trying not to allow his concern to show. He had to stay strong. They were counting on him. 'Thanks for the warning, Orian. Right now, my biggest concern is *him*. He's making an announcement today. Even *I* don't know what he's going to say.'

She rested a hand on his shoulder. 'Please, be careful. You're in the ursus den.'

'I can handle myself.' He tilted his head to her, then turned to the statue, patting a foot. 'Good dawn, old man,' he said with a genuine fondness, then walked away.

'Hope,' Elihus declared, standing with arms outstretched behind the podium at the top step of the town hall. Instead of the customary red Surprime robes, he wore a pristine white outfit, complete with flowing sleeves and intricate gold embroidery. 'As your Surprime, I will assure you that the actions taken by LunaTec were not unexpected.'

The onlooking crowd of media and residents gathered at the bottom step weren't as convivial as expected. Some waved banners and placards calling for his resignation. Others shouted unflattering statements, calling him a liar and a tyrant. Elihus harrumphed and moved on.

'Rumours that my government hid this from you is a lie. A lie perpetuated by the Lafian infidels. This will not stand.' He paused, and the crowd noise swelled. 'I assure you, our relationship with LunaTec has never been stronger. Even now, I am in communication with them, and they advise their launch went perfectly as expected. There is no better time for Hope to declare itself an independent nation. We no longer need their support. Hope is strong. We have outgrown the false preconceptions that we must suckle at LunaTec's teet to survive; the teet my feeble predecessors made us believe we depended upon. This is a lie. Hope is prosperous on its own. The time has come for Hope to be free.'

'What have you to say about the whereabouts of Minister Wyrm?' shouted a voice from a reporter in the front row.

'Ah, Ms Raine. Minister Wyrm's business is his own. He is doing whatever is necessary to keep Hope safe.'

'Does that mean justifying the heavy-handed actions of his HomeGuard officers?' Ms Raine added.

'HomeGuard officers are well-trained and will only use force when necessary to carry out their duties. They keep the peace.'

'Does keeping the peace mean evicting good, hard-working, and law-abiding citizens from their homes and beating them on the street in front of their crying children?'

'They're hardly law-abiding if they're being arrested now, are they? I'm very concerned about maintaining order and civility. Therefore, I expect the law to be upheld. I will not be held responsible for the actions of a few dissidents and troublemakers. But you make a good point, and that is a nice segue to my next announcement.' He raised his hands to silence any further questions. 'From this moment on, I am announcing additional peacekeeping measures—measures that will ensure order and civility is maintained in our great Hope. From this moment on, all protest activities, rallies, and actions deemed uncomplimentary to my government will cease. I will consider these actions treason, and they will be punished accordingly.

'Furthermore, we will finally weed out all Lafir insurgents who threaten to return Hope to the dark days before the war. As of seven tonight, a curfew will be in effect. Anyone of Lafian heritage out of doors without a permit and a valid reason will be arrested, charged with treason and taken to the border camps.'

The crowd erupted in outrage.

HomeGuard soldiers filed through the front door and around the building, moving in on those crowd members holding signs.

'You can't do this!' someone yelled.

'I have, and I will,' Elihus proclaimed, speaking loud to be heard above the crowd. 'Without order, there is chaos, and I will NOT have chaos reign in my town. To protect order and civility, these strict measures are necessary. One day you will come to see that as truth.'

'You're a tyrant!' another member of the crowd yelled before being tackled by two HomeGuard officers.

'No further questions.' Elihus turned and, with Jaxson and his guard trailing behind, went back inside.

As the heavy doors closed on the screaming crowd, Elihus, with his entourage, sauntered up the hall, where he retired to the comfort of his private offices. Jaxson followed in after, standing by the door, clasping his hands behind his back and pretending not to notice the three young buxom women lazing half-naked on the shiny, studded-leather couch by the wall. They smiled at him seductively with plump, glossy lips, flashing long painted eyelashes while Elihus removed his coat, poured himself a glass of malt, and joined them.

The moment he sat down, the three descended upon him like predators on a kill. Jaxson had to shy away when one plunged a hand down the front of the Surprime's trousers.

Elihus just gave an audible groan, reclining to lavish in the attention.

'What is it, my boy?' he asked Jaxson after a while.

'Sir?' Jaxson replied, eyes fixed on the wall above the old man.

'You look… stressed. Come. Join me.' He patted a space beside him and the women on the couch.

Jaxson cringed. 'No thank you, sir.'

'You sure?' Elihus probed. 'It's very stress-relieving.'

I'm never going to sit on that couch again, Jaxson thought, steadying himself and trying to ignore what was happening right in front of him. 'I'm sure it is. But I'm good, thank you, sir.'

'Suit yourself. You seem tense, is all. And I can't have the head of my guard tense. Tell me, boy, what did you think of my speech?'

The question startled Jaxson. He shifted his stance and tried not to let it show. 'Ahh,' he replied, clearing his throat. 'With all due respect, sir. I am just your guard. It's not my business to pass comment on what you do.'

'Correct answer. And be sure to remember that. Soon, the others will come to realise that also. What I do, I do to make this town great.'

'If you don't mind me saying, though, sir, it's not making my job easy.'

'Easy?' Elihus said, leaning forward. 'My boy, nothing worthwhile is ever easy. If running a town was easy, any imbecile would do it. As it happens, that's what was wrong here. Thankfully, I came along in time and now that I've corrected our course, things will improve. You'll see.'

Jaxson groaned inwardly.

'Ladies, give us some space,' Elihus said, refastening his pants and shooing the girls off.

As they slipped through the door, he stood, collected his glass, and ambled over to sit in his comfortable leather chair behind his desk. Jaxson remained standing at attention on the opposite side.

'Now, my boy, deliver your report. What did you find?'

'The LunaTec facility is completely empty. They've cleared the place out.'

'You mean to say you found nothing at all?'

'I didn't, no. Minister Wyrm, on the other hand, seems to have found something. But you're going to have to ask him what it was when he shows up because he's gone AWOL.'

'You were there to supervise him,' Elihus growled.

'Minister Wyrm doesn't need supervision, sir.'

'I beg to differ. I need to know what he's up to and why. How can I do that if I no longer know where he is?'

'Again, you need to ask him that. There was something else. Are you familiar with someone named the Commander?'

Elihus stiffened a little. It was subtle and no doubt unintentional, but Jaxson saw it.

'No,' he replied.

'Are you sure?'

'Yes. And never again question me like that, boy.'

Jaxson gave a small bow in acknowledgement. 'My apologies, sir. It's just curious that LunaTec has occupied those caves for eleven cycles, yet we haven't heard of such a person.'

'Perhaps that's something you should have raised with the previous incumbents? Now that LunaTec is out of my hair, I needn't worry about him or Ms Spriggs or anyone else, for that matter. My boy, you are about to witness the dawning of a new age for this great place. The previous leadership was weak and misguided. They had no direction. No purpose. Me, I wish to take this place to greater heights. We will be a global superpower. The world will be ours to conquer, and not even the sky's the limit.' Elihus ranted on, complete with hand flourishes. Jaxson cringed. The man was clearly enjoying listening to the sound of his own voice. As Elihus stepped around the desk to wrap an arm around Jaxson, he tried not to react to the malt on his breath and his overused aftershave.

'…I've enlisted the help of a very esteemed entrepreneur, and we have partnered to form a new alliance. Here he is now,' Elihus said to a knock at the door.

A flamboyant but acerbic man strutted in.

'Jaxson, my boy, meet Voltaire Catlow, Chief Executive Officer of OrbEn Enterprises.'

38 AND CONSEQUENCES

Excerpt from Book of the Progenitors:

Last of the Mighty Seven was the Progenitor Anima, the purveyor of life, for she could cure the ailments of all. Many came from far and wide in search of her healing. So great was her might; many believed the Progenitors themselves owed her their immortality. And immortal they were until the day they died, for the only condition she could not cure was death.

'Oh good, ya 'ere, luv,' Graylianne says as I wheel in a keg of ale and set it down behind the bar. 'We almost ran out an' had a riot on our hands.'

'By the looks of it, there's a riot brewing outside,' I reply sourly, pointing to the surging crowd through the window.

'Ah, yeah, that. Surprime announced a few more unfavourable changes today. I've been gettin' complaints from patrons all day, talkin' about new austerity measures, and now, a curfew. A curfew, can ya believe that?'

'No, I hadn't heard.'

'Thin's are gettin' tough, luv. Mind if ya tap that in for me?' she asks, handing me a spanner to hook up the keg.

'Sure.'

The door to the bar bursts open, slamming into the wall, and two men with their top hats, canes, and shiny double-breasted suits enter, surrounded by a flock of skimpy-clothed young women. They certainly aren't dressed for this cool weather, with only just enough fabric clinging to their bodies to hide their decency.

With their entourage in tow, the two men push their way through the crowd. It's no mistake; the arrogant pomposity of these two immediately give them away as Elihus Kinton and that drunken idiot from last night—Vol... *oh, who cares*? Two bulky men in plain black Surprime guard uniforms lumber in behind, followed by the neckless Creatch and Jaxson. From the red piping on his uniform, he's the apparent superior of the bunch. Despite that, he looks like he'd rather be anywhere else.

The horde moves to the opposite side of the bar, and when they find their seat is already occupied, the pompous duo stands back while the three black-suited brutes harass the current occupants, tossing their food and drinks on the floor and dragging them out wide-eyed by the collar. Once vacated, Elihus and friend, with their noses held high, take a seat, allowing the girls to get comfortable draping themselves all over them. All the while, Jaxson stands back, bulky arms crossed, taking in the abhorrent display with an expression that seems just as unimpressed as I.

Perhaps he meant what he said earlier about it just being a job? But that remains to be seen.

When they're all settled, Elihus yells out, 'your best malt, barkeep. And be swift about it. I haven't all night.' He laughs, then turns his attention to his sleazy companion. 'Voltaire, my good friend. So, what you're telling me is, I can have a seventy per cent share of all the technologies you sell in Hope?'

Voltaire gives an enthusiastic nod.

'And first rights on all commercial products?'

'Sounds perfectly cromulent,' Voltaire replies. 'Now, if you don't mind, I have to "liquidate some assets", if you understand me.' He turns to the thin blonde woman seated in his lap and whispers something in her ear. I can almost see her face redden under all that ornametics as she gives a cutesy chuckle. The two leave for the bathroom together, with Creatch trailing along at his usual distance.

'I'm done here,' I say, placing the tool on the bench. Before Graylianne begins priming the tap, I head for the loading dock.

From beneath the driver's seat of my truck, I retrieve my knives and strap on their sheaths.

Chef quickly melts out of my way as I storm through the kitchen, his eyes fixed on the large hunting knife at my belt. It's bigger than his.

And just before pushing through the kitchen door, I snatch a spare bar apron from its peg on the wall and put it on.

The evening is leading up to curfew, and it's apparent by the scant number of regulars normally packed into the bar. Of course, Elihus and his flock of floozies don't seem to care.

I pick up a tray of drinks from the bar and make for Elihus's table. He's too busy to notice me, but as soon as the tray touches the table, he roars. 'That's not what I ordered. Take it away, you useless imbecile! Get me malt! And the good stuff. Not that cheap shak…' His words falter when he glances up and finally recognises who's serving him.

'Hello, Elihus,' I say with a smirk.

He recoils in surprise. Clearly, he hadn't expected to see me.

Elihus raises his hand to his bodyguards. 'She cannot harm me,' he says with a nervous chuckle. 'She's sworn to protect me.'

'Are you sure about that, Elihus?' I reply, leaning on the table, and it's obvious he isn't as convinced as he wants to be.

'Are you challenging the rules?'

'Sorry, but not sorry, Elihus. Those rules burned with the Gord. And so should've you.'

His eyes widen with surprise. 'I should have guessed that was you.'

A meek smile is the only answer I provide.

'Well then,' he stammers a reply, sweat beading on his brow. 'I guess I should thank you. You freed me from that place. Drove me to bigger, better things. Come, join us,' he says, patting the padded seat next to him. 'I've always wondered what you'd be like. I mean, you're not the type I usually—'

'Shut up, Kinton.'

'If you're not here for some fun, what are you doing here, then?' He reaches out to grab my hand.

I grip his outreached hand firmly, and he looks up at me with fear in his beady little eyes.

'What are you doing?' he asks when I weave my fingers in between his.

'Making amends.'

'And how do you plan to do that, my dear?'

'This,' I say as I slowly bend his hand backwards.

His smile fades and then contorts in pain.

'Stop it,' he pleads. 'You're hurting me.'

'That's the point. It does hurt, doesn't it?'

'Yes,' he cries. 'I said, stop it! Please.'

Glaring into his pained eyes, he screams out. 'Stop it. Protect the chain of command.'

The tiny bones in his hand snap like twigs, and he wails in agony.

Two of the women with their breasts bulging out of their outfits scream and push past Jaxson and the other guards to escape the room.

The three remaining women, trapped in the corner of the booth, cower in fear, forced to watch in horror as Elihus howls in pain.

'Don't just stand there!' Elihus screams at his handlers with tears streaming down his face. 'Do something!'

'Wait,' I yell, causing them to halt. 'Have you told them?'

'Told them what, you crazy bikkja?'

'They don't know, do they?'

'Three against one. I think they are more than capable of handling the likes of you.'

'They don't know who I am, do they? Or *what* I am. What *you* made me. Tell me, *Patriarch*, are they as well trained as I am?'

'So, who is she, Elihus?' Jaxson asks, stepping forward.

'That's none of your concern,' Elihus snaps. 'Just do your job! Protect me!'

Jaxson shifts on his feet.

'I don't want to hurt you, Jaxson,' I say, turning to him. 'But I will if I must. You have no idea what this worthless excuse of a man has done.'

'Screw this,' a handler says from behind, and drawing a knife, he lunges.

Without taking my eyes from Elihus or releasing his hand, I twist, and the weapon jabs past. Striking the man's outstretched wrist, I snatch his knife away and kick him headlong through the kitchen door. In one fluid motion, I reverse the blade and drive it through Elihus's broken hand, pinning him to the table.

The three remaining women squeal louder than Elihus as they clamber over the privacy screen between the booths to get away. Jaxson holds his ground while the other brute rushes in. One of my throwing knives embeds in his weight-bearing knee, dropping the grunt to the floor.

My acutely trained senses detect movement just as the guard I'd propelled into the kitchen seizes me from behind. With his iron-like grip, he pushes me towards the bar. But I kick off it, and his footing falters. Whilst he regains his stance, I reach between my knees, grab his leg, and pull.

The guard drops to his back. Then knotting his leg up with mine,

I lay into his face with a fury of punches until his strength wavers, and he stops resisting.

Jaxson circles the room, moving to block the front door. No doubt observing and calculating.

With the two guards moaning like useless lumps on the floor, I remove the blood-splattered apron and throw it into the booth. Elihus is gone. Only a crimson pool and the knife remain where I had him pinned.

Jaxson stands by the door, and from his non-confrontational posture, he doesn't want what's coming any more than I do. 'Are you next?' I say to him.

'That's up to you,' he shrugs. Even as I approach him, he still hasn't taken a combat stance.

'I know you don't want to do this,' I try to persuade him. 'But you have to let me go. He can't be allowed to get away with what he's done.'

'I'm sorry, Jayne. I can't let you do that,' he says, sliding a foot forward.

There it is.

Even though I should be wary of him, his closeness feels comfortable and familiar, and I'm captivated by the warm, spicy aroma of his aftershave.

He's certainly not like the others.

He reaches out a hand to touch my shoulder, and instinctively I slap it away, returning with a full-force double-fisted punch to repel him. Whatever he's trying to do, I'm not interested.

His reaction is quick, though, using the distance to begin his attack. From an unguarded stance, he lands two hits before I find my wits, only just dodging his robust third and fourth.

Getting hit by just one of those feels like getting hit by a boulder thrown by Codan himself.

Finally, a fair fight.

He steps around his downed colleague with trained precision and corners me like a stray loaghtan. His jabs and punches come from a range beyond my shitak'na training, pounding at my blocks as I try to close the distance, each hit landing with painful accuracy.

The barrage of powerful attacks pushes me back to the bar.

His body flows smoothly, moving at the knees and hips with fists and elbows raised in a style I've never encountered before.

After delivering a startling strike to my head, he pauses.

'Are you okay?' he asks, giving me time to shake off the pain and disorientation.

'Just do this,' I growl.

He steps in again with a quick-fire succession of jabs. I sweep three tankards off a serving tray and wield it to deflect his attack.

Jaxson's brow furrows.

The next one, two, almost rips the tray from my grip, and I realise he's been pulling his punches.

I swing my now deformed shield at his face, pushing him back. But with every swipe, Jaxson delivers yet another powerful blow until the tray folds in my hands, and I throw it at his chest.

It's just the delay I need to grab another tray from a nearby table, and we begin again.

Blows and blocks are exchanged in an equally matched struggle for control. Gradually, I push him backwards while he keeps me beyond optimal striking range.

Until he stumbles.

Glancing back, an overturned table blocks his retreat.

Now, it's my turn.

In his moment of distraction, I throw the tray at him. Then, sweeping his legs, he drops, where I clamber amongst his arms and those fists and restrain him.

'What would your sister think?' he says with a voice strained from exertion as he struggles to break free.

'What is it with you and her?'

'I don't want to hurt you.'

'Yeah, well, I only do this on second dates,' I reply, twisting my body around his back while he rolls over to his hands and knees.

'Oh, no, you don't,' he says, dropping to his shoulder and landing with full force on top of me.

His weight compresses my chest, squeezing the breath from my lungs as I lock my arms around his neck.

He struggles against the choke. But I have him.

His hips drop, his arms flail, and soon, they fall limp to his side. His body relaxes, and he's out cold.

'Sorry, buddy,' I say, rolling him away. 'But falling asleep on the first date is really unattractive.'

Outside in the darkening street, protesters battle it out with HomeGuard soldiers in a choking haze of tear gas and smoke.

Kinton wouldn't have gone through that.

Five HomeGuard soldiers dressed in riot gear and bearing transparent shields turn to face me. The two closest rush forward, wielding their nightsticks.

Dodging the weapons, I swing off a shield, bringing it to the ground, kick the second officer over, and elbow the first in the face before taking off.

A light trail of blood on the pavement leads away from the protesters, and following it, I glance down the side streets, hunting for my prey.

Further up the road, a figure stumbles frantically under a street light, flashing a look over their shoulder.

It's him.

Two more riot gear clad HomeGuard soldiers appear from the darkness to storm me. The first strikes my right shoulder with his stick, sending ripples of pain down my body. The second steps around the first, blocking the road…

∞

Jaxson groaned, roused by the toe of a pointed shoe jabbing him in the ribs. He knocked the foot away and pulled himself up onto an elbow. As the fog in his head cleared, the image of Voltaire, looking as indignant as ever, sharpened in his vision.

With hands on his hips, the oily businessman loomed over Jaxson, considering him as one would consider an insect. 'What in blazes happened here?' he accused, glancing around the trashed bar. 'I go to, ahem, "do my business," and come out to find this. Seems to be a common theme emerging with this establishment.'

Jaxson hesitated. Then it all came flooding back to him. 'Jayne!'

Ignoring Voltaire, he leapt to his feet and steadied himself on the bar. 'Graylianne, which way did they go?'

The bartender pointed to the left. And with Voltaire's protests going unanswered behind him, Jaxson straightened his gun belt, with his pistol still strapped in tight, and sprinted out the door.

He hadn't expected the conflict outside and the choking haze of multicoloured smoke.

Four HomeGuard soldiers turned in a startle, ready with their batons, while a fifth gathered themselves off the road.

Jaxson yelled over the racket. 'Did you see a red-haired woman in a delivery driver's uniform come through here?'

The officer nodded. 'She's the one who attacked us.' He thrust his hand in the direction of the town hall. 'That way. And sir, the Surprime…'

'I know, thanks,' Jaxson yelled out as he turned to peer up the road.

Several protesters separated from the losing battle and ran for Jaxson, presumably having noticed his Surprime Guard uniform. To them, he was the enemy. As Orian had said, he was right in the ursus den. If he wasn't careful, they'd tear him limb from limb. 'Where's your boss?' they shouted with contempt, throwing rocks while they ran towards him. 'Kinton must die!'

Raising an arm to shield his face, he backed away.

Three HomeGuard soldiers turned and indiscriminately sprayed the group attacking Jaxson with rubber bullets, catching Jaxson with two shots in friendly fire. He bit his lip in pain and ran from the clash, escaping before other protesters came to their aid and beat into the soldiers' backs.

In the distance, illuminated by a streetlight, he caught sight of a soldier striking a person with their nightstick while another lunged forward with their weapon extended.

The person stumbled, straightened, and knocked the first soldier down, returning attack with startling skill and speed, disarming the other of their baton before effortlessly throwing them down.

That had to be Jayne, Jaxson thought, taking off in pursuit.

She continued toward the front entrance of the town hall.

Not wanting to startle Jayne, Jaxson instead sprinted for the back entrance. Perhaps he could cut off her escape. Reaching the door, he unholstered his pistol and cautiously pushed inside. He didn't care too much about Elihus, but he was employed to defend the position and failing to protect three Surprimes wouldn't look good on his record.

Raised voices echoed through the building's darkened corridors, and the only light came from the entrance hall.

'Please, Jayne, be reasonable about this.' Jaxson heard Elihus's quavering voice say.

'How reasonable do you want me to be?' Jayne's scorn-filled voice replied. 'Slow or extra slow? I could make your death very satisfying.'

Footsteps stomped over the timber floor in a scuffle. When Jaxson peered through the crack in the double doors to the ministerial chambers, Jayne had Elihus in her grip with a very large hunting knife to his throat.

The short-cropped bearded old man had his hand wrapped in a bloodied cloth, torn off from a section of his sleeve. His eyes darted frantically around the room, desperate for a way out.

Jayne growled into his ear. 'You want me to be reasonable? Tell that to Seraphin MonLantry, Ilona Mylaekar, Gaius Sempro and Sage Solon.'

Jaxson didn't know the first two names, but he certainly knew the last two. Palms sweaty, he adjusted the pistol in his hand and leaned in closer.

She continued. 'Oh, wait, they're all dead. BECAUSE OF YOU!'

'Look at you with all your misplaced sentimentality,' Elihus boldly remarked. 'You know what you are? You are a foolish little thviet, so naïve and simple you think you've developed a conscience. Like that even matters.'

'You don't get it, do you? IT ALWAYS MATTERS.'

'You are a tool. Nothing more.'

'I AM GAIAN!' Jayne yelled, thrusting Elihus to the floor. 'My purpose is my own. Not to be your instrument of destruction, killing innocent people so you can take their place.'

Despite the knife pointing directly at him, he cackled a callous laugh. 'Your purpose is to not question orders and do as you are told. You can't hope to comprehend the complex machinations of political manoeuvring and the delicate balance that is civility and order. Seldom even am I afforded access to such privileged information. It may surprise you, girl, there are fish even greater than I in those waters. We all do what we must.'

'What are you talking about?'

'If it makes you feel any better, I merely relayed Gaius Sempro's assassination order. It seems I was misguided in choosing MonLantry for the task. I cannot help she failed to complete her mission. But if you are to blame anyone for that bikkja's demise, the Commander is the man who set us on this course. He's the one you should be holding at knifepoint. Although that, my dear, would be unwise.'

This revelation came as a shock to Jaxson, but from the change in Jayne's expression, she, too, was unaware of this.

'The Commander?' she said, lowering the knife as she seemed to consider this new information.

'Oh yes,' Elihus hissed, climbing to his feet, dusting himself off, and pacing around the room with Jayne tracking his movements. It would seem that piece of information has given him something of a confidence boost.

'If I'm the Patriarch, the Commander is Supreme Master—a god, if you will. He created Garret Gord and trained the first of you. Even your precious Seraphin learned directly from the Master himself. The Mission is all his. Everything we did, we did at his order. Ever since he divided his time between that begotten LunaTec and us, we have been all the poorer for it. We needed resources, and Hope was supposed to provide that for us until that idiot Solon stood in my way. He gave me no choice.'

'So, you ordered Ilona to kill him?'

'What do you care?'

'Consequences, Elihus,' she said, brandishing the knife at him again. 'There are always consequences.'

'Now, now, young miss, don't be rash. I'm sure we can come to some sort of agreement. After all, I am Surprime. With the Commander gone, I am my own free agent. I can give you whatever your heart desires.'

Now it was Jayne who was laughing. 'Whatever my heart desires?' she said, mocking him. 'You have nothing my heart desires. You've already taken everything I care about. All I care about now is how much you need to pay for what you've done.' She advanced closer.

'You can't kill me, Jayne.'

She pounced on him, seized an arm and pulled Elihus to his knees again, pressing the tip of her large-bladed hunting knife to his neck so that beads of his blood seeped down the metal.

'STOP!' Jaxson yelled, emerging from his hiding spot, cocking his pistol, and levelling it at Jayne.

'Jaxson, my boy!' Elihus cried with relief. 'What in blazes took you so long? Apprehend her!'

'No,' Jaxson replied flatly. 'Not until I get answers. Someone needs to tell me what's going on here. Don't either of you tell me you don't know.'

'This is treason!' Elihus spat. 'How dare you question me, boy!'

'I never liked you calling me that,' Jaxson said, redirecting his weapon at Elihus, making him flinch. 'It's so degrading. Now, answer her questions!'

'Alright. Alright,' Elihus said. 'I should not need to explain myself to the likes of you. But if you must know, Hope was dwindling. How can we move forward when such a weak, incompetent Lafian miscreant as Sage Solon is at the helm? This town needed real leadership.'

'So, you ordered his assassination?' Jaxson demanded, ignoring the racial slur.

'And I do not regret it one midec.'

'I ALMOST DIED IN THAT ATTACK!'

'See, Jaxson,' Jayne said, looking up at him almost empathetically. 'This is the reason he has to die.'

Elihus's breath caught in his throat as he shied away from the blade cutting into his skin.

'No, Jayne,' Jaxson said in the calmest voice he could manage. 'I'm sorry, but as much as I hate to say this, I can't allow you to do that. Not like this.'

'You can't be serious?' she shouted, fiery fury blazing in her emerald eyes. 'You can't honestly still want to protect him after everything he's done? This pathetic excuse of a gaian killed my mother and Ilona. He even tried to kill me. But not before assassinating the Surprime and taking his place. And, as you said, almost killing you in the process. He's a misogynist, a paedophile and a rapist who preens and tortures his victims for pleasure. Sera once said I would make the world a better place. By ridding it of *this monster*, that is exactly what I'm doing.'

'Jayne, of all the people calling for Elihus's execution, believe me, my voice ought to be one of the loudest. What I told you this morning about Gaius being family was true. He was like a father to me. And Sage, we may not have shared the same parents, but he was my brother. I've known him longer than I care to remember, and he has saved my arse more times than I can count. I owe my life to both of them, and now I learn this man is responsible for their deaths. You bet I'm angry, but it is not for me or you to decide his fate. Right now, thousands of Hope residents are suffering at his hand too. They're out there protesting the austerity measures he has just imposed upon them. What they need is justice, not a martyr. And I mean real justice. That's what we need to give them. It's the only way we can make this right.'

'Hear hear,' Elihus said, but Jaxson levelled his pistol at the Surprime's head, and he quietened down again.

'And how do you suppose we do that?' Jayne asked.

'Give him to me. Let me put him on trial. Make him publicly answer for what he's done. It won't bring Gaius, Sage, your mother or Ilona back, but it will stop him from hurting others.'

Jayne lowered the knife. Although her face was still stricken with rage, Jaxson could see that in her glistening green eyes, he was getting through to her.

He moved forward to take Elihus's arm.

'How do I know I can trust you? I don't trust anyone. Just ask *him*,' she said, gesturing at the old man with the tip of her knife.

Elihus gave a wry smile.

'I'm a man of my word,' Jaxson replied with sincerity.

'Thank you, my boy—'

Jaxson tapped the muzzle of his pistol on Elihus's forehead as a reminder.

'Seems old canis can learn tricks,' Jaxson said, dragging Elihus to his feet.

Jayne re-sheathed the knife at her hip, then stood face to face with Jaxson. 'If you so much as think otherwise, I will hunt you down, and I will not hesitate to kill you.'

'Understood,' he replied as she turned to leave.

She took a step towards the back door.

Elihus lifted his good arm at Jayne, and a tiny gun barrel protruded from the cuff of his sleeve. At near point-blank range, he fired, the slug hitting the small of her back. She stumbled, grasping the tiny hole in her side where her clothing was already turning red with her blood.

In a state of deathly calm, Jayne slipped the knife from its scabbard and, like a dancer performing a perfect pirouette, spun, knife clenched against her forearm. Blood splashed across the blade as it sliced through Elihus's throat. And following through with a powerful but swift backward kick, she sent the stricken Surprime crashing through the solid timber front doors.

39 REDEMPTION

The Hope Town Hall doors fling open, and a crowd of angry townsfolk amassed outside watch in stunned disbelief as the Surprime bursts through. He staggers backward, clutching his throat. With his fingers and long flowing sleeves bleeding crimson, he stumbles as though drunk. In mixed dismay and horror, the horde watch on as their hated leader loses his footing and slips down the steps, landing at their feet with his throat slit and neck contorted at an unnatural angle. The crowd falls silent at the eyes staring blankly up at them. Then someone from the crowd yells out, 'Elihus Kinton is dead!' and they all burst out in raucous jubilation, for the man they had come to protest and denounce—the Tyrant of Hope—is no more.

I stand at the top step watching as the sea of stunned faces gaze up at me.

Eyes fixed on the crumpled body of the Patriarch lying dead before me; I only wish I could revel in this moment. But I can't. Pain flows over me like a torrent of water as I tentatively touch the wound in my back, the viscous slick of blood coating my fingertips.

'That fraking pistol!' I mutter. At least that solves the puzzle of where that ended up.

Jaxson rushes out and stands beside me, bearing a look of abhorrent shock.

'Ah, shak,' he curses, gazing down at his dead boss at the bottom of the steps.

I wanted so badly to punish Elihus for what he had done, to make him pay for the suffering he'd caused me and everyone I loved. Even looking at Jaxson, I wanted vengeance for him, too, for Gaius, Sage and everyone else who had died or had been corrupted at the hands of *that* monster.

But this is not what I had intended. This was too easy. Now, I felt hollow and lost.

'Jayne,' Jaxson says, not averting his gaze from the Surprime's prone body. 'I'm sorry. I can't help you. Though, I am supposed to give you this. I tried this morning, but it seems now is the moment I had to wait for.'

He passes me a folded piece of paper.

'What's this?' I ask, cringing as another wave of pain washes over me.

'Help, I think.'

I look at him, perplexed.

'Soon, my guard will be here, and they will want to arrest you. There's nothing I can do to stop them, but I'm not going to let them have you, either. I will only be able to hold them off for so long. You have to go.'

'Go where?'

He points to the paper. 'Something tells me you'll find the answer there. Now go.'

Clutching my back, I glance at the crowd already beating into Elihus, kicking his lifeless body around like a rag doll. Jaxson smiles and then urges me to go.

'Thank you,' I say, taking off into the night.

Jaxson was right. It doesn't take long before more Surprime guards brandishing weapons appear in the street behind me. Gritting my teeth through the pain, I sprint as fast as I can, weaving and dodging people down Main Street towards the address scrawled on the slip of paper Jaxson gave me. I can only hope I get there in time, and he is, as he says, 'a man of his word'.

That remains to be seen.

Exhausted and on the verge of collapse, I find a concrete building matching the address. There's no sign, just a number. Thankfully, the door is unlocked. With a bloodied hand, I pull it open and stagger inside.

It's a reception area, rather plain and simply furnished with a desk, chairs, and a water cooler. The walls are white, and nothing on them suggests where I am, aside from a poster that reads, "We Want You" in big, bold lettering.

I take a moment to sit in one of the chairs and catch my breath.

'Can I help you?' a man sitting behind the reception desk asks.

I hadn't noticed him there.

'Yes. I need medical treatment,' I reply, glancing down at my bloodied hand.

'Then you need a hospital. This isn't the hospital,' the young receptionist replies.

'I just need a medkit. Do you have a medkit?'

'I'm sorry, Ms, but I can only render assistance to members. Are you a member?'

'A member of what?'

'If you have to ask, the answer is clearly no.'

'Then, no,' I reply, pulling back the window blinds to look out onto the street. The people bearing weapons are approaching fast. 'How do I become a member?'

'Fortunately for you, you can sign up here.'

I let the blinds drop and approach the desk.

'Name?' the receptionist asks.

'Sorry?'

'What's your name?'

'Jayne Doe. Jayne, with a y.'

'Gender?'

'Jayne.'

'I asked for your gender, not your name. You look female.'

'And I told you. I'm Jayne.'

'Oh-kay then. Let's just write down "other" for now.'

Through the gap in the blinds, the people pursuing me are at the door, just about to barge in.

I stifle a groan from the pain.

'Okay then, sign here, and it's done.'

What am I doing?

Soon, the people after me will crash through that door, hungry for my blood. If my only option is to seek asylum through membership here, whatever this place is, I'll take it.

Hands shaking, I grab the scribe and scrawl my signature through a drop of blood at the bottom of the page.

'Excellent. You're one of us now. Recruit Jayne Doe; welcome to HomeGuard.'

∞

My name is Jayne. Despite losing my family, home and identity, what I found was Hope.

Time doesn't heal all wounds; it numbs the feelings and tempers down the memories. My childhood was but a fantasy—a distant memory of freedom and innocence corrupted by others who forced me to live off their dreams and nightmares. Then I grew up. I am who I am because of the circumstances that brought me here. And it all began when they burned the sky.

EPILOGUE - ANEW

TWO TENDAWS LATER

The warm morning light streamed through the window of the Kah-Pow café as Jaxson sat enjoying a fresh steaming cup of kahwah while reading the morning paper. Emblazoned across the front page was the headline:

Surprime Martell repeals Purge directive, Kinton assassin still on the loose

Thanks to Niklas, those persecuted by Kinton's Purge had been released, mostly unharmed, from the border camps and given back their lives. Some, like the café owner Islay, had been lucky, saved by a rebel few who chose to offer sanctuary to the Lafian pariahs instead of handing them in to the authorities—something Jaxson was more than pleased about.

Reading the article, he couldn't believe that someone seemingly so ignorant as Niklas Martell could undo most of Elihus's damage so quickly. *Looks like there's hope for Hope yet,* he pondered to himself, taking a sip. Although the town still had a long way to go before it would recover from the events of the past few treys. Authorities were still on the lookout for Elihus's killer. Jaxson was confident that case would go cold.

A tuft of red hair poked over the top of his page, and he lowered it to the smiling face of Lou, sitting across from him. He hadn't even noticed her enter.

'Well, hello,' he said, folding the paper and setting it aside. 'I wasn't expecting to see you again so soon.'

'Why?' she asked, green eyes sparkling. 'Didn't you enjoy our night together?'

'Of course, but I kind of left you stranded.'

'Meh, I've had worse,' she chuckled. 'And besides, quite a bit has happened since then.'

'You think?' he sniggered, clasping his hands on the table. 'About that. You did say if things should come to pass as you said, *and they did,* you would tell me everything.'

'I did, didn't I?' she said with a cheeky smile. 'So, what do you want to know? I take it you delivered my message?'

'Yes, although I didn't think she would take it. Your sister seemed confused, too. How'd you…?'

'My sister?'

'Yes, like that.'

She chuckled. 'Oh, Jaxson, how do I explain this?'

He stared at her blankly. She seemed to be enjoying this.

'She's not my sister.'

'Oh? Then, who is she?'

'Um…' she paused in contemplation. 'This is a little awkward, but… she's me.'

'Say what?'

'I thought you might say that,' she laughed. 'My name's not Lou. It's Jayne. She's me—well, a younger version of me.'

He laughed. 'You're kidding me, right? Is this a joke?'

'Nope, I'm serious. Jaxson, Jayne Doe and I are the same person. Just I had a little time travel "accident" and found myself, well, some time in the past. I can't really explain that. But there it is.'

He burst out laughing. 'You *are* kidding me. Time travel doesn't exist.'

Jaxson expected her to break out into laughter too, but she just sat there looking at him with a straight face.

'I assure you, it does. But you can't just do it whenever you like. My little trip was not intentional. Remember the scar on my back?'

He blushed. 'The dimple?'

'Yes, well, you saw how that happened. You were there when Elihus shot Jayne with that stupid pistol.'

'That was from that?'

'Yes.'

'If you knew that was going to happen, why didn't you warn me? I could have stopped him.'

'It doesn't work like that,' she said, leaning forward to speak in a lower voice. 'I learned a very hard lesson about trying to mess with the future. Don't do it. Just don't.'

'You mean to tell me I had "relations" with the same person who choked me out?'

'Yes, Jaxson. Yes, you did. She doesn't know it, and you can't tell her either, but yes, she—I—did that. Sorry about that. To be fair, she didn't know you, so… If it makes you feel better, she—I—enjoyed it. The fraking, not the choking you out bit.'

'Wow. That's heavy. But it was… ahem.' He rubbed the back of his neck nervously, then leaned forward, speaking discreetly. 'So… you killed Elihus Kinton?'

'*Jayne* killed Elihus Kinton. I'm not her. Not anymore. Are you going to arrest me?'

'What, ten or more cycles after the fact?' he laughed. 'That's not my area. Not anymore. Besides, I think we can all agree that the tyrant will not be missed. But don't go saying it out loud, though.'

'Noted,' she replied.

'Then why the name Lou?'

'That's a funny story. It was a name the other Jayne gave me. Yes, we met, but I couldn't reveal who I was. She heard "Lou Tenant Doe" and thought that was my name. So it stuck.'

'Ha-ha, cute. I'd probably call myself dickhead.'

They both laughed.

'You're a lieutenant?' Jaxson asked just as Islay came over to the table.

'Oh hello, ave didn't see you there. You want something to drink?'

Lou—Jayne smiled at her. 'I'll have a flat white kahwah, thanks, Islay. And good to see you're back in business.'

'Me too, and bless you, ave. This is a good one here,' she said, tapping Jaxson on the shoulder. 'You be good to her, you hear, Mr Jaxson. Anything else, ave?'

'Just the kahwah, thanks, Islay,' Jayne said.

'Right you are.'

As Islay turned to leave, Jayne smiled at him again. That smile was intoxicating.

'So what does that mean for us?' he asked, moving on.

'I don't know, Jaxson. What do you want it to mean?'

There was that smile again.

'I really enjoyed the other night,' she said. 'It was the first time I've felt like that in a very long while. So…?'

He looked at her sitting there. In the brighter light than the dingy Boart's Head, he was able to see just how beautiful she was. She may have had a chunk of an ear missing, but that smile of crisp white teeth was alluring. Her hair glowed in the sunlight like fire, and those green eyes sparkled like precious jewels, beckoning him. Then he remembered her body.

He leaned in closer to give her his answer, and they kissed.

Knowing now what he knew about her, answered a lot of questions. But a lot more rose in their place. Like how did she manage to travel through time? If she knew all these things were going to happen, why didn't she try to change any of it? Why was she still here, now? And why is she with him?

He pushed them aside and allowed himself to enjoy the moment.

'So?' she asked again.

'Relationships are hard to come by, especially for people like us. In times like this, it pays to grab what good comes your way while you can. I used to look at Sage and his family and be jealous of how lucky he was.'

'I didn't know much about him, except for what you told me the other night. How is his family doing?'

'Tough. What happened to Sage devastated them.'

'I'm sure it did.'

'But they're strong. They'll get by. I'm helping where I can. And now that I'm unemployed, I've got a lot more time on my hands.'

'You're not Surprime Guard anymore?'

'Ah, no. After Gaius, Sage and now Elihus, I didn't think it was a good idea to carry on in the role. Besides, I have more than enough to do. Jaylyn can always use me at the Co-op, and… well… there's um…'

'But what about you?' Jayne asked. 'You haven't told me how you're handling all of this.'

'I'll manage. I'm still processing all that time travel stuff, to be honest.'

She grabbed his hands. 'Forget that. We have an opportunity. As you said, grab it. Let's not waste it.'

'What will happen to *her*?'

'She has her own path to follow. I cannot intervene. I've learned that's pointless anyway, so I just live my life and try to keep out of hers. Eventually, she will do what I have done, but until then, she'll just have to figure it out as I did.'

'Where did you send her, anyway?'

'You never figured that out?'

'No. That was a matter between you and your… ahem… self. I knew it was an address, but that's all. So where'd she go?'

'HomeGuard.'

'You what? I would have thought that'd be the last place you'd want to go. Won't they be looking for her… I mean, you?'

'It's alright. That's the safest place she *could* go. The thing about HomeGuard is they look after their own. It doesn't matter what you do or did; you're protected as long as you remain enlisted. Even if they did find out—*and they won't*—they wouldn't do anything. It's HomeGuard policy.'

'Smooth.'

'Besides, HomeGuard will need protection from *her*. They're about to get a rude shock when they realise what kind of person they've just recruited. Few have received the training she has, and their cocky instructors will have no idea what they are in for. She'll give them a run for their money, I'll tell you that.'

Jaxson chuckled. 'Fair enough. There is one thing bothering me, though. Why didn't you stop yourself from killing Sage?'

'When I was her, Lou never told me about that or tried to stop me, so it never happened.'

'But you could have changed that!'

'No, I can't. It doesn't work like that.'

'But— '

'Let me put it another way. Did the other Jayne just this dec ask you about your morning?'

'Well, no…'

'Then it never happened, and nobody can change that.'

'And you're okay with that?'

'Can't do anything about it,' she shrugged. 'How would you handle it?'

He thought about that for a moment. 'Same, I guess. Then, why did you save me?'

'Ah,' Jayne said, leaning back, 'you really want to know that?'

He nodded.

'She's an assassin. At least I *was*. I think you got that from Jayne's conversation with Kinton. He assigned her girlfriend, Ilona, to assassinate the Surprime. She—I— wasn't aware Sage was the target. Jayne had planned to kill someone else.'

Jaxson leaned forward with intrigue. 'Who?'

'Sorry, I can't tell you that.'

'Fair enough.'

'But suffice to say, that didn't happen. Anyway, when she saw the occupants of the car weren't who she expected, she tried to stop Ilona. By that stage, she had already hit Sage. When she went for you, Jayne couldn't allow it. She may be a trained killer, but she has been taught to respect her power. At least, that's what I recall. Sera, Jayne's guardian taught her that, anyway. She doesn't kill for no reason. And that's it. Jaxson, you don't know how sorry she is—how sorry I am—about Sage. I know how much he meant to you …'

'Jayne,' he interrupted, 'it's okay.'

'So you're not angry for what happened to Sage?'

'Yes, I am. It hurts, and I'm still angry, but I know Elihus was responsible for that, not you. You were just acting on his order, as he'd trained you to do. Had it been me, I'd probably have done the same. Anyway, here in Hope, we have a saying; "What's passed is past. Everything happens for a reason".'

'Yes, I know it,' she said.

'That was one of Gaius's favourite sayings. It reminds us we can't afford to dwell on the past. And besides, you saved my life. If that hadn't happened, we never would have met.'

'True. Still, if there is anything I can do to fix it, I would do it.'

He gripped her hand tighter. 'It doesn't matter. At least something good came from it. And for that, I am grateful.'

She smiled.

'I'm curious,' he then said. 'When you talk about that, why do you speak about yourself in the third person?'

Her smile disappeared, and Jaxson could tell he'd touched on a sensitive subject. 'That's a story for another time,' she said, and he instantly regretted asking.

'I'm sorry. Anyway,' he mused, thinking for a moment. 'You may not be able to change it, but what if you could make things right?'

'This isn't some rhetoric about making the world a better place, is it? Because if it is, someone tried that on me once. Let's just say they died with a slug in their chest, and things turned out very differently.'

'No, well, maybe. I'll let you decide.'

Jayne will return…

GLOSSARY OF TERMS

THE DECAT (DECIMAL) TIME SYSTEM

Cycle (330 days with a leap year every six cycles): Year
Trey (110 days): Month
Tendawn (10 days)(singular) or tendaws (plural): Week
Day: Day (1 day)
Night: Night - nigh is used in conversation
Cendec (1/10 day): Hour
Dec (1/1000 day): Minutes
Midec: Seconds

MEASUREMENTS

Decameta: Kilometre
Meta: Metre
Micrometa: Centimetre
Nanometa: Millimetre

CREATURES AND OBJECTS

Ave: Bird-like creatures endemic to Jorth.
Billingar: a rare event when both of Jorth's moons, Askr and Embla, are visible in the sky.
Boart: a carnivorous wild boar-like creature with armour plates, long, upward-pointing tusks and razor-sharp teeth.

Bovis: a large bovine or cow-like creature.
Canis: Canine or dog-like creature.

Genet: A rare, lithe cat-like creature.
Kahwah: A black liquid, like coffee, often consumed with milk and sweetener.

Loaghtan: A woolly, herd animal like a Marino sheep, commonly raised for its prized fleece.
Megloinium: An extremely volatile and rare radioactive substance used for energy and as a destructive nuclear weapon.
Ornametics: Mineral-based make-up.

Rodentia: a small, furry rodent, like a rat.
Snaca: serpent-like creature that can either be venomous or non-venomous.
Tei: a hot drink made from an infusion of herbs and fruits, similar to tea.
Tomadai: a small, furry animal with long ears similar to a rabbit.
Ursus: A very large bear-like creature with thick white fur often hunted for its pelt.
Vaspa: stinging insect like a wasp.

PEOPLE

Abril Tope	Hope Ministry Treasurer.
Admiral Capenar	Admiral quoted in the Aster Herald following the Hillfar bombings.
Ajee Yond	Character in Jayne's story 'Be Yond the Horizon'.
Alessandra MonBrelstaff	Hope Minister for Health.
Alyx Blackthorn	Garret Gord bully.
Amity	Jayne's neighbour and babysitter. Is killed when Jayne's home is destroyed in the bombings.
Anaska Welandaz	Engineer from Gotthard who arrived in Hope with Orian.
Anima	The mighty Progenitor of life (the purveyor of life).
Aster	The mighty Progenitor of the sun (the sun mistress).
Averyx Solon	Sage and Jaylyn's eldest daughter.
Buck	Garret Gord guard.
Captain Branton Nash	Character in Jayne's story 'Be Yond the Horizon' - Captain of the Fenix.
Captain Fenton	HomeGuard officer.
Captain Siegfried Leaton	Aurora Liberation Army Commanding Officer.

Codan	The mighty Progenitor of land and stone.
Commander Fafnir Mylaekar (aka Commander)	Chief Commanding Officer of LunaTec and former Commander of The Watchtower.
Conrad MonBrelstaff	Personal Assistant to the Virtuous Surprime.
Creatch	Garret Gord guard.
Cristal Spriggs	Hope's Attaché to LunaTec and former Junior Lieutenant Radar operator of the Watchtower.
D'Tauro	Raider.
Dany	A member of Sage's small militia in Hope.
DelTasker (last name)	A guardian and Asset of Garret Gord. Instructor of 'resilience under duress' training.
Doctor Cherilyn Davi	Doctor at Garret Gord.
Doctor Dagley	Fenton's medic.
Elihus Kinton (The Patriarch)	The Patriarch of Garret Gord and Hope Minister for Education.
Ensign Arendt Prow	Watchtower Requisitions Officer.
Esmay	Young upstart in Hope.
Ester Megin	(*Mee-jin*) Jayne's childhood friend at Gotthard, taken by Commander and raised as a mathematical savant by LunaTec.
Fayanna	Remy's wife (deceased).
Ferne	Hope's apothecarist and herbalist - runs an apothecary in Hope.
Gaius Sempro	The Father of Hope - Hope's founder and first Administrator. Also known as 'The Smiling Administrator'.
Garan Tope	Hope Minister for Science and Research, husband to Abril Tope.
Gerriott (Ger)	Owner of Gerriott's Delivery Service in Hope.
Gotthard	The mighty Progenitor of storms and lightning.
Graylianne	Proprietor of the Boart's Head pub in Hope.
Hunter	Artimus's heavily armoured thug.
Ilona Mylaekar	Jayne's first love and companion at Garret Gord.
Indira Tryce	Hope Minister for Property and Development.
Islay	Proprietor of the Kah-Pow café in Hope.

Jarrek	Raider.
Jaxson Yanez	Head of the Surprime Guard and Sage's closest friend.
Jaylyn Solon	Sage's wife.
Jayne Doe	Main protagonist.
Kiera Solon	Sage and Jaylyn's youngest daughter.
Kiya	Smartarse girl in Jayne's class at Gotthard.
Lexi Colyar	Chief Surgeon at the Sempro Memorial Hospital and former Lieutenant Commander of the Watchtower.
Lieutenant Commander Levvit	Watchtower 2nd 2IC.
Lieutenant Ezechiel Coxon - Radar	Watchtower radar operator.
Lieutenant Montford	Watchtower grunt.
Lieutenant Tillman - LR Weapons	Watchtower long-range weapons operator.
Lou Tenant (Lou) Doe	Lieutenant who saved young Jayne from her destroyed home.
M'Shaksa	Raider.
Marra Pyke	Nurse and midwife at the Hope Sempro Memorial Hospital and Tobias's adopted mother.
Martok Wyllt	The mighty Progenitor of deceit.
Mayor Raydon Osman	Deceased Mayor of Curio.
Mrs Wolaver	Jayne's teacher at Gotthard.
Nanneral Mapp	Administrator at Gotthard.
Niklas Martell	Hope Minister for Food and Resources.
Orian Gracyn	Hope Ministry Speaker and Vice-Surprime under Sage.
Ossie	Comms officer in Sage's small militia in Hope.
Quinn Staff	LunaTec's Chief Engineer and former Lieutenant Engineer of the Watchtower.
Ragnar Mylaekar	Commander and Cristal's son.
Rear-Admiral Artimus Wrym	(*Arty-mus Worm*) Hope Minister of Defence and leader of HomeGuard.
Remy	Fishing gear-clad Admissions guy at Gotthard.

Rika Sempro	The Mother of Hope - Gaius's deceased wife.
Rodi Tope	Son of Garan and Abril Tope.
Sage Solon	First elected Virtuous Surprime (leader) of Hope and former vice-administrator.
Seraphin MonLantry (Sera)	Jayne's Guardian at Garret Gord.
Shibley	Warden at Gotthard.
Slugs	Garret Gord guard and Buck's mate.
Tide	The mighty Progenitor of water and abundance.
Tobias Megin	Orphan rescued and adopted by Marra Pyke.
Tracer	Raider.
Tur'coo	Raider.
Vic	Refugee from Gotthard.
Vina Blackthorn	Alyx's guardian and mid-range combat trainer.
V'nom	Garret Gord guard, and former raider.
Voltaire Catlow	Businessman and CEO of OrbEN Enterprises.
Weaons Shaddix	Ilona's guardian.
Wynter Raine	Hope reporter.
Xanthe Zurole	Media personality in Hope.
Xisnys Kacir	The mighty Progenitor of dragons and fire.

PLACES, GOVERNMENTS AND FACTIONS

The **Skoyca** (pronounced Skoi-ka) **Government** were allied with the Aurora Mining Corporation's Liberation Army **(Aurora Liberation Army)**, calling themselves the **Skoyca Government Alliance (SGA).**

They held provinces, including **Mon Loq** (capital **Hillfar**).

Grales - is a largely untouched Province within former Skoyca territory and is where **Hope** is located.

The **Lafir** (pronounced La-fear) **Government** were allied with the **Cedreau Corporation Militia (CCM)**, also a mining consortium, and held provinces including **Oclave**, **Aswela** and **Nusmore** (in which there was the small town **Plulvale**).

Together they called themselves the **Cedrean Coalition.**

Curio is a small, dilapidated village on the outskirts of Hope. It didn't survive the **Faction War.**

Garret Gord is a secret military facility located in the basin plateau of the Garret Mountains.

Gotthard was the name of an underground bunker that housed survivors of the **Faction War**.

Hope is a small town that prospered after the **Faction War** of AP1945. In NC06, the then Administrative council that ran Hope, led by Gaius Sempro, held elections to fill the newly created position of Virtuous Surprime. Following his induction, the newly elected Surprime, Sage Solon, dissolved the council and established in its place the **Hope People's Ministry**, the first democratic government of the new world.

ACKNOWLEDGMENTS:

First of all, we would like to thank Lee's mother, Margaret for being our first alpha reader and number 1 supporter, sales rep, ideas person, and for her contributions to the Book of Progentiors excerpts.

Our beta readers, Jeanette O'Sullivan, Kylie Fennell and David Shield, your feedback has proven invaluable and we are ever so grateful for your willingness to read our work in such a raw form.

Our team at Shawline Publishing, Bradley Shaw, our editor Kerry Wake.

Queensland Writer's Centre for their encouragement and support, especially all our fellow writers at Writers Fridays.

And last, but certainly not least, you, our readers. For without you, this story would remain just our story. Now it's yours too.

We'd love to read your reviews on Goodreads

SCAN ME

Shawline Publishing Group Pty Ltd

www.shawlinepublishing.com.au

SLP

SHAWLINE
PUBLISHING
GROUP